OF
BLOOD,
BONES,
AND
TRUTH

OF BLOOD, BONES, AND TRUTH

BRIMSTONE & FIRE, BOOK 1

T. M. LEDVINA

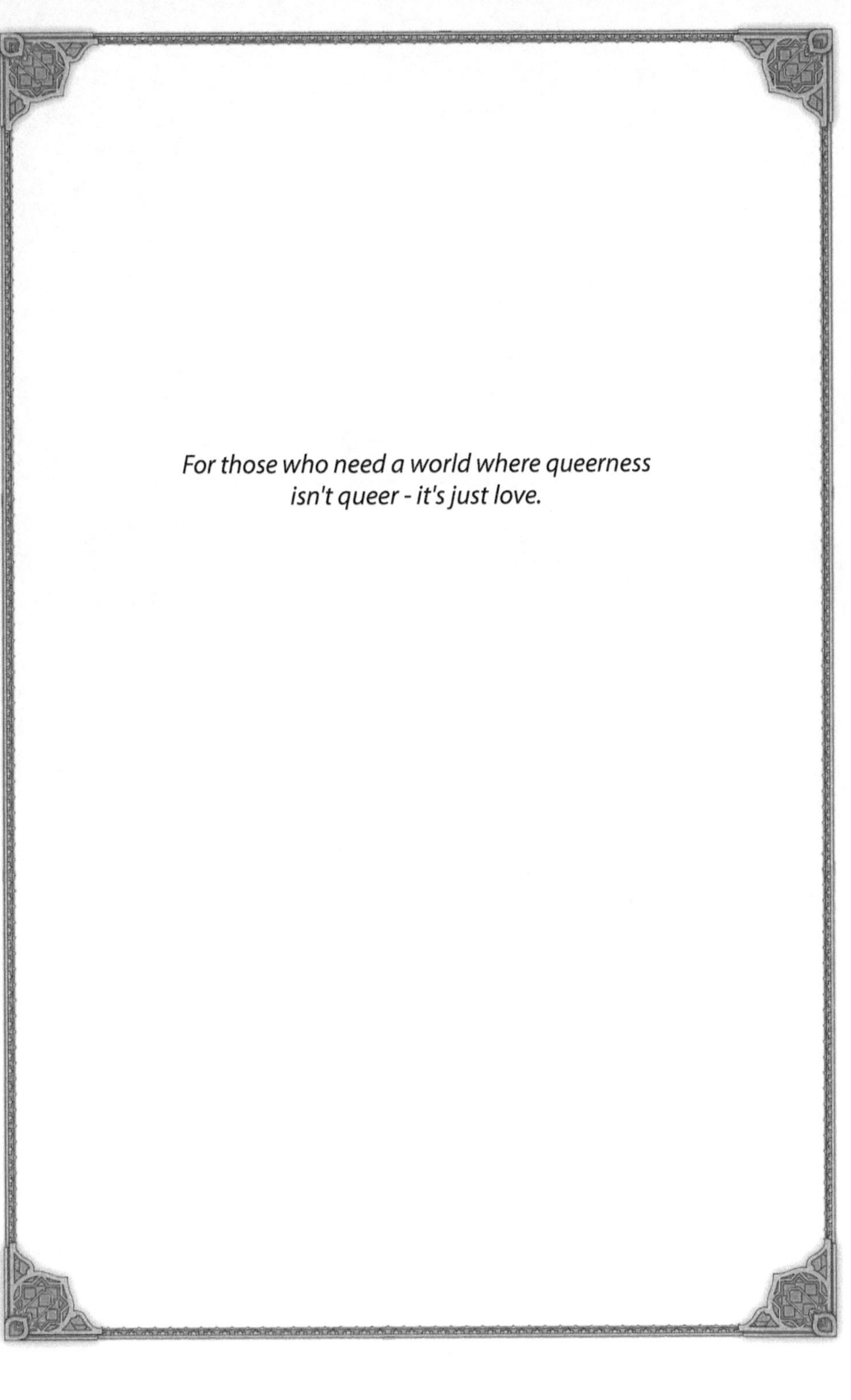

*For those who need a world where queerness
isn't queer - it's just love.*

TRIGGER WARNINGS

Dear reader, please be advised that this is a work of adult fiction. Themes include violence, gore, drug abuse, and descriptions of dead bodies. If any of the specific trigger warnings listed below make you uncomfortable, please do not read this work.

Blood
Violence
Descriptions of gore/dead bodies
Implications of child abuse
Implications of drug abuse
References to Rape/Sexual Assault
Kidnapping
Torture
Casual alcohol and drug use
Implications of alcohol abuse
Panic attacks

ALLERSEA
ISLAND

THE EASTERN NATIONS OF
ILERON
THE CERULEAN SEA
USWYE
THE BROGAN MARSHLANDS
THE ENSEN MOUNTAINS
TO THE FAR SOUTH

TO THE UNCHARTED NORTH
DENTEN
LEGEND
CAPITAL CITY
CITIES AND SETTLEMENTS
PROVINCIAL BORDERS
ALLIX
THE ASTRAN PASS
RIVENSTORM
RALIAH
CENTRILIR
LAKA
EBENFELL
NATHCON
NATRON
LACHIA
IVORYMORE
SPIRAL CITY
WEST MISERAN
WOLFWATER
ASTRA RIVER
KAZUTA
MIDLSET
KETTLEGUARD
LANAHEIM RIVER
WESTREACH
EASTREACH
ALDERBURN
GALZAGA LAKE
BALINDAO

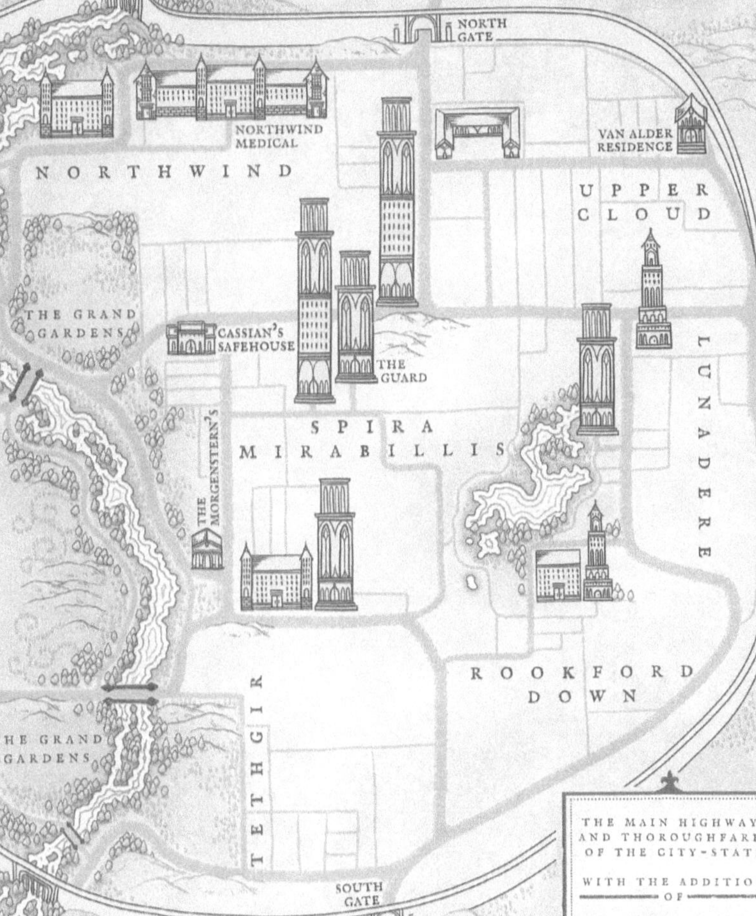

TO THE CERULEAN SEA
SPIRAL CITY
NORTH GATE
NORTHWIND MEDICAL
VAN ALDER RESIDENCE
NORTHWIND
UPPER CLOUD
THE GRAND GARDENS
CASSIAN'S SAFEHOUSE
THE GUARD
LUNADERE
SPIRA MIRABILLIS
THE MORGENSTERN'S
WEST GATE
BLOOMSIDE
ROOKFORD DOWN
TETHGIR
EAST GATE
TO THE EASTERN CITIES
THE GRAND GARDENS
SOUTH GATE
THE MAIN HIGHWAYS
AND THOROUGHFARES
OF THE CITY-STATE
WITH THE ADDITION
OF
NOTABLE BUILDINGS
AND LANDMARKS
mapped in the present age
TO THE UNCHARTED SOUTH

CHARACTER GUIDE

THE LEGION

KELLAN MANCHESTER: A private in the nineteenth division. A member of the Fallen subclass of the race of seraphs, Kellan serves as a military assassin.

VAIDA LARSEN: Another private in the Legion, serving in the eighteenth division as an analyst. She assists all divisions with data analysis, biological sampling, and other data-driven tasks.

THE COMMISSIONER: The leader of the Legion. He has served the Legion for over seventy years, but has only been in his current role for about eighteen years.

VICE COMMISSIONER FARROW: The secondary leader of the Legion and the commissioner's right-hand man. Has served the Legion for more than a hundred years.

SHARR RAZORBORN: A Lieutenant serving in the fifteenth division. Kellan's mentor when he first began working for the Legion.

CYGNUS CLEARVIEW: The first victim, Cygnus, was a corporal with the seventeenth division.

OTHERS

CASSIAN EVERMORE: An elven man from Ebenfell. Serves a man named Ragnor LaRoche as repayment for Cassian's father's debts.

SELWYN MORGENSTERN: An heiress to weapons and tech giant, Morgenstern Tech. Current head of the Research and Development sector and forming a deal with Northwind Medical.

PONTIUS MORGENSTERN: Selwyn's older brother and philanthropist. Serves a variety of charitable organizations across Spiral City.

SIDE CHARACTERS

MINA ROSEWOOD: Selwyn's best friend.

TARIN VEXNYS: Pontius' best friend and occasional philanthropic partner.

LEONARDO WHITBURN: An old associate of Cassian's, working under Ragnor.

RONSON BYRE: The current Director of Northwind Medical.

LIZA SARMANELLO: The first victim, died in conjunction with Cygnus.

ELIZA EVERMORE: Cassian's mother.

RAGNOR LAROCHE: Cassian's employer in Ebenfell.

Pronunciation Guide

Characters

Kellan Manchester: *Kel-ann Man-ches-tur*

Cassian Evermore: *Kah-see-ehn Ever-mor*

Selwyn Morgenstern: *Sell-win Mor-gin-stern*

Pontius Morgenstern: *Pon-chis Mor-gin-stern*

Mina Rosewood: *Mee-nuh Roze-wood*

Vaida Larsen: *Veye-duh Lar-sen*

Ronson Byre: *Ron-sun Bai-urr*

Sol: *Saul*

Hym: *Heim*

World & Setting

Illeron: *eye-lur-on*

Uswye: *oos-way*

Ellsemere: *ell-zuh-meer*

Illium: *ill-ee-um*

Denten: *den-tin*

Tethgir: *teth-gear*

Rookford Down: *rook-furd down*

Spira Mirabilis: *speer-uh meer-uh-bill-ihs*

Lunadere: *loon-uh-dare*

Raliah: *rah-lee-uh*

Lachia: *lah-chee-uh*

Centrilir: *sahn-trill-ear*

Midlset: *middle-set*

Kazuta: *kah-zoo-tah*

Nathcon: *nayth-con*

GOVERNMENT, POLITICS, AND LEADERSHIP

LUNAR CALENDAR

The calendar in Ileron is based upon their lunar calendar and follows the cycles of the moon. A new moon marks the beginning/end of a month, the full moon marking the middle. There are thirty days each month, and twelve months in a year.

The first Moon: Frost

The second Moon: Dawn

The third Moon: Earth

The fourth Moon: Blossom

The fifth Moon: Cresting

The sixth Moon: Day

The seventh Moon: Flame

The eighth Moon: Cerulean

The ninth Moon: Wind

The tenth Moon: Jupiter's

The eleventh Moon: Dusk

The twelfth Moon: Evergreen

Dates in Ileron are written as such: the X day of XXX Moon.

POLITICAL SYSTEM

Although named the Empire, the country runs on a democratic system. Spiral City is unique in its structure as a city-state, thus, its governmental bodies are different.

THE EMPIRE:

The Red Council is the Empire's ruling authority. It is a group of six individuals, nominated by their respective cities, to serve on the council for fifteen to thirty years. The nomination process happens every fifteen years. Three members are elected to stay on the board, two become seniors, and one becomes the Prime. The other three members retire from the council, and three new members are elected by the citizens of the realm to serve on the board. It is possible for a brand new member to become a senior immediately, although you cannot become Prime without serving as a member first.

In addition to the leadership of the Red Council, the White Court was established to serve as the secondary leadership council for the Empire. This court is a lifetime appointment, very similar to how the Supreme Court works in the U.S. The members, however, are not selected by members of the Red Council, but rather are also elected by the citizens of the Empire.

SPIRAL CITY:

The Governor is an elven man elected ninety-two years ago, named Caern Fenwyne. He is a strict and passionate man who is not necessarily adored, but most definitely revered by his citizens. Caern is a cautious man as well, rarely choosing to appear in public for fear of an assassination like that of his predecessor, Zephyr Dornwen. Although nearing the end of his term, he is still passionate about the protection of his citizens.

CURRENT DISTRICT COUNCILORS:

LUNADERE: Led by a shifter by the name of **Hazel**. She's a conniving and secretive woman, but is fiercely protective of her clan. The Councilor of Lunadere is also known as the Commissioner of Public Buildings and City Planning, and is in charge of development projects within the city as well as maintenance of public and government buildings.

UPPER CLOUD: Led by a seraph named **Bethor**. He's a kind and gentle man, if not a little proud. The Councilor of Upper Cloud is also known as the Commissioner of Public Finance and the Treasury, and is in charge of the city's finances.

NORTHWIND: Led by a seraph named **Roland**. Aloof and far removed, he is more interested in grooming the next leader of his district rather than actually governing it. The Councilor of Northwind is also known as the Commissioner of Public Health and Family Services, and oversees the city's public health services.

TETHGIR: Led by a Dragonborn named **Arice**. She is just as kind and gentle as her great-great-grandfather, Riveras, who was the original Councilor of Tethgir when Spiral City was established. She leads her district with a just and steady hand. Also known as the Commissioner of Public Information and Technology, this commissioner oversees the flow of information in and out of the city, and ensures technological advancements used by the government are safe and reliable.

ROOKFORD DOWN: Still led by the extremely old dwarven woman, **Gen**. She was a young woman when Spiral City was established, but is now old and gray. She is senile as hell, although her daughter, Erwen, has been helping her mother for the last one hundred years or so. Also known as the Commissioner of Public Trade and Consumer Safety, this commissioner oversees trade in and out of Spiral City and ensures standards are met to deliver high-quality and safe products to its citizens.

BLOOMSIDE: Led by a water elemental named **Exto**. He is incredibly proud of his district, focusing most of his efforts on conservation and water purification to keep the beautiful gardens flourishing. Also known as the Commissioner of Public Lands and Natural Resources, this commissioner oversees the Grand Gardens and other public parks within Spiral City and oversees any agriculture within the city's limits.

SPIRA MIRABILIS: Although technically not a residential district, Spira is represented on the council by none other than the Legion's **Commissioner**. Uniquely referred to as "The Commissioner," his official title is the Commissioner of Public Safety and the Legion. This is also the only member of the council not elected by their district's citizens, simply because there are none to elect.

THE LEGION

The Legion is made up of twenty-five total divisions, varying from accounting and magical facilities to the divisions like law enforcement, security, and investigatory units. In the law enforcement divisions, there are individual units, made up of Privates, Corporals, Sergeants, and Lieutenants.

RANKING STRUCTURE

PRIVATE: Indentured ranking

Same jacket style as the corporals. Each private is designated with the prison mark on the back of their necks. This is not unique to the Fallen. Every Fallen has a prison mark, every private has a mark, but not every private is a Fallen.

CORPORAL: regular/general members of the military divisions of the Legion ten and up, most common rank

Open-jacket style, worn with a white or black undershirt and matching necktie in their division's color.

SERGEANT: the leader of a unit within a division, corporals report to sergeants

Closed jacket style that buttons on one side of the chest and high neck, no undershirt or necktie. Matching solid color epaulets in the color of their division.

LIEUTENANT: the highest rank within a division, sergeants report to lieutenants

Closed-jacket style that buttons on one side of the chest with a folded down panel in the color of their division. Matching striped epaulets.

VICE COMMISSIONER: second-in-command of the Legion, functions as the Commissioner's right hand

Same jacket style as the lieutenant, but has three stars on the epaulets.

COMMISSIONER: the leader of the Legion, all positions report to him/her

Same jacket style as the lieutenant, but has six stars on the epaulets.

Medica: the secondary rank of all members of the tenth, eleventh, and twelfth divisions, nicknamed the Meds

> *Their first rank (Corporal, Sergeant, or Lieutenant) will determine their jacket style*

> *All Medica have an infinity-shaped ouroboros pin incorporated into their division pin*

THE DIVISIONS

The First Division: white piping; reports to the Legion Commissioner

> *Legal work & administrative law, mostly lawyers & judges, some paralegals, and admin assistants.*

The Second, Third, and Fourth Divisions: gray piping; report to Bethor, Roland, and Gen

> *Administrative work such as accounts payable/receivable, mailroom, purchasing, HR, employment relations, etc.*

The Fifth, Sixth, and Seventh Divisions: yellow piping; report to Hazel, Exto, or Arice

> *Facilities work such as maintenance, public works, civil engineering, magical security, etc.*

The Eighth and Ninth Divisions: green piping; report to Exto

> *Scientific research divisions, mostly in charge of exotic flora and fauna. Frequently works in cooperation with the University.*

The Tenth, Eleventh, and Twelfth Divisions: bright red piping

> *All first responder divisions, paramedics, firefighters, etc.*

The Thirteenth Division: black piping

> *Currently vacant. Has not been used as an active division for nearly a hundred years*

The Fourteenth and Fifteenth Divisions: navy piping

Private investigation units, can be hired by private citizens but primarily works for the government. These divisions do not have units, and each member has the rank of Lieutenant.

The Sixteenth, Seventeenth, and Eighteenth Divisions: cobalt blue piping

Regular law enforcement divisions. Traffic maintenance, domestic disturbances, security, etc.

The Nineteenth Division: blood-red piping

Labeled as another private investigatory unit, but most everyone knows this is a lie. They are essentially a "clean-up crew." Made up exclusively of draftees. The 19th also does not have a unit structure; each member reports individually to the Vice Commissioner and Commissioner.

The Twentieth Division: purple piping

A division that functions like a national guard. They are mobilized in extreme emergencies; otherwise, their members are split up into the other divisions when not mobilized.

The Twenty-First, Twenty-Second, Twenty-Third, and Twenty -Fourth Divisions: sky-blue piping

Special units, mostly investigatory, homicide, sex crimes, drug busts, etc.

The Twenty-Fifth Division: orange piping

The leadership division. Technically the Commissioner and the Vice Commissioner are the only full-time members of this division, but all Lieutenants have the Twenty-Fifth as their secondary division.

SECTION 1

MAGIC ISN'T FOR EVERYONE

Although the world of Ileron seems rife with magic, it's more uncommon than one would expect. Elves and seraphs are the most inclined to having natural, innate magic, although it isn't impossible for other races to have this sort of "wild" magic. This type of magic has no restraints, no specific set of rules by which it can be used, other than intuition of the user and practice. Many scholars with magical abilities dedicate their lives to practicing and understanding their magic. Beyond this wild magic, there are some wielders who must meet specific requirements to harness their talents, like imbuing their magic into objects, channeling their magic through sigils or emblems, or using verbal spells to focus their power.

Other types of magic exist as well. Before the Conjunction, many humans were blessed with specific magical talents, often one-trick sorts of abilities. These could include reading the future, conjuring fire, levitation, minor healing, and seeing magic. This type of magic is not nearly as prolific as the wild magic of the elves, but can be just as powerful if the user knows how to hone their abilities.

Elementals can use magic depending on their heritage. Fire elementals can create fire or variations of it. This could mean lava, lightning, smoke, or steam. Water elementals might create tidal waves, conjure rain clouds, or harness the moisture in the air.

Even with the wide variety of magic present in the world, it is still a relatively rare talent, one that each bearer wields a little differently. The amount of power available to a magic user is consistent and steady throughout their lifetime; and means to increase one's power have been researched, but nothing is conclusive.

The only exception is through demonic pacts. By summoning a demon, one can increase their innate well of power to vast depths. Of course, this is an uncouth way to gain power, and is strictly forbidden by world governments. Demons, as is well known, cannot be trusted. However, a pact will take more from the bearer than just a bit of blood.

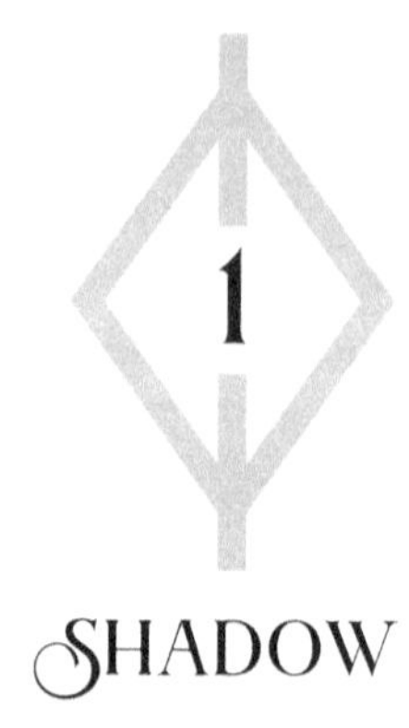

SHADOW

Unknown

The man pushed his long black hair back from his eyes, focusing on the ritual chant on the sheet of paper before him. He'd practiced the words many times before, but he would be an idiot to do this without them before him.

They were simple, as far as summoning spells went, but the power required to harness them wasn't. He sliced a thin line into his palm, letting the blood drip onto the floor inside the circle.

"*Guene hosth maalp, guene hosth zaalp, guene hosth senjit.*"

Of my blood, of my bones, of my truth. The beginning of the chant was meant to open the pact on his end, to prove he was willing to risk life and limb for this accord.

"*Mate hihyant meask, Alvemach, zuzagane gune ir oack guene zatoc gire mahoakk ec senjit.*"

I summon thee, Alvemach, to this plane to become a partner in truth. To bind the chosen demon to him.

"*Tunt tarth, hosth maalp, hosth zaalp, hosth senjit.*"

Come and be my blood, my bones, my truth. To seal the pact if the named demon accepted.

Alvemach had been his choice—the demon prince of the second layer of Hell. Who else would serve in the role he needed as well as a prince? A lesser demon wouldn't provide the powers he needed to carry out his plan. Yes, only a prince of Hell would do.

The enneagram before him glowed a pale gray, the bounding edges of the circle dull in comparison. Minutes passed in silence, but the man did not move. He knew this was a waiting game, a test to see who would break first.

He would not yield.

Finally, smoke rolled from the center of the nine-pointed star, billowing out as if a fire had begun. But it did not pass the boundary edge; it curled up against it as if contained in a glass jar.

From the center of the circle rose a seven-foot tall monster. Its skin was black, crackled with veins of fire that snaked over its entire body. It had no legs, rather, it was suspended upon a twisting tentacle of smoke that pulsated with lava. Its head was that of a tusked boar, its eyes filled with blackness and flames.

It turned to the man, its bulging arms crossed before its bare chest. It looked at him with contempt.

The devil named Alvemach did not speak.

The man smiled, if you could even call it that. The edges of his mouth curled dangerously upwards, revealing sharply pointed canines that were most definitely not natural. He stepped up to the bounding circle, but not beyond. Their pact must be sealed first.

"I've called you to form a pact," he began, staring unblinkingly into the demon's unnatural, fiery eyes.

The demon snorted. "Obviously. What are the terms?"

The man laughed, a harsh sound that would have grated on other ears. But the demon didn't seem to notice. "This world is dirty—fire cleanses. I shall remake the world, with your help."

The demon regarded him again with narrowed eyes. "What is your name, human?"

The man laughed again. "You may call me The Shadow."

The demon closed its eyes, obviously deep in thought. It didn't move, considering his offer in silence. The man knew not to press— even within the confines of the circle, a demon this powerful could easily find a way out if he so desired. So he waited.

Finally, the demon prince opened his eyes. He nodded once, then drove a long sharp tooth into the flesh of his hand, letting the blood well in his palm.

With that, the man entered the circle. This was the most dangerous part of the ritual, but he was not afraid. He clasped the demon's hand with his own, their black and red blood mixing and dripping onto the floor.

The instant their wounds touched, a flash of power threatened to drive the man to his knees. But he would not yield—he would not bow to the power that should bow to him. He stood firm, his grasp upon the demon's hand unforgiving and tight. He would make this power flowing into him his own.

Eventually it settled, coiling behind his navel like a snake waiting to strike. The feeling was incredible, indescribable. He thought he quite liked it.

They released their hands, the enneagram below them returning to a dull chalk picture on the floor as the pact sealed itself once and for all. Alvemach was here to stay—tied to the man with a blood pact that would not break easily.

"Tell me more of this plan of yours, Shadow," Alvemach said.

"All in due time, my friend," the man said. "I first need you to do something about your appearance. It's dreadful."

Alvemach's nostrils flared, but he obliged. The man had taken the first of the many steps in his plan. Uniting worlds was not a task to be done quickly. It was something that one had to work at for many years. He'd overcome the first and most difficult hurdle—acquiring power.

Now he must overcome the second. The smile that was not a smile reappeared. It was time to begin.

KELLAN

1st of Blossom Moon

The sky stretched out before him—cloudless, endless, blue. The spring air was cold through his wings, but he didn't care. The wind in his face was a welcome reprieve after four months of dreary winter.

Kellan loved this feeling. Like he was alone, above it all. Like whenever he let his wings free and soared through the skies, all his problems stayed firmly on the ground.

That was mostly why he was avoiding landing, despite the two winged legionnaires behind him blaring sirens and commanding him to halt.

He circled lazily above one of the Grand Gardens, debating landing in a thicket of trees and throwing them off his trail. But that would never work—they already knew who he was if they knew he was flying without a permit.

Kellan sighed and made his way down to a patch of grass within the garden, his combat boots tearing up the soil as he landed heavily. He pouted and turned to the officers landing behind him.

"Private Kellan Manchester," one of the black-suited figures said from beneath their visor. It covered most of the legionnaire's face, hiding their eyes behind mirrored black glass. "You are flying without a permit. This is grounds for punishment under Spiral City jurisdictional law section seven, subsection—"

"Thirty-seven, I know," Kellan said, cutting the legionnaire off. "I'm aware."

The legionnaire sighed. "Then you knowingly broke the permit law?"

Kellan shrugged. "I guess?"

The other Legionnaire, who'd been standing to the side watching this exchange happen, chimed in. "Since you're Legion yourself, we reserve the right to take you before your commanding officer."

This time, Kellan laughed. "By all means, please do."

The first legionnaire began turning a dial over their temple, presumably looking up his ranking structure. Kellan could see the exact moment they found his direct report—their mouth went slack, shoulders tensing.

"You're—"

"A Fallen, yes. Nineteenth division. Indentured servitude and all that. Take me to see the commissioner, then." He held out his arms in annoyance, daring them to chain him. Not that it was worth it to do so.

The second legionnaire stammered, "C-come with us then, Private Manchester. Regardless of your status within the Legion, someone must reprimand you for your flagrant disregard of permit laws."

Kellan smirked. "Take me away, boys."

The legionnaires who'd tried to arrest him had insisted on escorting him all the way to the commissioner's office. The elevator ride up had been incredibly uncomfortable. One had shifted on his feet the entire time while wringing his hands; the other had stood stock still and asked Kellan hundreds of questions about the commissioner without taking a single breath.

They now stood before the massive oak door that led into his commander's office. Both legionnaires stood still, staring up at the top of the doors in slack-jawed wonder.

"Well?" Kellan said, gesturing to the door. "Aren't you going to knock?"

The legionnaire to his left swallowed hard as they stared up at the doors. "Are you sure we can just—"

"We must report this disobedience," the legionnaire on his right insisted, but made no move to knock the door themselves.

Kellan sighed. "Bunch of wussies. He doesn't bite." He lifted his hand and knocked.

The answer was almost immediate. "Come in," a voice said through the door.

They pushed the doors open to reveal a massive office and a man sitting at a glass desk in the center, tapping away at a holographic display. He lifted his face to the door, expression never changing as Kellan entered, flanked by his two captors.

"Commissioner," Kellan said, bowing his head.

The legionnaires flanking him mumbled the same, bowing their heads as well.

The commissioner was not an imposing man, but he had an air about him that betrayed his years as a leader. His salt-and-pepper beard masked his age, and the delicate points of his elven ears poked out from behind a well-coiffed head of fiery hair.

His gray eyes shifted between Kellan and the legionnaires, the question on his lips obvious, but he refused to speak. They'd interrupted him, after all.

Kellan spoke first. "Sir, I was caught flying. Just thought you should know."

The commissioner sighed. "Private Manchester, we've discussed this before. Until you're provided with a flier's permit, you cannot fly over Spiral City."

Kellan bowed his head. "Yes, sir."

The commissioner cocked an eyebrow, then turned his attention to the legionnaires flanking him. "I have this under control. You are dismissed."

They didn't hesitate before turning on their heels and exiting the office without a single glance backwards. Kellan bit his lip to stop himself from laughing.

"Private Manchester," the commissioner said, "I know you want to stretch your wings, but the rules are in place for a reason; and, as a member of this organization, I expect you to adhere to them."

"I know, sir. It was only going to be for a few minutes, but I—"

The commissioner held up a hand. "I don't want excuses, Private. I'm letting you off the hook this time, but don't expect my generosity again." He sighed, rubbing his temples. "I have a job for you anyway, so this was good timing." He gestured to one of the black leather armchairs before his desk.

Kellan sat. "What's the job?"

The commissioner swiped a finger across the holographic display before him, bringing up a short file with a name in bold letters at the top—Levi van Alder.

He squinted at the file, reading the details below the target's name. Van Alder was apparently a medical researcher, but there was no reason listed for his elimination.

"What did he do, sir?" Kellan asked.

"The governor is displeased with his activities lately and has requested his immediate disposal. You'll be carrying it out tomorrow evening."

He nodded, unable to argue. He wished, not for the first time, that he hadn't been born a Fallen. He had no choice, no chance to refuse a request to eliminate someone the governor wanted dead. His fate was sealed at birth.

He simply nodded. "Yes, sir. I won't let you down."

He took one look at the dark clouds rolling in over the East Gate and swore under his breath. Kellan hated getting wet in the skintight stealth suits he wore for missions—they became unbearably tight when soaked. But there was no avoiding the fat drops that fell from the sky.

He was riding his motorcycle through Lunadere, the glow from his wheels' decorative lights reflecting off the now rain-slicked pavement. He slowed; he'd be in trouble if he took a corner too fast in these conditions.

Lunadere was quiet this time of night, or at least here in the residential area. The evergreen trees gave off a pleasant scent, mixing with the smell of the wet pavement. He didn't see many cars pass as he rode on—most people in this area were long asleep.

He took another corner at low speed, watching a street light flicker overhead as he turned. The rest of the city loomed to his west, a black outline against the night sky. A neon glow illuminated the brick and glass towers, signs for a variety of goods visible even from this far away.

The neon was probably his favorite part of the city. If he let himself stare long enough, he thought he could get lost in the glow. It made it feel alive, like the city was a sleeping, luminous beast ready to open its maw at any moment. Its roar was the sounds of horns honking and sirens blaring and music pumping loud enough to match the rhythm of his heart.

But not in this neighborhood. All was quiet here—serene. It was a small pocket of silence in the life that thrummed about him.

The rain was pouring now, soaking through his clothes and into his skin, making him shiver. Thanks to this gods-damned weather and the cold seeping into his bones, he knew he was going to have a challenging evening. Scaling the walls would be tough.

But the rain was also a blessing. It would cover any noise he might make; and if he was lucky, it would provide additional cover against security cameras or sensors. Nothing messed with magical security better than the weather.

He parked his bike on the side of the road, strapping the helmet to the saddlebags and praying it wouldn't be too wet by the time he got back. Part of him knew it was empty hope, especially with how heavily the rain fell now.

After removing the helmet, he replaced it with a visor. It covered both his eyes and ears, and enhanced his senses. He patted his belt, checking for the canisters of poison and his thigh holsters with his daggers.

He was as ready as he'd ever be.

Kellan slipped through the alleyways in the southern portion of Upper Cloud, the skyscrapers making him feel small. He shook the rain from his hair as he rounded the corner before his destination.

Levi van Alder's sprawling estate was, frankly, idiotic. The towering walls that surrounded the property weren't necessarily a challenge on their own, but the security cameras and alarm spells that blazed in his visor might be.

But Kellan hadn't come unprepared. The Legion had jammers, pieces of technology that could block alarm spell signals like the ones blazing around the manor. They could also temporarily disable cameras. He had a time limit, though, which meant as soon as he pressed the jammer's button, he'd need to be swift.

He took a deep breath, trying to settle into the calm he needed to do this. His last jobs had been simpler than this—much, much simpler.

A large drop of rain splattered obnoxiously on his nose. The sooner he finished this poor sucker off, the faster he could get back to headquarters and out of the rain. Not that he was in any rush to get back to the Guard, but he really, *really* hated the rain.

Kellan's finger hovered over the jammer on his hip. He took a breath in, let it out, then pressed the button swiftly.

The alarm spells glittering in his visor flickered and died. A mechanical beep confirmed the cameras were offline as well.

He retrieved a grappling hook from his belt, pressing the button to extend the clawed head up and over the wall. He clipped the cable to his belt, then let the pneumatic motor do the work to help him up the wall. The rain made the walls slick beneath his hands as he found the first handholds and pulled himself up.

He pursed his lips as he gripped the wall. This would be easier if he could fly, but he couldn't risk it after yesterday's escapade. Kellan rather liked the commissioner; getting on his bad side wouldn't do him any favors. So he sighed and pulled himself up to the next handhold.

The climb was challenging, but not impossible. His gloved fingers found purchase in small gaps between the bricks where the mortar had eroded away. Small chunks of loose brick ground under the steel toes of his boots only to be quickly washed away by the rain, falling beneath him in a gritty shower.

He reached the top of the wall, removing the hook's head from where it had landed in the gravel at the top.

The roof of the manor was one long leap away. Enough for a normal person to hesitate, but not for someone like Kellan. He backed up to the edge of the wall, another deep breath in steadying his footing as he prepared for the jump.

With cat-like grace, he swung himself across the gap and onto the southeastern portion of the manor's roof, the rubber soles of his stealth suit gripping the tiles even at the precarious angle. The muscles in Kellan's abdomen flexed as he adjusted for the steep grade.

The timer in the corner of his visor had begun counting down when he'd jammed the camera's signals. The time now read nine minutes and eight seconds. He was behind schedule.

The window he'd chosen as his point of entry led to a bathroom. It was small enough that most people wouldn't think about it as a security risk, especially not high-class people like Van Alder. Their trust in their security spells was too deep. They forgot easily that magic was fallible. But Kellan couldn't complain—their carelessness made his job easier.

He nudged the window, testing if it was locked. It shook but stayed locked against his test. He retrieved a set of lock picks from his belt, adjusting himself along the edge of the roof to get a better angle at the mechanized lock on the window. He'd picked locks upside down like this in practice, but this was the first time doing it on an actual assignment.

He breathed slowly through his nose to keep his fingers from shaking. He was freezing, but that wasn't the only cause.

The lock popped open with a soft click after a few good jiggles of his pick, and the window tilted in from the top. His feet went in first, then his torso, and finally his head was through the gap. His feet made no sound as he landed on the tile in the bathroom, his ears focused on any sounds he could pick up in the house.

Kellan turned the knob over his temple to switch his visor to infrared. So far, so good. A figure was sleeping in a bedroom two doors away—Van Alder. Just where he'd expected him to be.

Another figure was moving through the second floor. His stomach dropped. Van Alder had guards, but they were stationed on the grounds, not inside the house. Who in the world was walking around down there? A mistress? A maid? Had he changed his security protocols in the last few days?

He stayed in the bathroom, unwilling to move until he observed the patterns of the person moving about on the floor below. They hadn't moved much, standing in one spot and looking like they were rummaging through a desk or cabinet.

A nasty thought occurred to him—had the governor sent someone else because he didn't trust a Fallen to do the job? He'd never heard of such a thing happening, but he didn't know enough about the governor to guess.

If he didn't succeed today... Well, he didn't want to think about what might happen to him.

He continued observing the person on the second floor, but the timer was steadily clicking down. He had no choice. With less than seven minutes left, he needed to move, now.

He opened the bathroom door silently, then snuck across the hall to where Van Alder lay sleeping. In and out, leave no trace. That was what the poison was for.

Reaching back into his tool belt to grasp a canister, he shut the door behind him with a soft click. Kellan pulled the metal mask sitting around his neck up and over his mouth and nose, wincing as the sharp sides of the mask cut into his cheeks. Better a bit of a cut than death, he thought.

Through his visor, he watched the slow rise and fall of Van Alder's chest. The canister of poisonous gas was heavy in his hand, but he tightened his grip upon it as he approached the sleeping figure. This was how he'd killed the others—this was no different.

He pressed the button on the canister, placing it gently on the floor and rolling it to a stop beside Van Alder's bed.

Downstairs, the mysterious figure moved. He couldn't risk them discovering what he was doing. His heart raced as they moved from the second floor up to the third, slowly approaching the bedroom.

He readied his dagger, gripping the handle tightly as he waited. It would be a problem if he had to confront the trespasser in the bedroom, but if they didn't have a mask, the gas might take them out before he'd need to worry.

Kellan risked a glance, shuffling quietly to the doorway and peering out just as the figure rounded the top of the staircase.

He could see the mysterious trespasser's features clearly in his visor—delicately pointed ears, silvery blond hair, a wide nose, and a mouth that was tilted down in a frown. He was tall, moving down the hallway with a casual grace that Kellan knew was born of years of combat training. If the daggers at his hips and the sword sheathed across his back were any sign of his intentions, he was bad news.

He wasn't Legion. Kellan checked his chest for any sign of a divisional pin, but he couldn't see one.

The man wasn't wearing a Legion-issue battle suit, either. Although the elven man's suit was similar, with hard, black plates over his chest, thighs, and arms, the style and color were entirely different from Kellan's own all-black ensemble. The man had stripes of silver along his biceps, and the sheaths that held his daggers were a deep gray.

The man stopped, checking his watch and frowning. He hadn't spotted Kellan yet, but it was only a matter of time before that would change.

He had mere moments to decide his next course of action. Fight here, or lure him somewhere else. Fighting inside the house would be troublesome, especially since Kellan needed to confirm Van Alder's death before calling it in. But allowing this man to see what was happening in the bedroom was out of the question.

The sleeping Van Alder was now surrounded by a haze of poisonous belladonna gas, slowly suffocating him.

The other man was nearing the bedroom door on soft feet. Kellan shifted, his back to the wall just inside the bedroom. The mask was working to filter out the gas spreading through the room, and he hoped the man creeping down the hallway couldn't hear his mask quietly filtering his breaths.

And when the elven man finally reached the bedroom, he stopped. Kellan's heart pounded in his ears. Why was he stopping?

The man sniffed once just outside the door, then turned on a heel and retreated down the stairs.

CASSIAN

1st of Blossom Moon

Cassian's mouth tilted down into a frown as he crossed his arms. "Sir, if it's being handled, why am I getting sent to babysit?"

Ragnor waved a bejeweled hand dismissively. "The council paid me, and I pay you. You follow my orders."

Cassian Evermore hated Ragnor LeRoche more than anyone. He was rude, brutish, and arrogant—and to make matters worse, he owned Cassian. Thanks to his father's endless debt and poorly timed death, his young son had been forced to take up the mantle of hired hand. Cassian had started training under Ragnor over seventy years ago and had spent nearly thirty handling his dirty work. It wasn't a job Cassian enjoyed, but it kept Ragnor's collectors away from his mother, and that was enough for him.

Ragnor had been personally invested in him since he was young, overseeing much of Cassian's training directly. Although Ragnor rarely dealt with the multitudes of assassins in his employ, he never allowed anyone else to give jobs to Cassian. Ragnor had kept him close his entire tenure, and it was suffocating.

"Then clarify what I'm supposed to be doing once more. I'm not killing anyone this time. Why?"

Ragnor sighed, rubbing his temples. "You're toeing the line of my patience, Cassian. You are to retrieve the files and ensure Van Alder's assassination is completed. For once, this isn't an elimination for you to handle. Is that clear enough?"

Cassian squeezed his eyes shut to calm himself before he replied. "Yes, sir."

Ragnor turned his chair away to face the expansive windows looking down onto the city of Ebenfell. "It's not the first time the council has requested one of my employees to back up the Legion or the Red Guard, you know." Ragnor stood, clasping his hands behind his back, observing the view from the window as if he owned it. And in some way, Cassian supposed he kind of did.

He was the type of man who had his fingers in everything—money laundering, prostitution, and more legitimate business ventures like personal security and investments. His connections to the Red Council were unsurprising; he was the most influential man in Ebenfell, even if he was a criminal. They couldn't touch him, so instead, the council decided to work with him.

They allowed him free reign of his less-than-legitimate ventures as long as he wasn't causing too much trouble. Ragnor had long since learned what the Red Council would allow and what they wouldn't. As long as it benefited their goals, they didn't care what Ragnor did. Or, by proxy, any of his employees.

Ragnor stayed silent for several moments. Cassian didn't move; he'd found out the hard way what leaving before Ragnor dismissed you was like. It was not pleasant and usually involved more than one broken bone.

He was a violent man when he needed to be, and the multitude of times he'd broken Cassian's arms and wrists for insolence, real or perceived, had proven that not asking questions and waiting for Ragnor to speak was better than the alternative.

"The legionnaire assigned to the task is one of the indentured," Ragnor finally said, breaking the uncomfortable silence.

Cassian's eyebrows rose. "Is that why I'm being sent?"

"That's part of it," he said, but continued on before Cassian could ask another question. "You're leaving tonight. Arrangements have been made for you in the city. You're dismissed." He waved his hand, the light streaming in from the windows reflecting off the large gems embedded in the many rings on his fingers.

It had always been this way—Ragnor sending him away on a job, explaining hardly more than the bare minimum. Last week, it had been a business partner who'd failed to pay back money he owed Ragnor. The month before, a petty crime boss who'd encroached on Ragnor's territory in the east district. He had years of blood on his hands, blood he could never wash off, no matter how hard he scrubbed.

Cassian bowed his head to Ragnor's back and exited the opulent office into the hallway. He'd been sent to Spiral City before, but this would be his first time directly dealing with the Legion.

He had no idea what to expect, and that was enough to make him nervous.

That evening, Cassian tried his best to look stern as he handed his luggage to the girl behind the counter. "This is fragile, please be gentle with it."

She nodded, grasping the top handle with both hands. "Don't worry, sir, we always treat passengers' luggage with the utmost attention to detail. Your items will be safe with us."

He nodded once to her, grasping the small techpad in his hand that held his boarding pass. Techpads weren't a new invention, but it seemed they got sleeker and stronger with each passing year. Originally, they'd been bulky, black plastic things that allowed one to communicate over long distances. In more recent years, they'd finally figured out holographic technology, and now most resembled small pieces of glass with rubber grips.

Cassian had two—one of the handheld versions, which fit in the palm of an average humanoid's hand, and a larger version that he could use for more complex tasks like research and writing.

Ragnor had given him barely enough time to pack before he'd needed to catch the bullet train from Ebenfell to Spiral City. The ride was a relatively short one—about six hours. Cassian looked forward to sleeping in his own cabin.

Twenty minutes later, he settled into the first-class train car and stowed his backpack on the luggage shelf above his seat. He sighed, flicking the lock closed on the compartment door and pulling the privacy curtain over the glass. He opened the file Ragnor had sent him on his large techpad as he sat down.

The train shuddered to life beneath him, the file showing him a holograph of a young seraph boy smiling up at him. Blond hair sprouted from his head, shorn closely on the sides but left slightly longer up top. His eyes crinkled at the corners as he smiled, their rich, chocolate brown color still visible.

The file wasn't extensive—he'd been in the Legion for barely four months, not long enough to really garner a thick file. His experience came mostly from the training new legionnaires underwent with their mentorship program. Van Alder was only his third elimination.

In the grand scheme of things, this was a fairly standard elimination for any legionnaire.

Cassian shook his head. He'd never been able to figure out quite how the Legion operated. He knew at a base level that most of the people in the nineteenth were indentured, whether that be through the Fallen Crown Mission or other ways of servitude, and that they all answered directly to the commissioner and vice commissioner. Other divisions had a more militant reporting structure, but the nineteenth was special.

The other thing that set the nineteenth apart was where their missions came from—usually, they were handed down by the governor himself. Of course, he only knew this much because of Ragnor. The nineteenth's true objective wasn't common knowledge.

Often, they eliminated criminals or hunted down syndicates that had been a thorn in the side of Spiral City for a long time. Ones the usual system of justice would never be able to capture. But sometimes, they were sent to do the governor's dirty work.

Cassian shuddered and clicked the techpad off. The light was straining his eyes now that the sky outside was fading to a bluish purple. He twisted the small, silver pinky ring on his right hand as he watched the light fade. Night wasn't far off, and the train would arrive in Spiral City before sunrise.

He laid his head back on the backrest of the bench, knowing he wasn't going to catch much sleep during the ride. But he closed his eyes anyway, the image of Kellan's face burned on the inside of his eyelids.

He'd had this dream before, he realized as a familiar scene played out before him. The strong yet gentle hands of his father were as familiar to him as his own reflection. It had been nearly a hundred years since he'd died, and Cassian had long since forgotten what he'd looked like, but he'd never forget those hands.

The room before him was familiar, too. It was the living room of the house he'd lived in as a child. He could hear the sounds of his mother making dinner in the other room, humming a tune that was familiar yet unspecified.

His father's face swam before him, the features blurred as if a droplet of rain had obscured them. But his hands were clear, holding out an unremarkable silver ring.

"Take it, son," his father's voice said. It was hazy but deep—so deep that it reverberated in his chest.

He obeyed, grasping the silver ring with his child-sized hands and gazing upon it with wonder.

"That ring is special," his father continued. "It's a precious heirloom that you cannot lose. I'm giving it to you, so you must keep it on at all times. Okay?"

He nodded vigorously, and as he did, the walls of the house began to shake. The ceiling collapsed, massive chunks of plaster raining down around them. Giant cracks formed, crawling up the walls like massive, fast-growing vines.

But the blurred figure of his father before him never moved. "Promise me, Cassian. Promise me you'll never take it off."

He tried to answer, but his voice wouldn't come.

He opened his eyes. He always opened his eyes after that.

Cassian was still on the train, but it was slowing, the squeal of the brakes rising with every passing building. He glanced down at the ring still resting on his pinky and sighed. It hadn't happened like that at all, of course, but the dream had taken one of his few happy memories of his father and turned it into…well, that.

He stood and stretched as the train continued its deceleration into the central train station at the northern edge of Spira Mirabilis. The station itself looked like an old cathedral, built of a grayish beige stone and dotted with soaring arched windows. Inside, its lofty ceilings curved in arches above their heads, the central walkways filled with planters and benches for weary travelers.

Even though he preferred the old-world charm Ebenfell boasted, he had to admit, Spiral City had its upsides. This train station was one of them.

He navigated his way through the crowded platform and retrieved his luggage from the claim, double-checking the locks hadn't been tampered with. Confident that everything was as it should be, he headed out of the station to the hotel Ragnor had booked for him.

Cassian was a bit surprised he wasn't staying in a safehouse, but Ragnor had mentioned something about procuring new ones. They'd have to make do with regular establishments in the meantime. He wondered if the old safehouses had been compromised somehow.

Even though he'd been here several times during his career with Ragnor, he'd only used the safehouses twice. Once had been on his very first mission here. He'd been assigned to a mission with a man named Leonardo Whitburn.

At first, he'd seemed normal—kind, even. He'd taken Cassian under his wing, showing him the ropes of being in Ragnor's employ. He'd learned a lot from Leo.

But he'd come to realize that Leo was nothing like the man he'd pretended to be at first. He was cruel, sadistic, and delighted in torture. He had no remorse, no sense of guilt at all. In fact, Leo was the perfect assassin to work for Ragnor—smart, deadly, and had a thirst for murder that no normal man should have.

The longer he'd spent with Leo, the more obsessed he'd become with Cassian becoming his partner. Leo had seen something in him that made him want to keep Cassian close. What that was, he never figured out.

They'd parted ways nearly 20 years ago when Leo disappeared. No one had been able to find him, and Ragnor had simply assumed he'd died. No one had heard from him since.

Cassian shook his head as he left the station, clearing his mind of thoughts of Leo. He hadn't even thought of the man for so long, so it was pointless to think of him now. He flagged down a bright purple taxi, spoke the address of the hotel to the driver, then sat back and calculated his next move of the day.

According to the file, Kellan planned to strike sometime this evening. He'd need to be there before the legionnaire to ensure he could obtain the files Ragnor had requested. Truthfully, he had no idea what the documents were or what information they contained.

He didn't know if Kellan was going to be after the same information. All he knew was that he'd be there to kill Van Alder.

He leaned back in the back seat and rested his head against the headrest. The buildings flew by as the cab made its way through the streets of Spiral City, the grayish blur of metal and glass lulling Cassian back toward slumber.

4

SHADOW

Unknown

The man stood in a basement laboratory, the fluorescent lights above reflecting off the shiny metal table before him.

He'd just watched their researcher leave through the door in the back of the room. He was a weasel of a man, his face pinched and hair mousey. The man had hated him from the start, but they'd been stuck with him. At least, until now.

They'd taken every precaution to ensure Alvemach's transition into the material plane would go as smoothly as possible. So far, no one had raised a fuss except for that weasly man.

The man would have just killed him, but Alvemach would not allow it. There was a system of balance, he'd said, between them and those who were part of their plan. Balance didn't matter to the man, but he couldn't disobey Alvemach and Alvemach couldn't disobey him. Their agreement was mutual, so their decisions must be as well.

It ultimately didn't matter who killed the researcher. Alvemach had promised he'd handle it. The man knew he would.

But that was not their issue at the present moment. Their issue was what the researcher had left behind.

"We've gotten what we need from Van Alder," Alvemach said, clasping his hands behind his back. The man had to admit, the humanoid form he'd taken was much more pleasant than his demonic form. "He was useful for our genetic research, but I don't believe he has the skill to proceed to the next steps."

The man had little patience for roundabout talk, but he knew Alvemach wouldn't leave him hanging for long. The next steps required someone with more ambition than the researcher had ever shown. It didn't help that he had been a thorn in their backside for several years now. The mousey man had fought them every step of the way and questioned every decision the man and Alvemach had made. The man's patience had worn thin long before Alvemach's.

The man huffed. "Can we continue without him?"

Alvemach smiled. "Yes. The researchers we have are skilled enough for the next phase. We are close enough to begin actual tests. But I have my eye on someone who may be an ideal partner to round out the final testing and implementation."

The man cocked his head, but didn't pry further. Alvemach would offer the information when he deemed it necessary. He was in charge of this portion of the plan, anyway. The man had little patience for detailed research, which was why he'd trusted Alvemach to handle it.

But something itched in the back of his mind. He was restless. They'd been at this for several years already, but his vision for the future seemed as far away as it had the day he'd summoned Alvemach.

It wasn't that he'd lost faith in the demon's abilities—in fact, Alvemach had proven time and time again that he was the perfect choice. He was simply frustrated. Maybe with the annoying researcher out of the picture, it would make their plan move along much faster.

Alvemach's smooth voice cut into his thoughts. "I'd like to show you something."

The man smiled, the corners of his lips curling dangerously upwards. Now this...this was more like it.

5

KELLAN

2nd of Blossom Moon

Suddenly, the world slowed to a crawl. What had this mysterious man just done? Had he truly recognized the scent of belladonna and simply walked away? Or had he heard Kellan's mask and decided to retreat?

Kellan didn't know, and he didn't care. He couldn't let him just walk away.

He followed the man's retreating footsteps down to the first floor, then out the back door. The clock in the corner of his visor read five minutes and twenty seconds until the cameras were operational once more. He needed to get this over with as quickly as possible.

He opened the back door and saw the man retreating through the garden. He flipped his dagger, readying his aim, then released it, letting it fly at the man's head.

The man dodged, slapping the dagger out of the air with a flick of his wrist, a small spark flying as metal grated on metal. Kellan hadn't even seen him draw a knife. He ignored the swoop of surprise in his belly in favor of drawing a second dagger from the holster strapped to his thigh.

He didn't throw this one. He circled the other man slowly, carefully observing him and every breath he took, every twitch of his hands. The elven man stood casually, apparently content to let

Kellan observe rather than attack first. His behavior was strange. Why was he here? How had he known to retreat when he'd smelled belladonna? Who was he?

A thought settled in Kellan's mind as he came behind the elven man. Maybe he'd been sent here to kill him. Maybe he'd pissed off the governor. Maybe this Van Alder guy was more important than they'd expected. There were simply too many questions, and Kellan had no answers.

He risked satiating his curiosity. "Are you here to kill me?" he asked, stopping behind the man's back.

The man didn't move, nor did his expression change. "No," he answered simply, but didn't elaborate.

"Then why are you here? Did the governor send you?"

"No, he didn't."

"You're not being forthcoming, you know." Kellan couldn't help but express his frustration. The man was being obtuse, and he couldn't decide if it was purposeful or if this was just how he was. What was he supposed to do? Kill him? That course of action seemed like his only one; although, based on how quickly he'd deflected the first dagger, it wouldn't be an easy task.

The man simply shrugged, seemingly unruffled.

Kellan had had enough. "If you won't talk, then I'm sorry, but I have to do this."

The man looked from his face to his dagger, then back to his face. He sighed. "I really didn't want to fight you, but it looks like I have no choice."

Kellan smirked, the familiar rush of adrenaline washing over him in anticipation of the clash. He'd enjoy this challenge.

The man lunged, a sword still strapped to his back, a dagger in his hand. So he wouldn't use the advantage of a longer weapon? Interesting.

Kellan rolled out of the way, just barely fast enough to avoid the man's incoming attack. He felt him brush against his shoulder but didn't feel any pain from a slicing blade. The man rounded on him again, unfazed by the evasion.

They circled each other, blades at the ready, but Kellan didn't go on the offensive right away. He waited, observing the elven man's movements with a scrutinizing eye, waiting for an opening or any sign that he would let his guard down.

But the man was good—too good, if Kellan was honest with himself. His movements were smooth, practiced, and calculated, and he found himself lost about what to do next.

The timer was getting dangerously close to zero, and he'd made no further progress in taking care of the man before him. He tried a different strategy.

"Look, I don't know who you are, but I can't let you go. You know too much," Kellan said, relaxing his stance just a touch. Enough that he knew the man would notice.

The elven man finally threw him a confused look, relaxing his own stance in response to Kellan. "And it seems you know too little."

Kellan cocked his head at the man's words, confused. But he didn't have time to ponder for long—the man crouched again, then leaped forward with no warning. Kellan scrambled to move out of the way once more, but this time he wasn't quite fast enough.

He waited for the familiar sting of the blade to cut into his skin, but once again felt nothing. As he waited for the cold steel to cut his flesh, something hard connected with his temple, and he crumpled, vision fading to black.

6

CASSIAN

2nd of Blossom Moon

He'd knocked Kellan out with the pommel of his dagger. After all, his orders were only to confirm the kill, not to murder the assassin.

He felt a little bad for him, though. Cassian had avoided giving any information, which had clearly frustrated Kellan. It didn't matter. If he'd revealed anything about Ragnor, it surely would have made its way back to his employer.

Cassian retrieved his techpad from a side pocket on his thigh, pressing a series of three buttons before replacing it. He'd disrupted the camera feeds on his own, not risking the Legion jamming to do it for long enough.

He'd smelled the belladonna gas and known he couldn't enter the bedroom. What he hadn't expected was for Kellan to follow. Legion assassins were dedicated to their jobs, and confirming the kill should have been his priority. He really was green.

He left Kellan slumped on the patio as he went back inside to confirm Van Alder's death. The house was deathly quiet, his breaths the only sound as he climbed the stairs and opened the bedroom door once more.

The canister was now emptied, the gas dissipating as he approached. He held his breath before entering, sweeping across the room in one steady movement. The man's neck was still warm, but his heartbeat was nowhere to be found.

He reached down to grab the canister from the floor and tucked it into a pocket on his belt. Leave no trace.

Cassian left the room as swiftly as he'd entered, not daring to exhale until he reached the hallway once more. With the kill confirmed, his job here was done.

Moving back out to the patio, he looked down on Kellan's sleeping face and felt a twinge of guilt. He knew enough about the Legion's draft and indenture program to understand that any sign of weakness like this wouldn't be taken lightly.

And he wasn't the type to ignore his messes. After all, it was his fault for being so careless.

A tug in his gut encouraged him to listen to that instinct. He knew the feeling well, that pull. It had guided him for most of his life, saving him on multiple occasions and encouraging him to listen to the gentler side of himself. He'd learned to trust it when it occurred.

He carefully grabbed Kellan around his midsection, slinging him over a shoulder and carrying him out the back gate of the manor. He was light for his height and warm against his shoulder.

The night was dark, and Cassian stuck to the shadows as he left the manor. He needed a taxi, but he couldn't risk being seen too close to Van Alder's residence so soon after his death. Kellan wasn't that heavy, but dragging him several blocks away from the manor by his waist was awkward.

They finally ended up in the very northern tip of Lunadere, near a run-down bar with a neon sign of an elf chugging a frothy beer. The brilliant yellow lettering read "The Frothy Mustache." Cassian cringed.

He found a taxi soon after, painting a sheepish look on his face at the driver's questioning look when he threw Kellan into the backseat.

"Too much to drink," he said by way of explanation, gesturing to the nearby bar as proof of Kellan's state.

The driver looked suspiciously at the weapons strapped to their bodies but didn't ask for details. He just nodded when Cassian gave the address of his hotel, peeling away from the curb with a squeal of the tires.

Upper Cloud's buildings were tall and imposing, but they didn't bother him. Of all the districts in Spiral City, Upper Cloud's architecture reminded him most of his home in Ebenfell.

Northwind, however, was intimidating in a different way. The entire district screamed money, and a lot of it. The buildings here were white and cream, with columns holding up arches that were several stories tall. Everything about this district felt foreign, even in the middle of the city.

The journey was nearly complete when a groan from the backseat sent Cassian's heart into a panic. He might be helping Kellan, but he certainly didn't need to know that now.

Kellan's face was scrunched, his lips puckering as he roused from Cassian's attack. He pulled at the small well of magic in his gut, threading it out through his fingertip. It flowed in a purple stream at Kellan, sending him back into slumber.

The hotel finally appeared, and he thanked the driver softly as he unloaded a snoring Kellan from the backseat. He entered through a side door, taking care not to bump Kellan's head on the doorway.

His room was on the fourth floor, and he carried Kellan up the stairs rather than using a lift. It would be best for him to dump Kellan in the room and leave as soon as he could. The fewer people who saw them, the better.

Cassian opened the hotel door clumsily, still trying to balance holding Kellan with grabbing the keycard.

The bed was still made—he hadn't spent a night here yet, and now he wouldn't at all. His weapons trunk was packed, save for the sword still strapped to his back and the daggers at his thighs.

He made his way to the bed, gently placing Kellan down on it and cradling his head before it could hit the mattress. He'd already smacked him in the head once, it wouldn't do for him to do it again. Cassian didn't want to risk waking him, especially not now.

Kellan's hair shifted beneath his hand. It was short in the back, but the strands were soft, glimmering golden under the hotel light. The multitude of piercings adorning Kellan's ears caught his eye as he rested the man's head on the pillow. They ran the entire length of his ear, some hoops that circled the shell closely, some small sparkling gems that interspersed themselves between the hoops. Pointed cones that resembled the blade of a dagger decorated his lobes.

Cassian shook his head, removing his hand from beneath Kellan's head. He was wasting time. He didn't need to be staring at his piercings, not while he needed to pack and get out of here.

He concentrated on removing his thigh holsters, setting them firmly into their padded spots in his case. Next came his sword, which he inspected quickly before setting it into the last remaining divot in the padding.

He hadn't bothered unpacking anything else, so he shut his case quickly and latched it closed.

A sound came from the bed, startling him. But Kellan hadn't awoken—he'd simply turned over, his face toward Cassian now. His mouth hung open just slightly, and he snored once.

Cassian frowned, but a small bit of relief sparked in his heart. It felt good to complete a mission without killing someone. It had been many years since he'd been able to merely monitor a situation without needing to bloody his own blades.

Van Alder had died tonight, he reminded himself. But Kellan had done that, not him.

He glanced once more at the man sleeping on the bed. He didn't pity him, but something akin to concern pooled in his heart. He looked so young. The Empire was cruel to continue to do this to the Fallen, but changing the heart of the government would not be an easy task.

Kellan breathed deeply again, and Cassian gathered his trunk, heading toward the door without a second glance back.

7

KELLAN

"**B**eck Aenmar," the voice said in his dreams.

Kellan stayed glued to his chair, unable to move his feet, unable to stand. He knew what came next—Beck would hold his hand out over the water, and the column would drench him in a torrent of red water. And they'd never see each other again.

The scene before him was blotted, like it had been painted with watercolors that were too washed out. He could see figures move, he could see the column of water that erupted upon Beck's arrival to the podium, but he couldn't see Beck's face.

Kellan knew, yet he couldn't move. His ankle rested at his knee, his back against the chair as he watched Beck be led away silently.

Because back then, he'd hoped. He'd hoped he would go where Beck was too. But his water had turned black, and the commissioner's gray eyes had regarded him with pity as Kellan tried to explain why he couldn't go, why he couldn't leave his best friend behind.

The dream classroom faded, a dreamscape of white and blue leaving him floating before he opened his eyes to a white plaster ceiling.

He was in his bedroom at the Guard. Whitewashed brick walls, the bed standard issue and covered in gray sheets and a thick comforter—now on the floor after being thrown off during the night. His shallow closet stood wide open, stuffed to bursting with streetwear fashion, chains, buckles, and pops of bright color. His stealth suit hung off the back of the cheap wooden chair parked by his barren desk, carelessly thrown there after retrieving it from the cleaner's last week. He hadn't needed to use it since, but he never bothered to hang it.

The walls were too thick and too hard to do any decorating, so he hadn't bothered. It had been nearly nine months since he'd begun here, and the room looked no more his own than it had when he'd first arrived.

Kellan didn't bother throwing on a t-shirt over his bare chest and opened the door to his room. Legionnaires who lived in the Guard were given a room within a dormitory that shared a common space with four other members. The five rooms opened to a common area, usually equipped with a kitchen and a living space. They shared bathrooms with the entire floor, including showers and toilets.

Kellan was headed there now, hoping a short walk and a cool splash of water might help calm his racing heart. The hallway was quiet and empty, mercifully.

The water did nothing to help, although it woke him up a little.

The dream wasn't a surprise; he'd had similar dreams for months. Ever since the council had assigned Beck to the Red Guard and Kellan to the Legion.

It was pretty accurate to what had actually happened on Draft Day, his inability to call out, to stop whatever had been happening to them. He'd often wished he could change the dream, to force himself to stand, to say something. He might get away with it in his head.

His hand drifted to the back of his neck to where the diamond tattoo rested. Every Fallen had one just like it. It was a mark of their imprisonment, a testament beyond the wings and their heritage that set them apart from the rest. It forced them to obey. Because if they didn't, they would be killed in a heartbeat.

Touching the tattoo was a habit he'd formed young, a way to remind himself that he wasn't in control of his own fate; that should he step out of line, he'd be taken down in an instant. It was a sobering reminder and often kept him from letting his temper get the best of him.

He padded back to his room, the cold marble floor jarring his senses with each footstep. It was refreshing this time of year.

He slowly pulled on a pair of gray, loose-fitted pants and an oversized, neon green t-shirt, shoving his head through the neck hole with a grunt. His roommates must be out, he thought as he finished dressing. Their rooms were silent, only sounds of birdsong and cars coming from his window.

Avalan and Kindra were fine roommates, and had welcomed him with open arms when he'd been assigned to their dorm. They'd shown him around town, and he could always rely on them for a night out.

His first month after joining the Legion, they'd taken him to a nightclub in Lunadere and told him he wasn't allowed to leave until he'd tried every liquor in the display behind the bar. It did little, thanks to his seraph heritage, but he could tell what the intent was. Avalan had called him a cheater, but had always invited him out from that night on. Kindra had simply chuckled, slapping Avalan on the shoulder and telling him they should really invent a different game for new recruits.

They were indentured too, but neither was a Fallen like him. They'd earned their tattoos another way. It felt like too much of an invasion of privacy to ask, and they weren't close enough for that, anyway.

The day passed in relative ease. His assignments for the day included reviewing data on a group of young teens in Rookford Down who had been stirring up trouble. They weren't a threat now, but they someday might be. The governor was adamant about keeping tabs on any citizens who might someday become a problem. Kellan didn't love the idea, but he couldn't exactly ignore his duty.

A door slammed sometime around mid-afternoon, the sun in his window bright as he shuffled the papers around his desk.

Avalan was back. His dark hair was messy from combat, his suit torn in several places over his thighs and shoulders. He didn't say a word to Kellan as he passed through into his room, slamming the door as soon as he stepped inside.

Those first few hours after a job were always the worst. The overwhelming numbness that settled over the senses dulled the pain of flesh wounds after the killing was done. Although he'd become accustomed to it, the sensation was never something he would be "used to." He couldn't imagine it was any easier for veterans like Avalan.

Ten minutes later, Avalan opened his door, his lower half wrapped in a towel, the slight blue tint of his skin revealing his elemental heritage.

"Showering," he grunted as a response to Kellan's glance.

He didn't wait for a response before leaving their dorm, and Kellan simply watched him go. Avalan was normally cheerful, but his dark moods after a tough day's work were not uncommon. Even though he was supposedly descended from water elementals, his fiery temper was exactly the opposite of what you'd expect.

He scrolled mindlessly through the news on his techpad, not really absorbing anything. There was news of the governor, of course, and from the seven councilors that represented each district of Spiral City. There was news from other cities, too. Rivenstorm had apparently just celebrated their Founders Day with a massive parade. Eastreach was gearing up for more exploration of their pride and joy, the deepest lake in the Empire, Galzaga Lake.

A name caught his eye, and a sinking feeling pulled on his heart. Kettleguard's Founders Day was next up—and as was their tradition, the Red Guard would take part in their annual parade.

He wondered if Beck would be part of it. Would he be marching down the street in his brilliant red military uniform, his fellow Red Guard members at his side? The thought caused a familiar ache to stab through his chest.

Kellan's finger scrolled past the Kettleguard article, not wanting to dredge up any more painful feelings. He'd had enough of them already.

Another article caught his eye as the door opened once more, welcoming Avalan back to the room. A merger between Northwind Medical and Morgenstern Tech was on the horizon, it seemed, the deal brokered by Morgenstern's own Research and Development Director, Selwyn Morgenstern.

"I need a drink," Avalan said with no preamble. He looked slightly better, his dark hair now a wet mess against his head. His mouth was a straight line, which was an improvement from the frown he'd been wearing earlier.

Kellan shut off his techpad. "Should we wait for Kindra?"

He shook his head. "She's on assignment all week. She won't be back."

"Then I'm in."

Avalan nodded, a smile forming at the corners of his mouth as he turned on his heel to get dressed.

Two hours later, they stood together outside a pulsing nightclub in Lunadere named Fate. It wasn't Kellan's first choice, but Avalan had said he didn't want to hear himself think, and this was the perfect place for that.

While Avalan had opted for his usual clubbing gear, Kellan had gone a bit overboard. Loose-fitting black pleather pants stuffed into heavy combat boots that laced up mid-calf. He'd tucked a black shirt with a neon graffiti print into the waistband, adding a studded black belt over top for texture. He'd added a pointless black crop jacket that fell just below his rib cage.

People lined up around the block. The club was much busier tonight than it usually was, although Fate was frequently stuffed to the brim. They stood in line for a while, Kellan leaning against the red brick walls plastered in brightly colored advertisements and posters as they slowly moved toward the door.

This part of Lunadere was what had made him fall in love with Spiral City. Its tightly packed alleyways and brilliant neon signs made him feel transported to another world when he wandered through them. The posters covering nearly every inch of space called out a variety of events and deals, from a theater production fifteen years ago to a sale on techpads that expired in two weeks.

It was late enough that the sun had set, the neon glow casting deep shadows across the ground and bathing everything in almost sickly shades of pink and purple. People still wandered about as they hurried home, some on foot, some on motorbikes. Their high-pitched whine rang in his ears as they darted past Fate's line.

A part of him wondered how much more he could love the city if he hadn't been forced to live here. How much he could have enjoyed its twisty roads and cobblestone walkways without the constant threat of punishment and death hanging over his head.

But those types of thoughts were dangerous for a Fallen to even entertain. His life would not change, no matter how much he might wish it to.

Avalan didn't say a word as they waited; he seemed broody, and Kellan refused to pry. Sometimes it was better not to ask, and Avalan didn't seem in the mood for small talk.

When they reached the doors, Kellan recognized the bouncer waiting for them. He nodded Kellan and Avalan inside without a second thought.

Kellan stopped before the door to turn back to the bouncer. "Hey, any reason it's extra busy tonight?"

The bouncer looked down at him, his septum piercing glittering in the club's shifting lights. "Pontius Morgenstern is throwing a welcome back party tonight. Everyone's here for him—I assumed you were too."

Kellan shook his head, then chuckled. "Maybe I'll get some free drinks."

The bouncer snorted, turning back toward the line that still wrapped around the building. "Just don't cause any problems."

Kellan lifted a hand to wave as he walked through the doors, the music drowning out anything else the man might have said.

Avalan was already gone—typical. He liked to dance when he'd had a bad job, drowning himself in drinks and dancing, often stumbling home long after Kellan had already fallen asleep or not returning until the next morning.

Not that Kellan didn't like to party, he just had little interest in dancing. He'd found most people who frequented nightclubs like this to be fake and stuffy. And he especially hated the looks in their eyes when they spotted the tattoo on his neck.

It was never contempt. It was pity, and he hated their pity.

He slithered his way through the crowd, making his way through the packed dance floor over to the bar in the corner, its shiny black countertop calling his name. The underside was lit with brilliant white lights and reflected off the shiny pleather stools anchored to the ground.

Most people had cleared away from the bar, the few stragglers hanging on to half-finished drinks and chatting with each other. How they could hear anything was a mystery to Kellan, but he didn't care. He was here to relax and have fun, even if alcohol did little more than burn his throat.

He'd motioned to the bartender and ordered a whiskey when he heard a chuckle from beside him.

When he turned to find the source of the noise, he found himself face to face with one of the most beautiful people he'd ever seen.

The man's hair was black as night, pulled back in a half bun on top of his head. His elven ears pointed out beyond the curtain of hair left down. His skin was smooth and looked soft, and his deep blue eyes gleamed with mischief. He wore a maroon button-up shirt, unbuttoned enough for Kellan to see a well-toned chest and several glittering necklaces around his neck. His pants were tastefully tight, enough to show off his lithe figure, but loose enough to not restrict his movement. He was fashionable, and Kellan could tell the clothing wasn't cheap.

"It's strange to see anyone drinking a whiskey neat at a club like this," the man said, his smile bright and blindingly white.

Kellan returned the smile with a smirk of his own. "I mean, it does nothing to me, anyway. I like the taste."

"Ah, a seraph, then?" The man's eyes flicked to his arms, searching for the wing tattoos and finding nothing thanks to his jacket. They traveled up to his neck then, as they always did when someone put two and two together.

Kellan waited for the look of pity to cross the man's face, but was surprised as he watched it change from curiosity to what looked like fury. A seed of tension dropped into Kellan's stomach, his fingers tensing as they rested on the bar top.

"You're a Fallen," the man finally said. Kellan could barely hear him; he had to rely on reading the man's lips to understand.

The bartender returned, setting Kellan's drink down on the bar. He turned to the dark-haired man and asked if he'd like anything. He shook his head, never taking his eyes from Kellan's face.

Kellan's jaw clenched as he waited. He refused to say anything. He didn't know what this man wanted, or why he looked like that when he'd asked if Kellan was Fallen. It wasn't exactly hard to figure out. Sure, other seraphs had gotten the tattoo later in life, but it was a safer bet to assume one was a Fallen.

He knew it was probably unfair to make sweeping generalizations about the elves, but they'd committed so many atrocities in the past that he simply couldn't stand to be understanding. The elves were the ones who created the Fallen, the ones who'd enslaved the humans after they'd rebelled.

Most elves didn't have it in them to care about anyone but themselves, and he assumed this man was no different.

The man's face softened as he watched Kellan tense, and he rubbed his chin as he sighed. "I'm sorry, I just bombarded you with questions right off the bat. You don't even know me. I apologize." He held out a hand. "Pontius Morgenstern, it's a pleasure."

Pontius Morgenstern. The bouncer had mentioned this club was packed for a welcome home party for him. Beyond that, he knew a little of Pontius.

He had been instrumental in the movement for human equality over the last two decades. Activists around the country praised his work. He was one of the few elves that, in theory, didn't fall into the colonizer stereotype.

He didn't know what type of man Pontius truly was. Would he care as much about the fate of an indentured servant like he would about humans?

He took the offered hand, shaking it firmly. "Kellan Manchester."

"Well, Kellan, it's nice to meet you. If you don't mind, I'd like to buy you your next drink."

He frowned, but couldn't think of a good reason to turn him down, so he nodded. Pontius beamed again, then slid into the unoccupied stool next to him.

"I'd love to hear more about you," Pontius began.

Before Kellan could say much more, another man appeared at Pontius' side. He was tall and dressed similarly, but his hair was shorter than Pontius' and a shade of medium brown that soaked in the shifting lights of the dance floor. He noticed Kellan a moment after placing a hand on Pontius' shoulder.

"Oh, sorry, I didn't know you were in the middle of something," the newcomer said, his gaze friendly.

Pontius shot his smile to the newcomer, then turned back to Kellan. "This is my best friend, Tarin. Tarin, this is Kellan. I was just getting to know him."

Tarin smiled at Kellan, his expression shockingly less brilliant than Pontius'. "Nice to meet you, Kellan. I'm afraid I need to steal Pontius away for a moment; his sister just arrived."

Kellan held up a hand. "That's all right, I'm sure I'll see him again tonight."

Pontius stood but didn't move after Tarin. He turned back to Kellan, then gestured for him to follow. "Why don't you come with me? We've got a VIP room that's much quieter, and I'd love for my sister to meet some more people instead of always having her nose buried in her work."

He didn't have a reason to say no. Pontius seemed harmless, and his friend Tarin didn't seem like a bad person. Avalan was somewhere on the dance floor, and Kellan wasn't particularly looking forward to spending an evening alone.

He nodded, standing and grabbing his drink. "Let's go, then."

Pontius beamed once more.

CASSIAN

27th of Cerulean Moon

Cassian rubbed his temples as he stood across the street from a pulsing nightclub in Lunadere. He could already feel a headache closing in, caused by loud music and shifting lights.

Cassian knew this mission would be messy, and he really wasn't looking forward to it.

Pontius had given him the name of the nightclub and invited him to his welcome home party. He'd accepted, of course. But he wished Pontius was more of a jazz club or theater type. The pounding music was going to cause him problems, and he wasn't looking forward to spending an evening screaming over the driving bass.

Cassian had donned his tamest outfit tonight—the objective wasn't to stand out, but to blend in. He'd paired understated black pants that fit tight to his legs with a loose button-up cream shirt. He knew he'd probably give off the impression of being boring, but that was precisely what he was hoping for.

The bouncer nodded him inside, and he was hit with a wave of heat and loud music the instant the door opened. He shut his eyes for a moment but opened them again to scan the crowd for Pontius.

They noticed each other at the same moment, and Pontius' mouth spread into a wide grin upon seeing him. He gracefully swept through the crowd to join him, gesturing toward the back of the establishment.

"Cassian! It's wonderful to see you here. Thank you for accepting my invitation," Pontius said, moving through the crowd once more.

Cassian followed. "I should be thanking you for inviting me."

"What kind of person would I be if I didn't get to know those who work within my chosen field? Come, I want you to meet my dearest friend, Tarin. I think you two would get along splendidly!"

Cassian listened to Pontius ramble as they made their way through the crowd that parted like water before them. Pontius had an air about him, one that made you want to look at him, to pay attention to him, to listen. Cassian rather enjoyed the man's company.

It was a shame he had to kill him.

Unfortunately for Cassian, this wasn't the first time he'd taken a liking to a target, although the circumstances of his mission here made the relationship much different.

He'd ignored the regret for a long time, but the miniscule bubble of affection toward Pontius reminded him too much of previous friendships. He couldn't risk even feeling it. It was too dangerous.

Pontius led them to a VIP room in the back of the club. Through the door lay a circular room, a velvet cushioned couch running around the entire space and a massive table in the center. It was cozy, meant for intimate conversations and bottle service. The room itself was quiet, obviously soundproofed from the noise of the club.

"Please, have a seat," Pontius said, slipping into the left side of the booth.

Another man already sat behind the table. He was elven too, just like Pontius, with medium brown hair and dark eyes. He leaned back casually in the booth, one arm thrown over the backrest and his other hand resting on a mostly empty glass in front of him.

"Cassian," Pontius began, then turned to face the man already seated in the booth, "this is Tarin; he's my closest friend and biggest supporter. I think you'll find you have much to discuss."

Cassian nodded toward Tarin, who offered a friendly smile.

They exchanged pleasantries, and Cassian allowed himself to relax slightly in their presence. Both men were incredibly friendly and charismatic, and discussed many topics unabashedly.

After their conversation had taken a comfortable pause, Pontius stood. "I'm going to grab us a few drinks and talk to some of the other people here. Would either of you like to join?"

Tarin chuckled and shook his head. "Don't forget your sister will be here in a little while," he said, a smirk tugging up the corners of his mouth.

"Then all the more reason to find more people to introduce to her," Pontius said, mischief in his eyes as he opened the door, letting the brief swell of noise usher him out into the pulsing nightclub.

Cassian's preliminary research on the Morgensterns had turned up nothing surprising. While Pontius was the philanthropic sibling, his sister Selwyn had taken after their father, Galan.

He wondered what he would find on Pontius. Would he have some secret proclivities, dark dealings with the underbelly of Spiral City? Was he actually an agent of chaos masquerading as an activist? Maybe he could find something out from Selwyn—he didn't know what sort of relationship they might have. Hopefully, there would be something for him to exploit.

"So Cassian," Tarin began, leaning forward to weave his fingers together on the table. "Pontius gave me the smallest amount of information about you, but I'd like to hear it from you. He mentioned you work for a non-profit in Ebenfell?"

Cassian nodded. His cover story was that he was an outreach coordinator with a non-profit in Ebenfell. He was here to expand their influence and work with other philanthropic companies. Of course, Ragnor had concocted the cover story and ensured all investigations into his falsified background would check out if Pontius investigated.

"We're really looking to expand our influence and grow our network," Cassian said, keeping his smile relaxed.

He had a long timeline for this job, but not forever. Gaining

Pontius' trust was the first step, and ensuring he was good with Pontius' circle of friends would only help him in his endeavor.

Cassian hated undercover operations like this one. Spending copious amounts of time with a target made it much more difficult to do what needed to be done when the time came. He'd hardly spent more than a few hours with Pontius and he already liked the man. What would happen when the time came to cut his throat?

Tarin seemed satisfied with his answer and moved on to questions about his favorite hobbies and what he liked best about Spiral City. Their conversation was lighthearted and easy, and Cassian mixed in a few truths about himself to make his lies more believable. Tarin ate them up.

A dinging noise interrupted their conversation about Tarin's mother and her tradition of making his whole family wear matching fuzzy socks each day of the week-long Evergreen Festival.

Tarin glanced at his techpad lying face up on the table, then grinned.

"Looks like Selwyn is here. Want to come with me to grab her?"

Cassian shook his head. "No, I'll wait for your return. Navigating through the crowd is easier with fewer people."

Tarin laughed as he scooted around the bench to stand. "Fair point. I'll track down Pontius before I head back."

With a quick tug on the door and another brief barrage of noise, Tarin was gone. Cassian sighed, relaxing back into the booth.

Going undercover was exhausting, there was no way around that. Ensuring you said the right things, keeping your backstory straight, and always staying alert for potential traps was a lot to have on the mind all the time. But with no one in the room, he allowed himself to relax.

The silence of the VIP room was nice. He closed his eyes, leaning his head back on the top of the booth, allowing the faint pulsing of the music outside the door to lull him into an almost trance.

The door swung open once more, startling him out of his reverie what felt like only moments later. When he turned to greet whoever had come through, his heart stopped.

He wasn't here to enjoy himself, and the pull in his gut reminded him that death would greet him if he wasn't careful. And now, it seemed, he was teetering on the edge of a disaster.

Pontius had reentered, the assassin he'd met in a garden four months ago standing beside him.

Cassian had immediately dragged Kellan outside, pretending like they were old acquaintances who hadn't seen each other for years. Pontius was shocked initially, but had slapped him on the shoulder as he grabbed Kellan's shirt and pulled him outside.

They now stood in the alleyway behind the building, Kellan's back pressed up against the brick. Cassian had caged him in with both arms, their faces close enough that their noses nearly touched.

Kellan looked unruffled, a boyish smirk painted across his lips as Cassian scrambled to explain what he'd dragged him out here for.

Kellan broke the silence between them. "I usually like to learn the name of my conquests before I do this sort of thing in a back alley, but I can make an exception for you."

Cassian choked on air. "That's…not, no," he spluttered, shaking his head. "Listen, I needed to get you out of there before you blew my cover."

Kellan cackled, the laugh coming out in a short burst that seemed to take him by surprise too. "How can I blow your cover when I don't even know who you are?"

Cassian stopped. He was right. He'd never given Kellan his name or told him anything other than he wasn't there to kill him. Then he'd knocked him out and left him in the hotel room without another word.

But Kellan knew Cassian wasn't a philanthropist like Pontius believed. He might know almost nothing about Cassian, but he knew enough to ruin the entire operation before it had even begun.

"Look, I'm sorry about last time. I really am. I was just trying to do my job," he finally said.

Kellan frowned, tilting his head just slightly to the left. "So what do you want from me?" Cassian could feel Kellan's breath tickle his eyelashes as he spoke.

"You have probably guessed by now that I'm in a similar line of work as you," he began, the words coming slowly as he explained as much as he could without giving too much away. "My name is Cassian, and everyone in that room believes me to be working for a non-profit out of Ebenfell."

"Well, Cassian, I'm a little pissed at how our last interaction went. I have no reason to cover for you."

Cassian's stomach fluttered the smallest bit at the way Kellan said his name. His heart pounded loudly in his ears, the myriad of options he had at his disposal slowly diminishing as Kellan continued to glare at him between his arms.

"You're right, you don't. So how about I offer you a deal?"

Kellan quirked an eyebrow. "I'm listening."

"You can ask me for any favor as long as I'm here. Anything you ask, so long as it doesn't blow my cover or expose me to anyone involved in this operation. I won't ask questions, and I'll only refuse if it violates one of those rules."

It was a risk, a massive gamble to do this. But he didn't want to kill Kellan, and offering him a favor was the only valuable thing he had to give.

Kellan pondered his offer, making a show of tapping his chin with his finger and staring off into space. Cassian's heartbeat was so fast it felt slow, like every third beat was skipped entirely. If he refused...

"I accept."

"You do?"

Kellan shrugged, the motion forcing his shoulders to brush against Cassian's arms, which were still firmly planted on the wall on either side of Kellan. "Sure. You're obviously skilled, and having you at my disposal will be a great advantage."

Cassian sighed in relief. "Then we should get back."

"After you," Kellan said, his boyish smirk from earlier back. It was annoyingly attractive.

He pushed off the wall, freeing Kellan from his arm-prison before turning back toward the front door and ignoring the slight heat in his cheeks.

Kellan didn't follow. "By the way," he called.

Cassian turned to face Kellan. His heart beat powerfully once, the pulse in his neck so strong he could feel it under his skin.

"Who are you here to kill?"

"That's not your concern," Cassian replied, voice low.

Kellan chuckled, thrusting his hands into his pockets. "I'd like to know so I know what to ask for, obviously."

"I'll let you know if it violates the rules."

"I want to know."

"No."

Kellan pouted, his lips puckering in a way that had Cassian clenching his jaw.

The pull tugged in his abdomen, the sensation warning him something was coming. The hairs on the back of his neck stood, the air around him thickening as if time itself had paused.

A shriek pierced the night, rending the air in two and sending goosebumps up his arms. It was close. Kellan took off, Cassian on his heels as they ran toward the source of the scream.

9

SHADOW

27th of Cerulean Moon

The girl had run.

She'd gotten out of the building easily and had broken the ghoul's grasp on her with hardly any effort. Part of him delighted in the thought that the serum was at least partially working, but he was annoyed that the first test subject to have a modicum of success had escaped.

But her escape was a good excuse to see what action she would take. So he'd let her continue, curious about where she would go and what she'd decide to do.

He pursued her down the city streets, following the scent of fear and Alvemach's blood through the twisting pathways. She wasn't following any sort of pattern. Her movements were erratic, confused, and done out of pure instinct.

His chase brought him to the entertainment district of Lunadere. She'd stopped, but something about her scent had changed. He approached her position carefully, stepping across the rooftops on his toes.

The smell of blood wafted across his nose. Judging by its potency, there must be quite a lot. The man swore under his breath. Had he just lost his first test subject? What a waste. Finding a new one would take time he didn't want to invest.

He swung down off the rooftops, landing as softly as a cat on the concrete sidewalk below. His ponytail swiped across the back of his neck as he turned his head left, right, then back again. There was no sign of her here, but the smell of blood was overpowering everything else.

That was when he heard the growling.

Around the corner, he saw it. The transformation wasn't whole—she still had her head and her body was mostly intact. But she'd grown the talons, long and sharp and nearly the size of his forearm, hanging off each finger like she'd taped swords to her hands. Blood ran down each talon, dripping to the ground with soft plips.

She was the most beautiful thing he'd ever seen.

Beneath her feet lay a man, clawed and slashed to ribbons. She'd spared no part of him, and he was nearly unrecognizable thanks to the massive claw mark down the center of his face.

She whipped her head to him, snarling and gnashing her teeth. Her eyes had turned a vibrant yellow and were nearly glowing with bloodlust. He smiled, tugging at the coil low in his abdomen to bring her to heel.

She did not obey his tug as she was supposed to. Instead, she lunged for his throat, her talons extended.

The man drew his sword and promptly slit her throat as she lunged, clicking his tongue as she fell to the ground and gagged as blood poured down her white gown.

He watched as life left her eyes, and the talons shrunk. A waste of a perfectly good test subject.

Alvemach would not be pleased, but he didn't particularly care as he heard footsteps running from behind him. It would be too much effort to hide the bodies now, especially when he could save himself instead.

He opened a portal and stepped backward through it, the pool of blood nearly reaching his shoes as a scream sounded through the night.

KELLAN

27th of Cerulean Moon

They ran down the alleys, Cassian hot on his heels as he searched for the source of the scream. It had been close, no more than a block or two away, but the buildings were dense enough here that weaving between them often took you out of the way.

Kellan rounded the corner a block north of Fate and found a young woman kneeling on the ground, a bloodied body beneath her hands.

The scene was awful.

A woman lay on the pavement, her white hospital gown stained red as blood flowed down from her neck and pooled beneath her head. Her chest didn't move.

Another body lay several feet away, this one in significantly worse condition. It looked as if a sword had cleaved the body in half. He noticed with a jolt that it wore a Legion uniform, the signature black and blue piping unmistakable even when cut to shreds. The scent of blood was overwhelming, making Kellan stumble as he rounded the corner.

The young woman held her hands over the body of the girl, tears streaming down her cheeks as she wailed.

Kellan swallowed the bile that rose in his throat. He had to do something.

"Cassian, call Trauma Team." When Cassian hesitated, he raised his voice. "Now!"

The other man turned away, reaching into his pocket for his techpad and dialing the emergency unit. The Twelfth division would arrive soon to begin initial investigations, but right now Kellan needed to console the young woman who'd witnessed this gruesome scene.

He approached her slowly, unable to take deep breaths to steady himself thanks to the scent of blood overwhelming him.

"Hey, hey, it's all right. We're calling someone to help," he said in as calm of a voice as he could.

She whipped her head up to him, her eyes red-rimmed and puffy, the fear in her eyes apparent through the pain and tears. He held out a hand to help her up, and she flinched away from it. She stared at him, her mouth hanging open in terror.

"It's all right, I'm with the Legion," he continued in his calm voice. "I'm here to help you. Are you hurt?"

This time, she shook her head as she slowly lifted a shaking hand to grasp his, allowing him to help her up off the ground. Her hand was slick with the girl's blood but her grip was firm, as if the only thing anchoring her to the world was the feel of her hand in his.

He led her a few steps away from the scene, enough that the air was clear and he could breathe without being choked by the scent of blood. She seemed to calm a little with the change of scenery, her breathing less shallow.

He spoke again in the same calm voice. "Can you tell me your name?"

She looked at him again, breath hitching in her throat. "K-k-Kagome," she stuttered through stifled sobs.

"Well, Kagome, I'm Kellan. My friend Cassian over there is calling the emergency unit right now. Why don't we take a few deep breaths?"

Kagome nodded slowly, as if moving was painful for her. He breathed in once slowly through his nose, maintaining eye contact with her the entire time. She breathed in with him, hers much shallower than his.

He breathed out through his mouth, forcefully pushing the air out of his lungs. She followed his lead, the tears still streaming down her cheeks. She didn't blink; she continued to stare at Kellan, her eyelids fluttering as she repressed more tears.

They repeated this exercise several more times, her hand still in his as they breathed in sync. He did his best to keep her focus away from the scene behind her, to keep her focused on breathing and calming her heart rate.

Cassian had finished calling the unit a while ago and now stood watch at the mouth of the alleyway to keep any other passersby from stumbling into the grisly scene. They were far enough back that it was unlikely to happen, but it was still visible from the street if you looked hard enough. He felt a tug of gratitude to the man even though they'd just reunited under the worst possible circumstances.

Kagome's breathing became steadier as they stood together, hands still intertwined. She calmed a little, enough that when the twelfth got there, they'd be able to interview her.

Sirens reached his ears after what felt like an eternity, and they soon cordoned the scene off. The alleyway filled with several people dressed in black outfits with bright red piping, the "12" of their ouroboros pins glinting in the dim alleyway lighting.

One person approached him, their face grim. "You were the one who called this in?"

"No, my"—he searched for Cassian and found no trace of him. His jaw clenched.—"Yeah, I called it in."

The twelfth operative gave him a searching look but moved on. "I need to get your information as well as hers."

"Sure," he said, nodding. "Kellan Manchester, nineteenth division. This is Kagome."

They turned to Kagome, their face softening as they noticed her terrified face. "Kagome, can you give me a little more information about yourself?"

She looked at Kellan, and he nodded to encourage her. "Y-yes. I'm Kagome Ichinose; I live in Bloomside."

The operative smiled. "Thanks, Kagome. We'll have someone escort you to the Guard for questioning, is that all right?"

She nodded once more, but stopped abruptly and turned to Kellan. "Would he be able to take me?"

They looked at Kellan, regarding him with a suspicious eye. "You said you were nineteenth? Do you have your pin?"

He shook his head. "I'm off duty, but I can prove it." He turned away from them, baring the back of his neck and the tattoo there to the operative.

When he turned back, the traces of suspicion were gone. "Very well. Kellan, please escort Miss Ichinose back to the Guard. We'll handle the rest here."

Without waiting for a response, the operative turned on their heel and walked away, leaving Kellan and Kagome, still holding hands, alone in the alleyway.

Kellan left Kagome with the intake team from the seventeenth on the first floor of the Guard. He'd been called to speak directly with the commissioner.

He'd figured this would happen as soon as he showed the emergency operative his tattoo. It wasn't like he was in trouble—he hoped—but the commissioner would want to be briefed on the situation.

Kellan hadn't had the chance to find Cassian again after he'd disappeared. He figured Cassian didn't want to be questioned by the Legion and had snuck away as soon as he heard sirens approaching.

The door to the commissioner's office was at the end of a long hallway lined with similar oak doors. However, his door was much larger, spanning the entire wall from floor to ceiling. It was imposing, and he was positive it was built to be intimidating.

The commissioner's office was vast, and although he'd been here several times before, it still surprised him each time. The floor was made of a cool-toned stone and covered with a massive ornate rug in a style popular in the southern countries of Uswye and Ellsemere. The bookshelves lining the walls looked like pine, stained dark brown and filled with reference notes and leather-bound tomes. But the most interesting part of the office was a tall sliver of stone set upon one of those shelves—a stone that emitted a clear pitch like a siren song. It was a singing stone, one mined primarily outside of Laka, although the mines had long since collapsed. Because of the mines' demise, singing stones were nearly impossible to come by anymore.

The stone was lightly colored, this one nearly white with veins of sea-foam green weaving their way through the sliver. Although the note it emitted wasn't loud, it was distracting. Singing stones grew loudest at night, so at this time of the evening, it was nearly at its peak.

Kellan stopped before the desk, his hands behind his back in a rigid stance. The commissioner just waved him into a chair with hardly a second glance.

The commissioner glanced up at him, his gray eyes betraying nothing over his half-moon glasses as he watched Kellan lower himself into a chair.

"I heard you called in a double homicide—I'd like the details," he said, voice even and low.

The commissioner looked like he'd come from home, dressed in a white button-up and soft jogger pants. It was the most casual he'd ever seen the leader of the Legion, and most likely the most casual he'd ever see him again.

Kellan breathed in deeply, preparing himself. But before he could speak, the door opened once more, and another legionnaire entered with a techpad in hand.

The commissioner waved her over, and she sat in the chair next to Kellan, fingers ready to record their briefing.

He nodded to her, then to the commissioner before giving

his report.

Kellan changed only one detail—that Cassian had been present and called emergency services. Otherwise, he detailed the scene as he'd witnessed. He described what he assumed had been Kagome's scream, which had alerted him to the situation.

The commissioner listened quietly, one hand on his chin, the other resting casually on the desk before him. The clear note from the singing stone rang out underneath his story, adding a haunting soundtrack to the gruesome tale.

When he'd finished, the legionnaire beside him stopped typing, and the commissioner nodded once to her. She stood up, bowed, and exited the room, taking her techpad with her.

"I'd like to ask you something off the record," he said, leaning back in his chair to cross his fingers over his chest.

"Sir?" Worry burned yellow in his mind. Did the commissioner suspect something strange about his story?

The commissioner closed his stern eyes, sighing deeply before continuing. "I'm giving you the chance to say no to this, but I want to offer you an opportunity."

Kellan didn't know how to respond, so he didn't. He swallowed, aware of how loud the click of his throat was even against the hum of the singing stone.

"I'd like to give you the chance to investigate this, Private Manchester. The witness already knows you, you were the first on the scene, and this is a good opportunity for you to test the waters of another side of the nineteenth division."

Kellan paused, anticipation worming its way through his body. It sang in his ears, a high-pitched ringing like a bell had been struck far away.

"Why me?" he finally asked.

The nineteenth division, although made up of only indentured members, had other duties beyond elimination and espionage. Kellan imagined the disturbing death of a legionnaire made the governor want this kept out of the public's eye. Widespread knowledge of one of their peacekeeper's murders would cause panic.

The commissioner looked over his glasses at Kellan, his features stern but not unkind. "I thought I made my reasons pretty clear when I asked you before."

Kellan shook his head. "I should clarify—there are plenty of other senior privates and corporals who would be suitable for this. I'm curious why you'd assign this to me."

"Everyone must start somewhere, and I believe this would be a good stepping stone for you." He stood from his desk, hands clasped behind his back, staring at his bookcases. Even with his casual clothing, he looked commanding. "You've been on several cases with Lieutenant Razorborn, and he was confident you could serve in this capacity on your own based on his observations."

Kellan shifted uncomfortably in the chair, eyes straining against the bright lights of the office. He supposed the commissioner was right. He would have been assigned an investigation case like this eventually. The timing happened to be right.

"And Private, I'm afraid you are one of the few members of the nineteenth who isn't currently on long-term assignment. Even if I'd wanted to assign this to someone of a higher status, I can't." The commissioner turned back to him, his eyes tired. "I won't throw you to the wolves. You'll have help. Private Larsen of the eighteenth will assist you, and I'm sure Lieutenant Razorborn would be more than happy to provide guidance."

Kellan bowed his head. "Then I'd be happy to take the case, sir."

The commissioner removed his glasses, rubbed his eyes, then replaced them on the bridge of his nose. "I'm delighted to hear you say so. Private Larsen already has some information ready for you in her office. You're dismissed."

Kellan stood from his chair, balling his hands into fists to stop them from trembling. He bowed to the commissioner before turning to exit the large office doors.

The commissioner nodded back, lowering himself down into his chair and hauling a stack of papers toward him. It looked as though he was settling in to work for the rest of the evening.

The words left Kellan's mouth before he could stop them. "Aren't you going to go home, sir?"

The commissioner lifted his eyes to Kellan, the smallest smile brushing across his lips. "Thank you for your concern, Private, but I'm too awake to return home. I might as well get ahead on some of this paperwork." He lifted the stack as if to prove his point.

"But what about your family?"

The commissioner's face fell, his eyes downcast as the corners of his lips pulled down slightly. "There is no one waiting for me at home."

Kellan felt a pang tug at his heart but refused to press further. He'd pushed his luck enough talking so casually to the commissioner. It wouldn't do to push any further.

"I'm sorry to pry, sir. I'll take my leave." He turned on his heel without waiting for any further comment from his commander.

He heard a small sigh from behind him as he walked toward the door, the pitch perfectly in sync with the tone of the singing stone.

"K—Private?" The commissioner's voice drifted to him just as he grasped the handle of the office doors. "Good luck."

11

CASSIAN

27th of Cerulean Moon

After calling the emergency unit for Kellan, Cassian left the scene before the twelfth arrived. He refused to get caught up in the mess that would inevitably surround the situation. He returned to Fate and found Pontius in the VIP room once more, now accompanied by two women.

The one closest to Pontius had the same facial features, her oceanic eyes betraying their shared heritage. Her eyes were slightly upturned and her nose was delicate. She, like her brother, was quite beautiful. Her hair, however, set her apart from him. Instead of the deep black Pontius sported, hers was a brilliant, fiery red.

The other woman sat next to Tarin, her bubblegum pink hair done up in two buns atop her head, a sparkling set of hair jewels strung between them. If the first woman was regal beauty and fire, this woman was sunshine and fluffy clouds. Her sparkly blue dress left her voluptuous midsection bare, giving him a peek of a wing tattoo.

The first woman, Pontius' sister, turned her gaze to him, her eyes driving into him like she could see down to his soul.

"And who is this?" she said, not addressing him but also not turning to speak to Pontius.

"This is Cassian. I told you about him, remember? The one from

Ebenfell?" Pontius said.

The woman frowned, finally turning her eyes away from Cassian to glare at her brother. "I thought you said this would be a small gathering."

"It is," he countered, beaming at her. "There's only five of us—" He stopped abruptly as he looked back at Cassian, confusion written on his face.

Before he could ask, Cassian spoke. "Kellan wasn't feeling well, said he was going to go home."

Pontius' face fell for a moment, but he quickly perked back up. "Can't be helped. Cassian, let me introduce you to my wonderful sister, Selwyn Morgenstern."

Cassian nodded his head toward Selwyn, her face unreadable as she nodded back.

"And her best friend, Mina Rosewood." The girl with bubblegum hair smiled brightly at him, reaching her small hand out to shake.

He took her hand as she spoke. "It's wonderful to meet you, Cassian!" Her voice was high pitched and bright, exactly the sort of voice you'd expect from a girl like her.

"A pleasure," he replied, releasing her hand after a brief shake.

They spent the evening discussing various topics related to Pontius' work, moving smoothly through to discuss Mina's final year of university and finally landing on Selwyn's work with Morgenstern Tech. Cassian's ears pricked at the topic, his curiosity begging him to ask questions.

"Selwyn, if I may," he began, "could you tell me a bit more about your agreement with Director Byre?"

She cocked an eyebrow at him, her trepidation at his presence in their small group obvious. He knew he was the outsider here; it seemed the rest of them had known each other for years, but he'd be damned if he'd let that stop him from his mission.

Getting to know Pontius' friends would only make his objective easier. But part of him yearned for the closeness that came with the years of friendship shared between the group before him. Mina leaned on Selwyn, their shoulders pressed together as she leaned across to talk to Tarin about something. Tarin's arm rested behind Pontius, the casual gesture of intimacy accepted without a second thought.

He'd never really had the chance to make connections of his own since he'd been promised to Ragnor since he was young. Ragnor didn't share his possessions. The only people he'd really connected with at all had been Leo and a boy he'd fallen for many years ago named Aidyn. Both of those relationships had ended in tragedy.

Possibly because she noticed his genuine curiosity, Selwyn sighed. "Director Byre and I have an agreement to allow Morgenstern Tech to develop bionic limbs and assistive technologies."

Cassian raised his eyebrows. Most of Morgenstern Tech's output focused on security and personal protection—a deviation into bionics would certainly be a lucrative new direction for the company.

"Selly's always been interested in helping people, just like Ponty! But she uses her brain more than Pontius does," Mina interjected, chuckling at Pontius' flabbergasted noises at her statement.

Selwyn cracked a slight smile, the corner of her mouth just barely curling at the exchange between her best friend and brother. "Bionics has been an interest of mine since I was young. My efforts are simply for the good of society."

"It certainly sounds like a lucrative deal," Cassian said.

Selwyn's smile faded as quickly as it had come. "Profitability aside, it will be good for our company to expand into endeavors that save lives rather than end them." Her blunt tone made the temperature of the air drop several degrees.

He glanced at Pontius, who'd been listening to his sister with a vague look of pride on his face. But at Selwyn's latest statement, his face had also fallen. It seemed his opinion of the Morgenstern's main revenue stream was just as positive as his sister's. They not only led the industry in weapons manufacturing, but had exclusive deals with both the Legion and with the Red Guard.

Mina clapped her hands, a bright smile on her face as she stood.

"Anyway, I hear some great music playing out there right now. Why don't we go dance?"

Selwyn didn't move, but Tarin and Pontius both stood, nodding after Mina, who'd already put a hand on the door.

Cassian debated standing, but he knew following them wouldn't do much for his mission, and he wasn't exactly a fan of dancing to begin with.

Tarin and Pontius glanced at him once, questioning looks on their faces. He shook his head, and both men shrugged in unison, eliciting a small chuckle from Selwyn as they exited after Mina.

The silence was oppressive after the rest of their party left. Selwyn seemed to have no interest in starting a conversation with him. Instead, she sat with her glass of red wine, swirling it as she inspected the liquid within.

He debated leaving then, making an excuse to Pontius and calling it a night. But something told him to stay, that sticking around Selwyn might prove fruitful.

Before he could speak, Selwyn did.

"I'm curious why you're here," she said, her voice even. "Pontius told me you work for a non-profit in Ebenfell, but I'm not understanding why you've come to Spiral City to work with my brother."

Cassian swallowed but kept his face neutral. Pontius had been easy to convince with a few colorful words and a smile, but he could tell it wouldn't be nearly as simple with her. She was too observant to fool. So he mixed in some truths.

"My boss asked me to get in contact with Pontius because of the work he's done. Said working with him would be good for our organization and could really benefit our pro-human work in Ebenfell. His name is well known—connecting with him will be useful."

Selwyn chewed the inside of her lip as she stared at him, her eyebrows slightly raised. His heart beat annoyingly hard in his chest. Undercover work like this wasn't new to him, but something about her gaze was enough to make him squirm.

She made a noise, then leaned back into the booth, her eyes closed. "I didn't want to come tonight, but my brother has been gone for a month in Rivenstorm. Do you know what he was doing there?"

Cassian shook his head, then realized her eyes were still closed. "No, I don't. He didn't mention it."

She sighed. "He was hunting down the Resistance. You know, the Phantom Flame? But he found nothing. We know they exist, yet they totally ignored him. He tried his best and couldn't get a single person to speak with him."

Cassian stayed silent, unsure where the conversation was headed. He didn't want to interject before she finished her thought.

"I guess what I'm getting at here is what's the point? You do all this work and hardly have anything to show for it. He's wasting his time, and you're wasting yours. There are other, more effective ways to enact change. He had the right idea when he worked with the councilors on the Human Equal Rights Act a few years ago, but it feels like he's stagnated." She sighed, rubbing her temples. She spoke passionately, like she cared deeply for her brother and hated to see him fail. A doting sister, he thought.

Cassian breathed deeply. "I guess he'd say that the point is to change the hearts of the people. The most important thing when backing a societal change like this is to move their hearts along with their minds."

Selwyn's eyes flew open. Her stare was intense, enough to make him sweat. But it wasn't hostility in her gaze, it was surprise. Like she hadn't expected him to say such a thing.

"I…" she began, trailing off as if to search for the next words to say. "I suppose you're right. I never thought of it that way."

He gave her a soft smile, his shoulders relaxing. "It can be hard to see things that way when you've been told what to believe all your life."

She didn't return the smile. "Yes, it can be."

Selwyn picked up her glass, draining the last of the wine in a single swig before standing from the table and turning to face him once more.

"I rather appreciated our conversation, Cassian. Please do what you can for my brother—he deserves your faith."

He nodded to her as she exited the VIP room, her empty glass in hand.

He took his leave soon after his conversation with Selwyn, promising another meeting with Pontius before heading back to his safe house in Northwind.

Too much had happened tonight, but his mind was stuck on seeing Kellan again and the bloody scene that they'd found. He wondered if Kellan could handle that all right.

Cassian shook his head. There was no sense in worrying about a state-sanctioned assassin like him. Hopefully, they'd never see each other again. Staying too close to a legionnaire could only end badly.

His stomach dropped as he recalled the events of the night. He'd promised a favor to Kellan, and Cassian was a man of his word. Even if he skipped town, the guilt would eat away at him. It would be smarter to get it done quickly, so he wouldn't have to worry about it as he continued his mission.

What Kellan could ask for, he couldn't even try to imagine.

He arrived a block from the safe house, tapping his techpad against the meter of the taxi before exiting the cab. He took his time walking to the safe house, listening closely to the sounds around him for anyone following him and noting which buildings still had lights on.

The safe house was new—this one a nondescript townhome in a row of similarly beige townhomes, the front door painted a bland brown to blend in with the others. Even he had trouble remembering which it was. He'd never had an issue remembering where the old safehouses were, but Ragnor had decided to get rid of them. Cassian wasn't stupid enough to ask him why.

He stuck the old brass key in the lock, hearing the mechanisms register the security spells attached to the lock and the key.

Inside, the hideout was bare. Ragnor didn't believe in allowing his subordinates comfort. Instead, he was practical. A couch sat in the corner, the cushions sagging. A small end table with a single lamp was next to it. The walls were bare, and the kitchen was much the same. Up a small staircase in the corner were the bedrooms and bathrooms, as well as a small office. The bedrooms had a single bed with sheets and a pillow; the office came equipped with an old desk and chair.

The fact that there was furniture in here at all somewhat surprised Cassian—he'd been in previous safe houses with no furniture whatsoever. He'd often had to sleep on the floor after a mission, tossing and turning as the hard surface made his shoulders ache. Ragnor likely thought this house was positively luxurious.

He shut the door behind him, engaging the lock once more, the sounds of Spiral City nightlife dying as if sucked into a vacuum behind the door. The house might look plain and simple, but the real money lay in the security spells layered on every inch.

Cassian sighed, running his fingers through his hair as he tried to decide whether it was worth it to take a shower or not.

Before he could choose, his techpad buzzed, the number familiar. He frowned slightly before picking it up.

"Ragnor? This is a surprise."

Ragnor's voice was unamused. "This is a high-priority mission, Cassian. I thought I made it clear that I would check in with you periodically throughout the mission."

He was right, but Cassian hadn't taken him seriously. He'd never checked in on him before, only asking for a debrief after his mission was complete. But he supposed it made sense—this was a long-term undercover job, something he hadn't done in years.

"Yes, sir. I just assumed you would wait longer than two days before calling me."

"I want a debrief. Were you able to make contact?"

"Yes, sir. I just got back from an evening with the target. No information yet, but I believe he trusts me already."

Ragnor huffed. "I expect results, and quickly. You have a flexible timeline thanks to the council, but you know my standards are much higher."

"I understand, sir. I won't disappoint."

"Good, because you know the consequences if you do." With that ominous statement, Ragnor ended the call.

Cassian certainly knew the consequences. And there was no way in hell he'd ever let Ragnor lay a finger on his mother.

Even if it meant killing. Even if it meant pushing his own heart aside. Even if it meant a life of solitude and fear and resentment. Even then. Especially then.

SECTION 2

THE STARFALLEN REBELLION MADE THE FALLEN

The Starfallen Rebellion was one of Ileron's most significant historical events, its bloodshed and strife still felt even now, more than eight hundred years later. A clash between the displaced peoples of the Conjunction and the original occupants—the humans—the Starfallen Rebellion had ended with a massive battle between Sol and the original god, Hym.

Both the humans and their god Hym were left defeated at the battle's end, and other races were punished by the elves for their involvement.

The seraphs, celestial descendants of the gods of the old realm, were originally one race. Split into two by their support for either side of the war, the losing seraphs were forced into servitude for their crimes and rebranded the Fallen. Although no different genetically than their non-Fallen counterparts, the Fallen have been a tradition long upheld by the Empire.

The humans faced a fate even worse than that of the Fallen. They were stripped of their freedom, forced into slavery by the very people who'd invaded their land.

The times have changed, marginally. The humans are fighting to regain their freedom, the right to live in the land that was originally theirs. And their plight includes those punished for siding with them all those centuries ago.

12

KELLAN

28th of Cerulean Moon

After being dismissed from the commissioner's office, Kellan went to the interview rooms where Kagome was being held. Although they were required to hold any witnesses for questioning, he knew deep in his gut that she wouldn't have been capable of committing a crime like this.

Now came the part he'd been dreading. He knew, as the investigator for this case, that he'd have to force Kagome to relive that experience. It was the worst part of an investigation, but necessary.

He rode the elevator down to the subterranean floors. The Guard only had a few floors that went beneath the ground, all reserved for interview rooms and the temporary holding cells they used to contain criminals before they could be moved to the prisons outside of the city.

The interview room Kagome was in was not comfortable, but it wasn't as sterile and terrifying as the others. This one held a threadbare couch and a table, on top of which a steaming mug of tea sat untouched. Someone from the seventeenth must have gotten it for her before they'd left her here.

The room was brightly lit, with white flooring, white walls, and massive one-way windows that allowed observers to watch what was happening within. The windows were an almost reflective material, appearing clear on the outside but much like a mirror on the inside.

He could tell Kagome had been crying; her eyes were red-rimmed and puffy, and tear tracks stained her cheeks a soft pink. She wasn't crying now, though, her eyes dry as she lifted her gaze to the door.

He stepped through, actively forcing himself to relax his shoulders. As long as he stayed calm, she would feed off his energy.

Kellan sat in the chair opposite her, crossing his legs as he set a recording device on the table. "Hi, Kagome," he began, keeping his voice soft. "I'm sorry we had to keep you here for so long. Do you mind if I ask you some questions about what happened tonight?"

She bit her lip, then nodded. "Am…am I a suspect?"

"No, you're not," he replied quickly. "I just want to understand what you saw."

She flicked her eyes down to her hands folded in her lap. She'd already washed the blood off, but it still stained her clothes. He could tell she was hyper-aware of it as she stared downwards.

He spoke again. "Why don't you walk me through what happened this evening? What were you doing in Lunadere?"

"I was visiting a friend," she began, her voice quivering. "They live a few blocks away from the place where she…where I saw what happened. I'd run out to get us some snacks from the shop around the corner."

"And what prompted you to go to the alley?"

"I heard something growling," she said. "I was curious, so I followed the sound."

"Then what happened?"

She shuddered. "I came around the corner and saw the girl lying on the ground, but her hands…her hands were disfigured."

Kellan cocked an eyebrow. From the little he'd seen, the girl's hands weren't out of the ordinary. Maybe she'd imagined something from the trauma of seeing a dead person.

"Can you explain that a little more? What do you mean by

disfigured?"

"She had claws, long and sharp, and they were retreating as I watched her die."

Claws? He hadn't considered it, but maybe the girl was a shifter. Had she been coming out of a transformation? That was definitely a possibility, but he didn't have enough information about the victim to know what to ask.

Kellan shifted in his chair, crossing his leg over the other at the knee. "Okay, that's helpful, Kagome. Did you see what happened to the other man?"

She shook her head. "No, he was already like that when I got there."

"You said you watched her die," he began, and she flinched. Guilt welled, a sickly green color in his chest. "Did she say anything before she passed?"

Kagome froze as if the question prompted a memory she'd forgotten. "Yeah, actually, she did," she said. Her voice shook.

"Do you remember what she said?"

"It sounded like a name—Alfie? Alvin? Alvie?"

Possibly her killer? The fact she could get even a single sound out from the way her throat had been cut was surprising, but not impossible.

"Okay, Kagome, that's it for now," he said, and she visibly relaxed. He knew this interview must be stressful for her, and having to relive the events she'd just witnessed was a strain no one should have to experience.

He showed her to the door, letting one of the other legionnaires take her back up to the main floor and escort her home. She'd be under protection for the next few days, just in case the killer tried to target her.

Kellan's job, however, was far from finished. By the time the interview was over, it was well past the small hours of the morning, and light stained the sky as he finally made his way back to his dorm to collapse for a few hours. The coroner would need more time to do his analysis, and Vaida would probably need some time to gather enough information for a brief.

So he took the chance to collapse into his bed as the first few rays of a new day stained his gray sheets gold.

He prodded open the door to the crime lab later that day, letting his eyes adjust to the darkness of the room. The lab was large and open, one corner covered in computer monitors displaying various data and charts, another filled with a variety of microscopes, petri dishes, and vials. Vaida was sitting before the computer screens in the corner, typing furiously at her keyboard. The light from the screens reflected off her dark skin, making her look like she'd bathed in neon paint.

Vaida Larsen was a beauty. Her long dark hair reached down her back in tight braids that she frequently twisted into updos to keep from falling in her face. She wore large, rounded spectacles that made her gray eyes seem larger than they already were, and had perfectly pouty lips that she was currently chewing on as she stared at her screens.

It was rare to see Vaida in anything but her Legion uniform, and today was no different. The black, straight-fit pants paired with an open blazer with blue piping along its edges marked her as a member of the investigations team. Her white undershirt was buttoned all the way to the top, her matching blue necktie secured beneath her chin to precise Legion standards. He had a similar uniform, but the piping on his was blood red, a color unique to the nineteenth.

He'd first met Vaida while training with Razorborn. She was part of the eighteenth but assisted every law enforcement division. She was a brilliant hacker, scientist, and data analyst, and her skills had proved invaluable in solving hundreds of crimes. Although he didn't have to visit her as often as he did, he found he enjoyed her brusque demeanor and cool attitude.

While she'd probably deny it, he considered them friends.

"Hey, V," he said as he pushed the door closed.

At his arrival, she spun in her chair to face the door, a delicate eyebrow cocked. "I expected you hours ago," she said by way of greeting. She turned back to her computer screens, then pointed at the single chair parked next to her desk. "Sit. I have information to share with you."

He obeyed meekly, feeling like a dog with its tail between its legs after she scolded him for being late. He hadn't expected her to have anything to share this quickly, but it seemed his judgment was off the mark. He should have known better.

"First victim is Corporal Cygnus Clearview, seventeenth division. He was out on patrol in Lunadere when he was attacked."

"Okay," Kellan said. "Any reason he may have been targeted? Did he work a big case recently? Have a scuffle with someone?"

Vaida shook her head, her glasses slipping down her nose a bit. "Nothing I can see. He did a lot of regular desk work, mostly cleaning up after his fellow division members. He wasn't a standout person."

"Interesting. What else you got?"

She threw him an exasperated look, one he'd seen before when he'd interrupted her trains of thought in the past.

Vaida was what Kellan would consider fast-moving. She didn't have tolerance for small talk, as he'd discovered quickly, nor did she have patience for people with no motivation to learn.

She did, however, have patience for those who showed genuine interest in something she could explain. Kellan liked that about her— the way she'd soften just a touch when she'd talk about something she was passionate about. Her willingness to teach others was one of her best attributes.

Vaida's look of annoyance faded quickly at the sheepish look on his face. "The second victim is a young shifter woman named Liza Sarmanello. She was in her final year of undergraduate school at Spiral City University. Her parents live in Lunadere. It seems she was studying medicine."

Kellan looked at the picture on the screen—Liza had been a pretty girl, with big brown eyes, curly brown hair, and a wild, pointed smile that suggested she was a predatory shifter of some sort. That might answer the question of what Kagome had seen with her hands just before her death.

"Any connection between the two of them? Were they dating? Family?" Kellan asked.

Vaida shook her head again. "From what I've been able to pull up so far, no. Nothing. It's likely they never met. Who knows what they were doing together in that alley."

Silence hovered over them for several moments. It seemed Vaida's brief was done, but she stared at him with a concerned look on her face, her eyebrows knitted together as she waited for him to speak.

She'd been part of the training he'd received for investigations, teaching him about her involvement in a case. He'd always found her brand of direct explanation easier to understand than other lab technicians employed by the Legion.

But she knew what he normally did—everyone in the Legion knew that the nineteenth were hardly more than murderous errand dogs.

Vaida had never pitied him for it, but she seemed to somehow understand what it was like to not be able to choose a path for yourself, to not know how much blood you would have on your hands by the end of your life.

If anyone would understand the guilt he carried, he trusted that she could.

"I guess I'm just glad I get to help solve a murder instead of causing one," he finally offered with a small smile.

She returned the smile for a moment before leaning back in the chair. "It's a chance to do something worthy of that big heart of yours." She sighed as she pulled up a complex chart of ever-changing numbers. "I'll have an analysis of the blood and tissue sample the coroner sent as soon as I can."

"Thanks, V."

She tilted her head toward him again, the light of her screens reflected in her glasses. "Are you going to be all right?"

Kellan nodded, probably a bit too quickly. Her eyes narrowed, but he spoke before she could say anything. "I promise, I'm fine. I just…need to think of what to tackle next. It's a lot."

"Well, best advice I can give you? Explore all your options. Oh, and you should probably visit Liza's family."

He went cold. He'd forgotten that the lead investigator was usually the one who spoke to the victims' families. Razorborn had brought him along once when he'd done it. The memory of their horrified faces would forever haunt Kellan's dreams. And now he had to do it again.

"What about Cygnus?" Kellan asked quietly.

Vaida looked down briefly, a flash of sorrow passing across her features. "He had no one left, it seems."

He rubbed at his temples. He was out of his element with this, and he was so afraid that any step he'd take would end with failure. Was he even allowed to fail this? What would happen if he couldn't solve their murders?

He felt a hand on his knee. Vaida had a worried look on her face as he lifted his eyes to meet hers.

"Hey," she started, her voice softer than before. "You're going to be fine, you know. I'm here to help you. You're not alone."

"Thanks, V," he said as he patted her hand that was still on his knee. "I appreciate you."

She sat back in her chair, crossing her legs. "I deserve to be appreciated, so thank you."

He laughed, standing from the chair, then turned on his heel to face the door. "I should probably head out, then," he said.

"You probably should. I'll ping you when I have the analysis ready."

He nodded once, sending up a silent prayer to Sol to guide him through this.

KELLAN

28th of Cerulean Moon

The Sarmanellos lived in the expansive residential district of Lunadere, just along the wall by the East Gate. The houses weren't large, but they were full of character. Lunadere's architecture was an oddity in Spiral City; wood and stone were preferred over brick and glass. Many of the houses looked like they'd fit better out in the middle of the woods, and most were surrounded by trees.

Like Bloomside, the trees here were always alive. But this wasn't because of magic—most of the trees here simply never died. They stayed green eternally, providing a pleasant piney aroma all year round.

It took Kellan a few minutes to find the right house. It was tucked back into a side street, unassuming and shaded by the trees. A small stone walkway led to a wooden front door with a yellow flower-shaped window.

Kellan twiddled his thumbs as he stood before the door, shifting back and forth on his feet. He should have asked Sharr to come with him, but he'd been so focused on delivering her family the news that he hadn't thought of it until he was already here.

He reached up to grasp the small bronze knocker that took the shape of a snarling leopard, his stomach churning.

A kind-looking older woman answered the door, her graying blonde hair in a bun atop her head. The lines on her face suggested she was middle-aged, and the pointed teeth sticking out below her top lip gave away her animalistic heritage.

Her eyes widened at the sight of Kellan in his red and black Legion uniform, a shiny metal "19" pinned over his heart. "Yes? May I help you?"

"Is this the Sarmanello residence?" Kellan didn't move a muscle.

She nodded somberly. "The fact there is a legionnaire on my doorstep is unsettling. Please, dear, come inside."

He followed her, taking in the home as he did. Pictures of Liza lined the walls—her as a young girl, halfway between her human form and her leopard form; her as a teenager, in her school uniform on the front walkway; her graduation stole in a shadowbox. He couldn't see any indication of another child in the family.

"Ellis, there's a legionnaire here. Can you please come up?" Liza's mother called down the stairs off the main hallway.

A female voice rang back up. "Just a minute!"

"I'm Adelle, by the way," she said, talking over her shoulder to Kellan. "Would you like some tea?"

Kellan just nodded, trying to swallow the lump in his throat.

He sat at the kitchen table, the bright yellow wallpaper searing his eyes. Adelle busied herself with a bright blue cast iron kettle on the stove, taking her time measuring out the tea leaves and the water. Kellan tried to ignore how her hands shook.

"You never mentioned your name, dear," Adelle said after she finished measuring the leaves.

"My apologies. It's Kellan."

"Kellan, dear, do you like milk or sweetener in your tea?"

He shook his head. "No, thank you. I'll take it plain."

As Adelle served the tea, another woman appeared in the doorway. Her ashy blonde hair was cut in a short pixie style, and as she smiled, Kellan saw her pointed canines. She wore faded overalls with a button-up shirt, sleeves pushed past her elbows, and a yellow bandana around her head.

She approached Adelle in the kitchen and gave her a quick peck on the cheek before turning to face Kellan.

"To what do we owe the pleasure?" she asked, putting her hands on her hips.

Kellan cleared his throat, but before he could speak, Adelle appeared, a steaming cup of tea in her hand. She set it in front of him before taking a seat herself.

"Ell, sit down, please," Adelle said, gesturing to the seat between her and Kellan. "I'm sure whatever the young man has to say is important enough to warrant a seat."

Ellis shrugged and pulled a chair up to the table.

Kellan swallowed again, the tea doing absolutely nothing to soothe the lump in his throat. He laced his hands together in his lap to stop them shaking.

"I am...unsure how to begin, so I guess I'll just be blunt." He cleared his throat. "Your daughter, Liza, was found dead late last evening."

The utter silence that followed was deafening. Ellis didn't move, and Adelle's mouth dropped open slowly. No one breathed.

"We would appreciate it if you would come to identify the body." He reached a hand up to touch the back of his neck. "On behalf of the Legion—"

"You're sure it's her?" Adelle cut him off softly. "You're sure it's our Liza?" She stood, shuffling to the pictures he'd seen coming in.

"Delly…" Ellis said softly after her. She looked pale.

He could feel the shift in the air as the news settled over Ellis. She stared at the pin on his chest, unseeing. He didn't know what to do, and the helplessness made him feel physically weak. She hadn't even cried yet.

Adelle came back, holding the more recent pictures of Liza. "This is her. She's vibrant, full of life. She wants to be a medical researcher. She's so smart, so beautiful. She can't be…she can't…"

Kellan looked at the pictures despite knowing what he would

see—a picture of Liza, standing happily in one of the Grand Gardens, holding Ellis' hand. Liza, outside the house, planting flowers. Liza, reading a book on a swing in the backyard.

"I am deeply sorry for your loss," was all he managed to choke out.

With that, Adelle began to cry. The anguish of a mother who has lost her child tore Kellan's heart to shreds. He clenched his teeth to hold back his own tears. He was here on business—they were the ones who'd lost their only child.

Ellis held Adelle as she cried, cooing and shushing into her hair even as the tears rolled down her own face. Kellan waited, letting them do what they needed, not wanting to interrupt.

The guilt worked its way through his body, setting his nerves on fire, closing his throat, choking him. It was visceral and painful. He hadn't expected that—the physical pain of grief.

He didn't know what to do. He couldn't leave yet, but he had almost nothing more to offer them. Telling them the circumstances of her death was out of the question.

Almost as if she'd heard his thoughts, Adelle whispered, "What happened?"

He met her tear-filled eyes, willing his throat to open enough to say something. The first attempt came out as a croak. The second was more successful.

"It's quite distressing; I don't know if I should divulge details." He shifted, his shoulders pinching up toward his ears. He tried to remind himself to relax. It didn't work.

Adelle let out another short sob, her voice thick with pain. She turned back to bury her face into her partner's shoulder, her cries violent and silent as they wracked her entire body.

Ellis turned to him, more stoic than her partner but clearly in pain. "You'd like us to come identify the body, yeah?" she said, her voice wobbling.

Kellan just nodded, unable to loosen his throat enough to say more.

"Thank you, Kellan; we'll do that when we have a chance."

He swallowed, taking deep breaths and willing himself to relax. "Ellis, Adelle, I want to offer my sincerest condolences." He breathed again before continuing. "Liza seemed very loved, and I can't begin to imagine what you must be feeling."

Ellis' lip trembled, but she listened silently while Adelle kept her face buried.

He pulled out his contact card and held it out to Ellis, which she accepted with shaking fingers.

"I'm only a call away if you need anything at all," he said softly.

She looked down at the card, tears wobbling off her lashes to fall onto Adelle's shoulder. She didn't say anything, and he hoped she'd heard him.

He stood, placing a hand on Ellis' shoulder. "I'm so sorry."

"Thank you," she whispered back.

He moved to leave, only turning around to look once on his way out. The picture was much different than when he'd first arrived. Even the loud yellow wallpaper seemed dimmer.

Is this what happened to the families of those he'd killed? He fought off a new wave of nausea by breathing in deeply, the fading scent of spices and tea leaves filling his nose. No, no—he only killed people who had done harm. No one like Liza. Never anyone like Liza.

He shut the door behind him and finally allowed himself to lose his composure for a minute. He sank to the ground, head in his hands, and cried.

29TH OF CERULEAN MOON

The morgue was a drab building located on the eastern side of Spira, squat and built of yellowing gray brick. It was unwelcoming and unassuming—understandable for a building whose only customers were the dead.

He parked his motorcycle in the front, not bothering to straighten it out before unclipping the helmet from beneath his chin. He locked it to the bike, checking his hair in the small side mirrors. It was short enough that the helmet usually didn't screw it up; he was just wasting time.

The door was made of polished chrome and glass, and a chime sounded somewhere deep in the bowels of the building when he opened the door. A single hallway stretched out before him, lit poorly with yellow-tinted fluorescent lights. They flickered almost imperceptibly, just enough to threaten a headache if he spent too long under them.

A receptionist waited at a desk just to his left, typing at a keyboard and looking bored. Her form-fitting pink dress had an asymmetrical keyhole just over her collarbone, elongating her neck beautifully. She barely gave him a passing glance as he approached.

"Name?" she asked in a monotone voice.

"Kellan Manchester, nineteenth division." He flashed the pin over his heart as he said it even though she wasn't looking at him.

She paused, squinting at her screen before finally turning to face him. "Not on the appointment list. You working on a case?"

He nodded, sticking a hand in his backpack to reach his techpad. Before he could, she turned back to the computer and typed something else faster than he thought possible.

"You can go sit over there; Doctor Hanlin will be with you shortly." She pointed to a small waiting area filled with plastic chairs attached to metal rails. He obeyed, awkwardly pulling his hand back out from the backpack.

The morgue was deathly silent, as was expected. But the silence was almost oppressive, like the air was too thick to speak into. The knowledge that these walls held the dead was enough to quiet his mind.

After an uncomfortable silence spent staring thoughtlessly at the popcorn ceilings, a well-groomed elven man appeared in the waiting area from the hallway. He smiled at Kellan when he appeared, his teeth blindingly white.

"Mister Manchester, I assume you are on the Sarmanello case, yes? Quite a tragic one, that is. Follow me, please. I have a few things to point out to you."

He turned on his heel and didn't wait to see if Kellan followed before heading back the way he came. Kellan scrambled up from his seat, hurrying down the hallway behind him.

They passed several closed rooms before finally stopping about halfway down the hallway in front of a door that read "Examination." Hanlin opened the door for Kellan, stepping aside as he gestured for him to enter.

Inside was a sterile room of stainless steel. One wall was entirely made of small doors, behind which Kellan assumed were bodies. The thought made him shiver. Was this where his victims ended up?

The center of the room hosted a large stainless steel table surrounded by several trays on wheels filled with a variety of tools, some of which looked an awful lot like torture devices. A massive light hung low above the table. The heat from the light made him sweat as he moved closer.

Doctor Hanlin approached the table, which held a body covered by a sheet. He swallowed. Liza must be under there. He wasn't sure he could handle seeing her body again, not after what he'd seen in that back alley.

"I won't show you too much," Doctor Hanlin said, apparently eading his expression as queasiness. "But there are a few"—he paused for effect—"oddities I'd like to point out to you."

Kellan just nodded, not trusting his voice enough to say much of anything as he approached the table.

Hanlin lifted the sheet off the body with extreme care, folding it back just enough to produce one of Liza's hands. Kellan gasped.

He hadn't seen it when they'd found her, but her fingers were purple and bruised, like every single one had been broken before she died. Her nails were gone; instead, the beds were bloody and ragged. Was this a result of those claws Kagome had mentioned?

"What in the…" Kellan whispered under his breath.

"These wounds were obviously inflicted before her death—if I had to venture a guess, I'd say she got them fighting against whatever they were attacked by. The bruising on her wrists and ankles suggests she was bound. However, I am unsure what happened to her nails. I've never seen anything like it."

"Could—" Kellan began, then stopped to swallow. His throat felt like sandpaper. "Could someone have pulled them off?"

Doctor Hanlin shook his head, replacing her hand back under the sheet. "I thought the same, but the wounds aren't consistent with that sort of torture. Plus, it's usually only a nail or two that is missing, not all of them."

Kellan just nodded, his mouth dry.

He moved to the top of the table, folding the sheet down to expose Liza's pale and lifeless face. He didn't give Kellan time to react before opening one of her eyes gently with his fingers.

"This is the strangest thing I've found yet," he said, gesturing with the other hand for Kellan to approach. "Her files say her eyes were brown, yet…"

Kellan looked down to see a bright yellow eye staring back at him. It wasn't like yellow eyes were unnatural—in fact, they were quite common in shifter races. But Kellan didn't know of a phenomenon that caused eyes to change colors.

"Could it have been caused by her trying to shift, maybe? The witness said she saw claws before Liza died too." It was the only logical explanation he could think of.

Doctor Hanlin shook his head. "Shifter traits like eye color and hair color don't change that drastically when shifting between forms, especially not for predatory breeds like she was. Her eyes would have stayed brown even during a shift. And her fingers certainly wouldn't have ended up broken for her own claws."

Kellan shook his head. "Can you think of anything that might have caused it?"

The doctor looked sheepish as he pulled the sheet back up over her face. "Honestly, I wish I could give you a better answer, but no. I have no idea what could have caused a change like this right before her death."

Kellan stared down at the sheet, gears turning in his mind. Nothing made sense, and he wasn't sure if it was due to his inexperience or if the clues truly did not add up.

He knew Razorborn had done what he could to train Kellan properly for an investigation, but he didn't know if any training could have prepared him for this. It wasn't Razorborn's fault he couldn't figure it out—it was his own.

"Anything else of note?" he asked, worried for the answer.

Hanlin pulled over a metal rolling stool and took a seat. "As you know, her throat was cut, which was the cause of death. She lost a lot of blood very quickly. But there was something else. Which is the third thing I wanted to talk to you about." He sighed, crossing one ankle over the other knee. "She had a heart attack at some point pretty quickly before her death. She was twenty. She was healthy. No shifter girl her age and health should have been having a heart attack. And why, when an officer was ripped to shreds next to her, was her throat cut while she was having a heart attack?"

He sighed again, rubbing his temples. "But I suppose that's why you're here, isn't it? You get to ask those questions; I'm just here to tell you the facts."

Kellan scratched his chin thoughtfully. "Could it have been from fear? You know, like she was so afraid she gave herself a heart attack?"

"No, that looks entirely different than what happened here." He shook his head as he swiveled back and forth. "This type of attack was from too much strain—her blood was either too thin or too thick for her heart to pump. Eventually, it just gave out from trying too hard."

Kellan had no idea what that meant, and he hadn't even asked about the legionnaire yet. He was almost afraid to, worried that asking after him would make the case even murkier. But he couldn't leave without asking, not if he wanted to do this well. He had a duty to Cygnus to find his killer.

Kellan reached up to scratch the back of his neck. "So what about the corporal, then?"

"He's much more clear cut, although I won't show you what's left of the body. Cause of death was blood loss and the lacerations, although I'm sure you could have assumed as much."

Kellan nodded.

"I did check his fingers and eyes, but they weren't changed or broken. Strange, considering their times of death were nearly simultaneous."

"Who died first?" Kellan asked. "You said nearly simultaneous, but they weren't at the same time, right?"

He nodded. "The legionnaire was first, the girl followed by three to five minutes, according to the medical team."

Yet another piece of information that made no sense. He was overwhelmed, burdened by all the knowledge he'd gathered today. He had no idea how to interpret any of it, and he had a feeling that if he asked any more questions today, he'd end up completely losing it.

"Thank you, Doctor," he said, shifting on his heels.

Hanlin just shrugged and turned back to face the door they'd come in. "That's all I've got for you right now. Your lab technician should be doing the rest of the analysis and bloodwork, so you'll have to go visit her if you want more information."

Doctor Hanlin held the door open for Kellan, who nodded his thanks as he passed through it. His thoughts churned, twisting and forming a plethora of half-baked theories, but nothing stuck. Maybe Razorborn or Vaida would have a better idea of what all this meant.

"If it's any consolation, I've been doing this for many years and the facts make no sense to me either," Hanlin said quietly as they continued back down the hall.

It didn't make him feel any better.

14

CASSIAN

1st of Wind Moon

Cassian's techpad dinged as he sat in his hotel room, reading articles that mentioned Pontius Morgenstern by name. He'd had little time to do his usual preliminary research before being ushered away for this job, so he was trying to catch up on it now.

Most of the articles mentioned his work with the Human Equality Act that had passed three years ago. The law had ended the use of humans for medical testing and had freed most of them from indentured servitude in the Empire. It hadn't fixed the inherent inequality they'd founded the entire country on, though.

It was, however, a step in the right direction. And many who wrote of Pontius' accomplishments expected more great things from him.

Pontius was, according to several lifestyle interviews, a busy man. He made appearances around the city nearly non-stop, his face plastered on every event from animal welfare to human-focused charity groups. His schedule would be inconsistent, making it a challenge to plan a strike. Which was why Cassian was determined to find at least one constant in Pontius' on-the-go lifestyle.

Hence his surprise when he discovered a message from Pontius waiting for him on his techpad.

**I've gotten a hold of your old friend, Kellan.
We've made plans to meet up in a few days. You
should join us!**

Cassian sighed. After their meeting in the alleyway, he'd been hoping to avoid Kellan as long as he could. It seemed that fate, or rather Pontius, wouldn't let him off the hook that easily.

He realized he'd been reading the same line for nearly ten minutes, completely lost in his thoughts of Pontius and Kellan and not having a damn clue why he couldn't just concentrate on the task at hand. But Cassian knew a lost cause when he saw it, and this was certainly it. He had to get his mind off this. A walk would do it.

He found a small restaurant a few blocks away with outdoor seating overlooking a small park and requested a table. The small halfling server stared up at him in awe as she nodded and showed him to a small table in the corner.

He stared down at the park for a long time. Several couples were taking advantage of the warm, sunny day to have picnics. Children flitted about with kites and throwing discs. A few tossed balls back and forth, shrieking in delight. He remembered doing something similar with his own family, back when he was very young.

Cassian had been a reserved child. His father had died when he was relatively young, so most of his treasured memories were with his mother, Eliza. She'd fostered his love of the stars early, taking him to the planetarium in Ebenfell each year on his birthday. Parks and kites and throwing discs had been fun, but he treasured those planetarium trips the most.

Elves aged significantly slower than most other races in Ileron; most didn't reach maturity until they were about a hundred years old. Ragnor had drafted Cassian to his current job on his one-hundredth birthday. The fact he'd never truly belonged to himself had always bothered him. He'd never gotten to dream about his future because he'd known what awaited him.

The longer he considered, the more he realized he didn't even know what he would choose to do, if given the chance. It had never been an opportunity, and it wouldn't do him any good to think about it now.

The only choice he'd ever made for himself was Aidyn, and he'd carried that regret with him even now. He wasn't allowed those feelings, those thoughts. Because somehow, Ragnor always knew.

As the sun began its descent, Cassian's senses prickled like he was being watched. He glanced around the patio, wondering if maybe the hostess who'd stared at him earlier was still watching. She was still at her post, preoccupied with wiping off the menus rather than watching him. No one else on the patio seemed to care that he was there.

He continued observing his surroundings with even more focus now, paying attention to shadowy corners and rooftops. There was definitely something off, he just couldn't pinpoint what it was.

A server set a cup of coffee and a plate of creamy pasta before him before retreating with a bow. He didn't pick up his fork—the buzzing in his veins that signaled the pull was growing in intensity, begging him to stand up, to move, to go.

He didn't listen, not this time. He waited, letting the food cool as he observed his surroundings. The feeling faded slightly as he ate, but never fully went away. It was as if whatever had been watching him had left…but something was still wrong.

Cassian couldn't stand the buzz in his veins any longer. He stood from the table, draining the cup of coffee before paying the bill at the front desk and leaving the patio, hands in his pockets.

If he appeared too on edge, whatever was stalking him would leave. So he made a show of walking down the block, watching the rooftops out of the corners of his eye.

Nothing caught his eye. Nothing was unusual.

The pull in his gut led him up to a building, tugging endlessly at him, urging him to listen. He climbed the fire escape, putting hand over hand as the metal warmed under his grip. He felt a little stupid, climbing to the roof of a building for no reason other than his instincts told him to. But he'd trusted the pull before. It never led him astray.

He headed back the direction he'd come, hoping to gather a clue from the rooftops around the restaurant. It took only a few minutes to find something—and it unnerved him greatly.

A white envelope sat on a rooftop next to the patio of the restaurant, taped to the low brick railing. As Cassian approached, he could see the flowing script read his name on the front. His stomach dropped.

He gingerly peeled the envelope off the railing, taking great pains to ensure it wasn't trapped or magicked. Once he confirmed it was safe, Cassian tore the envelope open with his index finger. The note was short but terrifying.

Nice to see you, Cassian.

The note had no signature, no sign of who it might be from. He tugged at the small bit of magic that settled in his navel, commanding it to burn the paper as he held it. His fingers shook the entire time.

Despite his unsettling lunchtime experience, Cassian had plans that evening with Pontius that he couldn't back out of. They'd agreed several days prior that they'd be visiting one of the career centers in Tethgir that Pontius had helped start up. Its goal was to assist humans in finding jobs across Spiral City since the passing of the Human Equality Act. Pontius had, apparently, been instrumental in its creation.

When he arrived in the industrial district, smog and a cacophony of loud machinery assailed his senses. The streets were concrete, the buildings concrete, the roofs flat and made of even more concrete. It was as if the entire district had been poured into a giant mold.

Pontius was waiting for him in front of the center, wearing a gray button-up and black slacks. It was the most casual Cassian had ever seen him look, but he still made the look seem lavish.

"Cassian!" Pontius beamed as Cassian's taxi pulled away. "So glad you could join me. I've not met with Director Sylva here for weeks."

Cassian nodded as he approached. "Thanks for inviting me."

Pontius beckoned to him, and they entered the squat building side by side. Inside, he found a welcoming interior. Bright orange couches and yellow armchairs dotted the space, interspersed with low glass tables. People occupied these seats at random, talking with blue-shirted counselors. It gave the impression that it wanted to be a hospitable space but not boring or drab.

He followed Pontius to a set of yellow chairs near the entrance, where a dark-haired human spoke with a counselor. They both smiled when he approached, turning their smiles to Cassian when he trailed behind Pontius.

"Pontius!" the counselor said with excitement. "We haven't seen you around for a few weeks. How did Rivenstorm treat you?"

Pontius chuckled. "It seems I'll be making several more trips back if anything will come of it. But it was certainly a lovely city." He turned his attention to the other person, shooting his best smile at them. "You're quite lucky—Cort is one of the best counselors here. They'll find you the perfect position, I promise."

The human smiled even wider, bowing their head once to Pontius before turning back to Cort. "You really think the plant will like me?"

Cort nodded. "With your experience, they'll be thrilled to have someone like you on the planning team."

Pontius patted Cort on the shoulder before moving on, Cassian trailing on his heels.

He had several more conversations like that one as they moved through the room, each counselor more excited than the last to see Pontius. Many of the humans didn't greet Pontius with the same enthusiasm, but it was obvious they knew who he was and met him with polite nods or soft greetings.

Pontius introduced Cassian to many of the counselors and

explained their partnership in excited tones. They greeted him with the same enthusiasm they'd given Pontius, asking questions about his work in Ebenfell, if he planned to model career centers there after this one, and what other services his organization wanted to implement.

Lying to them was difficult. Each time he'd assure them of his dedication to introducing more services in Ebenfell, his heart would sink lower in his chest. He wished this wasn't a farce, that he really could bring back information about the movement here to his supposed organization. He wished he was the one to bring positive change. Not murder.

As they said their goodbyes to one of the last pairs of people in the room, a woman dressed in a blue shirt approached them. She had thick, curly brown hair and heavily lidded eyes that made her look like she was always sad.

But the moment she saw Pontius, her expression opened up, her eyes widening with joy.

"Pontius! It's so lovely to see you, dear," she said, grabbing him by the arms and kissing both his cheeks.

"Sylva," Pontius said, returning her greeting in kind.

Her eyes slid to Cassian, her smile dying down to a knowing smirk. "I see you've brought a friend?"

Pontius stood aside, holding his arms toward Cassian. "Indeed, I have. Director, this is Cassian. He comes to us from Ebenfell and hopes to gather some information about the programs we've helped start here in Spiral City for his own organization's efforts."

"Well, that's absolutely wonderful," she beamed, holding a hand out to shake. "I'm thrilled you're taking some notes on Pontius' endeavors. He has done much for the human rights movement."

Cassian took the proffered hand, shaking it with vigor to cover the nasty feeling rising in his throat. What would these people think when Pontius was dead? They'd never know it was Cassian who'd wielded the knife, but they'd never see the fruits of his supposed labor come true in Ebenfell. All this effort they were putting forth to teach him would do nothing, would go nowhere.

Cassian hated how it made him feel.

"I'm looking forward to learning from you," he said after what felt like too long of a pause.

Sylva didn't seem to notice. "Let's take a tour of the facility, yes? Show our guest here what we do."

Pontius held a hand out, gesturing for Cassian to follow Sylva while he trailed behind.

The facility was well-equipped beyond the initial room they'd entered. An entire room of desktop techpads was just beyond a set of glass doors, allowing anyone who needed access to apply for a job digitally the means to do so. Sylva explained with pride how Pontius had supplied the funds for the techpads, while Morgenstern Tech provided security and data administration.

Sylva explained the rigorous training their counselors underwent as well. Counselors from Spiral City University provided training to a new hire, once again paid for by Pontius and his giving fund.

Cassian was noticing a theme as they continued on their tour—it seemed Pontius' role in his philanthropic efforts focused on his monetary contributions. Unsurprising, in some way, but Cassian wondered what even made Pontius want to do this in the first place.

The tour concluded with a final bit of praise for Pontius, and they returned to the first room, where Sylva bid them farewell. Cassian bit his tongue until they'd exited the building.

"Pontius," he began, guilt and curiosity warring for their place within his body. "Why do you do this?"

Pontius looked slightly confused. "What do you mean?"

"I mean, this"—Cassian gestured toward the center—"help humans like this. Get involved in their lives."

He smiled vaguely at Cassian, but the edges of it were melancholy. "You know, when people ask me this, they usually just want to know why I'm throwing all my money away for a cause that doesn't even concern me."

Guilt overtook the war within him. That was exactly what he'd meant by his question.

Pontius continued, leaning against a concrete wall. "Because I care about the humans of the Empire. I know what it's like to have a life of privilege. Why wouldn't I want that for everyone?"

Cassian frowned. "But that's not reason enough to dedicate your entire life to them, is it?"

"It's starting to sound like you're doubting your own career path, Cassian." Pontius' voice had a hint of laughter as he spoke.

"Call it professional curiosity, then," Cassian replied. He didn't know why he was even pushing. Maybe something in him called to the struggle of humans, their never-ending imprisonment and suffering at the hands of those more powerful. He knew it well, that feeling of helplessness.

Pontius chewed his lip in thought. The silence stretched for what seemed like hours until he finally spoke.

"I'm an oppressor, I know that," Pontius said. "I didn't know how to approach it for the longest time. But when I was a teenager, my mother took me to the auctions they used to hold for slaves. All she brought with was her techpad and an envelope. I didn't know what the envelope was for."

Cassian cocked an eyebrow but said nothing, waiting for Pontius to continue.

"It was horrible. They kept the humans in iron cages next to the stage, and when it was time to auction one off, they'd bring them forward in chains. They even sold children." He took a shaking breath, then continued. "She'd bid on every single one. And she'd win. I didn't understand—we didn't keep slaves at our house, so why was she purchasing so many?

"When the auction was finally over, she paid for every single slave she bought. They were terrified of us when the auctioneers showed us to their cages. One even tried to bite my mother. But she never flinched away. She instead told them she'd bought them to free them."

Cassian raised his eyebrows. He knew the Morgensterns were

wealthy people, and the number in his mind had increased as he'd listened to all Pontius had paid for at the center. But to purchase an entire auction of slaves? The number boggled his mind.

Pontius continued, eyes downcast. "She handed each of them a ticket from that envelope and told them they were to take a special train that ran from the station just outside the auction arena to Rivenstorm, where they'd be able to live in peace. Many of them didn't take it. A few did, but most simply stared at her like she'd sprouted an extra head or she'd lost her mind. Which I'm sure was what they thought of her. A wealthy elven woman, buying their freedom? A ridiculous notion."

Cassian was speechless. A ridiculous notion, indeed.

"They all took that chance to leave, though. I don't know where they ended up, if they were captured again, or if they found their own way to Rivenstorm. But I do remember what my mother said when I asked why she did it."

He breathed deeply again, clenching his fingers so hard the knuckles were white. "She said it was because it was what she could do. She didn't have influence over the council, she didn't have friends on the court. No one would listen to the partner of a wealthy elf, no matter how much influence he carried. But what she did have was money, and she was going to use it to help in any way she could."

It certainly wasn't enough to only free a single auction of humans. But actions like that, over time, would build up. They would create tangible change, little by little. Even if it wouldn't change in a human's lifetime, it could change in an elf's.

Pontius finally lifted his eyes. "I understand it must seem ridiculous, the ways my mother and I are going about trying to help. But she's right. I don't have influence over the council, I have no friends on the court. But I have money, and I am going to do the best I can with the means I do have. And I intend to make those connections in the future to have influence over the people who truly can change things. That's why I do it. It's because it's what I can do."

Cassian couldn't think of a response. What could he possibly say to a speech like that? He couldn't fabricate a reason that would match the intensity of Pontius' commitment to the cause.

Pontius sighed, pushing off the wall. "I'm sorry if I am a bit intense—I haven't told that story for a long time."

Cassian finally recovered enough to speak. "Pontius, that's—" He stopped, struggling to find the words. "I know my blessing means nothing, but I think it's a worthy reason."

Pontius' smile was bright as he turned to Cassian. "Thank you, Cassian. I just hope those I'm trying to help think so too."

15

SHADOW

1st of Wind Moon

The shipment of humans had finally arrived—later than it was supposed to, much to his annoyance. The human rebellion had interfered in his plans, frequently sabotaging his shipments and causing delays. That rebellion would need to be quashed, but that was a different problem for a different day.

He gazed upon the human who was being bound to the table by the ghouls. He thrashed and strained against his bonds, but the ghouls were stronger. It also helped that they couldn't feel anything, including pain. They were mindless, though, and he needed something with more…spunk.

His frustration over losing the girl had faded. After all, he'd seen what she'd become just before death had claimed her. They were close. So close.

He'd realized they'd made a mistake in the calculations when she'd disobeyed him, however. They'd been making small tweaks to the formula for the last week.

It had been Alvemach's idea to try a human instead. It was the humans who made the best demons after death. Why not start the process sooner?

Two syringes laid on a tray next to the table where a ghoul finished strapping the human in.

"I'd advise you to stop struggling. You'll need your strength," the man said through a sly grin.

"What are you going to do to me?" the man on the table asked. His voice shook, and the sound sent a jolt of glee through the man's bones.

He just laughed. It didn't matter anyway; once the drug was administered, he wouldn't remember a thing. Other than his master, of course. He turned to the syringes again.

The first syringe contained a light blue liquid, designed to deaden any magical affinity the subject might have.

The second contained a viscous, reddish-black liquid. The coloring came mostly from Alvemach's blood, although some of it was from the other ingredients included. He'd measured this batch perfectly.

He administered both carefully into the human's right arm, watching as the veins turned purple, then blue, then black beneath his pale skin. His breath came in shorter and shorter gasps until, finally, they stopped altogether.

The man waited patiently, observing every twitch, every shift the human made. Soon, the transformation would begin.

Suddenly, the man jerked up off the table; the bonds holding him down snapped. He convulsed, choking on air as foam gathered at the corners of his mouth.

His fingers elongated, becoming sharp and shiny. His eyes snapped open, the irises turning yellow and the pupils becoming slitted. Elongated canines forcefully popped his mouth open, his breath coming in labored gasps.

But the transformation stalled, and the man slumped back down on the table, breath gone. The claws stayed.

The man didn't move. They were getting closer.

16

KELLAN

1st of Wind Moon

Vaida's office was still as dark as it had been two days ago. She'd messaged him during his morning workout that the blood analysis was ready. He'd cut his routine short to come see her.

Before he could even open his mouth, Vaida shooed him to a chair in the corner. She put a vial into a refrigerated case, labeling it in small, neat handwriting.

He waited while she finished preparing the samples. She flitted about the lab for a few minutes, putting labels back in drawers, pens in holders, and straightening the piles of papers on her desk before finally sitting at her computer and starting up its three screens. Her uniform jacket hung over the back of her chair, her necktie completely missing.

She cocked one finger at Kellan, motioning for him to come closer. "I have some…confusing results I need to share with you," she said promptly as he leaned over, not bothering with a greeting. "About the blood analysis."

"Okay?" Kellan said, confused. "What's so weird about it?"

"Have you ever looked at a blood analysis or a toxicity report, Kellan?" she asked, still staring at the screens.

He shook his head and then realized she wasn't looking at him.

"No. Razorborn showed me something similar, but nothing of this complexity."

"Then I'll explain." She pulled reports up on the screen. There were four total, each as confusing as the last. She pointed to the first. "This is the preliminary analysis I did for regular or recreational drug use. Standard for homicides. See this line right here?" She pointed at a thin purple line running up the scale.

"These are the control results. They took these from a regular drug user. Now compare that to this line here." She pointed again at the chart, this time at a thin red line that ran almost perfectly along the bottom of the scale until the very end, where it peaked higher than the purple line. "This isn't normal. It's like she condensed years of drug use into a single night."

Kellan shook his head. "What does that mean?"

Vaida shrugged. "Honestly, Kellan, I've got no gods-damned clue. I've never seen a result like this. But that's not the only weird thing." She moved to the second report. "This was a platelet count. I wanted to see if maybe the weird results were a cause of some sort of infection. Turns out that wasn't it; her platelet count is significantly lower than a healthy shifter her age should be. That isn't normal either. And so I thought maybe I should further analyze her blood, see if maybe it was some kind of poison. Want to guess what I found?"

"Something abnormal, I'm guessing?" Kellan replied, shifting.

Vaida sighed, rubbing her temples beneath the arms of her glasses. "Something extremely abnormal, even more abnormal than all the other abnormal shit I've shown you already. This girl had *different* blood in her system. Do you know how transfusions work?" She finally looked at him over her spectacles.

He shook his head.

"Usually, if the blood is a compatible type, the body simply accepts it as its own. No fuss. If it's the wrong type, you could face some serious medical complications; your body will attack the transfused blood."

"So is that what happened?"

Vaida shook her head. "No. And that's the confusing part. The blood isn't the right type for her; it's not even shifter blood. Her body should have been attacking it. But it didn't. It just accepted it as if nothing was wrong."

Kellan frowned. Confusing results, indeed. Paired with the results of the autopsy, things were getting murkier and murkier. He was so far out of his league.

"And, as if that wasn't weird enough, I found trace amounts of some sort of acid in her blood. Acid I don't recognize. Its structure is completely foreign to me."

He narrowed his eyes as he stared at the screen, as if that would help make things clearer. It did not. "Okay, so what does that mean? Does that have something to do with her weird drug results?"

Vaida leaned back in her chair. "Probably, but I can't be sure. I have nothing to compare these results to. She's a one-of-a-kind case, and I firmly believe those don't exist."

"The coroner said she died of blood loss, but she had a heart attack just before she died. Do you think that the acid caused it?"

"Who knows? There's no way to tell, honestly."

Kellan sighed as he glanced back at the screen. "You've told me about three of the reports, what's the last one?"

Vaida leaned forward once more, pointing her mouse to the last graph. "A toxicity report. I did a more in-depth one after the strange spike in the preliminary drug one."

"And?"

"And," she said, glaring at him for interrupting, "she had a combination of inorganic substances present in her bloodstream. Unsurprising, considering the abnormal results I got from nearly every test. But I've never seen this combination before."

"Would Northwind Medical know?"

Vaida shrugged again for the millionth time and flicked the computer screen off with a click. "Most likely, yes. They have more resources at their disposal, and it might be worth your time to ask.

They won't be as fast as I am, though."

Kellan rubbed his temples and stared at the ground. It was a lot to take in, and almost none of it made any sense to him.

He'd have to get in touch with someone at Northwind and ask for expedited results. He was sure the commissioner could help with that. But the despair and confusion over the facts were causing his head to swim.

He felt a cool hand cover his own—Vaida. Her glasses flashed as she held his hand tightly in her own.

"Look, I know this is confusing, and I know this seems like it's out of your league. But you aren't alone."

A pang of gratitude, orange and bright, flashed through his system. Although Vaida might seem like she was cold and unfriendly, it was small moments like these that made him believe she actually might like him. Just a bit.

Another pang flashed through him, this time of loneliness. How much easier would this have been with Beck at his side? Beck had always been smarter than him. He was sure he would have figured out some sort of common thread by now if he'd been here.

Vaida must have sensed his spiraling thoughts and squeezed his hand again. "You know who you should visit?" she said quietly.

"The commissioner will help me get into Northwind at least—"

"No," she cut him off. "Razorborn. You admire him, don't you? I saw the way you followed him around like a lost puppy when you trained with him. He might have some insight."

Kellan nodded slowly. She was right; he'd looked up to Razorborn since the moment they had been assigned together for training. He was warm and kind, not what you'd expect from a hardened investigator within the Legion.

But he supposed that was why Razorborn was so popular. His energy was magnetic, and Kellan couldn't deny it also pulled him in.

He smiled at Vaida weakly. "You're right, V. He'll probably have an idea about what to do."

She returned the smile with one of her own. "That's it. Now shoo;

you can probably catch him in his office this time of day."

He nodded, turning to face the door. Before he left, he turned back to face Vaida.

"Thanks, Vaida. I'm—"

She flapped a hand at him, cutting him off. "Don't get sappy on me. Now scram."

He smiled again as he rose to leave, shutting the lab door with a decisive click behind him.

Lieutenant Sharr Razorborn's office was on the sixth floor, mixed in with the first division's legal team. It was set farther back, and he got turned around a few times on the way there. It had been months since he'd visited his office.

Razorborn had been his mentor when he'd first been assigned to the Legion. He'd been tough on Kellan, but he always knew his limits. They'd spent those first three and a half months of Kellan's tenure together every single day. Once Kellan had finished his training and they'd gone their separate ways, Razorborn had left behind a void, a loneliness that still haunted him.

His mentor had proven to not only be skilled at his job, but a wonderful confidant, too. When they'd had the time, Sharr had shown him around the city, introducing Kellan to his favorite restaurants and bars around town. They'd spent large swaths of time exploring, Sharr letting Kellan lead the way.

He hadn't realized it, but Razorborn had been his first real friend in the Legion.

Kellan idly wondered if that was why the commissioner had left them together to train for so long. Normally, training only took two months, but they'd been together for nearly double that. Did the commissioner simply not trust him to have learned as quickly as other recruits, or was it something else?

When Kellan finally arrived, he saw the dragonborn man sitting behind an almost hilariously small desk, his clawed fingers tapping slowly at a keyboard. When the man saw Kellan, though, his face broke into a massive smile, showing two rows of pearly white and extremely sharp teeth.

He also wore the Legion uniform, but his piping was navy, the color of it nearly blending with the black of the rest of the uniform. His uniform differed slightly from Vaida's—the jacket wasn't meant to be worn with an undershirt, thus, the neck came up farther, folding over at the shoulder and creating a square neckline. Only the vice commissioner and lieutenants had this style of jacket, marking their ranks with stars along their breasts, just above where their unit pins rested. Sharr's had three, marking him as a long-standing officer with fifteen or more years of service in the Legion.

"Kellan! What can I do for you?" Sharr asked, pushing himself away from the desk to lean back.

"Sharr, it's great to see you," Kellan said, leaning against the doorframe.

His old mentor gestured to the chair in front of the desk. "Come on, sit down. You don't have to give me that tough-guy routine, always leaning against shit."

Kellan chuckled and obliged. "Are you trying to say I'm not tough? I'd say that reflects on the master more than the student, wouldn't you?"

Sharr laughed. "I see your tongue is as sharp as ever," he said, leaning down to the bottom drawer of his desk to pull out a bottle of whiskey. "Want a glass?"

"Why not?" Kellan said as he watched the amber liquid fall. Whiskey was his favorite, and Sharr knew that.

"So, Kellan," Sharr said, thudding the small glass down in front of him. "What brings you to my office?"

He swallowed. It was hard to ask for help, but he knew he wasn't getting anywhere. Sharr was experienced in investigations like this; he'd know what to do. "I need your help."

"My help, eh? What's the case?"

"Murder investigation."

Sharr's brow raised, the black of his scales gleaming in the fluorescent light. "Really? It seems surprising they'd assign you one so early in your tenure."

"One of the victims…he was Legion." Kellan scratched the back of his neck awkwardly. "The commish thought it best to give it to me since I was the one who called it in." He frowned. "And apparently none of the other senior officers in the nineteenth have the time."

Sharr leaned back once again, swirling his whiskey thoughtfully. "Interesting. Well, no matter. I'm happy to assist my little hatchling. What do you need me to do?"

Kellan explained the basics—what he'd learned about Liza and Cygnus, the unsettling circumstances of their deaths, the confusing autopsy and blood analyses, and where he was stuck now. As he described it, Sharr's brow became more and more furrowed, and a hint of some emotion Kellan couldn't place flashed in his green pupil-less eyes.

"Well, you're not wrong, Kellan. This is a confusing case."

"That doesn't make me feel better."

Sharr chuckled, the sound throaty and deep. "Not saying it's impossible, though. Your instincts will guide you more than you think. You said you were hoping to get a sample to Northwind Medical?"

He nodded.

Sharr scratched his chin. "That's not a bad idea. The commissioner should be able to assist you with that. They've cooperated with us in the past."

"Is that what you'd do?"

Sharr nodded. "I think that will open some doors for you, hatchling. But take a moment to slow down, analyze the facts. In your rush to finish something, you might end up missing an important clue."

The way Sharr spoke slowed down his heart rate. He knew Sharr was right, but hearing someone as experienced as he was tell him the case wasn't clear-cut made Kellan feel less like a complete failure.

He took a sip of the whiskey, letting the liquid swirl around his tongue first before swallowing. It left a pleasant, smoky taste in his mouth.

"Kellan," Sharr's voice cut through his thoughts. "It's okay, you know. To not know what you're doing. This is an enormous task that the commissioner gave you. It's okay to be unsure. I'm glad you came to me for help." The man reached over to rest a clawed hand on his shoulder. "You're not alone."

Kellan cocked a small smile at his mentor and friend. "Thanks, Sharr. You've been a big help."

Sharr released his shoulder and sank back into his chair once more, swirling his whiskey in the glass. "Have you spoken with Beck lately?"

Kellan could feel the grimace as it passed over his face. "I haven't had the chance to call him."

"Well, that's part of your problem," Sharr admonished. "He's your best friend, you must be missing him."

Kellan sighed. "I know, I know." He ran a hand over his face, then through his hair. "But he's busy too. Last I heard, he's on protection detail for one of the White Court members."

Sharr whistled, then took another sip of his whiskey, teeth clacking against the glass. His massive hands nearly swallowed the glass entirely; if you weren't looking closely, you'd think he wasn't holding anything at all.

Kellan sipped from his own glass, reminding himself to unclench his jaw. It had been too long since he'd talked to Beck, and he missed him desperately.

Their silence was comfortable, wherein Sharr finished most of his whiskey in a few sips. He set the glass back on his desk and sighed.

"You know, I remember when you first came here," he began.

Kellan groaned. "Please don't remind me."

Sharr chuckled. "You were so skinny, and you couldn't remember where my office was for the first two months. There were so many things you didn't know after you were assigned here."

"I'd like to think I've grown since then," Kellan grumbled good-naturedly.

Sharr smiled, his toothy grin wide. "Of course you have. But now, I look at you, not even a year later, and you're running your own case? I couldn't be more proud of my hatchling."

Kellan could feel the blush rise up through his neck and into his cheeks. "Sharr—"

Sharr held up a hand before he could say anything more. "I may not have hatchlings of my own, but I am proud of you like a father would be. Have faith in yourself, like I have faith in you."

His blush refused to fade, his heart pounding noisily in his ears. He knocked back the rest of the whiskey, savoring the slight burn as it slid down his throat. He didn't know how to respond, but the knowledge that Sharr believed in him so deeply gave him courage.

"I should go, Sharr. Talk to the commissioner."

"Go on, get out of here." Sharr waved his hand, returning Kellan's smile with a smirk of his own.

He found himself once again in the commissioner's office after his discussion with Sharr. It had surprised him that the commissioner could meet with him so soon, but he didn't think about it too hard—it was lucky for him, anyway. He wouldn't ignore good luck.

The commissioner was behind his desk, his uniform neatly pressed, the orange piping a bright compliment to his hair. Upon Kellan's arrival, he looked up over his half-moon glasses, a small smile spreading across his face as his eyes met Kellan's.

"Private Manchester. It's a welcome surprise to see you back so soon. What can I help you with?" he asked, gesturing to the chairs before his desk.

Kellan didn't sit. This would hopefully be a quick meeting. "I'd like to ask a favor, if you don't mind, sir."

The commissioner leaned back in his chair, a pensive look crossing his face. "It sounds as if you've sniffed out a trail to follow already. I'm happy to aid you."

"I'd like you to get me in contact with someone at Northwind Medical who can do a deeper analysis of a blood sample. Upon discussing things with Lieutenant Razorborn, he recommended this course of action, and I agree with him."

The commissioner's eyebrows rose as he listened quietly to Kellan's request. "Was Private Larsen unable to provide a satisfactory report?"

Kellan shook his head. "No, her report was well done, but I believe I need someone more specialized to investigate something she didn't recognize."

The commissioner was silent for a few moments as he considered Kellan's proposal. Normally, the businesses within Spiral City were required to assist the Legion in any investigation when asked. Northwind Medical wasn't exempt from this. But they were trying their best to keep this investigation as confidential as possible, and adding yet another person into the mix would only create more opportunities for the case to leak and the details of the crime to go public.

But even Northwind couldn't escape the ramifications of a crime like this getting out. The commissioner must have recognized this, as his expression changed from one of careful consideration to one of agreement.

"I don't see why not," the commissioner finally said. "If this is your recommendation, with influence from Lieutenant Razorborn, I don't see a reason to turn it down."

Kellan bowed his head. "Thank you, sir."

"How is the investigation going otherwise?"

He tilted his head, then scratched his neck, debating where to begin with all he'd learned over the last two days. The commissioner liked detail, but Kellan wondered if providing all the details would be cumbersome. He erred on the side of explanation. The commissioner was his superior—it only made sense to be as honest with him as possible.

He described everything Vaida had discovered about Liza's blood, intentionally describing the mysterious substance she couldn't identify in precise detail. He nodded along, never once appearing bored or uninterested.

When Kellan described Cygnus' state, his brows furrowed. For the cause of death to be so dramatically different in such a short time seemed to concern him too. It seemed Kellan's instincts had, at least, been on point.

When he finally finished, the commissioner was silent for a few moments, scratching his beard as he pondered the case.

"It seems you are doing well, Private," he finally said, his words slow and deliberate. "I am satisfied with your progress. But I would like to request one thing."

Kellan bowed his head again. "Sir."

"I'd like regular updates from you. They don't have to be in person. I am interested in your progress on this case."

The nineteenth reported directly to the commissioner and vice commissioner themselves rather than through a ranking structure like the other divisions. But for him to be this interested in a case was strange, as he usually allowed the nineteenth more freedom without this sort of direct oversight. Kellan supposed the commissioner simply found it fascinating.

"I am happy to oblige, sir."

He clapped his hands, then picked his techpad up off the desk. "Then you are dismissed, Private. Remember, regular updates."

Kellan bowed his head once more as he turned toward the door. "Yes, sir."

17

CASSIAN

3rd of Wind Moon

The Bronze Paragon was built in the old architectural style of Northreach, from which Spiral City had been born several hundred years ago. The outside was made of graying whitewashed brick, the corners covered in filigree carved from sandstone in the shape of dragons. Over the door, a massive bronze dragon's head welcomed visitors, its gaping maw frozen in a silent roar.

Inside it was entirely refurbished. The walls were dark and reflected the neon pink and blue lights installed in the ceiling. The bar was made of what looked like fiberglass, dyed black and soaking up the lights like a dark void. Behind it, glass boxes lit from below with more colored lights showcased the club's most expensive liquors in a display that stacked nearly as high as the soaring ceilings.

Cassian followed Pontius through the club, claiming seats at the bar as Selwyn trailed behind. Kellan was on his way, according to Pontius, who deemed it necessary to update Cassian on his every interaction with the man.

He regretted his cover story for his relationship with Kellan—it seemed Pontius had latched onto the idea that they were long-lost friends. He didn't know why it resonated with Pontius so deeply, but it was exhausting to keep up with. But he couldn't very well backtrack on it now.

They'd ordered two rounds of drinks. Cassian's head was getting fuzzy, and he knew if he drank any more, he'd be in serious trouble.

By the time Kellan arrived, the fuzziness had gotten worse.

He appeared next to Cassian, dressed in tight-fitting black pants with pockets along his thighs that didn't seem to serve a specific purpose. His shirt was color-blocked black and gray—one sleeve missing and the other reaching down to his wrist. The sleeveless side showed off his wing tattoo brilliantly. Something in Cassian's stomach fluttered. He was definitely drunk.

"Kellan!" Pontius said, his words a little slurred. Selwyn looked on with concern but didn't move.

Kellan's face broke into a brilliant smile as he took the seat next to Pontius, which placed him far from Cassian. "Pontius, nice to see you again. Thanks for the invite."

"Oh, no bother, Kellan, no bother. I found it an opportune time to reunite old friends and make some new ones for myself," he replied, waving down a bartender and raising his nearly empty drink to Kellan. "Go on, order something; tonight is on me!"

Cassian watched Selwyn frown as the two men talked. Their discussion was animated and lively, comprising many hand gestures and barking laughs. He watched the way Kellan's cheeks rose when he laughed, how his throat moved when he sipped his drink, how his fingers curled on the glass.

Something was definitely wrong with him.

He stood abruptly, and Pontius turned to him with a cocked eyebrow. "Cassian?"

"Bathroom," he muttered back.

"Don't take too long," Pontius' voice flitted to his ears as he retreated.

He was too warm. The alcohol was getting to him even though he'd been sipping water. He couldn't lose his composure, not here, not with so much hanging in the balance. But cavorting with Pontius was a necessary part of the job—people often revealed things when intoxicated, especially with those they trusted.

He didn't know how Pontius felt about him yet. Their relationship still felt like a business exchange. He was already much more open with Kellan than he'd been with Cassian.

Cassian knew, in some part of his mind, that he was part of the reason for that. He wasn't the most sociable. People like Pontius were intimidating to him, able to connect with others in ways he couldn't even fathom.

And Kellan…apparently, he was like Pontius, too. They'd hit it off almost immediately, acting like they'd known each other for years when it had only been a few minutes.

Something twinged in his head at the thought.

He entered the club's bathroom, standing before the sink and splashing cold water on his face to cool himself down. His cheeks were flushed and his eyes slightly bloodshot. He'd been sleeping poorly; combined with the alcohol, he looked worse for wear.

"Pull yourself *together*, Cassian," he whispered to himself as the door to the bathroom opened again.

"Talking to yourself?" a voice echoed. "I'd say I came because I was concerned, but honestly, I just needed to pee."

He whipped his head around and saw Kellan leaning against the doorframe, arms crossed. A smirk played across his lips, and Cassian felt the heat rising once more to his face. He swore silently that he'd never drink again.

"Ignore me," he finally said, mouth dry. "I'm just a little tipsy is all."

"You sure that's smart?" Kellan retorted. "After all, aren't you on some super secret undercover mission? You were all worried about me blowing your cover, but you might blow it yourself the way you're acting."

Cassian straightened his back as he felt his brow furrow at Kellan's words. "I don't appreciate being scolded by you."

Kellan chuckled, then turned toward a urinal before looking back over his shoulder. "Sorry, sorry. I didn't realize you were so sensitive."

"I'm not sensitive. You're just an ass."

"I know, but that's part of my charm."

Cassian rolled his eyes, the heat from his face finally dissipating. He felt steadier on his feet, thankful for the break from the darkness of the club and the barbs from Kellan apparently helping to sober him up.

"I'm leaving," Cassian announced, turning toward the door.

Kellan made a noncommittal noise, and Cassian let the door swing shut behind him.

After returning to the bar, Pontius handed Cassian yet another drink. He tried to politely refuse, but Pontius was insistent. He sipped it slowly as Kellan returned to their group.

Selwyn kept a careful eye on Pontius, waving off the bartender each time he approached. Finally, she got agitated.

"Pontius," Selwyn said, the concern in her voice palpable. "You should really slow down."

He waved a hand at his sister, taking another swig from his glass. "Selly, I'm not here to impress anyone. Let me have a bit of fun."

She huffed, crossing her arms as she glared at her brother. "Fine. But let's find a table instead of sitting here at the bar."

"Great idea," Cassian said, eager to move somewhere quieter.

A second floor beckoned them up a set of spiral stairs. Massive cushioned booths surrounded low tables in spaces cozy enough for groups small or large. Most were already occupied, but Selwyn found them an open one toward the middle of the space.

A young shifter woman with brilliant purple hair flitted about, refreshing drinks, clearing empty glasses, and taking new orders with a practiced ease. Cassian watched her as they sunk into the cushions, Pontius nearly tripping down the two steps to get into the booth.

"All right, Pontius, that's enough, you're cut off," Selwyn said, grasping his upper arm as he sank into the cushions.

"I'm…" He paused, breathing in deeply through his nose. "I'm fine," he said.

She frowned, then flagged the waitress down with an elegant lift of her hand. She ordered a round of water for everyone, to which Pontius laughed and insisted he was fine once more.

Kellan and Pontius continued talking amicably, while Selwyn kept a close eye on her brother and Cassian did his best to seem pleasant. It seemed neither Pontius nor Kellan really noticed their discomfort.

That was until Pontius' eyes came to rest on Cassian and a guilty look flashed across his face. "Cassian, I'm so sorry; I've hogged all your precious friend's time and haven't even given you the chance to catch up!"

"It's really all right, Pontius. You two seem to be getting along nicely. I didn't want to interrupt," he said.

"Nonsense!" Pontius stood, Selwyn springing up after him. "I'm going to go hunt down some drinks, why don't you two catch up in my absence?"

"Pontius, I really don't think——" Selwyn began. Pontius cut her off. "Selwyn! Come with me?"

She frowned, then gently smacked him on the shoulder. "I wasn't done speaking, you brat. Let me finish before you say something."

Their argument continued as they walked away and disappeared down the stairs, leaving Kellan and Cassian alone.

They stared at each other for a few moments, Cassian's words stuck in his throat. The warmth had returned to his face, thanks to the third drink Pontius had given him a few minutes prior.

"So," Kellan began, "I'm going to guess you're here to kill either Pontius or Selwyn. Which is it?"

Cassian remained stone-faced. This part of the job was easy for him—withholding information was something he'd practiced ever since becoming Ragnor's property.

"Like I told you before, it's none of your concern."

Kellan flapped a hand at him, then downed his drink in one gulp. "Yeah, yeah, you can drop the broody act with me. I figured you wouldn't tell me, anyway."

"Then why did you ask?"

Kellan shrugged. "Curiosity."

Cassian felt his eyebrows rise. Was this sort of flippant behavior normal for legionnaires? It made them such a liability. But he supposed Kellan was less of a liability than most, thanks to the tattoo on his neck.

"Look, I promise I won't pry anymore, all right? You still owe me a favor, though."

Cassian nodded. "I didn't forget."

Kellan looked down at his empty glass, his thumb brushing the condensation off the sides. "I may have a request for you, then."

"I'm listening."

Kellan glanced around the space, and Cassian, even through the fuzziness in his head, could sense the other man's hesitation. Whatever he was about to ask was uncomfortable for him. His thoughts spun wildly into territory he dare not acknowledge, especially not now.

Just as he opened his mouth, Selwyn returned, an even more inebriated Pontius in tow.

"I'm so sorry, gentlemen, but Pontius is the most irresponsible man I've ever met. I'm taking him home," she said.

Pontius had an arm thrown over his sister, his head lolling off toward his shoulder as he tried to smile. He mumbled something that sounded like "I'm fine," but it came out so muffled that Cassian couldn't be sure.

"What happened?" Kellan asked.

"Someone offered him a shot at the bar when I was calling a cab. One shot turned into three, and I can officially never leave him alone ever again." She hefted her brother up once more. "Seriously, you are nearly two hundred years old, act your age!"

Pontius swayed again and shot his sister a toothy grin, but didn't respond. She rolled her eyes, looking back at Cassian and Kellan once more.

"Again, deepest apologies. I'll have him give you both a call in the morning. Good evening." She dipped her head and, without waiting for a response, dragged her brother back toward the stairs.

Cassian turned back to Kellan, waiting for their conversation to continue, but Kellan looked rattled.

"Kellan?" he said quietly, but it was enough for the other man to hear him.

Kellan shook his head, his dangling earrings swaying. "I'd rather not ask here, honestly. Would you be willing to come back to the Guard with me?"

Cassian went cold. Absolutely not. Non-government-sanctioned assassins like himself were taboo, illegal, and certainly not welcome at a place like the Guard. Even though they wouldn't know unless he said something, he wasn't willing to risk it. There were far easier ways to get himself killed.

"No," he said simply. Kellan furrowed his brows. "But I have another place we could go."

Why he was willing to reveal the location of the safe house was beyond him, but the fogginess in his head was messing with his decision-making skills. He knew it was, but another, louder part of him didn't care.

He tried to silence that louder part of him, to no avail.

Kellan shrugged. "You're not gonna ditch me in a hotel room again, are you?"

He shook his head. "No, but I can't promise the accommodations will be as nice."

"I don't really mind. Let's go, then."

Cassian stood, feeling the alcohol rush from his stomach to his head. He swayed slightly but swallowed hard, keeping his balance by digging his toes into the ground. His blood was loud, pumping through his ears in a steady rhythm. He walked to the beat, only paying the mildest attention to where he was going. He simply followed Kellan's back as he weaved his way through the crowded bar and outside into the late summer evening.

He was in deep shit, wasn't he?

18

KELLAN

3rd of Wind Moon

Kellan stuffed Cassian into the back seat of a waiting purple cab, the taller man staggering just enough to need Kellan's support down the stairs.

He climbed into the cab after him, poking him when the driver looked back expectantly for an address. Cassian didn't give one, instead asking to be dropped at an intersection in Northwind.

The car wound through the streets of Spiral City, the structures flying past the window in a neon blur. More than once, Cassian fell slightly forward, not entirely held in place by the seat belt. Kellan had to reach an arm across his chest to hold him in place.

He tried not to notice the hard planes of Cassian's chest beneath his plain blue tee as he held the man back in his seat. He didn't know why he was doing it, but he couldn't take his hand away. So he left it there while Cassian closed his eyes and seemed to fall asleep.

His ears and face grew hot, but he pretended not to notice, willing them to cool before they reached their destination. Wherever that was.

Once the cab pulled to the stop Cassian had requested, Kellan gently shook him awake, murmuring in his ear so as not to surprise him. He tapped his techpad against the meter, then helped Cassian out of the car.

The cabbie shot him a knowing look before peeling away, leaving them standing on a street corner in Northwind, Kellan holding Cassian's arm in a death grip.

"Where to?" he asked as Cassian slowly observed their surroundings with bleary eyes.

He sighed. "This way."

Kellan dropped his arm but stayed close as Cassian meandered down the left turn of the intersection. He was positively lackadaisical in his walk, more relaxed than Kellan had ever seen him. It was hard to reconcile the man before him with the man he'd met in Van Alder's garden all those months ago.

Beck probably would have liked him, Kellan thought bitterly. They both had an air about them that reminded Kellan of stone, tough and unwavering.

Yet, while Beck was granite or corundum, Cassian was more like marble—built up over the years of various experiences to form a stone whose beauty was entirely unique and sturdy.

He started. Why was he comparing Cassian to a stone? He had more important things to focus on than Cassian's attractiveness.

Cassian stopped before a row of beige townhomes, each more boring than the last. He approached one nested in the middle, its door painted a medium-toned brown. From his pocket, he produced a heavy, old-fashioned key. Its antiquity surprised Kellan. Why would such a modern townhome use a key?

"Is this your place? I didn't know you owned property here," he said casually, watching as Cassian inserted the key into the lock. He understood the key's uniqueness when it flared purple after being put into the door.

Cassian shook his head. "Not mine, but my boss'. I probably shouldn't even be bringing you here, but we're well past the point of *should be*. I moved into *I stopped caring* territory a long time ago."

Kellan couldn't understand why his heart raced at the comment, but he hoped if he ignored his reaction, it would go away.

Sure, Cassian was stunning. His profile was bathed in gold from the streetlamps, diametrically opposed to his natural silver tones. He had a strong nose, something Kellan hadn't noticed before but now couldn't tear his eyes away from. And his lips…

"Kellan?" Those lips moved, the way they formed his name melodiously ringing in his ears.

"Hmm?"

"It's open," Cassian said, moving into the space beyond the door.

Kellan followed, biting the inside of his cheek to bring himself back to reality. It wasn't like he hadn't noticed that Cassian was attractive before. It just seemed more pronounced now, in this intimate situation.

He'd been flustered that night Cassian had pushed him against the wall in the alleyway and begged him not to reveal his secrets. The memory of that night brought a deeper flush to his cheeks, but it was soon doused when he remembered what had followed.

After all, Liza and Cygnus' deaths were the reason he was here.

Cassian closed the door behind him and flicked the lights on, washing them in the pale, warm light of the townhome. Kellan looked around, noticing the sparse furnishings and the pallid yellow walls. Heavy curtains covered the windows facing the street. It was a simple place, completely lacking in personal touches.

"Wow, love what you've done with the place. Such charm," he said, monotone.

Cassian chuckled as he headed toward the staircase. "Like I said, not mine. I need to change. Sit wherever."

Kellan threw himself into the sagging couch in the corner, tossing an arm casually over the back of it, and listened to the thumping of Cassian upstairs.

He was risking a lot, asking a total stranger like Cassian to help him. But he'd bothered Sharr enough, and he didn't know how to ask anyone else in the nineteenth for help. He doubted they had the time to spare, anyway. Not even Avalan or Kindra could assist him; he hadn't seen Avalan since meeting Cassian again, and Kindra hadn't returned for nearly three weeks.

Kellan was aware he was probably being stupid for even asking, but something in his gut said he could trust Cassian. That something about the man banging around upstairs was safe to believe in.

Cassian ambled down the stairs a few minutes later, dressed in soft gray sweatpants and a white T-shirt. He was barefoot, and something about him looking so domestic set off a swarm of butterflies low in his gut.

"So," Cassian started, heading for the kitchen as he spoke, "what was the favor you were hoping to ask of me?"

The kitchen was open to the living room where Kellan was, so he watched as Cassian made coffee for himself. Apparently, he noticed Kellan's gaze.

"You want a cup? Might help sober you up."

Kellan shook his head. "I'm not drunk."

"Right. Suit yourself." He shrugged, turning back to the hand grinder he'd pulled from a cupboard.

He sat in silence for a few moments, simply watching Cassian move about the kitchen. Before he finished, however, Cassian turned back to face him, an eyebrow cocked.

"You can start talking, you know. I'm listening." His tone wasn't accusatory or rude; it was simply a statement.

Kellan scratched the back of his neck. "Right. About that favor…" He trailed off, biting his lip and unsure where to even begin.

It seemed Cassian knew he was searching for the right words; he said nothing more, just continued to prepare his coffee in silence. The sounds of him grinding the beans and filling the electric kettle with water calmed Kellan's heart.

"I can't believe I'm asking you this, but I need your help with an assignment. Frankly, I don't even know if you *can* help, but it's worth a shot."

Cassian poured the ground beans into a paper filter atop a glass carafe, then poured the boiling water over them slowly in circular motions. Even tipsy, his movements were slow, practiced, and precise.

"Something for the Legion? I would rather not deal with any of your co-workers, honestly."

Kellan shrugged. "I figured. But I'm on the case alone."

Cassian waited as the water dripped through the grounds slowly, filling the carafe beneath with the bitter drink. Kellan cared little for coffee, but he had to admit, it smelled nice.

"Who are you supposed to kill?"

Kellan breathed slowly out his mouth, the puff of air whistling slightly between his lips. "No one, for once. I'm investigating a double homicide."

"I didn't think the nineteenth did investigations?"

He laughed dryly. "Only in special circumstances…which I suppose these are."

"Go on," Cassian said, his voice quiet.

"It's that case we stumbled on last week. With the girl in the alley. And the legionnaire."

Cassian sucked in a breath through his teeth, his face pinched. "And you want my help with…?"

"Investigating, like I said. I'm out of my league with this damn case, and I don't know what to do with the information I have. Nothing makes sense."

Kellan waited as Cassian sighed, then swirled the coffee that had dripped into the carafe. He didn't respond for some time, instead waiting for the last of the water to sift through the grounds and pouring himself a cup. He looked at Kellan one more time as he grabbed a mug, to which Kellan simply shook his head.

He sipped once from the cup, closing his eyes as he did. He moved to sit next to Kellan on the couch before turning to look him in the eyes.

"I'll help, but only as long as it doesn't interfere with my current objective."

Kellan shot Cassian a withering stare. "I heard you the first time you said that, you know."

Cassian smiled.

The sight knocked Kellan breathless. It was clouds parting on a rainy day, blossoms blooming after the winter snow melted, or the first note of his favorite song. He'd never seen someone smile in such a way before, nor had a smile affected him so.

Goosebumps pricked up his arms, over the wing tattoo on his triceps, up the back of his neck, and through his scalp, forcing the short hair on the side of his head to stand on end.

"Um, great. Then it's settled." He coughed, aware that the tips of his ears were now burning.

"All right then, update me on the situation." Cassian seemed to ignore Kellan's obvious flush, instead sipping at the coffee in his hands like nothing was amiss.

Kellan loosed a breath, willing his heart to calm, but it ignored him. He slowly walked through what he knew—the weirdness about Liza's hands, her eyes, the drugs in her system. Cassian listened with intention, nodding occasionally as he soaked in the information.

He didn't ask questions. Cassian simply sipped his coffee once more, then held his techpad out to Kellan.

"Give me your information. We'll need to stay in contact."

Kellan nodded, silently accepting the techpad from Cassian's hands, heart in his mouth.

He was in deep, deep shit.

KELLAN

7th of Wind Moon

After his appeal to the commissioner, he'd gotten a meeting with a researcher at Northwind Medical to do an additional analysis on Liza's blood sample. Vaida was an incredible lab technician, but even she wasn't able to get the results a medical researcher could.

They needed time, he'd said, to analyze it themselves as well as review Vaida's findings. So he'd twiddled his thumbs for four days and waited for their scheduled appointment time.

Northwind Medical was an imposing building, comprising nearly a hundred floors—over half of which served as the city's main hospital and emergency care unit. To the naked eye, everything was made of glass, but Kellan knew better—the building was covered in top-of-the-line anti-shatter spells, wards, and protective spells to keep disease out.

The front doors slid open smoothly as he approached, not even requiring handles or a knob.

The lobby was built of white marble and a light blue stone, with imposing columns stretching up toward the sky. Behind the large glass reception desk sat a startlingly beautiful elven woman typing furiously at a keyboard. Her delicate spectacles drifted slowly down her nose as she typed until she stopped, pushed them back up, and sighed.

Noticing Kellan, she waved him forward with a flick of her hand tipped in silver-colored, perfectly manicured nails. She looked over the top of her glasses at him. "Hello. Name?"

He cleared his throat. "Kellan Manchester, nineteenth division. I'm here to see one of the chemists."

She popped her gum loudly, fingers flying across the keys as she typed his name into the system. "Hm. Okay, I see you here. Says you're supposed to meet with Doctor Renata. She's on the seventy-second floor."

She swiped a white access card against a reader on her desk, attached a red lanyard to it, then handed it to him. As he took it from her, she snapped her gum again. He barely contained a flinch.

"All right, this will get you up there. I've let the doctor know you're here. She'll meet you at the elevators."

"Thank you," he said, inclining his head in thanks.

"Lifts are that way, sweets." She pointed her sharp nails toward the shiny elevators across the space, one of which was opening.

Two men stepped out of the elevator. The first was thin and reedy and held a mid-sized techpad in both hands like his life depended on it. He murmured something in the second man's ear, at which he smiled.

The second man's skin was deep tan, his eyes a deep bluish green that seemed to twinkle as if he was always smiling. He wore a fitted gray suit and a blue tie that nearly matched the color of the sky outside. His shoes were shiny enough that Kellan thought he might see his reflection in them.

The well-dressed man approached the counter, a debonair smile spreading across his face as he stopped to face the receptionist.

"Director Byre. You didn't inform me you'd be leaving so soon." The receptionist batted her eyes at the director.

The air around Kellan became thick with the aura of someone in power. The director was an intimidating man, that much was obvious. He'd risen to his current position a few years ago and had led Northwind Medical with a determined but steady hand. From what he'd heard of the man, he took no nonsense but was kind to his employees.

Kellan had heard plenty about the director even though he'd been living in the city for less than a year. Byre wasn't an elf, a fact he was forthcoming about. But no one knew what his heritage was. Obviously, he wasn't a human—his pointed ears proved that enough. But was he a half-elf? Half-seraph? People had certainly theorized, but no one knew for sure. Something about the man had grabbed ahold of the public's interest, whether it was his mysterious heritage, his dashing good looks, or his immense wealth.

Kellan couldn't be sure, but he had a feeling it was a combination of all three.

The director's eyes shifted his way, and the smile never faded as he took in Kellan's gold legionnaire pin on his chest.

"A legionnaire in my building? Interesting. Whatever my staff are assisting you with, young man, I can assure you they will do their best to deliver good results." His voice was like honey on a summer's day. It was soothing.

He bowed his head again in a gesture of respect. "Director Byre. I appreciate it, and I certainly hope I can get some good results. Your staff are the best in the city, after all."

The director laughed heartily, a sound that tickled Kellan's ears and nestled into his brain. "They certainly are. Well, I must be on my way, busy day and all."

He nodded again to Kellan, then to the receptionist before turning on his heel and exiting the building, the man with the techpad following in his footsteps.

The receptionist stared after the director, looking like she'd forgotten that Kellan was even there. So he turned on his heel and approached the elevators without a glance back.

On the seventy-second floor, the elevator doors opened to reveal a severe halfling woman with jet black hair and horn-rimmed glasses.

"You must be Kellan, I presume?" she asked, her voice even.

He nodded. "That's me. I'm here for the blood analysis."

"Sure. I'm Doctor Renata. Follow me."

She briskly led him down the hallway. The walkway was open on his left, a glass railing separating him from the long drop to the first floor. On his right was a white hallway, lined with wooden doors inset with frosted windows. Exam rooms or labs, he assumed.

Hanging from the ceiling was a massive chandelier, its droplets of glass rectangles hanging at intervals and gradually thinning as they worked their way down. At this level, the glass rectangles were thick, enough to nearly block his view of the other side of the floor.

"This way, please," she said, opening one of the many wooden doors to reveal a sterile white room. Two chairs sat before a massive monitor on one wall, a small desk before them.

She gestured to the chairs, and Kellan took a seat in one as she flicked the lights off and booted the screen up.

"Now, I won't review what your lab technician already told you. I assume you understood her analysis," Doctor Renata said as she sat in the vacant chair next to him, picking up a remote for the screen.

"Correct. She explained it well," he replied.

She nodded, then looked toward the screen. "Good. Her analysis was very thorough, as is expected of Miss Larsen."

"You know her?"

She laughed, a breathy sound from her nose. "Yes, we work with her frequently. Shame she can't be recruited to work for us; she's absolutely brilliant." She clicked the remote once, bringing up charts he recognized from his visit with Vaida. "That aside, her analysis, like I said, is spot-on. We couldn't find anything further than what she'd concluded about the drug results, nor about the acid in her blood. However, we were able to find something more conclusive about the foreign blood in her system, as well as the compounds there."

He leaned in as she advanced the slide, now showing a pie chart with impossible names and a list on the right side of the screen. He recognized some of the words in the list as the names of drugs.

"What's this?"

"An analysis of the foreign compounds in her system. This combination isn't anything we know of, but it's made of several substances we are familiar with. I've listed the potential recreational and prescription drugs that could have created this combination on the side."

He scanned the list, but nothing stood out to him as particularly interesting. He didn't recognize half the names listed there to begin with.

She clicked again, this time showing a complicated chart with percentages and a bar graph. "Now, this is the most fascinating part. Miss Larsen was correct about the different blood being present in Miss Sarmanello's system. We analyzed this blood and found something quite disturbing."

"What do you mean, disturbing?"

"It's demon blood."

The color drained from his face. "Demon blood? But why? How?"

She shook her head, clicking buttons on the remote to end the slideshow and turn the lights back on. "I don't know, to be honest. There are many things unknown even to science, and the demonic rituals and arts are one of them. We simply do not have enough information."

"Then what should I do?"

"I suggest the Library of the Ancients. You know of it, yes?"

Sure, he did. It had been on this land long before Spiral City was built, and it had stayed through Ileron's tumultuous history. Kellan had never needed to visit it, but now it seemed his path would finally collide with the old building.

He nodded. "Thank you for your analysis. I'm not totally sure what these results may mean for the investigation, but at the very least, I'm grateful for your time and assistance."

Doctor Renata stood and made her way to the door. "I'm glad to have helped, Kellan. I've already sent a more detailed file to Vaida, so she'll be reviewing it as we speak. In the meantime, I suggest you brush up on demonic lore."

The Library of the Ancients was a massive stone building, towering over the smaller buildings around it from atop a large hill. University students lingered about, sitting on the stone stairs leading up the hill, some resting on blankets in the grass next to it.

Spiral City University had built itself up around the library as the city was established, and thus, to reach the library, one first had to pass through campus. SPU was one of the largest universities in the Empire, second only to the Sequoia Institute in Ivorymore.

The library itself was beautiful. As the oldest building in the city by far, Upper Cloud's councilor and the regents of the university carefully oversaw its maintenance. The brick was a soft shade of ivory, the vines growing from its base breaking the monotony of color. Toward its roof, the building sported an inaccessible balcony, the railing made of beautifully carved granite.

The entrance was just beyond a series of grand pillars, the doors to the library itself made of intricately carved wood. Kellan approached the massive doors, wincing as they creaked open. But once they shut, the silence was overwhelming.

A large marble and wood desk stood in the center of the atrium, barring entrance to the library beyond. A tall, willowy figure stood with its back to Kellan, sorting through a return cart of books. But as the doors closed, the figure turned.

Kellan had heard tales of The Bookkeeper, the ancient guardian of the library. He was completely bald, with grayish skin and black eyes with no irises. His nose looked as if it had once been smashed into his face and never reconstructed. But the worst part was his mouth. His mouth was sewn shut with several x-shaped stitches.

This library is a dangerous place—books that should not exist live here. Books that never have existed live here. I cannot simply let you walk inside. Prove to me you are worthy. He heard the Bookkeeper's voice in his head, but his lips never moved.

Kellan panicked. Several students walked past the desk without so much as a glance toward the Bookkeeper. He ignored them, his attention fully on Kellan.

"What does that even mean?" Kellan asked, glancing around the atrium, hoping for some scrap of evidence as to what proving your worth meant.

The Bookkeeper simply gazed at him with lidless eyes, his mouth set forever in a gruesome, stern line. *Only you can decide what your worth is.*

What the hell could he do? All Kellan knew was fighting, sneaking, assassinating, and being a legionnaire. He didn't know what his worth was. He didn't know what he could give to prove any part of his worth.

The Bookkeeper seemed to sense his frustration and turned around to face the stack of books he'd been sorting through earlier. Presumably to give Kellan time to think.

But he couldn't think. His life had been so bland and boring; he'd been raised to do nothing more than serve the Empire with every last breath. He'd been born into service and he would die in it. What was his worth? His fighting prowess? His remarkable wit?

He sat on the hard marble benches that lined the atrium wall next to the door and crossed his legs, arms thrown casually over the bench.

"What if I said you had to let me in on official Legion business?" He didn't think that would work since a place like the Library of the Ancients was exempt from Legion laws and business. But it didn't hurt to try.

You have answered that question for yourself, young man.

Kellan sighed and rubbed his eyes with the heel of his palms. All he wanted was to get in and find out how to close this case.

He thought of Liza's parents, the way they'd cried and held each other when he'd delivered the news of their only daughter's death.

He had to get in for them—to make sure he never had to do this again for any other family. No one should be made to suffer the way they had. He needed to get in for their sake. For Liza.

The Bookkeeper sighed softly, his stitched mouth curving slightly into a small smile. *Ah, I see.*

"See what?" Kellan said, looking up.

Your worth.

Kellan cocked an eyebrow. "What do you mean?"

The Bookkeeper simply sighed again, turning back to the books on the return cart, now neatly sorted. *Welcome, Kellan, to the Library of the Ancients.*

The door next to the desk swung open, revealing an expansive library the size of an amphitheater. The Bookkeeper walked through, pushing the cart before him. He gestured one long, spindly hand toward Kellan, motioning for him to follow.

You are indeed worthy to enter. What you seek is on the third floor, stack forty-two. He stopped, the wheels of the cart squeaking in protest. *You will find that when you listen with your heart, the searching will not be as challenging as you thought.*

With that, the Bookkeeper wheeled his cart into the shadows of the stacks on the first floor. Kellan stood in the doorway, mouth agape. He'd never seen a place so large.

The worn carpet was the color of the forest floor. The oak bookcases reached to the ceiling and were filled to bursting with books. They looked haphazardly stuffed into the shelves, but judging from his interaction with the Bookkeeper, Kellan seriously doubted there was anything haphazard about it.

Students clustered at tables set just inside, their heads bowed over books larger than any he'd ever seen before. Each table held a lamp with a bright gold base and a dark green shade, their light muted like liquid gold.

He spotted a large marble staircase in the far corner that presumably continued up to the third floor. How he'd find stack forty-two was beyond him at the moment, but he'd cross that bridge when he came to it.

Kellan took the stairs slowly, his fingers trailing up the cold marble railing. Ancient frescoes framed with carved marble, painted forests, and brilliant starscapes lined the walls as he climbed. Their colors were dark, muted with time but not sullied or dull. It was beautiful, he thought.

Upon arrival on the third floor, Kellan took a detour to look over the railing that kept him from falling to the first floor. The library was even more impressive from this angle. The light from the lamps didn't reach this far, but a massive chandelier lit the rest of the library from above. He hadn't noticed it upon arrival; the domed ceiling soared high enough that the chandelier's sparkling gems hadn't caught his eye until he was further up.

Kellan sighed and turned to face the stacks behind him. Did he need to count? Which side started from one? He approached the nearest one, hoping for a number or a sign or something. He was rewarded with a small brass plaque that read "six." Great. Thirty-six more stacks to go.

The forty-second stack looked exactly the same as the previous stacks, but a sense of understanding, of rightness, flooded Kellan's senses. Was this the ancient magic of the library? He shook his head and looked at the books.

Titles he couldn't read in characters he'd never seen before were the majority here. What was this language? The titles he could read were things like *Demonology and the Nine Hells*, *Historia Daemonia: The History of Demons*, and *Planar Study: The Nine Hells and the Astral Plane*. He hardly knew where to start.

Before long, a title popped out at him; *The Nine Hells and The Nine Demonic Princes*. It gave him the same feeling he'd felt upon arriving at the stack. Kellan shrugged and grabbed the book. Nothing to lose by simply reading.

He flipped the pages, hoping that the same feeling he'd gotten with the stack and book would return. But it didn't, and he was instead left reading something he wasn't sure even related to the case. He flipped pages, searching for that feeling of rightness, hoping a passage would spark something.

He didn't get too far before the feeling returned. He stopped, reading the first few paragraphs of the page.

The second layer of hell is named Dis. Be warned, this plane is nothing like the hells of your dreams. It is a place that will trap and ensnare your senses, for it appears as a regular city.

The skyscrapers loom tall in Dis, and demons of this layer are exceptionally cunning and tricky. Many are skilled in stealth and deception and are the hardest to discover when they infiltrate other planes. Often, they enjoy hiding in plain sight, using their wits to trick those around them into believing they have existed in that plane for days, years, or centuries.

One such tale is of one of the demonic princes of Dis, Alvemach. It is said that Alvemach was once an elven general in the Starfallen Rebellion. His thirst for blood and treachery eventually landed him in the hells after death, whereupon he was made into a prince. No one has seen him in the material plane since his mortal death.

He cocked an eyebrow, setting the book back down flat on the table, the passage still open. What did the second layer of hell have to do with anything?

Kellan spent three more hours scouring the shelves of the library for more information on demons, searching for that same feeling again, but it evaded him. He wondered if he should talk to the Bookkeeper again, but he wasn't sure that would work. What had he said before? Something about searching with his heart?

His eyes drooped as he continued searching the shelves, but nothing else stood out to him. It was getting late, and he had made little progress toward finding out why Liza had had demonic blood in her system.

So he re-shelved the books, leaving a few on the table when he couldn't figure out where they belonged, and left the library, his heart sinking deep into his stomach.

JUPITER'S COLOR IS RED

Jupiter, the Goddess of Night and Death. Her color is red. When people die, their spirits are sent to the ethereal plane, where Jupiter presides with Sol and their four daughters. It's said that if one is a decent person while living on the material plane, Jupiter will welcome you to her eternal hearth. Thus, her color is red for those comforting flames.

Celebrations of life are common to honor the dead. They are meant to send the deceased's soul to its final resting place, to remind Jupiter of the good they'd done in their life. Essentially, they are a trial to prove the deceased worthy of spending the rest of existence by the fires of eternal rest.

These celebrations tend to be large. The remaining family gathers as many people as possible who'd known the deceased in order to increase the chances of their stories being accepted by Jupiter.

20

CASSIAN

9th of Wind Moon

Cassian's research and subsequent evenings spent with Pontius had proven fruitless. The worst thing he could find on Pontius was his penchant for overindulging when partying. But his sister Selwyn stymied any consequence that could come from being too drunk. She was his guardian angel, keeping him clean and protecting him from himself.

So when Ragnor called again that week, he knew how poorly the conversation was going to go.

"You're telling me it's been two weeks since I sent you and you've done absolutely nothing?" Ragnor's voice was cold, emotionless. Cassian knew that tone meant trouble.

"That's not entirely true, sir," he started, but Ragnor cut him off.

"I expected you to at least have a trail to follow by now, Cassian. I spent a lot of money on you, training you, making you into the ideal version of yourself. But you know what will happen if you fail me."

"Yes, sir."

"Tell me again about your target."

He drew in a deep breath, sorting out the facts in his head. "Pontius Morgenstern pretends to live up to his reputation of being the city's number one bachelor, but strangely, I never really see him go home with anyone but his sister. He's very dedicated to his work, however, and I've found he takes his job seriously. He has a tendency to overindulge when partying, but Selwyn keeps him from ruining his reputation."

Ragnor sighed. "You must get his sister away from him."

Cassian hesitated for a moment, mulling over the implications. The moment was too long for Ragnor, however, who barked another order over the line.

"When I say to do it, that means to do it."

"Yes, sir," he replied immediately.

"I'm being very flexible with you, Cassian. Next time I contact you, I expect results." Without waiting for a response, Ragnor hung up.

Cassian hardly ever got a word in edgewise, but it didn't really matter as long as he got results.

He *had* to get results. After all, Ragnor had his mother.

His father had been in Ragnor's employ since before Cassian was conceived. He hadn't been Ragnor's property, though. He'd chosen to work for the man, hunting down rare artifacts from around the world. He'd made good money from it too.

But somewhere along the way, he'd met Eliza, fallen in love, and gotten on Ragnor's bad side. Cassian didn't know how Briar had done that, but he suspected it had something to do with Cassian himself.

After Briar had passed, he'd left behind massive debts that Ragnor had demanded be paid. Cassian was still a child at thirty, and his mother couldn't pay them. So, he'd taken Cassian as payment instead.

Cassian had never been able to hate his father—after all, the memories he had of the man were happy, fuzzy, and warm. He'd never despised him, but his father frustrated him. What had he done to incur all those debts? And how large were they to reduce Cassian's entire life to servitude?

He knew, logically, that the debt had probably been long since paid. But Ragnor would never admit it—he'd keep Cassian forever as long as he could hold the threat of Eliza's life over his head. And there wasn't a damn thing he could do about it, so he obeyed.

That was why, even if he was beginning to like Pontius, he couldn't stop. He had to do as Ragnor commanded, or his mother would die.

As he laid his techpad down on the side table, he caught a whiff of fresh laundry and something spicy—a scent he recognized as Kellan's. He'd been sitting on this very couch and speaking with Cassian in soft tones. He'd refused a cup of coffee and blushed until the tips of his ears turned red.

Cassian put a hand over his mouth as he recalled Kellan's red ears. He'd insisted he wasn't drunk, and Cassian knew it was true.

So why had he been blushing?

A rustle outside his window had him springing from his seat. Rationally, Cassian knew it must have been a bird or some other small creature resting in the trees along the front of the townhouses.

But his heart was already thumping too loudly in his chest, and something about the blood coursing through his veins made him more paranoid than usual.

He stood from the laundry-and-spice scent on the couch, mourning its disappearance for a moment before moving toward the window and yanking the heavy curtain aside.

The quiet street was empty; no animals or cars moved outside. No one walked along the sidewalks or hung ominously from rooftops as he'd apparently been expecting. There was nothing, no one there.

But the feeling of being watched only grew as he observed the street, scanning the sidewalks at the corners of his view. The longer he looked for something, the more ominous the feeling got. The longer he searched for movement, the stranger it seemed that there was none.

Just as he moved to draw the curtains, cursing himself for his paranoia, he saw something—a shadow moving across the rooftops, a blur just barely darker than the light-stained sky beyond the trees.

He swore, jumping toward the door and not bothering to put

any shoes on.

Leo had stalked him like this once, back when he'd been seeing Aidyn. Back when things had been so much easier, but also so much harder.

He'd followed Cassian everywhere, stalking him on his missions, following him around on dates, even watching him when he'd return home. He'd watched from rooftops, from trees, silently laughing as Cassian went about his day.

But then, Aidyn had died. Shot by a gang whose leader Cassian had killed a week earlier for owing money to Ragnor. They never should have known it was Cassian who'd targeted him, but they'd known exactly where he would be and who would be with him. And how to hurt him.

Cassian had always suspected Leo's involvement but had never gotten the chance to confront him about it. Because as soon as Aidyn died, Leo had disappeared.

What he was feeling now, this lingering sense of being watched, of being observed from afar, was not unfamiliar to him. It was reminiscent of that time in his life when he'd been the sole focus of the most bloodthirsty man on the planet.

The pavement was still warm from the sun, which had only just set. It was rough on his feet, but he didn't care.

He raced across the street, frantically searching for a ladder, a fire escape, or even a convenient set of bricks to climb the building where he'd seen the shadow. But it took too long. Once he'd located the fire escape, the shadow was long gone.

He searched for a note like when he'd gone to the restaurant, but there was nothing there. There was no trace of his stalker at all. So he returned to the townhouse, shaking his head all the while.

Before he went to sleep that night, he fortified all the windows and doors with a touch of his own magic, just in case.

21

SHADOW

9th of Wind Moon

The man sat on a rooftop, staring across the street at a house he did not recognize.

He could sense the power that sat inside.

He wondered if the man inside knew he was here, watching him. Something about him not knowing was thrilling.

A curtain fluttered in the window across the street, and the man knew Cassian was aware of his presence. A tingle rolled through him, pushing his blood through his veins, circulating it through his fingertips like liquid fire. The thrill of the chase always gave him a high he couldn't replicate anywhere else.

Chase me, he begged silently. *Come find me.*

But nothing moved. No one left the house across the street, and the curtain didn't budge. Disappointment was not a feeling he experienced often—in fact, he knew how to avoid it well.

It swarmed through him now. It creased the space between his eyebrows, clenched the muscles of his jaw. The discomfort was almost too much for him to bear. He needed to move, to get this feeling out and away from him.

The curtain moved again as he stood. A smile crept across his lips, stretching them thin over his pointed canines.

He was coming after him. *Finally.*

But he wouldn't be caught now. The man simply wanted Cassian to chase after him, to acknowledge that he was there and watching.

There was so much more to be done before he could be caught, before he would let Cassian close enough to see what he'd done. The beauty he'd become.

It wasn't time for that just yet. No. There was more to be done before he could reveal himself.

But he needed Cassian to chase him now. Just a little taste of the thrill that was to come.

He moved away from the house he didn't know, listening for the sounds of pursuit. They came moments later; the door slamming and feet hitting the pavement. The echo bounced off the rooftops and reverberated in his ears.

Oh, the thrill of the chase gave him chills. The goosebumps ran up and down his arms, making the hairs on the nape of his neck stand on end.

He could feel the power Cassian radiated, could smell it, practically taste it on his tongue. It was divine, heavenly, ethereal.

He wanted that power so badly it hurt.

But patience—patience was his friend. It would come in due time.

The pursuit began in earnest as he heard Cassian cross the street. But he wouldn't get up here so easily.

The man savored the crackle of power in the air, the thrum of it vibrating his skin as Cassian grew closer. But he let himself taste it only for a moment before he departed, leaving the rooftops behind him in a blur.

KELLAN

10th of Wind Moon

The Archangel was not Kellan's usual haunt. Located in the business district of Bloomside, ever-blooming cherry trees and dogwood surrounded it, painting it in shades of pink and white. The building was lovely, built of a whitewashed brick and decorated with gold filigree. Celestial wing motifs adorned each joint of the building, and the attention to detail in the carvings was so fine that they looked almost lifelike.

Kellan snorted, looking away from the winged motifs, and walked through the sliding glass doors, Cassian following close on his heels.

They were here tonight at the request of Pontius again, but apparently, he was only a proxy for his sister. It seemed she'd decided that they were overdue for an evening at "a proper establishment." The phrasing seemed to bring Pontius a lot of joy, as he'd described it in his message to Kellan when he'd invited him along.

Cassian had surprised him, showing up in loosely fitted denim jeans and a short-sleeved button-up with a floral print tucked into the front. He looked breezy, casual, and it set something off in his mind that had him stealing glances every moment he could.

Mina awaited them at the bar, her legs crossed as she waited for the bartender. She'd donned a sparkly golden dress tonight, the fabric sleek and flattering on her curvy frame. It fell just past her knees, a single slit running up to mid-thigh to give her freedom of movement. She'd curled her hair and clipped one side of it back in a polished style. The look suited her, Kellan thought.

The bar itself was sleek and black, with soft white lighting on its underside. Lights overhead twinkled like tiny stars and reflected off the wall of wine bottles stacked in hexagonal patterns behind a white-haired seraph bartender. His wings were fully manifested and appeared silver beneath the lights above.

Mina waved as they approached, her face brightening into a smile when she spotted Kellan.

"I'm so glad you could make it!" She beamed. "Selly, Ponty, and Tarin are waiting for us in a room in the back. I'm just out here to grab us some drinks."

The bartender finished pouring two glasses of bubbly wine, setting them down before Mina and cocking an eyebrow at Kellan.

"Why don't I order us something and join you in a minute?" Cassian's low voice rumbled behind him.

Kellan breathed in deeply before turning to look over his shoulder. "Thanks, Cassian."

Cassian just shooed him away with a flap of his hand, and Kellan turned to face Mina once more.

She jerked her head down a hallway just beyond the bar before turning on her heel. Kellan gave Cassian one last look before following her.

Mina led him down the hall, brushing aside a heavy velvet curtain to reveal a cozy rectangular room with two plush benches flanking a black table. It was large enough for at least fifteen people.

Selwyn sat on a bench, legs crossed at the ankles and an empty flute in her hand. A pair of sleek taupe pants that came to the perfect spot on her ankles accentuated her long legs. Camel-colored, strappy sandals were a perfect compliment to the color of her pants. She wore a loose-fitted white button-up, a dark brown under bust corset cinching her small waist. Her hair was down, loose and curly.

She looked bored, but her face brightened upon their entry. Kellan wasn't delusional enough to think it was because of him.

"I've got another glass for you, Selly. Same stuff, right?" Mina said as she handed a flute to Selwyn.

"Thank you, Mina; that's perfect." Selwyn's smile was soft, and Kellan thought she wore the expression beautifully.

Pontius sat across from Selwyn, dressed in an ostentatious white suit that would have looked ridiculous on anyone but him. His friend Tarin, who Kellan vaguely remembered from the night he'd met Pontius, sat beside him. He was dressed much less obnoxiously in navy blue.

It was Tarin who greeted him first, not Pontius. "Kellan! Pontius told me you'd be joining us. I feel left out; I haven't gotten the chance to get to know you."

Kellan smiled. It was forced, but he didn't think Tarin could tell. "Pontius has been very kind to continue to invite me out like this."

Tarin beamed, then slapped Pontius on the back. "That's my Ponty boy, always making friends wherever he goes."

Pontius rolled his eyes good-naturedly, but Kellan could see the smile parting his lips as Tarin continued buttering up his best friend.

Mina selected a seat next to Selwyn, leaving a space perfectly suited for two more people. Kellan sat there, fidgeting with the collar of his oversized black shirt to distract himself from the fluttering of his heart.

Selwyn sighed after taking a sip of her drink. "So, Kellan, tell us more about yourself."

Kellan felt his eyebrows raise in surprise. He hadn't thought Selwyn was interested in him at all. "I'm a legionnaire, nineteenth division."

"Admirable," was all Selwyn said.

Mina covered what would have been an awkward silence quickly. "Oh! That's wonderful, Kellan. What does the nineteenth do again?"

"Special Ops. Unfortunately, I can't tell you much more than that. Undercover work and all," he replied, winking at her for effect.

Mina giggled. Selwyn regarded him with slightly narrowed eyes.

The curtain lifted once more, and Cassian appeared, two glasses of whiskey in his hands. He set one in front of Kellan, then looked between the couches, unsure of where to sit.

Kellan gestured next to him, and Cassian took the invitation. He nodded at Pontius and Tarin, then again at Selwyn.

"Nice to see you again, Mina, Tarin," he said softly.

Mina giggled again. "It's nice to see you both as well," she said as she glanced toward Kellan, lashes lowered.

Their conversation turned light, the sort of discussion people have when they don't know each other all that well. That seemed to bore Selwyn, though, Kellan noticed. She was silent through most of it, only offering small tidbits of information when spoken to directly. After she'd sipped half of her sparkling wine, she finally seemed to decide upon a topic for conversation that interested her.

Selwyn turned to her brother, gently setting her glass down on the table before her and weaving her fingers together.

"My dearest brother, why don't you tell us about your experience in Rivenstorm?" she said with the barest hint of a smirk.

Pontius laughed. "Come on, Selly, you know it was a disaster. You just want to hear my pain all over again."

"You're absolutely correct. It's hilarious," she said, chuckling.

"I'd love to hear more, if you don't mind," Cassian chimed in quietly. Kellan stared at Cassian's hand holding the glass for a moment longer than he intended. Swallowing, he forced his gaze back to Pontius.

"Well, I'd heard whispers that there was a bar they all gathered at, but no one there would talk to me. It seems elven kind aren't exactly welcomed in Rivenstorm."

"Of course not. It took them over four hundred years to separate themselves enough from the Empire to establish their own anti-slavery laws," Selwyn said.

Pontius nodded. "Indeed, but even when I told them who I was, they entirely ignored me. I spent three weeks trying to earn someone's trust in that town and not one of them would have anything to do with me!"

"Why were you there, anyway?" Kellan asked casually.

"Looking for the Phantom Flame, of course. They're quite famous, supposedly led by a descendent of Queen Ameloria herself!"

Kellan had heard of the Phantom Flame. They were a human-led rebel group that had amassed quite a force in Rivenstorm. There was nothing the Empire could do about them, though, since they weren't violent in the slightest.

Most of their work focused on taking in refugees, finding them work and shelter in the city. Sometimes, they helped them to leave the Empire all together. Even with the new anti-slavery laws in place, the Empire still apparently found it hard to let old habits of obsessively corralling the human population within their borders die.

"You really believe their leader is a long-lost human queen?" Kellan finally said, cocking an eyebrow.

"Why shouldn't I?" Pontius said, tilting his head. "It's not totally implausible; they never found the Queen after Starfallen."

"Didn't they find her remains like two hundred years later or something?" Mina asked, leaning slightly into Selwyn.

Pontius shook his head. "No, they thought they were hers, but scans proved that to be false. She escaped, and now her descendant is fighting for equality. It's just so…poetic," he said, eyes shining.

"Can I ask you a potentially rude question?" Kellan asked, leaning forward to set his glass down.

"No rude questions here, only curious ones."

"Why?"

"I'm sorry?"

"Why do you do it? Why do you fight so hard for the dismemberment of a system that has done so much for you?" Kellan wove his fingers together in his lap. There was something about

Pontius' demeanor that both surprised him and threw him off.

After all, it made no sense for someone like Pontius to care or pretend like he did. Kellan hadn't been able to figure out if the man actually cared or if he was simply using this as an outlet for boredom. He knew Pontius probably meant well, but were his actions going to cause more problems than they'd solve? Was he actually changing things or just pretending to?

Pontius was silent for a moment, considering. "You know, Kellan, I like you." He pointed at Kellan, shaking his finger and smiling. "I don't get asked that question often."

"Really," he replied, monotone. He saw Selwyn's eyes slide to him, narrowing a touch.

He shook his head. "Most of the time it's just 'why do you bother,' or 'who even cares?' But I care. I do. I understand what life is like when you are afforded freedoms. I understand how good life can be with no barriers or stumbling blocks. And I can't be selfish—I can't claim that life is only for me. I can't in good conscience live my life without wanting that for others, for everyone."

"That's incredibly selfless of you," said Kellan. "But what are you actually *doing?* The sentiment is nice and all, but it means nothing if you aren't actually creating change. You have the power to do so."

Pontius pondered for a moment. "Well, I had a hand in enacting the Human Equality Act that passed a few years ago, and I personally support many humanitarian efforts across the city."

Kellan could feel the fire burning in the pit of his stomach. "And? Just because humans can't be slaves anymore doesn't mean the world is magically better. They're still suffering, many of them still enslaved in different ways. They can't find work, they can't leave since they have no money, and many of them have to stay where they were before the act passed simply because they have no choice."

"Well, that's—" Pontius began, but Selwyn held up a hand to stop him.

"Kellan, I understand freedom and oppression are subjects that are…well, very personal to you," she began, and the rage simmered hotter in his stomach.

How dare she? How dare she assume anything about his life, about how he felt about the issues Pontius was pretending to fight?

"But," she continued, ignoring Kellan's rising anger, "Pontius is trying. Change doesn't happen in a day. It takes years of hard work—long years. Years that humans don't have. Elves can oppress multiple generations of humans in a single lifespan. So doesn't it make sense that someone like Pontius becomes an advocate for humans?"

The rage cooled a touch at the logical tone of her voice. "Look, I get it. You're not as bad as the other 'activists' I've seen try to change things. But all you're doing is making yourself feel better. That's just as bad."

"I'm not." Pontius finally found his voice, gesturing for Selwyn to stop before she could say more. "I mean, it may have started that way, but I truly care about helping the humans here in the Empire."

"Then that goes back to my original question—why?" Kellan couldn't stop the words from leaving his mouth even when he knew this conversation was getting him nowhere. He *liked* Pontius. So why couldn't he stop them?

Pontius wrung his hands for a moment, everyone's eyes on him. Selwyn didn't speak again, and both Mina and Tarin had stayed silent while Kellan interrogated Pontius. Kellan didn't even want to look at Cassian.

But it seemed Cassian wouldn't let him off so easily.

"Because he's doing what he can, Kellan," he said softly.

Pontius nodded. "My strength lies in my privilege, a privilege I can share with others. I have been blessed to have more than I could ever need. It's only right that I share it."

The room was silent for a few moments as Pontius' words sunk in, the fire in Kellan's belly dying. It seemed like forever before Mina finally broke the silence.

"Did you give the humans in Rivenstorm that speech? It might've helped," she said with a tentative smile.

Pontius laughed, and the intensity of the room dissipated some. "If only I could have; I was trying to save the good stuff for the Phantom Flame, but alas, no such luck."

He took a long drink of his sparkling wine, downing the whole glass before standing. "I need something different to drink. Besides, I'd like to stretch my legs. Cassian, would you like to accompany me to the bar?"

Kellan's eyes finally found Cassian's as he stood to join Pontius, but nothing in his expression betrayed his thoughts about the conversation they'd just had. A knot formed in Kellan's stomach. He tried ignoring it as the rest of the group fell into conversation, but it wouldn't go away.

CASSIAN

10th of Wind Moon

Cassian followed Pontius out of the VIP room, his head still spinning from their conversation.

He'd gotten to know Pontius over the last two weeks, and he turned out to be nothing like Cassian expected. He'd been expecting a rich snob wanting to play rebel for a day, not someone who seemed to truly understand the cause he was fighting for. A lot of activists in the elven communities of the Empire weren't as driven as Pontius was. They lost interest quickly or just stopped caring when things didn't go their way. Many simply didn't want to face the ugly truth—that the Empire wasn't a promised land. It was deeply flawed and broken, and to fix it would take a lot of hard work.

But Pontius understood. He'd shown that in their conversation moments ago. He expressed a dedication to the cause that Cassian had never seen from someone like him before. And it made his mission so much harder.

"So, Cassian, tell me a bit more about Ebenfell," Pontius said as they approached the bar.

He smiled softly as he leaned up against the shiny black material. "My mother grew up there, and her mother, and her mother. Being from Ebenfell is just in our blood, I guess." The truth wouldn't hurt.

"I see," he said, sitting on one of the white stools, the lighting under the bar reflecting off his dazzlingly white pants. "I've been there a few times. Lovely place. The cherry trees in spring are truly a sight to behold."

"Don't those in Bloomside stay flowering all year?"

"They do, but there's something about the ephemeral beauty of the Nathconian cherry trees that Bloomside's magic simply cannot replicate."

Cassian simply nodded in agreement. The cherry trees were his mother's favorite, and she'd always taken him to see their blooms fall in late spring. He remembered the way the pink petals drifted to the ground like falling snow. How soft they were when you scooped handfuls of them off the ground. He used to throw them around like confetti, laughing as they fell around him. A tender smile spread across his own face at the memory.

"Thinking of something good?" Pontius asked.

Cassian started, not realizing he'd been daydreaming. "Oh, yeah, just my mother. She loves the cherry blossoms."

"My mother is quite fond of them as well, although I'm not sure she's ever seen the ones in Nathcon."

The white-winged bartender approached them, holding two glasses of a drink that could only be described as molten gold. Pontius must have ordered it while he was zoned out.

Pontius grabbed a glass, tipping it toward Cassian with a small smile. Cassian grabbed the remaining glass, holding it up. It surprised him to find that the drink was warm. Pontius took a sip first, eyes closing as he did.

He tested it, taking a small sip first. It tasted like honey and cinnamon when it hit his tongue, warming the inside of his mouth pleasantly and coating his tongue like chocolate. But as he swallowed, the taste changed. It turned warmer and fuller, tasting of apples and coriander and star anise with a slight burn that only came with alcohol.

"What was that?" he asked, staring at the swirling drink in his hand.

"Ambrosia," Pontius said. "It's the Archangel's specialty. You like it?"

He'd tasted nothing like it in his life. "It's delicious."

"It's my favorite drink. I'm glad you enjoyed it."

They sat in silence for a few moments, Cassian sipping the ambrosia thoughtfully. It truly was one of the most delicious things he'd ever tasted.

He watched Pontius out of the corner of his eye as he drank. The other man didn't seem fazed by the conversation in the VIP room. In fact, he looked almost invigorated, like talking about it had unlocked something inside him.

Cassian could understand Kellan's frustration—after all, he'd been given the short end of the stick in life too, forced to bear the sins of his ancestors. Although it may have appeared harsh on the surface, he understood it had been important for Kellan to question Pontius.

Pontius interrupted his thoughts. "So, I haven't asked yet, but I'm curious—how did you and Kellan come to know each other?" The question was natural, but not one Cassian had been prepared for. This was what he got, he thought bitterly, for making up a cover story on the spot.

His stomach swooped, panic rising in his throat as he scrambled to come up with an excuse that sounded natural. After all, how in the world could he have known someone from the Mission? They were sequestered their entire lives until they were assigned to one of the Empire's cities.

"My organization," he began, testing the waters. Pontius' expression didn't change. "Worked with the Mission a while back. Or tried, I guess is a better way of putting it. But I did have some contact with the kids there. Kellan was one of them. He's grown a lot."

It was the best he could do. He'd have to update Kellan on their backstory at some point, but for now all he could hope was that Pontius believed him.

"Ah yes, I've heard of some organizations doing mentorship

programs and such with the Mission. You must tell me more—"

He was interrupted by a hand appearing on his shoulder. Cassian looked up to see Tarin smiling at them, an unlit cigarillo in his mouth.

"Tarin, hi," Pontius said, setting his glass down. "I'm sorry we lost track of time, I didn't realize we'd been gone so long."

Tarin shook his head. "No, no, you're fine. I'm just going out for a smoke, wanted to see if either of you wanted to join me."

Pontius shook his head. "No thanks, Tarin. Enjoy."

He turned to Cassian, who followed Pontius' lead and shook his head. He'd never liked the taste of the smoking weed they used in the packed cigarillos; they made him lightheaded.

"Cool. See you guys soon." He pushed off the bar and walked toward the door, hands in his pockets.

Pontius sighed, grabbing his drink and motioning to the bartender. "Send a round of six ambrosias to VIP room three, please." The bartender nodded, and Pontius turned back to Cassian. "I suppose we really should head back, shouldn't we?"

"Couldn't hurt," Cassian replied, grabbing his own drink from the bar and nodding to the bartender as he made more of the liquid gold. Relief was cool as it flowed through his veins. He could avoid the topic of his relationship with Kellan for at least a little while longer.

They reentered the suite, and Cassian noted the way Kellan's eyes immediately found his when the curtain was pushed back. Even with the ambrosia still in hand, his mouth was dry.

Mina and Kellan were now sitting close together, her upper arm touching Kellan's shoulder. She looked flushed, and part of Cassian understood.

They spent the next half an hour discussing music and a movie Selwyn had taken Mina to last week when the curtain drew back to their room. Tarin returned, looking worse for wear. His skin had paled, his eyes were unfocused, and he swayed slightly upon entering.

Pontius rose, concern filling his eyes as he grabbed his friend by the shoulders.

"Tarin?" he said, shaking him slightly. "Tarin, are you all right?"

Tarin didn't reply. Instead, he swayed forward, his head falling onto Pontius' shoulder.

"Tarin? Tarin!" Pontius shook him again, his body now almost fully limp in his grip.

Cassian rose and made his way to them, gently taking control of Tarin from Pontius. "Let me," he said gently. "We should lay him down."

Pontius nodded, letting his friend's shoulders go. Tarin was colder than he should be, like his body heat was slowly being leached away. It wasn't cold outside, so why was he like this?

He lifted the now shivering man onto the bench he'd just vacated, tilting his chin up to open his airways in case he couldn't breathe. His chest rose and fell in shallow breaths as Cassian checked his pulse. It fluttered inconsistently like he'd had too much caffeine. He pried open one of Tarin's eyes gently. It was bloodshot and red. But even more concerning was the color—the irises had a yellowish tinge to them where they'd once been soft brown.

Suddenly, Tarin convulsed, his back arching off the couch and his legs flailing, nearly kicking Cassian in the face. He shook violently, and froth appeared at the corner of his lips.

"Call the trauma team, now!" Cassian commanded no one in particular as he struggled to hold the flailing Tarin down.

"Already on it," Kellan replied.

It took the twelfth division four minutes to reach them, and in that time, Tarin scratched Cassian's arms so badly they bled. He'd kept him from hurting himself, at least. They injected him with a sedative that caused his convulsions to stop. Another of the team members held their hands over his chest, fingers splayed and hands glowing purple. Whatever spell they cast stabilized him enough to lift him onto a stretcher and out the door.

After Tarin was gone, the rest of the group stayed silent. Minutes passed and no one moved. Finally, Pontius stood.

"I'm going to go to Northwind. He needs me."

Selwyn stood as well. "I'll take you." She turned to the rest of the group, still sitting in stunned silence. "Mina, are you coming or staying?"

Mina looked pale, her head resting in her hands as she stared at the ground. Cassian's heart twisted for her. While it wasn't easy for him and Kellan to deal with, she wasn't a hardened warrior like them. Injury, illness, and death would all be a major shock to her.

"Coming," she squeaked. Kellan helped her to stand.

Selwyn looked back to Cassian, her blue eyes intense. "Will you two be all right?"

Cassian nodded dumbly, his hands numb. The twelfth had taken a moment to patch his arms up with that same glowing purple light they'd used on Tarin. He didn't have a scratch on him.

Selwyn nodded and followed her brother out the velvet curtain, her arm linked in Mina's.

It was Kellan who broke the silence first.

"What the hell happened?" he said softly. "He just said he was going for a smoke."

Cassian shook his head. What had happened, indeed?

24

KELLAN

10th of Wind Moon

Kellan watched as the curtain fell back into place, still not quite able to process the events that had just taken place.

"We should probably look around," Cassian said, resting a hand on Kellan's shoulder.

The gentle contact made him startle, and Cassian looked guilty as he removed his hand and made for the curtain as well.

"Sorry, I didn't mean to surprise you."

"It's okay," Kellan said, his shoulder still tingling.

He followed Cassian to the curtain, taking a moment before stepping outside to glance around the room once more. He spotted something on the floor by the bench Tarin had laid on. It was a small syringe.

"Cassian," he said, reaching a hand out to stop him. "What is that?"

Cassian followed his gaze. He dropped the curtain and approached the bench, cautiously picking up the discarded syringe.

"It looks like it had liquid in it, something reddish," he said, turning the syringe over in his hand. It was smaller than his palm. "I don't like this, Kellan."

"I don't either."

"We should have this analyzed."

"You think this caused Tarin to collapse?" Kellan said, approaching Cassian. "If that's the case, I have someone who could do that."

"Don't know until we try," Cassian said, shrugging. He handed Kellan the syringe. It hardly weighed anything, barely enough to even register when he took it from Cassian's outstretched fingers.

"Kellan." The way Cassian said his name made him want to close his eyes and savor the sound. "There's something else."

He cocked an eyebrow. "Something else?"

"Tarin's eyes." He breathed deeply through his nose. "Maybe we should sit for a minute." He found the bench again, sitting so that his elbows rested on his knees.

Kellan followed suit, sitting on the other side of the short table. "What is it? What happened?"

"They were turning yellow."

Kellan's heart stopped beating for a moment. "Are you sure?"

"Positive."

He looked at the syringe in the palm of his hand. Was this what had been in Liza's bloodstream? Was this the unknown substance Vaida couldn't identify? What was Tarin doing with something like this?

It wasn't like drugs were a new problem for Spiral City. In a city as large as this, underground crime networks were bound to pop up no matter how hard the Legion tried to squash them. A bit like weeds, the seedy underground grew between the cracks of the lawful.

Kellan swore as he stood from his seat. "I doubt anyone is still out there, but just in case…"

Cassian stood as well, placing a hand on his shoulder once more. His eyes gleamed with determination as he nodded to Kellan before disappearing behind the curtain.

Kellan stayed glued to the spot for a moment, staring at the small syringe in his hands. How lucky and yet unlucky he must be for this clue to have dropped itself into his lap. How else would he have attained it if he hadn't come here tonight?

He shook his head, gripping the syringe as he pushed through the curtain and left the bar, nodding once at the bartender as he exited.

It was dark outside, the night sky a hazy smog of light pollution and clouds. Cassian stared up at the sky, a somber expression on his face.

"It's really quite unfortunate," he said softly as Kellan approached.

Kellan said nothing but moved to stand next to him as he leaned up against the whitewashed brick of the Archangel.

"You can't see the stars here," he continued. His hands were in his pockets, his hair falling over his forehead in perfect, silvery curls. "You can't really see them in Ebenfell either, but I still look. Every time I'm outside."

"The stars were pretty amazing at the Mission," Kellan added, leaning back on the brick as well.

Cassian turned to face him, his mouth a tight line. "I used to look at the stars every time I'd finish a job. For some reason, seeing the vast unknown above has always grounded me."

Kellan just nodded, not entirely understanding.

"But lately, I haven't been able to see the stars. Especially since coming here. It has left me feeling…untethered." He shook his head, curls bouncing. "I know I sound insane—"

"Not at all," Kellan interrupted. "We all have to find what gives us peace, and if that's stargazing for you, then it's not insane."

Cassian looked at him, the gray in his eyes dissolving slowly and the green becoming bright. His lips quirked up in a small smile. "Thank you, Kellan, for understanding."

Kellan chuckled. "I don't completely, but I know how you feel."

"It's enough."

They stood there for a few moments, the silence comfortable, before Cassian pushed off the wall with a grunt. "You've got someone who could analyze that stuff?"

Kellan nodded, also pushing off. "Yeah, although I doubt she's in the lab right now."

Cassian's eyes met his own, and he paused, unsure of what to do next. Their night had ended prematurely, but Kellan was hesitant to leave.

Cassian made the choice for him. "I should get going, Kellan. I'm tired."

"Oh, sure," he said, his heart falling. "I should probably go as well."

Cassian hailed a cab, turning to Kellan once more before getting in. "Sleep well, okay?"

Kellan nodded, glued to the pavement until the cab disappeared around the corner and out of sight.

14TH OF WIND MOON

The sun was high as he sat at his desk in the Guard, staring once again at the papers strewn about. Nothing was making sense. It had been over three weeks since Liza and Cygnus' bodies had been found, and he'd gotten absolutely *nowhere*.

The only thing he had left was that syringe—hopefully it would prove to be something he could use. He'd dropped it off with Vaida over the weekend, and she'd promised to expedite the testing. These things took time, though, and all he could do now was twiddle his thumbs and hope maybe he'd missed something in the smattering of information he had already collected.

He'd updated the commissioner several times over the last week, but even he didn't have any ideas about what might have been in that syringe. Drugs were a common problem in Spiral City, new ones cropping up every few years and giving the divisions trouble for a few months before they'd quash the problem altogether. But they'd had no reports of strange new drugs recently.

His techpad lit up and dinged, Pontius' information on the screen, breaking his train of thought.

He pushed the answer button, leaving it on speaker. "Hi, Pontius."

"Kellan, hi." Pontius' voice was strained. Kellan felt his eyebrows raise. Of all the people to be calling him, why Pontius? "I'm sorry to call you so suddenly. I desperately need your help, and I have nowhere else to turn."

"My help? What for?"

"Tarin's missing."

"What? Wasn't he at Northwind? Did he get released?"

Pontius sighed. "I'd rather not talk about it this way—can you meet me somewhere?"

Kellan chewed his lip. This was definitely not protocol, but he wasn't getting anywhere in his current case. A different quandary might help clear his mind.

"Sure, I can do that," he replied.

Pontius rattled off an address in Bloomside and asked to meet in an hour. Kellan agreed, and Pontius thanked him profusely before hanging up.

An hour later, he walked through the residential area of the westernmost district of Spiral City. The houses here were ostentatious. It was the only word Kellan could think of to describe them. They were all tall, with large windows and ornamented doors, complete with large yards surrounded by wrought iron or white wooden fences. The flora was just as bright and luscious here as it was in the commercial districts, but none of that surprised him. This was where the elites lived, the Morgensterns included.

He found the Morgenstern residence at the end of a tree-lined street, its front walkway shaded by rows of hearty oak trees. It was just as obnoxious as the other houses, built from a light terra cotta stone, its window sills painted bright blue. The enclosed yard had a white wrought-iron fence, and blue hydrangeas, yellow daisies, and still-blooming pink peonies covered the lawn. He rang the bell, reaching up to scratch the back of his neck as he waited.

The door opened to the sound of two voices arguing softly and a haggard-looking Pontius. A black-suited man standing just behind him looked annoyed but simply bowed when Kellan glanced at him. Pontius gestured for Kellan to come in.

He looked uncharacteristically unkempt, wearing a pair of navy sweatpants and an old graphic tee with holes by the bottom hem.

"We'll be in the second-floor sitting room, Dean," Pontius said to the man standing behind them. Dean simply nodded and bowed his head, turning on a heel to disappear down the hallway.

The house was just as beautiful on the inside as it had been on the outside. They were currently in the home's foyer, a curved staircase running up both sides of the circular room. The gray tiled floors were home to several plush white rugs, and soft light filtered down from the floor-to-ceiling windows that flanked the front door.

Pontius led him up one side of the double staircase, his gaze fixed ahead. His calm playboy demeanor from a few days prior was gone. Kellan followed, one hand trailing up the wooden railing.

The second-floor sitting room was the second room to the right, just beyond what looked like a rec room. It was painted white, like much of the rest of the house, and furnished in monotone black and white. A whitewashed fireplace was barren on the far side of the room, two squishy black velvet chairs placed before it.

Pontius made a beeline for a mirrored bar cart in the far corner, not even bothering to check if Kellan followed.

"Would you like something?" he asked, finally turning to face Kellan, who was still standing by the doorframe. Pontius held up a bottle of red wine.

"I'm all right, thanks," Kellan said. "Doesn't do much for me, anyway."

"Right," Pontius said, pouring himself a generous glass. "I'm terribly sorry to be drinking like this, but I am…not doing well, to put it bluntly."

Pontius steered himself toward an armchair, unceremoniously plopping himself into it with a sigh. He gestured for Kellan to take the other.

"I'm sorry to be so vague about my request, but I just didn't know who else to call," Pontius said, staring at the dark red liquid in his glass.

Kellan settled into the chair next to him. "So tell me why you can't go through the Legion properly to find him? I apologize for saying it, but it's kind of unorthodox for you to come to me directly. I don't usually—"

"Because I think Northwind Medical kidnapped him."

Kellan was dumbstruck. He'd suspected that Liza and Tarin were connected, but the connection was flimsy. The only thing he had was the changing eye color. But this was leaps and bounds ahead of his own theorizing.

If this was what Pontius believed, it made sense that he'd called Kellan privately. Northwind Medical was a public organization—its ties to the government ran deep.

If Pontius truly believed Northwind Medical was behind Tarin's disappearance, of course he would want to keep it from the prying eyes of those who wouldn't believe him to begin with. It mattered little, though. Kellan couldn't believe it himself.

"Why?"

"Where else could he have gone?" Pontius said, his voice cracking. "He wasn't even awake when I visited him yesterday." He sighed, setting his untouched wine glass down to rub his temples. His shoulder-length hair was unstyled, looking for all the world like he'd just woken up even though it was nearly noon. "Look, I know Tarin had some…problems, let's say. But he wasn't a bad person. I've never seen him that messed up before."

"You mean he didn't normally take strange drugs?" Kellan didn't mean for it to come out so harshly, but the words were out before he could stop them.

Pontius ran his fingers through his hair. "No, he didn't. But what if he got them from someone he already knew? Or what if they attacked him outside and ran away? What if Northwind somehow laced his cigarillo—"

Kellan held up a hand. "Pontius, wildly theorizing like this is only going to drive you insane."

Pontius bit his lip as Kellan spoke, guilt deepening lines on his face.

Kellan rubbed his temples before leaning forward to rest his elbows on his knees. He knew little about Northwind beyond what he'd seen for himself in his brief visit last week. The director had certainly made an impression on him, but it wasn't a negative one. Doctor Renata had been helpful and polite. He just simply couldn't imagine them kidnapping someone. There was hardly enough evidence to connect Tarin and Liza, never mind connecting them both to Northwind.

"You must think I'm insane." Pontius' voice cut into his thoughts.

He shook his head. "No, I don't. But I need to investigate this carefully before we theorize." He laced his fingers together in his lap. "Can you tell me more about what's happened?"

Pontius nodded. "His phone is off, and he isn't home. I can't find him anywhere he usually hangs out, and none of our other friends have heard from him either."

"So he just vanished?"

Pontius nodded again, gripping the arms of the chair so hard his knuckles were white.

Kellan swore to himself. He didn't even know where to look for a missing person, especially not when he already had Liza's case on his hands. But he knew he couldn't say no, not when Pontius looked so desperate.

"Why not go to Northwind Medical yourself? I'm sure the director would see you personally since you're a Morgenstern—"

Pontius interrupted him with a short burst of laughter that took Kellan by surprise. "I may be a member of an influential family, but that doesn't mean I can just walk in and demand a meeting with one of the most powerful members of the city. My father maybe could, or even my sister, but not me."

Kellan just stared, openmouthed. "I guess I assumed you had more power than that. I'm sorry."

Pontius just waved a hand, turning back to his forgotten wine glass and taking a deep swig. "So, will you help me?" he said.

"I'll see what I can do, but I'm not a skilled investigator." As much as he hated admitting it, he couldn't lie and pretend it would be fine. Especially not with how poorly his current case was going.

Pontius took another drink before turning to him once more. "It's better than me trying to find him." He sighed. "Thank you, Kellan, truly. From the bottom of my heart. I didn't have anywhere else to turn."

Worry lined Pontius' face and aged him several hundred years. His blue eyes were lined with the silver of unshed tears, his mouth a tight line. He flicked his gaze to the door of the sitting room.

"Dean, it's all right, you can come in."

Dean opened the door a few moments later, bowing upon entering. Pontius simply waved at him vaguely from the chair. Kellan didn't know what that gesture even meant, but Dean seemed to.

"Mister Manchester, if you'll follow me, please." Dean gestured at the empty doorway.

Kellan nodded, following Dean out into the hallway with a single backward glance at Pontius, now slumped over his hands in the chair.

Yet another thread woven into this complex tangle he couldn't unravel. Kellan's head hurt.

25

CASSIAN

14th of Wind Moon

Cassian was sitting in the living room in the safe house, the midafternoon sun streaming through the half-closed blinds and casting lines over the faded gray couch. He hadn't bothered to change, still wearing his sweatpants from the night before. His cold coffee still sat, almost empty, on the small side table he'd moved in front of him.

He'd spent most of the morning researching Selwyn, hoping to find a way to lure her away from Pontius for an evening. He still had no plan. He could distract Selwyn all he wanted, but he was only one person. He needed to be there when Pontius dug his own grave.

A knock at the door cut through his stupor. Panic rose for a terrifying moment as he thought of the night he'd seen the shadow across the street. But logic took over a moment later, reminding him a stalker wouldn't knock on his door in the middle of the day. Whoever knocked wasn't here to kill him.

He didn't bother putting on a shirt before going to check the peephole. His heart dropped to his stomach when he saw Kellan waiting for him on the other side.

"Cassian?" Kellan called from the other side of the door. "I need your help, open up. Please."

He removed the deadbolt and opened the door.

He'd forgotten he wasn't wearing a shirt until Kellan's ears turned bright red. He felt his own blush creep over his cheeks as he motioned for him to come in and directed him to sit before running upstairs for a shirt. He stuffed it over his head quickly before running back downstairs to Kellan, who now sat on the couch Cassian had vacated moments ago.

"You said you needed my help?" he asked.

Kellan nodded. "Tarin's missing and, frankly, I don't know what to do anymore."

Cassian's eyes widened. "Tarin's missing? What? Did he get released from the hospital already?"

"No, that's the thing. Pontius said he was in a coma when he visited yesterday. Suddenly, today, Tarin is gone. Supposedly discharged. But there's no way…" Kellan trailed off, and Cassian could practically hear the wheels turning in his head.

He wasn't sure what he could say, so he waited for Kellan to speak again. Before he could, though, Kellan reached both hands up to his head and messed up his hair, groaning angrily.

"None of this makes any gods-damned sense and I now have to find Tarin on top of it? I didn't sign up for this! I don't even know where to begin."

Cassian's heart squeezed. He'd promised to help Kellan, but he'd hardly done anything to assist him since they'd agreed upon it. Before he could think better of it, he sat on the couch beside Kellan and reached forward to gently grab his hands from his hair.

Kellan looked at him, lips slightly parted, his hair sticking up at all angles. Surprise was a mask he didn't think Kellan wore often, but it suited his features. Cassian stared unblinkingly at Kellan's face, squeezing his hands.

"Look," he started, dropping Kellan's hands quickly, "I said I'd help you. But this is getting dangerously close to my mission, and I'm not so sure it's safe for me to do anything."

Kellan sighed, leaning back into the couch. "I'm not asking for you to go out and investigate with me. I could just use someone to talk to."

His heart leaped into his mouth. "Don't you have someone back at the Legion you can speak with?"

Kellan shrugged. "Sure, but Pontius asked me to keep this from the Legion for as long as I could."

"Why?"

"He's got a theory—he thinks Northwind Medical has something to do with Tarin's disappearance."

Cassian froze. That was a major accusation—the only unethical concern that had been raised against Northwind Medical over the last thirty years had been human trafficking. The claim had been proven false and had fallen out of the memory of the public. Claiming they were doing so, and with non-humans, was a major and potentially deadly claim.

"You think it's stupid." Kellan's voice was soft, unassuming.

His stomach turned. "I can't honestly say *what* I think. What evidence does he have to support that kind of claim?"

"He doesn't, really. I don't know if I believe it either, but I have to start somewhere. I just can't shake the feeling that there's a connection between Tarin and Liza."

"What do you want to do?" Cassian said. "Investigating Northwind Medical could be really, really dangerous."

"I don't know; that's why I came to you."

"Because…?"

"Because I know you're here for either Pontius or Selwyn, and you must have some information on Northwind if you're investigating Selwyn."

He remembered reading about Morgenstern Tech's deal with Northwind when he'd done his initial research on the family earlier, but since his target was Pontius, he hadn't read up on it as much as he should have.

"I'm sorry to disappoint you, but I've got nothing."

Kellan frowned, the curve of his lips somehow beautiful even with the expression. "So your target is Pontius."

Cassian mimicked Kellan's frown but didn't confirm or deny it. He had a feeling Kellan wouldn't say anything, but he still didn't want to put his mission into words. Not here. Not now.

Instead, he moved on. "Is there anything else I can help with? Not with Tarin, but with the other case."

Kellan nodded, reaching into his backpack to reveal a manilla folder and handing it to Cassian. He accepted, staring at Kellan's face. He looked tired, the bags under his eyes darker than usual.

He opened the folder to see a page of text and a few photos. "What are the photos?"

"Crime scene. Maybe you'll see something I didn't."

He nodded and unceremoniously dumped the contents of the manilla folder on the table. Several photos spilled out, but only one landed face up. It showed a girl, caramel hair splayed out on the pavement, her throat cut. It was a brutal way to die, and Cassian felt a small wave of nausea creep up from the pit of his stomach. Not for the gore, but out of pity.

The scene was brutal, but it was just how he remembered it— the gash on her neck, the wrong angles of her arms and legs, the blood that had stained the white hospital gown she wore.

But as he stared, he noticed something he hadn't seen when they'd found her, when it had been too dark to see details. It looked like she'd been bound, based on the bruises around her wrist. But he couldn't make sense of the man. Slashed to ribbons like the largest, sharpest knife he could imagine had cut him in two. What could have done that to him?

He lifted his eyes to Kellan to ask what he thought. He was asleep.

The afternoon sunlight streamed through to shine on his golden hair, which was now overly mussed at the top. It looked freshly cut, shorn close to his head on the sides, but slightly uneven. Did Kellan cut his own hair?

He must have rushed getting ready today. His outfit wasn't as flashy as Cassian was used to. He'd donned a pair of light khaki pants, white sneakers, and a dark thermal t-shirt. The chipped nail polish on his fingers was a testament to Kellan's state of mind.

He looked younger than he actually was when he was asleep. His cheek pressed against his own shoulder, forcing his lips open just slightly. Cassian ignored the urge to touch them, to feel how soft they must be.

Kellan flinched, surprising himself out of his impromptu nap, much to Cassian's disappointment. His eyes found Cassian's, blinking slowly as he came to. His normally bright eyes were heavy-lidded, the lashes brushing against his cheek with each blink. Cassian couldn't stop staring.

Kellan, slightly more lucid, smirked. He shook his head, running fingers through his hair, then flicked his eyes down to the photo Cassian had been looking at.

"Weird, isn't it?" he said, gesturing with his chin at the photo. "She was bound. I wonder how she escaped."

"Did the coroner say anything of note?"

Kellan rubbed his eyes, the frustration in his movements apparent. "The full autopsy report is in there too, but none of it really makes sense."

"How so?"

He shook his head. "She had a heart attack right before she died. And her fingers were broken. Cygnus' death was completely different from hers, but they were nearly simultaneous."

Cassian frowned, turning the paper over in his hands and chewing his lip. He'd never seen a double hit that used different methods before. It was ineffective and risky. But someone had deliberately done it that way. He wondered why.

Kellan stood slowly from the couch, stretching both hands above his head. His shirt pulled up slightly to reveal a sliver of his stomach, and Cassian felt a lump in his throat form at the sight.

He was here to kill, not to ogle, he chided himself, and swallowed the lump, willing it to disappear. It only mildly cooperated.

"Well, if you notice something, let me know. The witness

interview is also in there, in case you're interested in what Kagome had to say."

"Did anything stand out to you?"

He shook his head again. "She said Liza said something before she died, but it doesn't make sense..." He trailed off, looking like he'd just pieced something together. The dawning of an idea was obvious on his face.

"Kellan?"

"I just..." He shook his head. "No, no way. If this is what I'm thinking, we're in a lot more trouble than we bargained for." He shook his head again as if he was trying to clear the thoughts that were distressing him.

Cassian set the file down and stood to join him. "Look, if it might help the case, share it with me. Maybe I can help."

"Let me confirm something first, okay? I gotta go see Vaida," he said as he slipped back toward the door. "I'll call you if anything happens."

Cassian nodded somberly, then watched him leave through the front door, his lips pursed. Whatever was bothering Kellan must be big.

He shook his head and sat back at the table once more, picking up the crime scene photos and ignoring the discarded techpad with Selwyn's face on it. That could wait a few hours.

Cassian returned to the crime scene.

It was just after dinner, and people strolled leisurely along the sidewalks, their chatter indefinite and lively. The piney scent of the evergreen trees drifted to Cassian's nose, and he inhaled deeply to steady himself.

He was sure there would be nothing left, that coming here would be a mistake. But he needed to be back in that moment, see if there were details he could recall from that night. He'd brought the photos with him, hoping he could compare what was in them to what was there now.

He'd never really done this before, so he wasn't totally sure what Kellan was hoping to achieve by using his favor for this. It was certainly obvious that he'd overestimated Cassian's abilities, but he wouldn't let that stop him. After all, he'd spent nearly thirty years in the killing game. It wasn't like it was surprising to him.

He made his way to the back alley where they'd found her, the scene different in the fading dusk. He grimaced at the bloodstains still visible on the concrete. They had faded, but you could still tell what they were. Apparently, no one had tried to get them out.

Glancing around the space revealed nothing new. The garbage was piled high in the dumpsters. A cat leaped out from behind a pile of wooden pallets and chased some small creature into a branching alleyway.

But there were no sinister people about, no one lurking in the shadows, having returned to the scene of their crime.

Suddenly, he felt stupid. He'd wasted his time coming here. Of course he wouldn't find anything. It had been three weeks since they'd found Liza. Any evidence was long gone by this point.

A flash of purple caught his attention. It was far enough away that he could have dismissed it as a security spell or something else.

But the pull in his abdomen told him not to. It tugged at him insistently, like a hound on a scent. Follow, it said. You must.

A sense of foreboding crept up on him, traveling up his spine in a slither. He turned his gaze up to the rooftops, the memory of a stalker long past creeping back into his memories.

There—a flash of movement, outlined by the almost completely faded light. The figure moved across a rooftop next to where he stood.

And this time, a fire escape was directly ahead.

It took him less than fifteen seconds to scale the escape. Two roofs over, he saw a flash of black as someone jumped to a lower building. He took off after them, his breath coming in short, calculated gasps.

What was he going to do if it really was Leo? The man was at least a hundred years his senior and an advanced magic user. He could probably choke the air from his lungs with a snap of his fingers if he wanted. But the pull wouldn't let him stop. It urged him onwards, and he listened.

The next roof came quickly, and Cassian made the leap at full speed, landing on his shoulder a little too hard as he rolled out of the jump. The black blur ahead of him was still running, heading west, into the heart of the city. The Guard stood out against the lower buildings in the distance, and Cassian had to wonder where this person was heading.

Another leap (and another jarring hit to his already sore and throbbing shoulder) and he was finally on the same roof as the person in black. Their hair was shorn roughly to their shoulders, and they wore a heavy black overcoat, much too heavy for the late summer heat.

"Stop!" Cassian shouted, willing his voice to boom over the rooftops.

The person in black continued running, leaping to the next rooftop with an ease Cassian couldn't replicate. He was gaining, slowly but steadily, and the next leap only brought him closer. The wind felt like it was egging him on, pushing gently against his back, spurring him forward.

He hit the next rooftop harder than he intended, rolling out of the leap clumsily. He felt warmth bloom across his shoulder and knew he'd cut it open through his shirt. It didn't matter.

He closed the gap between them until he could finally reach out and grab their coat with one hand, sending them both sprawling across the gravel roof.

Cassian wrestled his way on top of the person, pressing both his hands into their back, one knee on top of their shoulder blades.

They laughed, chilling Cassian to his bones. He knew that laugh.

Leonardo Whitburn sat beneath him, his shoulder-length black hair tangled in his beard. "My, my, Cassian, you've gotten quite good." His voice was slightly muffled from being pressed into the gravel.

"Shut up," Cassian growled. "Why are you here?"

Leo cackled. "I could tell you, but what's the fun in that?"

Cassian pressed his knee deeper into Leo's back, leaning more of his weight into it. Leo didn't even flinch. He looked completely unaffected by the additional pressure.

"Leo, gods damn it—"

Another laugh cut him off, although cackle might have been a better word for it. It was high-pitched and hysterical, but not frightened. It was more like he was enjoying himself.

Cassian had had enough. He flicked open his pocketknife and twisted Leo's hand up hard enough to hear the joints pop. Leo looked thrilled, a wild look coming over his features.

"Do it, Cass, I dare you," he said, low in his throat, like he was suppressing laughter.

Cassian pressed the knife into the soft flesh between Leo's pointer and middle finger, a line of red blood, deeper than any he'd seen before, welling down the blade. He said nothing to Leo, instead just studying his face.

The wild look in Leo's eyes hadn't changed. "Glad to see Ragnor finally beat that soft side out of you."

"Did you kill that girl?" he said, pressing the blade deeper.

Leo said nothing, staring unblinkingly at Cassian, a sinister smile spreading across his lips.

He'd seen enough. He lifted the knife to position it at the joint of Leo's thumb, but in the brief moment it took to adjust, Leo broke free. His injured hand swung back just far enough to catch Cassian in between his legs. The spike of pain through his body toppled him, and he let go of Leo's hands, the knife clattering to the ground.

Leo stood, not even bothering to look back at Cassian, dusting himself off casually. The blood still dripped from his hand, splattering across the stones.

Cassian glanced up at him, tears in the corners of his eyes as he struggled to unfurl himself. He couldn't let him get away, not after he'd avoided all of his questions. He willed himself to stand, but the strength wouldn't come.

He watched as Leo licked the blood from his fingers and made a sweeping gesture with his hands. Before he could uncurl himself, a shining purple portal opened up before Leo. He swore to himself and fought even harder against his own aching body to stand.

But just as he got his feet beneath him, Leo cast a backward glance at him, a smirk twisting his features.

"How unfortunate," he said. With a dramatic salute, he stepped through the portal.

It shrunk and disappeared behind him, and Cassian was alone, bleeding on a rooftop, a colorful string of curses on his lips.

26

SHADOW

18th of Wind Moon

The man was frustrated. He'd lost one good candidate, and the only time the drug had been successful recently was with the human test subjects. He couldn't get it to work on the non-humans. Except for the girl—she'd been close. But she was dead now. And the lanky man in front of him wasn't nearly as susceptible as the girl had been.

And then there was Cassian. His former companion had grown considerably since last they'd met, both in strength and mind. He'd always known Cassian could be something great if only he could get him away from that man who owned him.

He gritted his teeth and turned back to the white chair to gaze at the elven male strapped to it.

"Please," he said weakly. His voice was barely a whisper. "Please, just let me go."

The man said nothing as he picked up the syringe full of deep red liquid. The first syringe had been administered long ago, and they didn't need to do it again. Instead, he flicked the top of the needle to release any air bubbles and unceremoniously stuck it into his arm, covered in bruises and poke marks from previous administrations. None of which had worked, of course.

"No, please…" the brown-haired man said with no force behind his words. He was too weak to fight back.

The red liquid drained sluggishly from the syringe into the man's arm, and he clicked his tongue as it did. Much too slow. Something was wrong.

The man strapped to the table made a choking noise, then convulsed. Foam formed at the corners of his mouth as his eyes rolled back in his head. He held the convulsing man down, waiting for him to finally breathe his last. He'd seen enough failures to know when one was coming.

The man swore to himself and called for the ghouls. Yet another body to dispose of.

"Get rid of him," he said to the nearly transparent figures that appeared in the room. The ghouls couldn't speak, they simply obeyed his orders—a gift of the power of Alvemach.

The ghouls obeyed, dragging the now lifeless body off the chair. If his vision wasn't so good, it would appear almost as if the body was floating on its own.

The man sighed, then closed his eyes, reaching for the pit of power that sat behind his navel. Calling Alvemach was second nature at this point.

It took nearly two minutes for the telltale pop of interplanar shift to echo in the medical chamber. Alvemach appeared before him, a slight frown quirking his mouth downward at the corners.

"Status?" Alvemach asked.

"Subject deceased," he said. "He was much weaker than the girl."

Alvemach sighed, reaching up to rub his nose. "And is there a particular reason you took one that was close to Miss Morgenstern?"

The man smiled toothily. "It seemed fun."

Alvemach frowned. "Don't do that again. She's off-limits, as I've said before. We need her."

The man continued to smile. When someone told him not to do something, it was practically an invitation to do exactly that. He knew if he didn't do it perfectly, Alvemach would be displeased.

But he had a plan.

"The ghouls will take care of the body."

"Good. I'll leave you to it." Another pop, and Alvemach was gone once again.

The man's next move was going to be big.

27

KELLAN

19th of Wind Moon

Vaida was quick, he had to give her that. She'd had just under a week with the syringe and already had results.

All her screens were on when he entered the lab, but she wasn't sitting before them this time. Instead, she was bent over a lab table in the glass-walled section of her lab, a white coat covering her shoulders and a large pair of goggles over her eyes.

"Vaida?" he said, knocking softly on the door.

She whipped around, holding two vials in her gloved hands. "Gods, Kellan, you scared the shit out of me. What do you want?"

"How are you, V?" Kellan said, leaning against a wall. She wouldn't answer him, but he knew it would drive her nuts.

She proved him right by rolling her eyes and carefully replacing the vials she'd been holding. "Just fabulous. You're here for the substance test results, yeah?"

"I'm also here to see your smiling face, but yes, the test results would be great."

"Shush. You'll keep your snide comments to yourself, thanks." She flapped a hand at him as she pulled a chair up to her computer, hanging her lab coat up on a peg on the wall. Her necktie was missing again, but her button-up undershirt still fastened all the way up.

Kellan followed suit, pulling a chair around to sit next to Vaida.

"Here's the compound's analysis. It's a pretty standard hallucinogenic. They're usually a latent drug, so it takes a bit for it to hit, which is why people OD so often."

"Okay, so you're saying it's nothing special?"

Vaida frowned, clicking to another chart. "Not at all. In fact, your hunch was correct."

"What?"

"I said—"

"I heard what you said, but what do you mean? Liza took this stuff?"

Vaida nodded. "A less potent version, but yes. It's got the same makeup as that compound I couldn't identify in Liza's analysis."

Kellan sat in stunned silence. He'd been right? Liza and Tarin were connected. Which meant his search for Tarin wasn't unrelated.

He didn't know what else to do. Searching for Tarin was of the utmost importance now, considering he was most likely wherever Liza's killer was. If that was the case, that meant they were running out of time to find him alive.

"Kellan, where in the world did that guy get this stuff? This shouldn't be legal—or even exist, frankly. I have no idea how to synthesize something like this. I couldn't even guess."

He sighed, resting his face in his hands. "I don't know. I can't even go talk to him."

Vaida turned to face him, her glasses slipping down her nose. "Did he die?"

"No, but he's missing."

She cocked an eyebrow, clearly waiting for an explanation, but Kellan had almost nothing to tell her. He couldn't vocalize Pontius' suspicions about Northwind here, and he didn't feel comfortable sharing a half-baked theory with her anyway. Although, with these results, it might not be half-baked anymore.

He shook his head instead. "I'll talk to Pontius, see what he knows."

He stood, putting the chair back in its place. Vaida didn't move. She stayed perched at her desk, her fingers still hovering over the keys, and watched him move toward the door.

Just before he left, she spoke in a soft voice. "Please be careful, Kellan."

With one hand on the door, he turned back to her with a nod.

20TH OF WIND MOON

He was underwater, unable to see, unable to breathe. He opened his eyes to dark, murky waters that were bone-chillingly cold, watching vague shapes move past him in the darkness. They didn't move closer to him, only past him, as if he didn't exist.

A light shone in the distance—it was a pinprick of light, only a small gleam in the vast inky darkness that swirled around him. He swam toward it, his lungs already straining against the pressure of holding his breath.

The light appeared before him, bright and vivid, pushing away the shadows that swam past him. He reached out to touch it, but as his fingers met whatever it was, he gasped for breath. Water poured into his mouth and nose, clogging his senses, choking him.

It had been salty and briny, and he'd awoken from the dream gasping as if he'd truly been drowning.

And so here he was—sitting up in bed, drenched in sweat, trying to calm his breathing and steady his nerves. The dream had made his heart pound. He shook his head. He needed a shower.

The sky outside was a hazy rose color as he shuffled to the bathrooms, and he groaned. He was never awake this early on purpose, and he'd been up late enough last night that the lack of sleep was making him feel like a mess.

The shower did little to wake him up, but he felt semi-coherent as he shoved his legs into his uniform pants and buttoned up his undershirt, forgoing his blood-red necktie but throwing his jacket over his shoulder.

The knock at his door was short and sharp, a rapping he knew well—the vice commissioner.

Vice Commissioner Farrow was the commissioner's right-hand man. He also functioned as the lieutenant for the twentieth when it mobilized in times of crisis. His dwarven stature often meant people underestimated him, which Kellan had discovered quickly was a mistake. There was a reason they had selected him as the vice commissioner, and it wasn't because he was kissing anyone's ass. The only person the vice commissioner outwardly respected was the commissioner himself.

"Kellan? In there?" Vice Commissioner Farrow's gruff voice sounded through the door.

"Gimme a sec," he called, tying the laces of his boots before standing and opening the door to see the vice commissioner scowling. "Where's my service with a smile, Vice Commissioner?"

The vice commissioner's frown grew even deeper. "I ain't dealin' wit yer shit today, Manchester. Commissioner thinks you've got 'nother body," he grunted. "Astra River, North Bloomside, by the city walls. I'm comin' wit yeh."

"The commissioner thinks it's related to my case?"

The vice commissioner shrugged, turning toward the door. "Don' know, yeh should check it out anyway."

Kellan shrugged, following Vice Commissioner Farrow out the door and to the parking garage. The Legion vehicles awaited them; large, bulky, and painted all black, they were incredibly intimidating. They reminded him of fancier, more militaristic versions of the wyvern racing chariots they used outside the city.

"When did the call come in?" Kellan asked as he settled into the passenger seat of one of the smaller buggy-like vehicles. Vice Commissioner Farrow strapped into the driver's seat, adjusting the dials to accommodate his small stature.

"'Bout ten minutes ago. Found it floatin' in the river, belly-up.

Twelfth's still there."

They drove through the city in silence. They encountered very little traffic, their vehicle's bulk forcing any other cars to make a path for them through the narrow boulevards. The vice commissioner was an efficient driver, navigating the tangled web of interconnected streets with ease. He wasn't much of a talker, though, and it was much too early still for Kellan to be much of one either.

The scene was hectic when they arrived—the twelfth had the area cordoned off with holographic markers that read "do not cross" in bright red lettering. Kellan could barely make out a gurney surrounded by several medical team members, denoted by their bright red armbands, red piping on their uniforms, and the telltale sign of soft purple magic that glowed around their hands. The rest of the trauma team was scouring the shoreline, obviously looking for clues. One brown-haired halfling noticed their buggy pull up and sauntered his way over to them.

"Vice Commissioner, thank you for coming," he said flatly. "Body's over here."

Vice Commissioner Farrow just grunted and motioned for Kellan to follow him into the throng of people.

The body was laid out on a gurney, and Kellan nearly retched from the smell. It was awful, like wet, rotting garbage mixed with old sour meat. And the body didn't look any better than it smelled.

After spending what had obviously been several days in the water, it was hard to tell who this person may have been when they were alive—their face was swollen, skin blackened and cracked, and the hair was falling out in clumps. But Kellan's stomach dropped when he noticed the clothing. The body was dressed in a white hospital outfit, exactly like the one Liza had had on when she died.

"Well?" Vice Commissioner Farrow's voice behind him made him nearly jump out of his skin, and he heard the man chuckle. "Didn't mean 'ter scare yeh."

Kellan just shook his head. "It's fine, I was just…" He paused. "Thinking, I guess."

"So? He one of yers?"

"I think so."

The vice commissioner clapped his hands. "Great. Ye can stay here, then, I'm headin' back to the Guard."

Kellan nodded absentmindedly before finally processing what the vice commissioner said. He whirled around and grabbed the shorter man by the shoulder. "Hang on, you drove here."

"So?"

"So? I can't get back without you."

"Ye got wings, don' yeh?"

"I don't have a flier's permit yet!"

Vice Commissioner Farrow just shrugged, then continued walking, leaving Kellan dumbstruck next to the body.

The halfling man that had approached them earlier came to stand next to Kellan, his black legionnaire uniform pressed finely, the red piping along the seams assigning him to one of the first responder units. His jacket crossed over his chest, securing near his armpit in a line down the side of his body in the style granted to unit sergeants. Matching bright red epaulets sat atop his shoulders, their color vibrant against the black. Two stars adorned his breast, the infinity shaped ouroboros pin with the number twelve just below.

"Brigir Conlan," he said, holding his hand out to shake. "You must be Kellan. The commissioner told me about you. Mentioned you'd stop by with the vice commissioner."

Kellan took the outstretched hand, surprised at just how firm the man's grip was. "It's a pleasure, Sergeant."

The sergeant smiled. "Please, call me Brigir. I know you upper divisions love your formalities, but I can't stand the title. My name is enough."

Kellan nodded, although he couldn't quite get himself to call the sergeant anything but his title in his mind.

Sergeant Conlan continued, "I heard you mention this guy might be related to a case you're working on?"

Kellan nodded. "Yeah, one of our own and a girl were found

murdered in Bloomside. But the circumstances of this death are, frankly, very different." He paused, gathering his thoughts. "Can you tell me more about what the trauma team's found?"

The sergeant nodded, leading him back toward the body and the medical team whose purple glow was now fading. Their investigation would, at the very least, give a preliminary cause of death if one wasn't immediately apparent. The medical team could save someone with their abilities, but those abilities had limits. Magic was such an integral part of a person that using it meant giving a part of yourself away—thus, healing often left people with those abilities tired, weak, and drained after a difficult or long healing session.

Of course, determining the cause of death or disease was much easier since it required no actual action on the healer's part. It was more like a scan, one that showed the healer what parts of the body weren't working right—sometimes that was internal bleeding, a weak heart, a drug overdose, or a brain aneurysm.

The medical team began packing up their instruments, and Sergeant Conlan stopped one of them with a hand to the arm. A small, button-nosed girl turned to face them, her eyes as big as dinner plates.

"Sergeant?" she asked, and Kellan noticed her slightly pointed ears. A half-elf?

"This is Private Kellan Manchester of the nineteenth. This body might be related to his investigation. Can you tell us more about what the team found?"

The girl nodded, setting her tools back down gently before taking a deep breath. "Looks like our victim had signs of drug use in his system, although that's not the cause of death. He had a heart attack and a stroke at once, so he must have been under some seriously intense pressure. Our preliminary scans can't do toxicology reports, so I can't tell you what he might have been on, but my guess is a cocktail of bad stuff."

"So he didn't drown?" Kellan asked.

She shook her head. "No, the body was dumped here after he died. I'd estimate around a half an hour to twenty minutes after his time of death. This is just what happens to a body when it's submerged in water for that long."

"Anything else of note? Identification on the body or anything?" Kellan said, glancing again at the white hospital outfit.

"He appeared, drug use aside, to be a relatively healthy elven male in his mid hundreds. No distinctive markings, tattoos, or piercings, and no identification was found. It appears he was restrained at some point, specifically over his chest, wrists, thighs, and ankles. Most likely, he was prone with that sort of binding."

"So what, like he was lying on a table or something?"

She nodded. "Precisely."

Kellan shuddered as he remembered how Liza had been bound as well.

Realization washed over him as he remembered Liza. Hadn't he just proven that Tarin and Liza were connected? He looked at the body again, shame washing over him. If this body was Tarin…

He turned away from the girl, breathing in deeply through his nose, which he instantly regretted when a new wave of nausea washed over him. A purple glow shone, and the smell disappeared, his nausea gone.

She was holding his lower arm gently with her hand, her eyes closed as she erased his nausea. He didn't even know how to react to her kindness, so he just mumbled his thanks under his breath.

The sergeant had stayed through their whole conversation, but he now turned to Kellan with a serious look in his eye. "The vice commissioner ditched you here, huh? Need a ride back to the Guard?"

Kellan just nodded, still lost in his own thoughts.

28

KELLAN

20th of Wind Moon

Kellan rode the elevator up to the commissioner's office later that day. He wasn't even sure what he would say, but it felt better than doing nothing. The guilt was eating him alive.

He shook his head. If he started thinking like that, he'd never get an opportunity like this again. He'd drown in his own self-doubts and continue being nothing more than a legalized assassin. And that was a fate he couldn't resign himself to any longer now that he'd tasted what life outside this small box was like.

But if their dead body really was Tarin, what in the world was he going to do? Cassian definitely wouldn't help him, and he would have to let Pontius down. He'd been unable to save his best friend and hadn't even been able to prove if Northwind Medical had something to do with it.

Kellan chewed his lip, peeling small chunks of dry skin away as he pushed open the commissioner's massive oak door. He felt like he was drowning, not unlike the nightmare he'd woken from that morning.

The singing stone's clear tone greeted him as the door swung open, the soft note weaving around his head as the panic rose higher and higher in his body.

He wasn't ready for this. He'd let so many people down. He

thought of Liza's moms, how they'd cried when he'd told them of Liza's death. He didn't even want to know how Pontius was going to take the news if that body truly was Tarin.

The commissioner sat behind his desk, swiping through reports on his techpad.

"Private Manchester, what brings you here?" he asked, not looking up from the report he was reading.

"Sir," he started, swallowing the lump in his throat, "the body you sent me to investigate with Farrow…"

"Was it one of yours?"

Kellan nodded before he realized the commissioner wasn't looking at him. "I strongly suspect so, but I need more information."

They sat in awkward silence for several moments, only the sound of shuffling papers and the soft hum of the stone interrupting it. The commissioner finally set his report down, folding his hands beneath his chin and regarding Kellan with a watchful eye.

"Something wrong, Private?" he asked kindly.

Kellan took a deep breath. "Sir, I don't think I can solve this. If I'd been faster, this victim might have—"

The commissioner held up a hand, something like pain shining in his eyes. "I'm going to stop you right there, Private. I'm going to give you a piece of advice that will save you from torturing yourself in the long run. You cannot blame yourself for every death you could not prevent." He breathed in deeply. "Unless you are the one holding the knife, a death cannot be yours to claim. If you take responsibility for every death on your watch, you will torture yourself into madness."

"Sir, with all due respect, I don't think that's entirely true—"

"I'm not looking for a debate, Manchester. I am offering you advice. You'd be smart to take it. Is that clear?"

Kellan snapped his mouth shut, nodding once.

The commissioner leaned back in his chair, spreading his arms out to stretch. "I know it's hard not to feel guilt for death. Your instinct to take responsibility simply means you have a good heart. But in this line of work, it's sometimes all that keeps us sane. You'd do well to remember that."

Kellan nodded as he reached up a hand to scratch the back of his neck. "Yes, sir."

"Private Manchester"—the commissioner's eyes bored into his—"I know you can do this. Ask Lieutenant Razorborn, Private Larsen, whoever you need to. But I didn't take you for a quitter—don't prove me wrong."

He swallowed against the lump that had formed in his throat. He'd done nothing to earn the commissioner's trust other than do what he was told. The fact he wasn't treating him like someone who was little more than a slave was enough to give Kellan goosebumps.

The techpad on the desk rang, its shrill sound jolting through Kellan and shocking him from his thoughts. The commissioner answered it with an earpiece, quietly listening to the voice on the other end, his brow slightly furrowed.

"You're sure? Mhm. He's with me. I'll update him personally." He paused, waiting as the person on the other line spoke again. "No, have them sent to Private Larsen, please. She's already working on the case. Yes. Thank you."

The commissioner turned toward him, the line between his brows deepened. "You know how the medical team couldn't ID the body?"

Kellan nodded slowly, a sinking feeling in his stomach.

"Well, the coroner just finished his exam. We've got an ID. His name is Tarin Vexnys, elven, one hundred and forty-five years old. Apparently, he's a well-known associate of—"

"Pontius Morgenstern," Kellan said without thinking.

The commissioner cocked an eyebrow. "Yes...how did you know?"

"I was afraid of this. I was with him the last night we saw him alive and well."

"You what?"

His heart was in his throat. He'd failed again, but the commissioner's words rang in his heart. He had to do something to prevent more people from dying like Liza, like Tarin. He couldn't afford to fail ever again.

Determination turned his bones to steel. He would succeed.

"Please excuse me, sir; I've got a couple people to follow up with at this point. What did you tell them to send to Vaida?"

The commissioner looked taken aback by Kellan's sudden shift in mood. "Blood samples and DNA analysis."

"Good. I need her to confirm something for me." He stood, then bowed his head to the commissioner. "Thank you, sir, for your words. I appreciate your faith in me."

"Private, please talk with Lieutenant Razorborn. I know you're perfectly capable of doing this on your own or I wouldn't have given this task to you. But I also don't want you to fail."

Kellan simply nodded as he retreated from the office. "I'll talk to Sharr again, and I won't fail you, sir."

He heard nothing as the door to the office closed. He knew exactly what he needed to do, and he wasn't looking forward to it. But he didn't need Sharr's help—he needed Cassian's. He just hoped the man would still be willing.

The trip to the safe house felt too short. He hadn't even warned Cassian he was coming; he just hoped he'd be there.

His blood pounded in his ears so loudly it nearly overwhelmed the sound of the motorcycle as he wove his way through traffic. It was still midmorning, but the traffic was always heavy in Spiral City. He caught glimpses of himself as he wove through the cars, his neon green helmet reflected in their shiny exteriors.

He swerved left, cutting off a shiny silver sedan and earning a swift honk in return. He just held up a hand in apology, never slowing down. Because if he was right, and he was sure he was, he was in a deep, *deep* pile of shit.

He was sure Liza and Tarin were connected, but did that mean

Pontius' theory was also correct, that Northwind Medical was kidnapping citizens of Spiral City and drugging them for some experiment? The thought sent chills up his spine.

Kellan pulled up alongside the townhome, flicking the ignition off and locking his helmet to the bike in two swift movements. His hand shook as he rose to knock on the door, praying that Cassian was actually here. Maybe he should have called beforehand.

Luck was on his side—Cassian answered swiftly after he knocked, wearing soft gray sweatpants and a white t-shirt. His hair was wet, and he still held a towel up to his head. Kellan's stomach did an annoying somersault.

"Kellan," Cassian said, surprised. "Come in."

Kellan did, and Cassian disappeared to the bathroom. Kellan assumed to get rid of the towel.

When he returned, he set about cleaning off the table by the couch, full of research notes and multiple mugs of coffee. Cassian returned to the kitchen and set about making another cup for himself.

"You want some, Kellan?" he said, reaching up toward the cupboard with the mugs, wincing as he did.

Kellan frowned. "No, but you're in pain. What happened?"

Cassian shook his head. "Nothing you need to be concerned about. I hit my shoulder a little hard, that's all."

Kellan wanted to ask more but decided against it. He didn't have the right to pry, anyway. Instead, he breathed in deeply through his nose, readying himself for the inevitable disappointment that was about to happen.

Cassian said nothing else as he finished pouring himself a cup, then joined Kellan on the couch. "So what brings you here?"

Kellan looked down at his hands. "Another body showed up. It's related…in more ways than one."

He continued staring at his hands as Cassian shifted next to him. "What do you mean, more ways than one?"

"Let me explain." He breathed once again through his nose,

exhaling out his mouth. "A body turned up in the Astra River today. It had signs of drug use and a similar cause of death as Liza."

"So you have a serial killer on your hands?"

"That's not all," he continued. "The body was Tarin's."

Cassian didn't respond right away, but Kellan didn't dare look up at him. He'd been clear when they'd struck their deal that if his case got too close to his own mission, he would back out. And Tarin had been Pontius' best friend. Helping him would only make this messier.

Cassian sighed. "Want to know how I hurt my shoulder?"

At that, Kellan looked up to meet his eyes. "What?"

Cassian licked his lips, then set the mug down on the table. "I chased a man across the rooftops in Lunadere. I hit my shoulder as I was in pursuit. It's a pretty nasty bruise, but it will heal."

Kellan knew he looked like an idiot with his mouth hanging open, but he couldn't help it. "Not that I'm not concerned, but what does this have to do with anything?"

"I'm not sure, but I have a feeling," Cassian continued, twiddling his thumbs, "that the man I chased across the rooftops has something to do with your killer. And I think this man is after me. He's a very old associate of mine…and he's stalked me in the past."

"But why would he be killing people in Spiral City? And why is he after you?" Kellan's confusion was palpable. He couldn't keep it from his voice as he spoke.

"I don't know, Kellan, and I wish I did," he said. He rubbed his temples, squeezing his eyes shut. "Look, I know I said that if this got too close to my operation, I wouldn't help you. But I can't leave you to face Leo alone."

Kellan's heart stopped. "So you're going to keep helping me?"

Cassian nodded, his face somber.

Kellan chewed his lip. Pontius' theory was that Northwind was conducting illicit medical testing on citizens from Spiral City. If Cassian's theory that this Leo character was involved, then it would seem the Northwind theory was incorrect. But something nagged at him, something that was unwilling to let the Northwind theory go.

"Could Leo have teamed up with someone at Northwind Medical?" Kellan asked quietly.

Cassian frowned. "He's not the type to work with someone else unless it's of great benefit to him. It's improbable, but not impossible."

"So he wouldn't make a deal with anyone who couldn't benefit him…" Kellan began, thinking out loud. He thought back on the passages he'd read in the library about demonic princes. "Do you think—"

Cassian winced. Kellan looked to his shoulder and noticed a small red stain appearing on his shirt. Whatever had happened to his shoulder, it was definitely more than just a bruise.

"Cassian, I hate to ruin the mood, but you're bleeding."

Cassian swore under his breath, then stood quickly from the couch. "I'll go re-bandage it. Don't move, I'll be fine."

Kellan ignored him, standing as Cassian did. "It'll be easier if I help you. You said it was your shoulder? That's hard to bandage alone."

"You really don't have to—"

Kellan stopped him with a hand. "Don't care. Where's your first-aid kit?"

Cassian's shoulders deflated a bit, but he conceded. "In the bathroom. Follow me."

They crowded into the small bathroom down the hall, Cassian stripping off his shirt before sitting on the closed toilet seat, Kellan standing over top of him as he carefully cut the old bandages away. They were close enough that he could feel Cassian's warmth as he worked.

He hissed when he saw what was beneath—there was quite a nasty bruise, but a massive bit of road rash cut itself into the back of Cassian's shoulder. It wasn't deep enough to require stitches, but it was large.

It looked several days old, the edges of the bruise fading to a sickly greenish yellow while the center looked nearly black. Most of the road rash itself had healed over, but there were a few cuts in the center that had opened themselves back up.

Kellan cleaned them gently, dabbing the open cuts with a cotton pad. Cassian's skin was warm to the touch, his upper arms smooth, the muscle firm. Kellan ignored the flush rising to his cheeks as he worked, instead focusing on the task at hand.

"Kellan," Cassian's voice was low and thick like he'd swallowed honey.

Kellan didn't respond, switching out a bloodied cotton pad for a fresh one.

Cassian continued, "Will you tell me about it? Your life at the Mission?"

He started at that, the cotton pad jerking to the side. "And why do you want to know about that?"

It had been hell, but he hadn't realized it until after he'd left. They'd been *children,* raised to be the weapons of the Empire, never allowed time to simply grow up or make mistakes or fall in love. They were raised to fight, to kill, to kiss only to steal secrets, to form bonds only to get close enough to stick the knife in further.

And it had only gotten worse after the Draft. Kellan had been ripped away from everyone he'd ever known and forced to separate from Beck, the one person he'd ever been able to consider family. He hardly ever saw the other Fallen who'd been assigned to the Legion.

He'd never needed to explain it. Never needed to tell anyone about it. They'd either already known, had lived it themselves, or never asked. No one had asked. Yet Cassian had.

"Honestly, spending this much time around Pontius is rubbing off on me," Cassian said.

The cotton pad was sufficiently bloodied, but the skin around the cut looked less inflamed. He threw it away for a final pad, then breathed in deeply, Cassian's nutty coffee scent tickling his nose.

"There's not much to tell, to be honest. It's…difficult to describe what it was like."

He could see the pulse in Cassian's neck fluttering, begging for someone to notice it, to address it. A curl of silvery hair lay next to it, and Kellan ignored the urge to take the lock between his fingertips.

Cassian didn't press him for more. "I entered Ragnor's employ when I was a child too. I had no choice."

His heart felt like it had collapsed in on itself. He hadn't realized that Cassian had as little choice in his life as Kellan had in his own. He'd experienced his own fair share of hardships—why had it never occurred to him that others had just as many?

"I-I didn't know," he said stupidly, the cotton pad forgotten in his fingers as he stared at the lock of hair on Cassian's neck.

"I never said anything, so why would you?"

"I don't know, I feel like I should have sensed it or something. You know, assassin's intuition or some shit."

"Kellan," Cassian said again, shifting so he could meet Kellan's eyes. His shoulders pulled away as he turned. "That's the stupidest thing you've ever said to me."

He couldn't help the smile that spread across his face. "Yeah, okay, that's fair."

Cassian returned his smile, the corners of it soft as if he was seeing it through a fuzzy lens. He turned back to face forward, bringing his shoulder back to Kellan's hands.

"Thanks, by the way," Cassian said as Kellan resumed his work. His voice was softer now, softer than he'd ever heard it.

Kellan swallowed, his throat dry as he laid a bit of gauze over the cleaned cuts and began wrapping the wound. "Don't mention it."

Cassian stayed still and silent as Kellan continued wrapping, the only sounds in the bathroom their intermingled soft breaths.

29

KELLAN

21st of Wind Moon

He sometimes wondered if Vaida ever slept.

Kellan pushed open the door to her lab once again in the morning. It was early, especially for him.

She was sitting in front of her screens, reading something with the intensity of someone who'd tuned out the rest of the world around them. He'd inevitably startle her no matter what he did.

"V?" he said long before approaching the desk.

His prediction was right—she jumped out of her chair, her glasses sliding far down her nose as she stared at him.

"Oh, for fuck's sake, Kellan!" She wheezed, a hand over her chest. "Why do you always scare me when you come here?"

"Because you never pay attention to your door."

She rolled her eyes at him, then sat back down. Her hair was down today, her tight braids falling nearly to her mid-back. She flapped a hand at the chair next to hers in an invitation to sit.

He obeyed, gripping his knees tightly.

She watched him from the corner of her eye, her brows furrowing as she took in his grip, his posture, and the hard line of his mouth.

"Before we start," she began, pushing away from her desk to face him, "talk to me. How are you doing?"

He felt his jaw clench. Tarin was dead. The commissioner's words rang in his heart again, but he still couldn't fully believe them. He thought of his talk with Cassian about Leo. There were too many moving pieces in the puzzle, and he didn't know how any of them fit together.

"Kellan," Vaida said in a sing-song voice. Her hand was in front of his face, snapping him out of his trance.

He shook his head. "Sorry. It's been a long couple of days."

"So I've heard. Your latest body was someone you knew?"

He nodded. "Not well, but yeah. It's my fault he's dead."

Vaida sighed. "I know the commissioner gave you that speech. Don't you dare pull that on me." She leaned in, lowering herself so she could see Kellan's face even with his head lowered. "He already told you, and I'm going to say the same. You can't dwell on those you couldn't save. They will haunt you for eternity."

"It still doesn't change the fact he's dead." He was avoiding admitting she was right, but he didn't really know why.

Vaida sat back, crossing her arms over her chest. "Yeah, you're right. It doesn't change the fact he's dead. But you can prevent more if you stop wallowing and get to work."

Kellan looked up at her, lips slightly parted. Her support wasn't coddling—she said what she meant, and you had to decide if you could handle it. Part of him wanted to be offended by it, to ask her to tell him everything would be okay. But he knew she was doing this for his sake. He needed to do something, or Tarin would have died for nothing.

"Are you ready to hear about Tarin?" she asked quietly.

He nodded.

"Good."

She pulled up charts on her screen, and he recognized them this time as the ones she'd shown him for Liza's death. They looked similarly confusing, but he remembered most of what Vaida had told him last time.

"As you can tell, most of the results are the same. Although, Tarin seemed to be a bit more recreational of a drug user than Liza was.

However, his drug results still skyrocketed the last few days before his death."

Kellan nodded. "And what about the demon blood?"

She pointed at one of the charts. "Present in his system as well. It seems the genetic makeup is the same between the two, although I did a really primitive test on that. I'd need more time to confirm for sure, but it's safe to assume it was the same demonic blood."

He sighed. None of the results were surprising, considering how strange Liza's case had been. But he was frustrated—even though the results proved Liza and Tarin were connected, it didn't give him any new clues as to who was actually doing this.

Pontius' Northwind theory rattled in his brain once more, and he shook his head. It was stupid to even consider it. There was no evidence. It wouldn't sway him, not when he had other evidence to interpret.

"V," he began, "are you able to tell what demon the blood in their systems came from?"

She cocked an eyebrow at him. "Not without a sample of the demon in question. It's not like we have records of demonic blood types and who they belong to."

"I figured, but I wanted to at least ask."

She shrugged. "At least now you know that they're connected. Indisputably."

Kellan had already known that, but it was good to have confirmation. He was sure that the demon prince Alvemach was connected to this, but he couldn't understand how. Was the drug his invention? How was Leo tied to this?

Cassian had said last night that Leo would only do things if they benefited him greatly. He wondered if working with a demon could be considered of great benefit.

Vaida was typing away at her computer as he thought, her glasses reflecting the light of the monitors so that he couldn't see her eyes.

"Can I ask another question?" he said quietly. He wasn't even sure she'd know.

She spun to face him. "Sure."

"How would someone summon a demonic prince to the material plane?"

She stared at him a moment too long, taken aback by his question. "Why do you want to know that?"

He pointed at her monitors. "I talked to Cassian last night, and I have a theory that whoever is behind this is partnering with a demonic prince named Alvemach to manufacture whatever this drug is that killed Liza and Tarin."

Vaida's mouth hung slightly open as she listened. "I mean, a demonic pact is certainly possible with a demonic prince, but they'd have to have some magical ability already to even summon one. Kellan, why in the world would someone need a demonic prince to help them manufacture a drug?"

He sunk back in his chair, deflated. "I know it doesn't make sense."

"It doesn't, but that doesn't mean it's not true."

Kellan rubbed his neck as Vaida spoke. He was lost and had no idea what direction he should be moving. Vaida's eyes sparkled as if something he'd said had sparked her interest.

"Cassian, huh?" she finally said, a smirk pulling her lips up at the corners.

He hated himself immediately as a blush rose to his ears. "He's just…a friend."

"Mhm, because me saying a friend's name to you definitely makes your ears bright red every time."

Kellan pouted, crossing his arms as he looked away, unwilling to meet Vaida's eyes again. "It's nothing."

"Pfft. Nothing, my ass. Spill."

"I'm telling you, he's just a friend. Besides, even if I wanted to start something, I doubt he'd go for it. We can't mesh like that. It won't work."

Vaida chuckled, turning back toward her screens once more. "All right, all right, I won't push you on it. But I'm here if the 'mesh' happens."

"Vaida!"

She shrugged. "What? Don't be such a prude. You're obviously attracted to him, and maybe a night with someone would be a helpful distraction for you."

"He'd never do that—and besides, I definitely can't ask. That would be mortifying." His head spun, but he refused to even consider the possibility of spending an evening with Cassian like that. Sex was fine, but it had never meant anything to him.

Vaida continued typing. "Suit yourself."

"I will."

"Good."

Kellan stood. "Good. I'm out of here, then."

Vaida lifted a hand as he retreated out the door. "Sex is good for you, Kellan!"

He slammed the door a little too hard on his way out.

30

CASSIAN

22nd of Wind Moon

I t was Selwyn who reached out to Cassian this time.

Apparently, Pontius had taken the news of Tarin's demise as well as anyone would have hoped, but he needed a pick-me-up, and he'd requested that both Kellan and Cassian attend a celebration of life for Tarin. Although Cassian didn't think they should be part of the grieving, it seemed Pontius had been insistent.

Selwyn hadn't begged, but he could tell she'd been desperate.

And so, he'd come. He'd dressed as well as he could but had to purchase a red tie before arriving. Red was Jupiter's color.

Tarin's twilight celebration of life was being held at an outdoor event center in Bloomside, in one of the district's Grand Gardens. The pavilion was lovely—a small pond burbled pleasantly beside the stone-paved clearing where the celebration was to be held. The plants in the Grand Gardens were like all of the plant life in Bloomside, eternally beautiful. Peonies of every color blossomed, their petals fluttering gently in the breeze. Lilac bushes interspersed between other brightly colored flora had grown taller than him. Their scent drifted over his nose, a nostalgic sort of smell, although he couldn't place why.

People had already arrived. Many were as well-dressed as

Pontius had been each time they'd seen each other. There was no doubt that this event would be full of Spiral City's elite, and Cassian felt even more out of place as he stepped into the space.

Several people wore suits in the fashionable asymmetrical style, their buttons uneven and running up the sides of their torsos. Many people wore combinations of suits and dresses, the variety of styles and shades of red almost overwhelming. It was a sea of red mourners, the color reminding him of blood.

It wasn't long before he felt a slim body sidle up next to his own. Selwyn was there, clad in a silken burgundy dress that reached mid-calf, a small flame pinned to her chest to signal her as a host. She didn't smile as she came to stand beside him.

"I appreciate you making an appearance, Cassian," she said softly. Her demeanor was calm and collected, but he watched her hands squeeze as she spoke.

He nodded his head to her. "You said it was important that I be here. I wouldn't have missed it."

"Pontius is…not doing well," she stated. "I probably shouldn't be talking about this with you, but he seems to trust you. And I love my brother, but I am…" She trailed off, looking down at her hands.

Cassian waited for her to finish, still staring out at the crowd.

"Worried," she finally said. "He's been theorizing wildly about Tarin's murderer, claiming Northwind Medical had something to do with it."

Cassian willed his features to stay neutral. He'd already heard this theory, of course. Kellan had been clear with him that he believed, at the very least, Northwind was involved.

"And why does he believe that?" Cassian replied, feigning ignorance.

"Because Tarin was receiving care there and because…" She trailed off again, apparently realizing she was treading into dangerous territory with her words. "Never mind. The theory is ridiculous anyway."

"Selwyn, I know it's probably presumptuous of me to say this, but I'm here if you want to talk. I've been told I'm a good listener." The last part stung; the only person who'd ever said that to him was Aidyn.

Ragnor's warning flashed in the back of his mind. *You must get his sister away from him.* He felt an instant pang of guilt—this wasn't the time.

If he'd been a better assassin, he would have taken this opportunity in stride. Isolating Pontius would be easier in grief. But he wasn't a better assassin, and the only thing he could think to do was give them space to grieve.

"Anyway," she continued, "I do hope you'll take the time to talk Pontius down from the ledge he's on. I've done all I can, but my conversational abilities do not lie in emotional discussions."

He nodded, and she bowed her head, walking away to blend seamlessly into a crowd of mourners standing beneath a blooming white tree. He watched her go, breathing as slowly as he could to calm his thudding heart.

A hand landed on his shoulder gently, and he jumped. The following chuckle was brief.

"Sorry, I thought you knew I was here," Kellan said in his ear.

Cassian shook his head. "I was lost in thought."

"I couldn't tell."

He glanced at the man standing beside him, clad in a fashionable black suit, the buttons running up the far left breast in the style he'd seen others wearing. His tie was also red, a deep crimson. He'd done something with his hair that made it look more sleek, although with hair as short as Kellan's, Cassian couldn't figure out how he'd done it.

Something small fluttered in his stomach. But before it could fully form, he looked away, back toward the people here to mourn Tarin's passing.

"I'm not sure what we're supposed to do here, you know?" Kellan said softly, staring out into the crowd of well-dressed elites.

Cassian felt the trepidation in his bones, knowing what Kellan was feeling exactly. "Honestly, the last celebration of life I attended was my father's, and that was a century ago."

Kellan turned to look at him. "Your father's?"

Cassian nodded. "He was…killed in action. Our careers were similar."

"You followed in your father's footsteps, then?"

Cassian smiled bitterly. "Not by choice, but yes."

Kellan stayed silent for a few moments. Cassian watched his hands as they moved—they relaxed by his sides, then wrung around each other, then lifted to his neck, then relaxed once more. He could sense the question on his mind.

Why?

Honestly, Cassian hated that question almost as much as he hated the answer.

Because he had no choice.

"I'm sorry."

Kellan's eventual statement wasn't what he'd been expecting. It wasn't like Kellan had anything to apologize for, yet Cassian knew what that statement really meant. *I'm sorry that you had as little choice as me in this life.*

He found it comforting.

"You have nothing to apologize for, but I appreciate it anyway," Cassian replied.

Kellan sighed, then rolled his neck in a circle. "We should probably go find Selwyn and Pontius, shouldn't we?"

"I already talked to Selwyn—but yes, we should find Pontius."

Kellan nodded. "Let's go, then."

They wove their way through the mourning crowd, attempting to find Pontius. For once, he was difficult to find.

The pavilion got more packed as they searched, people arriving as time passed. And still, Pontius was nowhere to be found. It was strange that he was absent at his best friend's celebration of life, but Cassian had a feeling he was grieving on his own somewhere.

People paid them little mind as they milled about, conversations drifting past as Kellan and Cassian mingled. Talks about Tarin as a child floated by. One woman mentioned his rebellious phase, another talked about his accomplishments in university.

It seemed each person here truly did care for Tarin, in their own way.

He spotted Selwyn again about a half an hour later, bowing her head to a particularly stuffy-looking couple. As soon as they turned away, she spotted them through the crowd and headed their way.

"Kellan, thank you for coming," she said, bowing her head at Cassian to acknowledge him once more.

Kellan shot her a small smile, inclining his head toward her in thanks. "Any idea where Pontius is, Selwyn? We'd like to pay our respects to him as well."

She nodded, then inclined a finger at them to follow, her dress swishing around her legs as she spun and headed off toward the pond.

A small gazebo sat on the pond's edge, a small structure made of whitewashed wood and beautiful latticework. Inside was a small wooden and wrought-iron bench that faced the water. A beautiful spot for reflection, and, apparently, the perfect spot to mourn on one's own.

There Pontius sat, head hung low, his hair styled halfheartedly. He wore a deep burgundy suit that matched Selwyn's dress, a flame pin identical to his sister's pinned to his lapel.

"Ponty?" Selwyn said gently as they approached. "Cassian and Kellan are here to see you."

He lifted his head at the sound of her voice, his eyes red-rimmed and bloodshot. Cassian couldn't help but notice that he looked horrible. A five o'clock shadow graced his chin in patches. His eyes were hazy and unfocused, like he wasn't fully present. Of course, his suit was perfectly pressed and his black shoes were just the right amount of shiny, but Cassian suspected that part wasn't up to Pontius to begin with.

"You came," he said. His normally smooth tenor voice was scratchy and rough, like he'd swallowed sand.

Cassian gave him a halfhearted smile, but Kellan walked to sit beside him, plopping unceremoniously on the bench next to him.

Selwyn nodded her head as she turned to leave, stopping by Cassian to whisper in his ear.

"Don't talk about Northwind, please?"

He nodded his agreement, and she walked away briskly, her heels clicking on the paver stones that snaked over the garden.

Kellan had already started chatting at Pontius, his words inconsequential. He commented on the beauty of the garden, how there was an entire floor of the Guard dedicated to plant research, about how his ride over here had been nice because of the fading light.

Pontius listened with glossed-over eyes, his unfocused gaze pointed toward the small fountain in the center of the pond.

Kellan kept talking. He didn't expect Pontius to answer, and that was part of the beauty of it. He didn't mention Tarin—that conversation had already happened. What Pontius needed now was a reminder that the world still turned and existed, even when someone he loved had left it.

As the light faded from the sky, lights began to twinkle on throughout the garden. Lights had been strung in trees, floating on invisible lines between sign posts and wrapped around the ceiling of the gazebo and the pavilion.

"Pontius," Kellan said, his monologue over, "look. Isn't it beautiful?"

Pontius' eyes lifted to the scene before him, swiveling left, then right, then back to center again. He looked at Kellan, his lips tightening.

"Thank you, Kellan," he said.

Kellan gave him a small smile, and Cassian felt his heart swell. He'd never understood how to handle grief—even when he'd been through it himself. No one taught him how to deal with other's emotions all that well, and the little he knew he'd learned through trial and error. After all, a pawn with emotions was more likely to betray. Ragnor didn't encourage empathy.

He'd stood by and let the two men talk, unwilling to interrupt and possibly ruin the moment. But something had changed now that the world was darker and Kellan had given Pontius a small spark of life back.

Pontius turned to him, his mouth still drawn in a line. "And thank you, Cassian, for coming. I really appreciate it."

"It's really no problem."

"Still, the gesture is welcomed. I know you didn't know him well, but I'm sure his spirit appreciates your presence."

Kellan stood, brushing his pants out. "Speaking of his spirit, we should head back, tell some good stories for Jupiter's judgment."

Pontius finally cracked a small smile. "Yes, we probably should. He'd never forgive me if I didn't tell our fair goddess about his trysts."

The three men headed back together, Pontius standing a little taller.

After hours of telling and exchanging stories to honor Tarin's life, the celebration dwindled. Cassian and Kellan stayed the entire time at Pontius' behest. He asked them to stick around, introducing them to the rest of his friends who'd known Tarin.

But it was finally late enough, the crowd thin enough, and Cassian's social battery drained enough, that he turned to leave, bidding Pontius a goodnight.

Kellan moved to leave with him, but before they did, he stopped Cassian with a gentle hand to the arm.

"We should say goodbye to Selwyn, too," he said.

Cassian nodded.

Selwyn was, apparently, taking a break at the same gazebo they'd found Pontius in a few hours earlier, Mina at her side.

As they approached the gazebo, something in Cassian twisted. That gut feeling he knew so well pulled at him. A nasty feeling tickled the back of his neck, like he was once again being watched.

He thought back to the chase across the rooftops a few days ago. Leo wasn't stupid enough to target him here, was he? There was no way.

He chalked it up to paranoia and ignored the sinking in his gut as they walked up the winding pathway to the small pond. The path was quiet; the only sounds were the distant hoot of an owl and the rustle of leaves in the night breeze. It was lovely, really.

The gazebo was still well lit; the lights reflected in the water along with three shadows hunched together in the center of the structure. It was just as Pontius had said—the girls and another guest.

But his skin turned ice cold when he saw who accompanied them.

Leo.

He looked pleasant, his face softened into a kind smile as he nodded along with whatever Mina was saying. Selwyn seemed pensive, her legs crossed as she watched their conversation.

Kellan looked unperturbed, approaching the scene as if nothing was wrong. Before they got close, though, Cassian grabbed his arm, his urgency betraying him in his grip.

"Cassian?" Kellan said, cocking an eyebrow at his grip on his arm.

He could barely speak. Fear coursed through his veins as he choked out, "Leo. That's Leo with them."

Kellan's face hardened. "What do we do?"

"We need to get them away, but I'm afraid of what he will do if he sees me."

"Stay there, then. I'll get them."

Cassian nodded, crouching down behind a large lilac bush to observe the scene.

Kellan approached, his demeanor calm and collected, as if he didn't know of the man who sat betlveen Selwyn and Mina. Cassian couldn't hear them, but he watched Leo as he observed Kellan thoughtfully.

Their conversation wore on, and Cassian grew nervous.

Something wasn't right. The situation felt like it was teetering on the edge of a cliff.

"Cassian," he heard a voice call. "I know you're there."

His heart pounded so loudly that he couldn't hear, but he knew that if he stayed hidden, Leo would only drag him out. Or worse, hurt someone.

He stood, then rounded the corner as he forced himself to breathe slowly. It was better to stay calm and hopefully resolve this without bloodshed.

Leo smiled. He was standing now, Selwyn to his left and Mina to his right, both still within arm's reach. His throat was dry.

"Cassian, so good of you to join us," Leo said. "I was just wondering where you were."

Selwyn looked at Cassian, confusion written on her face. "Cassian, you know this man?"

Leo didn't let him answer. "But of course, we're old colleagues."

"Oh, I see," Mina said, her voice bright. They didn't know the danger, then.

Selwyn, however, looked skeptical. Her mouth had become a thin line, her arms crossed. He tried to send her a look that said *stay quiet,* but he couldn't tell if she understood. At the very least, Kellan knew of the danger they were in right now.

"What brings you here, Leo?" Cassian asked, trying his best to sound casual.

Leo chuckled. "I wanted to see what all the fuss was about."

Selwyn flinched.

Cassian silently willed her to stay where she was. "You've seen it. Now, let's go; I have a few things to discuss with you."

Leo laughed again, the sound like two rocks grating against each other. It was harsh and violent, nothing like a true laugh should be.

"I'm rather bored. I've come here with a purpose, you know. But I think I'm done with the pleasant chit-chat."

Cassian felt the magic crackle before it appeared, but he was unarmed save for a small knife in his pocket. Before Kellan could reach them, Leo grabbed Mina by the neck and threw a hand toward Selwyn, purple ropes snaking out to wrap around her.

"See, you weren't my goal today. I've gotten what I came for this time." He waved a hand again, a portal opening behind him. "But I'll be back for you, Cassian."

He couldn't throw the knife—his aim wasn't good enough from this distance to ensure it would hit Leo and not someone else. Kellan was frozen in place, his hands twitching by his sides.

Leo threw Mina and Selwyn through the portal and followed them through, lifting two fingers to his brow in a cocky salute as it closed behind him.

31

CASSIAN

22nd of Wind Moon

"No," Cassian screamed, throwing a hand forward in an attempt to stop the portal closing.

He had little magic—a small well that allowed him one or two uses a day. He'd rationed it well throughout his life, using it to his advantage whenever he could. Today's use: a desperate attempt to stop the portal closing.

Shockingly, it worked. The portal was just big enough to step through and follow Leo wherever he'd gone.

The funny thing about portals was that they were limited in scope. They had to point toward the destination, and there was a limit to how far a portal could take you. For example, a portal might get you from one end of Spiral City to another, but it couldn't take you much farther.

The strain of holding the portal open was draining his strength fast as Kellan called out to him.

"I'll go after him," he said, stepping up to the portal.

Cassian couldn't allow him to go, not after Leo, and certainly not alone. His chances of surviving against the man were higher. Not much, but enough to make a difference.

"No, Kellan. I have to. Go get the Legion, or at least some backup. I'll send you my location."

Kellan opened his mouth to protest, but after seeing the expression on Cassian's face, apparently decided against it. "Just… be careful, okay?"

Cassian's heart flipped. "I know how to hold my own against him. I'll be waiting for you."

He stepped up to the portal as he watched Kellan's eyes widen, then soften.

"Find me quickly, please," Cassian said, his voice barely a whisper.

His strength waned as he stepped through the portal and into the night.

He was in an alley in a residential neighborhood he didn't recognize. Leo was nowhere to be found, but that didn't mean he was gone.

Unfortunately, his well of magic was dried up. It would take some time to refill, so he'd need to rely on his senses to find where Leo had taken the girls.

Theoretically, he would have needed to use a lot of power to pull three people through a portal. He probably wouldn't have done it twice, so more likely than not, he was in the vicinity. Although he didn't recognize the area, he figured Leo must have some ties to this part of the city.

He walked toward the corner, hoping to get an idea of where he'd ended up. But when he stepped out onto the sidewalk, recognition hit him like a gut punch.

Cassian knew exactly where he was.

The very first time he'd come to Spiral City nearly thirty years ago, he'd stayed in a safe house that now no longer belonged to Ragnor. After purging the old ones, Ragnor had stricken this one from the list.

He'd stayed in this very safe house with Leo. It was only natural he'd come somewhere that Cassian would know to follow.

He was in Northwind, along the wall of the city, in a small residential area. The particular safe house he was now searching for was an unassuming two story home on the end of a cul-de-sac.

His footsteps along the sidewalk were quick and light as he sent a message to Kellan with a pin on his location. He didn't know how quickly Kellan would arrive, but he hoped for his sake that he'd bring something to fight with.

The house was a block from where he'd ended up, its windows blocked from light with heavy wooden shutters.

Cassian didn't know if the security spells were still active or how much the house had changed since it had been in Ragnor's possession. He decided it was better to assume nothing had changed.

He snuck around the back, using the alleyway to access the garages beneath the homes on the street and keeping an eye out for cameras on the neighboring houses. He'd rather not get the Legion called on him for being suspicious.

There was a secret back door that Ragnor had installed into the home—he had it done for all his safe houses. Of course, the location varied by house, but they were a trademark of Ragnor's.

This one was in the back, just after the garage. To access, you simply needed to know where to push.

The wall popped open upon applying pressure to the siding. With a sigh of relief, he opened the door.

The inside of the house was dark, but he could hear someone moving upstairs and the muffled cries of someone in pain.

He swore silently to himself, looking around for anything he could use as a weapon. The only thing he had on him was his pocket knife, and he wished desperately for his sword.

He made his way to the kitchen, looking for a knife or any sort of blade. Although he needed to move quickly, Cassian forced himself to observe everything with a calm eye. If he rushed, he'd only put himself, Selwyn, and Mina in more danger.

Finally, he settled on a large butcher's knife. Not the ideal weapon, but it would have to do.

The stairs were located toward the front of the house, opposite of where he was in the kitchen. He crept along the wooden floor silently, willing his shoes to stay quiet on the hard flooring. He knew Leo would expect Cassian to chase after him, but having the element of surprise on his side wasn't a bad idea.

He made it to the stairs silently, keeping his heels hovering above the floor just enough to muffle the sound of his footfalls. The stairs would be harder, but he willed his heart to stay calm as he placed a foot on the first step.

His caution was for naught—he felt the crackle of magic the instant he stepped on the stair. An alarm blared through the house, high-pitched and whining, like a small animal whose leg was stuck in a trap.

"Someone's here to play," he heard Leo scream over the alarms. It was hard to hear anything else over the cacophony.

He removed his foot from the staircase, but the noise didn't cease. He had moments to decide where he wanted the inevitable battle to take place and decided the ground floor would be more suitable. He didn't want to get Mina or Selwyn more involved than they already were.

Leo appeared moments later at the top of the staircase, a whip coiled at his hip and a dagger in his hand. He looked unsurprised to see Cassian at the base of the stairs.

"I always knew you'd come for me," he said. Leo said the words like he was speaking to a long-lost lover, their edges gentle as he smiled maniacally at Cassian.

"Let them go, Leo, they have nothing to do with you." He doubted words alone would be enough to convince Leo to release Mina and Selwyn, but he had to try.

Leo laughed, the sound grating on his ears and sending goosebumps down his spine. "Oh no, dear, I can't do that. I need them for something very important, you know."

"And what would that be?"

Leo laughed again. "Enough chit-chat. I see you've armed yourself." He began descending the stairs, adjusting his grip on the dagger in his hand. "Let's dance."

Cassian nodded as Leo came to meet him, taking his time as he walked down the stairs; it was as if he wanted to savor the moment.

He wished, again, for his sword. He'd be in deep trouble if Leo resorted to his whip when all he had to defend himself with was a kitchen knife and his wits.

Leo jumped down the last three steps, coming face to face with Cassian. His nose was close enough to nearly touch Cassian's. His smile was wicked.

"Boo."

Leo swung his dagger up and then back down in an arc, his movements fast enough that Cassian had to scramble to keep up with him. Their blades met, the sound of metal against metal clanging through the house.

The alarm continued to scream as they fought, Cassian matching Leo movement for movement, swipe for swipe. Their fight took them away from the stairs and into the living space, cleared of furniture. Leo used every trick to his advantage—distracting Cassian with a feint to the left, disappearing behind corners, talking about their jobs together to throw him off his guard.

But he never used his magic. Why? Leo would win easily if he cast a spell. He could make Cassian stand still; he could bind his arms and legs like he had to Selwyn.

This fight could easily be his if he used it. So why wasn't he?

They circled each other in the empty living room. Leo had landed a few cuts on Cassian, his nice clothing cut along his arms and stomach. But Cassian had returned the favor, tearing the simple t-shirt Leo wore in several places.

He'd apparently never reached skin, though, as Leo wasn't bleeding anywhere.

Their fight dragged, time slowing to a crawl around him as their blades met over and over. He didn't have time to wonder where

Kellan was, how much time had passed, or even if Selwyn and Mina were all right. All he could focus on was keeping his breathing steady, his muscles relaxed enough to meet Leo's moves, and keeping himself alive.

He didn't know how much longer he could keep this up, though. He was okay now, but Leo was fine too. He didn't seem tired or even mildly challenged. It was like this fight was a dance and he was simply enjoying the movements.

Suddenly, Leo stopped, catching Cassian's butcher knife under his own blade and popping it free. It flew across the room and embedded itself in the wall, wiggling back and forth from the force of the throw.

Leo's face darkened. "Your skills have improved, it seems. Our little encounter on the rooftop wasn't a good judge, I suppose."

"Shut it," Cassian said, backing away from Leo, whose dagger was still pointed toward him.

Leo laughed and advanced, his blade facing Cassian. "Oh, don't worry, I won't kill you."

A noise brought Cassian's attention out of the tunnel vision that had formed during his fight with Leo. It was a cracking noise, like splintering wood. The wail of the alarm had grown even louder, another scream joining its lament.

The front door cracked in two—the glass panes shattered inwards, their glittering fragments like dangerous confetti.

Cassian's heart leaped into his throat when he saw who stood there. Kellan. Kellan had come, and he'd brought reinforcements.

Two individuals stood behind him—a man with dark messy hair and eyes like the sea, and a woman with auburn hair and a set of circular weapons sheathed at her hips. Both wore the same stealth suit he'd seen Kellan wear.

But Kellan himself hadn't changed. He'd only grabbed a sword.

Leo frowned. "You've gotten tricky in your adolescence, Cassian. I didn't expect you to have backup."

"Well, he does. Get on your knees, hands behind your head,"

Kellan said, his voice strong and loud over the blaring alarm spells.

Leo made a show of thinking about Kellan's request; he tapped his finger against his chin and looked pensive. But Cassian knew he wouldn't surrender.

"Hmm. I don't think so, little legionnaire. You see, you're in a rather difficult position."

"What do you mean?" Kellan motioned for his two companions to enter the space. The woman's hands came to rest on her weapons. The man's hands, Cassian saw with surprise, had become translucent.

"I mean, you must be here for those women I took, aren't you?"

Kellan's frown grew as he glanced at Cassian. He simply flicked his eyes up the staircase and hoped Kellan understood.

Kellan motioned to the woman, gesturing toward the stairs. She nodded once, then took off, not bothering to look back. Leo laughed again.

"Set foot on those stairs and they will die."

The woman stopped. It was like someone had sucked all life from the air. Leo was no longer smiling.

"I do not appreciate being ignored. You've broken in here intending to take things that belong to me. And worse, you don't even greet your host."

Cassian slowly continued backing up toward where the butcher knife was still embedded in the wall, never taking his eyes from Leo. He was thankful Kellan had appeared—it had inevitably saved him from a long fight. But now that he was here, fear had fixed itself in his stomach, a clenching, cold fist that squeezed the air from his middle.

He needed to take advantage of Leo's momentary distraction. He knew it wouldn't take long, but any time he spent not looking at Cassian's movements was a moment he needed to use to his benefit.

Kellan bowed his head mockingly. "Oh, I apologize, I didn't realize I needed to greet kidnappers and murderers."

"You should extend common courtesy to everyone, child," Leo said, spitting out the last word like it was a bitter taste on his tongue.

"I don't extend courtesy to criminals. Give Selwyn and Mina back."

"I already told you, no. They're mine."

The woman by the stairs stood just before them, her eyes shifting back and forth from Leo, to Kellan, to the staircase, and back again. The man whose hands had turned translucent was still standing by the door, just behind Kellan. His hands were entirely shapeless now, dripping water to the floor. *A water elemental,* Cassian thought dryly.

Kellan slowly advanced toward Leo, a hand on his sword. "People are not property. They don't belong to you."

Leo laughed, the joyous, maniacal smile from earlier returning. It seemed Kellan had risen to whatever silent challenge Leo had issued.

"And *that's* where you're mistaken," Leo said, unfurling his whip and lashing it toward Kellan.

Something broke then. Whatever silence and stillness had descended over them was gone, and suddenly, the room was a flurry of movement.

Kellan lunged out of the way of Leo's studded black whip, rolling along the floor to avoid its sharp points. The man behind him extended his dripping arms toward Leo, a wave of white-capped water rushing toward him.

The woman at the base of the stairs seemed to decide to risk running up them, taking them two at a time and barely touching as she flew up them.

Cassian took his chance to lunge toward the butcher knife. He yanked it from the wall, leaving a massive scar in the drywall, then turned toward where Kellan, Leo, and the water elemental man were facing off.

Leo was drenched, but he didn't seem perturbed. His smile was even worse than it had been before, his upper lip nearly gone as his sharpened canines poked his lower lip.

Cassian lunged, using the space between Kellan and the other man to his advantage. But Leo seemed to know he was coming and spun out of the way.

The three assassins circled Leo, but he didn't seem worried. In fact, the smile on his face only grew the harder they fought.

A thump came from the stairs, and Cassian whipped his head to see the redheaded woman carrying Selwyn. She was slumped over, but looked whole. The relief was palpable—both he and Kellan visibly relaxed.

"I'd appreciate it if you didn't take what belongs to me. How many times must I repeat myself?" Leo suddenly appeared before Selwyn and the redheaded legionnaire, whip hanging lazily from his hand.

Selwyn lifted her head, a fire of defiance burning in her eyes.

"Fuck you."

Leo giggled. "Oh, I do love your spark. But please, there's no need for that sort of language."

Selwyn spat in his face. "I said, *fuck you,*" she snarled, power behind her words.

Leo clicked his tongue. "*Tsk tsk,* miss. I'm willing to be gentle with you, as I need you in one piece. But you can still perform for me if you lose a few fingers."

He reached forward, and the woman supporting Selwyn shifted, tucking Selwyn behind her and swiping one of her circular blades at Leo. He easily avoided her attack, but stopped advancing. He tilted his head in thought, but before he could come to a conclusion, Kellan and the water elemental man rushed forward.

Foreboding washed over Cassian. "Wait!" he screamed, but to no avail.

A massive wave of purple magic swept out from Leo, knocking Kellan and the dark-haired man off their feet and sending the woman and Selwyn slamming against the wall. The wave didn't reach Cassian, dissipating in a flash of purple.

"You lot are quite annoying and have been so rude. I am simply protecting my property, yet here you are, destroying my house and all my hard work." He sighed, rubbing his temples as the others slowly picked themselves up off the ground.

And then he turned, heading up the stairs slowly as if daring them to follow.

"I told you that if you set foot on the stairs, they would die. It seems you need me to prove that to you."

Cassian felt the blood drain from his face as Leo disappeared up the staircase.

32

KELLAN

22nd of Wind Moon

Everything hurt. Whatever that wave had been that knocked him and Avalan to their asses, it was *painful*. It seemed Selwyn and Kindra hadn't escaped the wave either, Kellan noticed as he stood from the floor.

Cassian, however, seemed unscathed. But he stared up the stairs in horror, his face colorless.

"We have to follow him," Kindra said, wincing as she held Selwyn up.

Kellan shook his head. "You and Selwyn stay here. We can't risk him taking her back." He looked at Avalan first. "You stay here with them. Cassian, you come with me."

Cassian nodded blankly.

They needed to hurry—whatever Leo had planned was sure to end poorly for them. Selwyn looked pale but unharmed. He hoped desperately that Mina was the same.

"Mina wasn't with me," Selwyn said, her voice hoarse. "He took her to another room."

Kellan nodded, then turned and ran up the stairs, skipping them two at a time. He heard Cassian follow him up, his footfalls heavy.

Once they reached the landing, Kellan stopped. It was quiet, the alarm silent, with no sign of where Leo had gone.

Cassian laid a hand on his shoulder. "We should split up—you check that side, I'll check this one."

Kellan nodded to him, heading off to the opposite side of the hallway and opening doors. Cassian turned and entered a bedroom on the left, out of Kellan's peripheral vision.

The first door led to what looked like an office, although the entire space was completely bare. He remembered how barren Cassian's safe house had been—apparently, this was the norm.

The second door yielded more of the same. But when he reached for the final doorknob, he heard a muffled sob.

"Cassian!" he whispered, jerking his chin toward the door.

Cassian joined him quickly, his movements smooth. He held the butcher knife in his hand, his knuckles white.

Kellan whispered, "Here, take this."

He unsheathed the sword at his back. He had daggers, anyway. Cassian had nothing, and it already looked like Leo had gotten him a few times. Blood leaked through small cuts on his arms and torso, but nothing looked too serious.

"Are you sure?" he said, hesitantly reaching his free hand toward the offered hilt.

Kellan nodded. "I have my daggers. I'll concentrate on getting Mina out. You distract him."

"Thank you," he said as his fingers brushed Kellan's on the sword. It was a shock—his hands were freezing, and the contact sent a small wave of electricity through his arm.

Cassian didn't wait for him to open the door. He threw the butcher knife down the hall before opening the door with a violent twist of his wrist.

Mina slumped against the wall, looking terrified but ultimately unharmed. Leo stood before her, his whip uncoiled in his hand. Its studded end slithered along the floor like a snake, the silver studs scratching along the floor ominously.

He paused as the door flew open, his smile vile.

"So good of you two to join me just as the fun is about to begin."

Cassian didn't waste his breath. He lunged, brandishing the sword at a perfect angle for an uppercut.

Leo jumped away, toward Mina. Before Kellan could get between them, he grabbed her, pulling her in front of him and stopping Cassian short. Leo wrapped his arm bearing the whip around her waist, his other hand holding a dagger to her throat.

"One more step and she dies," he said, his voice full of ice.

Cassian lowered his sword point to the floor but never removed his eyes from Leo. Kellan stayed in the doorway, his grip tight on his daggers.

"Give me the other woman back. Now."

"Release Mina, and we'll think about it," Kellan replied. Selwyn would forgive him for dangling her in front of Leo as a prize. He hoped.

Leo chuckled, the knife point digging deeper into Mina's neck and drawing blood. "Honestly, what do you think is stopping me from just killing her now?"

Kellan considered the question. He didn't know Leo like Cassian did. He didn't know what Leo wanted with Mina or Selwyn. It seemed that of the two, Selwyn was his main target. But he wouldn't let go of Mina. Kellan wondered why.

"Because you need her," Cassian responded. "I don't know what you're plotting, Leo, but I won't let you use her."

Mina was silent, not even letting a whimper escape as Leo dug the point of the blade in deeper. Her jaw muscles were tight, her lips a thin line. A small trickle of blood ran down Mina's neck, the droplet disappearing beneath the collar of her shirt. He could see her fear, but she was doing an exceptional job of staying silent and calm.

With Leo's attention on Cassian, Kellan caught Mina's eye. He nodded once at her, a small gesture to let her know they were going to get her out of here alive.

Her eyes widened a fraction.

Then Cassian was moving, drawing a blade from his pocket. He threw it in one smooth motion, the blade turning end over end as it flew and embedded itself in Leo's leg.

Leo screamed, and Kellan watched in slow motion as he released Mina, dropping her to the floor to clutch his thigh.

Before Leo could take her again, Kellan lunged, grabbing Mina under her arms and lifting her to her feet. Cassian met them there, positioning himself between Kellan and Mina to protect them.

"Get her out of here!" Cassian said as he held up the point of his borrowed blade. Leo had pulled the knife from his thigh, and viscous reddish-black blood pulsated from the wound. Kellan had never seen blood like that, but not every creature bled red.

Mina wasn't walking quickly like he'd expected. As he held her up, he noticed her ankle was swollen and bright red.

"Mina, can you walk?"

She shook her head. "I think he broke my ankle. I can barely stand, if I'm being honest."

Kellan swore to himself. Of course. No wonder she hadn't just escaped from the bedroom while they'd fought downstairs. She wouldn't get anywhere without help.

"Hold on to me; I'll carry you."

He sheathed his blades, lifting her beneath her knees and cradling her back. She wrapped her arms around his neck and held on tightly. He could feel her trembling in his arms, and a pang of white-hot guilt ran through him. She never should have been involved in this.

The sounds of a whip clanging against metal resounded behind him as he made his way carefully but quickly through the door. Once they made it safely outside, he could put her down. But for now it was faster to carry her.

As he reached the end of the hallway, he heard the sounds of fighting behind him grow louder. It sounded like they were moving toward the hallway. He couldn't risk Leo sneaking up behind him.

But he trusted that Cassian would protect them if that happened.

The stairs would be treacherous—he was holding someone, and walking down steep stairs was precarious without that added obstacle. Mina looked, then frowned.

"Put me down," she said. Her amber eyes were raging.

"No," he said, and held on tighter. "It'll go faster this way."

"No, it won't, not if you fall. Let me down." She hoisted herself out of his grip, putting her good foot down first, then holding her broken ankle off the floor. "See? I can hop down the stairs one at a time."

He couldn't argue, not when she was already out of his arms. "Fine. But hold on to me."

She nodded, her lips set in a stubborn line as she grasped the handrail in one hand and his waist with the other.

Halfway down the stairs, he heard a thump, then a triumphant whoop. It didn't sound like Cassian.

His heart thundered in his chest as he tried to move behind Mina. The stairs were the worst place for them to be caught. They were high enough up that a tumble could injure either of them badly, and Mina couldn't move much faster than she already was with her ankle. His only hope was to protect her as best he could while she moved down the stairs.

Kellan looked over his shoulder to see Leo standing at the top of the stairs, his clothes torn, blood trickling down his arm. Whether it was his own or Cassian's, Kellan couldn't tell. His heart sank, but he didn't stop moving. Whatever he did, he had to get off the stairs and get Mina to safety. Whatever Cassian's fate was, he couldn't worry about it now.

"I thought I made myself quite clear, little legionnaire," Leo began, his voice colder than he'd ever heard it. "I don't appreciate people stealing what's mine."

"I'm not your property!" Mina shrieked from the stairs. She shrugged out from Kellan's grip to face Leo, her eyes burning with defiance.

Leo's hand flicked, and Kellan moved in slow motion.

"Mina, *move!*" Kellan said as he lunged, but not fast enough.

A thin stiletto knife flew down the stairs, embedding itself through Mina's neck.

She fell, tumbling head over heels down the stairs, landing with a final thump at the base.

A scream sounded, and Kellan's vision went white.

Mina's body tumbled, landing at the foot of the stairs in a heap, limbs at unnatural angles. Kellan shook. The scene before him moved in slow motion, just as it had when the knife had flown.

A slow laugh sounded behind him. Leo still stood at the top of the stairs, his smile positively feral.

"A shame, really. But in a city this large, she is easily replaced."

The world swam red before his eyes. "You're disgusting."

Another laugh. "No, dear legionnaire, I'm practical."

He didn't have the chance to lunge—Cassian appeared behind Leo, slapping the pommel of Kellan's sword against his temple. Leo collapsed to the ground, knocked out cold.

Relief swept through his veins, but its cooling sensation didn't last for long.

He heard a choked sob from the base of the stairs and turned to see Selwyn bent over the body of her friend, bleeding out from the puncture in her neck.

"No, Mina, no, hold on, please, please," she pleaded.

Kindra was already on her techpad, calling the emergency response teams to their location. They'd already had them on standby, but for fear of spooking Leo, they'd only brought a small team. He regretted that decision now.

Mina blinked slowly, looking up at Selwyn as the blood leaked too quickly from her throat. She couldn't say anything. Kellan felt sick as he descended the stairs.

He didn't know what to do for Mina. Sure, he had first-aid training. He could stitch gashes together, bind a broken bone, or stabilize someone with many injuries. But this was beyond his abilities. Unless the trauma team showed up quickly, there was nothing they could do for her.

Selwyn looked at him expectantly, obviously hoping he'd have some trick up his sleeve. He looked back at her helplessly, searching the room for Avalan or Cassian. Maybe they'd know.

Avalan was behind Selwyn, hands held before him, his eyebrows pinched. His magic wouldn't help here—after all, elementals could only conjure their own element. While there were certainly creative ways to use it, closing a gaping wound with water wouldn't do much.

Cassian came to stand by him, fists balled at his sides. When Kellan turned to face him, Cassian's face was tight.

Leo had obviously knocked him around—a lump was forming on his forehead, and he had a nasty gash down his forearm. Kellan could tell that his greenish bruises would turn dark.

There was nothing he could do either. This wasn't a wound you could simply stop bleeding with a wadded up t-shirt or ripped pieces of cloth.

"Please," Selwyn gasped. "Someone, do something."

Mina lifted her hand feebly to grasp Selwyn's. Her eyes said enough.

Let me go.

"The trauma team is close," Kindra said as she approached. "All we can really do is try to make her comfortable and hope they make it in time."

That was how she'd always been, practical to a fault. But something about her words made Kellan's spine straighten. She wasn't dead yet—there was still time.

Kindra kneeled, gently taking Mina's torso off Selwyn's lap. "Sitting her upright will help keep her airway open."

Selwyn nodded dumbly, her eyebrows drawn together. She said nothing but watched Kindra's gentle hands lift Mina to an upright position.

Mina was pale, the color in her cheeks fading. She looked tired, and the entire front of her clothes was stained dark red.

Mina took a rattling breath, the sound both wet and sharp. Selwyn grasped her hand, and Mina tried her best to force a smile.

"I'm…sorry," she rasped. Her voice was barely a whisper, shredded by the knife still embedded in her throat.

Selwyn stroked her best friend's hair, smearing a bit of blood in its strands. "You have nothing to be sorry for."

Mina closed her eyes then, a small smile spreading across her lips. She did not open them again.

33

KELLAN

23rd of Wind Moon

The moon was high as Mina's body was taken away.

Avalan returned to the Guard with the trauma team.

Kindra escorted Selwyn home, who'd clung to her after Mina passed.

Kellan couldn't bring himself to follow either of them, so Cassian took him back to his safe house, his hands gentle as he led him up the stairs and into the bedroom.

He was numb.

It wasn't like he'd never seen someone die before. It was a routine part of his everyday life. But he'd never watched someone die who shouldn't have.

Someone he'd wanted to save.

And what was worse, when they'd returned upstairs to arrest Leo, he was gone. He'd failed in every way. He'd allowed Mina to die, he'd lost the culprit, and he hadn't figured out if Leo was connected to his murders. He hadn't even gotten a tidbit of information.

Cassian didn't speak as he moved about the space. His jaw stayed tight, the muscles flexing and relaxing every few seconds as he ground his teeth. Wordlessly, he turned down the bed, fluffing the pillows and adjusting the sheets.

He stepped away once his task was complete and gestured for

Kellan to take the bed.

"Where will you sleep?"

Cassian shrugged. "Couch, floor, a chair. I'll figure it out."

Kellan said nothing as he stripped off his battle suit, letting the top half fall to the floor. As he reached to remove the pants, he heard Cassian clear his throat. He didn't have the energy to be embarrassed.

"I didn't know if you knew I was still here," Cassian said, hand on the doorframe.

Kellan shrugged. "I don't honestly care if you see."

Cassian turned his face away without responding and left, lingering for just a moment before shutting the door. Kellan felt something rise in his chest—a tight feeling, the bright lime green of panic over being left alone.

"Cassian?" he called quietly.

The door opened again, just a crack.

"Stay," he said, not taking the time to think through what he'd just asked for, what it could imply. All he knew was he didn't want to be alone. He needed Cassian's presence, another beating heart, if he was ever going to sleep tonight.

The door cracked open a little more. "Are you sure?"

"Please." His voice sounded pathetic in his own ears. "Please, I don't want to be alone."

The door opened all the way. Cassian's face was neutral, but he could sense the shift, the tightness in the way he carried himself as he came back into the room.

"I'll stay."

Kellan awoke the next morning, sun streaming through the windows directly into his eyes. His head was resting on a fluffy down pillow, not the hard one he usually slept on back at the Guard. He blinked the sleep from his eyes, groaning as he sat up. He froze when he saw Cassian sleeping peacefully at his bedside.

He'd forgotten he'd asked him to stay in such a pathetic voice. He'd forgotten that Cassian had agreed like it was nothing. Something sparkled at the memory, the understanding that being alone was the worst thing for Kellan.

He watched the sun dance over Cassian's sleep-mussed curls that fanned out over the comforter. He looked serene as he slept, a small smile playing over his lips as he dreamed. Kellan's insides turned to liquid.

There weren't many memories in Kellan's mind like this one—soft, hazy, warm. The few he had, he treasured. But they were mostly with Beck, a few of them fuzzy memories of his mother. But none were like this. None of them involved someone he felt more than just general affection for.

Someone he…

He reached a hand out, tempted to touch those silvery locks. But before he could, Cassian stirred. He opened his eyes to Kellan, still staring at him, and smiled. It felt like a dream, waking up like this in a sun-drenched room, a beautiful man at the edge of his bed. But as the fog of sleep faded, the horrors of the previous night came crashing down on him.

Cassian moved to sit next to Kellan's legs on the bed. "Kellan…" he began hesitantly, "last night wasn't your fault."

Kellan pulled his knees to his chest, letting his head rest on top of them. "The rational part of me knows that. But I can't stop feeling like it was. There was so much more we should have done."

"You can't dwell on what-ifs, Kellan," Cassian said calmly. "And it's not your fault—you know Leo targeted both of them because of me."

"I should have saved her. I should have been faster."

"You did save her—as much as you could have in that moment."

Kellan sighed and pulled his knees even tighter. The blackness of his wing tattoo peeked out from behind his elbow then ran up his tricep, as black and whole as it had always been. He could still fly tomorrow—Mina never would again.

A wave of tears cut hot lines down his face, marking him as weak for all eternity. The tears themselves were not what made him weak, the fact he could not save her did.

He should have been faster. He should have called for more backup. He should have done a lot of things. What good was it for him to continue? He'd failed four people now. Who knew how many more he'd fail if he didn't figure out what was going on?

"I'm sure you don't want to hear this right now." Cassian's voice was soft, gently cutting through Kellan's spiraling thoughts. "But you were so strong last night."

Kellan lifted his head to look at Cassian, still seated at the edge of the bed. Somehow, he looked more handsome now than he had before, his hair messy but his eyes bright. His slightly furrowed brow made Kellan's heart squeeze.

Cassian scooted down the bed to sit right next to him and reached out a hand to brush away a tear that had escaped down his cheek. The touch was too gentle, too kind. He didn't deserve such tenderness, not after he'd failed like this.

"You haven't failed, you know," Cassian whispered, somehow knowing exactly what was on Kellan's mind.

He swallowed, sandpaper in his throat. "I have, though, Cass."

Suddenly, both of Cassian's hands were on his face, grabbing him and pulling him close, their noses nearly touching. "You. Have. Not."

Kellan was too stunned to move, instead blinking several times in surprise. He felt his eyelashes brush against Cassian's cheek. He didn't let go of Kellan's face, instead holding him there until Kellan finally closed his eyes.

When he let go, Kellan felt the guilt a little less, like Cassian had helped himself to part of the weight that sat upon his shoulders. It felt like he could breathe again.

"Thank you," he said quietly to Cassian's back.

The man turned back to him, silvery curls bouncing with the

movement. He offered one brief, small smile, as if to say *I understand.* And Kellan knew he did.

Northwind Medical & Morgenstern Technology Group

Morgenstern Technology Group was founded 250 years ago by its current chairman and CEO, Galan Morgenstern. Selwyn and Pontius' father is an incredibly intelligent and enterprising man, focusing most of his development efforts on security and heavy weaponry. The company holds exclusive deals with both the Red Guard and the Legion, as well as many individual companies and private investors. Morgenstern Tech develops most of the Empire's top-of-the-line security technology and has been a trusted leader in the industry for nearly its entire existence.

However, Selwyn Morgenstern, slated to be the company's next CEO, has a different vision for the company. Her desire to improve the lives of the citizens of the empire has turned her into a visionary for Morgenstern Tech's future. She sees a future for the company that involves helping people. She has her sights set on bionics, and her partnership with Northwind Medical is the first step in her plan.

Northwind Medical has existed for nearly as long as Spiral City has been around, beginning as a hospital and eventually expanding into medical research in partnership with Spiral City University and Sequoia Institute in Ivorymore. Their current director, Ronson Byre, rose to his current position not long ago after the previous director retired.

The partnership between the two companies is a massive deal for the denizens of Spiral City, so it's understandable that the news has been the talk of the town.

34

CASSIAN

23rd of Wind Moon

Kellan went to shower after their talk on the bed, and rather than twiddling his thumbs while he waited, Cassian polished his blades.

His jaw twitched in frustration, thinking about Leo's laugh and Mina's stoic silence, her final apology to her best friend. She'd deserved an honorable death at a ripe old age, after a life well lived. As his cloth slid against the metal of the blade, he thought about all the people whose lives he'd taken before their time too. Had they deserved the death he'd given them? Most had been as awful as Ragnor. But some had not.

He frowned, an unpleasant feeling unfurling in his gut. He'd spent as long as he could *not* thinking about the lives he'd taken. He'd crafted a perfectly cool bubble that should have lasted until he was free of his debts and could absolve himself in whatever way he saw fit.

That was the problem—he couldn't think of a fitting way to pardon his actions. He'd done awful, terrible, horrible things. And only now, presented with someone with the same struggle as him, did he realize how much time he'd spent *not* thinking about those things.

Maybe he should feel worse. He should be distraught like Kellan.

But he wasn't. He felt empty, numb, like he had after his father died. Like he had after every kill he'd made. He'd learned to turn off the pain long ago. Would he ever be able to turn it back on? Did he even want to? He didn't know.

Cassian heard the shower stop and re-sheathed the blade, gently packing it up along with the cleaning cloth and various polishes and oils he used to keep it clean and sharp.

He wondered if Kellan would notice the clothes he'd laid out for him in the bedroom. Cassian had gone downstairs to give Kellan privacy, but he was worried about Kellan's well-being. He'd felt his stare this morning, the intimacy of sleeping at his bedside the night before boring a hole in his brain.

He refused to entertain the idea of what Kellan looked like fresh out of the shower.

Instead, he stood and stopped at the base of the stairs, hoping his voice was loud enough to reach Kellan in the bedroom upstairs.

"I should visit Selwyn, I'm positive she'll have questions," Cassian called, his voice slightly raspy.

A grunt let him know Kellan had heard, and a few moments later, he emerged at the top of the stairs, wearing a pair of Cassian's soft sweatpants and a plain black tee. Something about seeing Kellan in his clothes sucked all the air from his lungs.

"I'll go with you," Kellan finally said, his hair a wet mess on his head.

Cassian shook his head. "You don't have to, take it—"

"If you say take it easy, I'll punch you," Kellan interrupted. "I'll be fine. I *am* fine. I need to be there, though. Take responsibility."

His eyes shone with an emotion Cassian couldn't place that hovered between determination and sorrow. It was heartbreaking. He nodded to Kellan, sure that if he tried to leave him behind, he'd never be successful.

"I talked to the commissioner this morning, too," Kellan added, descending the staircase slowly, his movements deliberate.

"Will there be trouble for you?" Cassian asked. He hadn't even considered how this might affect Kellan's status within the Legion.

But apparently, he needn't worry—Kellan shook his head. "The nineteenth gets pulled into stuff like this more often than you'd think. Some units patrol specifically for this kind of shit." He made a face.

"I see," Cassian added lamely. He realized how far out of his league he was whenever Kellan talked about the Legion. Even though most people in the Empire had some idea how they worked, it was an entirely different thing hearing about it from a legionnaire himself.

The Red Guard was more widely known since they served the whole Empire, not just their base city. And although the Legion modeled themselves after the Red Guard, their operations were much less complex.

Cassian looked mournfully at the empty coffee maker, wishing he'd taken the time to make himself a cup. But they couldn't delay this conversation any longer. He shivered, then strapped his daggers to his hips.

"Why the heat?" Kellan said, stuffing his clothes from last night into a bag.

Cassian shrugged, attempting to be casual. "I'm being cautious. I've been caught without them too many times now."

"Hmmm," Kellan hummed back.

They hailed a cab a few blocks from the safe house, and he opened the door for Kellan, gesturing for him to climb in first. Kellan obliged, and Cassian scooted in after him.

He turned over what he could say to Kellan, knowing he'd done what he could last night and unsure what he needed now. Kellan didn't look inclined to talk.

His voice floated over a few minutes later, however, soft enough so the cab driver couldn't hear. "You've done enough for me, you know. You said if it jeopardized your cover, you would stop. I'd say this is that threshold."

He shook his head. "I'm in too deep now, Kellan. Selwyn saw me last night, and I'm sure she's going to have questions."

Kellan looked down at his legs. "I'm sorry. I really am. I never meant to blow your cover."

"I can still fix it, I'm sure."

Kellan frowned.

The car ride continued in silence. It was heavy, full of words left unsaid. The pressure weighed on Cassian's chest until he couldn't bear it any longer.

He realized he'd been chewing his lip. "I know what it's like, Kellan, losing someone you should have been able to save."

Kellan stayed silent, his hands balled into fists on his knees. Cassian resisted the urge to reach over and hold his hand, opting to copy him instead.

"Does it get easier?" Kellan said, his voice small.

"No, it doesn't."

"That's somewhat of a relief, but also frustrating."

Cassian smiled softly. "It just means your heart is big enough to take it."

"I know." Kellan paused, letting a deep breath slowly stream out of his mouth. "Thank you, Cass. For last night."

This time, Cassian really did lean over, grabbing one of Kellan's hands in his own. "We're in this mess together now. And we'll avenge Mina, I promise," he said, squeezing.

Kellan squeezed back, nodding.

Cassian didn't know what he'd expected to see when they arrived at the Morgenstern mansion, but it wasn't this.

He had to admit, Bloomside was beautiful with its everlasting blooms and perfectly manicured lawns. But the wealth on display was borderline obscene.

The Morgenstern mansion was no exception; colorful flowers and fragrant bushes of all shapes dotted the front lawn, tastefully arranged in a way that was perfectly manicured chaos.

Thankfully, Kellan seemed just as uncomfortable as he felt. He watched as he wrung his hands, twisting them in random circles, occasionally cracking his knuckles. Cassian resisted the urge to reach out and hold Kellan's hands to stop him from squirming.

Dean, the butler, answered the door and immediately ushered them inside. Cassian glanced at him sidelong but followed Kellan into the opulent foyer.

Apparently, Selwyn was waiting in the parlor. They followed Dean as he led them down a hallway to an ornate room decorated in reds and deep blues. Selwyn sat in one of the long fainting couches placed in the center of the room atop a plush rug dyed an impossible shade of red. The color made him queasy.

He angled his head to look at Kellan, gauging his emotions as best he could. He looked pale.

"Thank you for coming to see me, although I didn't ask it of you," she began. She sounded exhausted. "We need to discuss what happened last night."

Before either of them could say anything more, she gestured to the couch across from her, then asked Dean for coffee. He bowed, shutting the parlor door behind him.

Cassian sat, uncomfortably, on the corner of the fainting couch. Kellan perched beside him, his hands balled into fists in his lap. He watched the other man out of the corner of his eye, noting the way his eyes stayed firmly planted on Selwyn, how he never once glanced at the blood-red carpet beneath their feet. He wondered if Selwyn noticed, too.

Selwyn's eyes stayed soft, their usual steel nowhere to be found. Although tears didn't make an appearance, the sorrow she felt was palpable.

"Mina didn't deserve this," she said softly, her voice steady. "What did she do to deserve this? Was it because of me?"

"No, Selwyn, no; not because of you," Cassian cut in, his words coming slowly to keep his tone even. "I'm afraid I put you all in danger."

Selwyn said nothing. She stayed frozen, her head held high even as the tears welled in her eyes. She didn't make a sound as they fell; somehow, her silence was worse than an outburst. Kellan stayed still, his hands clenched so tightly the knuckles had turned white. Cassian glanced back and forth between the two of them, finally deciding to stand and cross the room to sit next to Selwyn.

"Selwyn," he said gently, bowing his head to her but not daring to touch her. "I promise you, I will catch the man who did this to her. I'll make him pay."

With that, Selwyn turned to look at Cassian. A fire burned in her eyes, red-rimmed and spilling tears down her cheeks. Even a crying mess, she was still beautiful. "You had better make him pay tenfold," she whispered fiercely.

He nodded and allowed Selwyn to sink into the joint of his shoulder as the rush of tears finally overtook her. Kellan continued to stare at his hands.

They spent a fair amount of time sitting in the front room, consoling Selwyn and eventually discussing Mina. She'd wanted to be a veterinarian and had been in her final year at Spiral City University. Her dad had always been fiercely protective of her, and her mother was the sweetest woman Selwyn had ever met. She'd had a younger brother, James, who was in his second year of high school. They hadn't gotten along that well when they were younger, but as Mina had grown older, their relationship had gotten much better.

At some point, Dean had come back into the room and delivered coffee. It sat upon the ornate table between the couches, untouched.

Selwyn talked about Mina for what seemed like hours. Finally, her tears stopped. Cassian handed her another tissue, and she dabbed at her eyes.

"You know who that man is, don't you?" Selwyn asked, head still in her hands. "And you're not actually who you say you are." She didn't frame it as a question, rather, it was a statement.

He sighed, glancing over to Kellan. He looked back with worry in his eyes, but they couldn't say much in front of Selwyn.

"Your hunch is correct. And, unfortunately, I can't tell you much more, but I mean you no harm. However, I believe you and your brother may be in danger now because of me."

"Is that why someone targeted Tarin, too?" she asked, her mouth turning into a hard line.

Kellan cleared his throat, and Cassian stayed silent as he explained.

"Look, Selwyn, I can't believe I'm about to tell you this, but I think I might need your help," he began, sighing and unfurling his fists. Cassian saw nail marks in his palms as he opened them to rest on his knees. "I think Pontius' theory about Northwind Medical being involved in Tarin's disappearance might be right. But I don't know if Mina was connected to that."

Selwyn's brow furrowed as she bit her lip. "I expect this from Pontius, but not from you. What evidence do you have against them?"

Kellan sighed. "Not much, honestly. Each of the victims had the same substance that Tarin took the night he overdosed in their systems, and they share some key similarities that are too suspicious to ignore. I have to explore all possibilities."

"That's awfully thin evidence, you know," Selwyn said matter-of-factly.

Kellan nodded. "I know. That's why I was hoping to get your help. Have you noticed anything when you've visited the director? Anything weird going on?"

Selwyn shook her head. "No. Nothing out of the ordinary. He seems to conduct a lot of medicinal research, but that's what they do."

Kellan sighed, pinching his nose. Cassian knew how frustrated he must be—his case was essentially at a standstill.

"Why trust me with this information?" Selwyn asked softly. "After all, you barely know me."

Kellan just shrugged. "You don't seem like the type of person who would have believed me if I tried to be vague."

She snorted, a sound that surprised both Kellan and Cassian, eliciting a small flinch from the latter. Cassian sighed, chewing the inside of his lip as Kellan continued.

"But I don't know how to continue, and you're the best chance I have," he said.

She sighed, sitting forward and tenting the tips of her long fingers. "You want me to get you in with Director Byre somehow, don't you?"

Kellan just nodded, staying silent. It was probably a smart move, Cassian thought, letting Selwyn decide if she even believed them. He knew it wasn't much, but he hoped the genuine concern in Kellan's face was enough to convince her.

She took a deep breath, then shook her head. "It's just not enough. I can't go risking my neck just to give you a shot at him on a one-in-a-million chance that there *might* be something shady going on. He's a good man—he has proven it time and time again."

Kellan didn't let it show, but Cassian could almost feel his heart stop. How could he convince her to get Kellan in to see Byre? Just talking to him might change the tide of this whole case.

Cassian tensed at the sound of footsteps approaching. Was Dean back with more coffee? He glanced at the cold coffee sitting before them. Surely not…

The parlor door swung open to reveal a haggard Pontius. His hair was in disarray, his eyes sunken and dark like he hadn't slept in weeks. He wore an old t-shirt with the words "Enya's Fire" written in curling elvish script and baggy sweatpants with threadbare knees.

"Why are you two here?" he said flatly.

"Mina is—" Kellan started before Selwyn interrupted him.

"Mina is dead, Pontius," she said, her voice even. Her throat bobbed as she finished the sentence, her eyes wide. She held her head high, as if keeping herself still would stop the tears from reappearing.

Pontius simply stood, frozen in place, unwilling, or possibly unable, to move from the doorframe. Cassian's heart broke at the sight.

"Come sit," Kellan said, standing up from his spot on the couch and gesturing to Pontius to take it instead.

He moved at Kellan's request, albeit jerkily, like his body wasn't quite his own. Almost like he wasn't completely in control of it anymore. When he at last plopped onto the deep blue velvet sofa, tears were streaming down his face.

"What happened?" he asked, but then immediately held up his hands. "Never mind. I don't know if I can handle it. Just tell me, does it have anything to do with Tarin? Is it because they were friends with us?"

Kellan laid a hand on the man's shoulder, the gesture gentle. "No, Pontius, we believe her death was an entirely separate matter. And neither has anything to do with being associated with you."

Although the words were meant to calm him, the tears ran even faster down Pontius' face. He slouched forward, dropping his head in his hands. His hair fell limply through and around his fingers, streaming like dark water toward the floor. Kellan continued holding his shoulder in an attempted gesture of comfort. Cassian watched with clenched teeth. He could practically feel the man's anguish from across the room.

"What," Pontius blubbered between sobs, "were you talking about just now? Before I came in?"

"They were just telling me how they believe Northwind Medical might be responsible for Tarin's death," Selwyn said.

Pontius' head whipped up, flinging tears across the carpet.

Kellan turned to face Pontius, confusion written on his face. "You haven't talked about it?"

Selwyn shook her head. "No, we have. I'm just..." She trailed off, biting her lip. "I'm just finding it rather difficult to believe such outlandish theories."

Pontius stared at Selwyn like he could see through her, his gaze intense for a man who'd been sobbing moments before. "You could be of use to them, Sel. You have a direct connection to Director Byre."

She stared back at him with equal intensity. "If you are implying the same thing they were asking, I refused them, and I will refuse you too."

He stood suddenly, the movement scooting the couch back a few inches with the force of his gesture. Kellan raised an eyebrow, and Cassian felt himself copying the movement.

"You must help them with the director," Pontius said, staring unblinkingly at Selwyn. "If there is any chance we can figure out what happened to Tarin, we must take that chance."

"It's entirely too risky," she shot back. "He has next to no evidence, a flimsy case at best. I would risk my entire career to do this."

"To the hells with your career, Selwyn; we'll outlive the bastard anyway!" Pontius practically screamed. "Tarin will never get that chance!"

Selwyn stayed silent, calm as a rock against the stormy sea that was Pontius' fury. She stared at him. Her stoicism impressed Cassian.

"And neither will Mina," she said after a long pause.

The room felt as if all the air had been sucked from it. Pontius deflated, sinking back into the couch like someone had punched him in the stomach.

All four of them stayed silent for several moments, Cassian waiting with bated breath to see who would be brave enough to break the silence.

To everyone's surprise, Selwyn was the first to speak.

"I have an…opportunity. To get you close." She sighed, then turned to face Cassian. "And I'll need you there too."

He was surprised, but he didn't let it show. Instead, he simply nodded, letting her continue.

"I've been planning a gala to announce the partnership between Morgenstern Technology Group and Northwind Medical. A deal I struck several months ago has finally been confirmed, and we are looking for donors. Byre will be in attendance. Come as my protection—it'll get you close to him."

Cassian raised his eyebrows. It was the perfect opportunity—Byre would also be under heavy protection, but it mattered little. It wouldn't seem out of place for Selwyn to have protection too.

Pontius raised his head to look at her, the question on everyone's minds undeniably on his lips. But when he opened his mouth to speak, Selwyn simply held up a hand.

"I'm only doing this out of love for you, brother," she said. "Only because I hate to see you eaten up over Tarin and because I refuse to act the same for Mina. They wouldn't want this for us, Pontius. They wouldn't want you to starve yourself, to forget who you are simply because they are no longer with us." She sighed, the shaking of her breath the only sign of the intense emotion she must be feeling. "I am doing this because I believe in you and because this route presents the smallest risk to me."

Pontius didn't move, staring at his sister, mouth slightly agape.

Kellan bowed his head to Selwyn, interjecting, "Thank you, truly, for helping me. I am in your debt."

Selwyn turned her severe blue eyes to Kellan, and Cassian noted they were once again lined in silver. "I am trusting you not to tarnish this relationship, legionnaire. I have worked far too hard to be where I am for you to trample it before it even begins."

"I won't let you down," he said, his face shining with sincerity. It made Cassian's neck prickle.

"No, you won't." Selwyn held Kellan's gaze, the tears in her eyes refusing to spill.

35

SHADOW

26th of Wind Moon

"I am unimpressed with your antics, Shadow," Alvemach said. His voice, contrary to his form, was icy.

The man bowed his head, something he would never do for anyone else. But he felt it too—his last attempt to find a candidate and speed their research progress along had failed spectacularly. He wasn't used to failing.

"I told you once before that I will work on her myself. You have your duties to focus upon. If you so much as lay a single finger on her again, I will violently end this pact, regardless of your agreement to it or not."

"I understand," the man replied. He hated the sound of his own voice.

"Then let this serve as a reminder to never disobey me again."

The man's legs hurt as the veins pulsated, the already dark bruising under his skin becoming black. The pain was enough to send spots along his vision, nearly forcing him to his knees and cry out in pain. He did not feel pain. But Alvemach could make him.

The veins grew as he winced and writhed, spreading from where they'd stayed below his knees to spread up his thighs and wrap around his hips and lower abdomen. The process would happen naturally as their accord continued, but Alvemach could force it along if he wanted to.

The process was extremely painful if forced. Alvemach had taken to forcing it as punishment.

The man knew, somewhere in his mind, that if given the chance, he would do it all over again. The result of their pact would come to pass eventually, and truthfully, the man did not mind the process being expedited.

Pain was progress, after all.

Alvemach released him, allowing the veins to slow their progress across his body. Little by little, they would grow, creeping up his body until they finally reached his heart. Once they did, the ritual pact they'd engaged in would be complete.

But until that day, they had work to do. And the man understood his part. He needed to trust Alvemach. He'd been the one to call him here, after all. And Alvemach had proven himself capable of all that the man had wanted.

Trusting one another didn't come easily, but the pact made the choice to try easier.

"I won't fail you again, Alvie," the man said, a sadistic smile spreading across his lips.

Alvemach made a face. "I told you not to call me that."

The man shrugged, the pain already a distant memory, a fuzzy, hazy past that was forgotten as soon as it was over. He had gotten his punishment. Dwelling upon it would do nothing.

Alvemach rolled his eyes, then disappeared in a flash of purple laced with black.

The man shook his head, the smile from earlier still carving a thin line across his face. It was time to move to the next phase—and this time, he would not fail.

36

KELLAN

28th of Wind Moon

The dream was less of a dream and more of a nightmare.

It started with the crime lord Kellan had killed, the first person whose life he'd ended. His blood dripped through Kellan's fingers, rushing to meet the floor as it pooled at his feet. The man stood before him, his face blank, featureless.

Then they morphed into the mage he'd killed soon after. More blood pooled, this time covering his shoes and swirling about his ankles.

The next was Van Alder, his blood leaking from the ceiling, running in deep vermillion rivulets down the walls. It reached his knees.

Then it was Tarin. The bath of blood rose over his thighs, soaking through this clothing and weighing him down.

And finally, it was Mina. The blood leaked slowly from her neck. His hands were stained deep red. The pool reached his hips.

Kellan stood stock still, frozen in place and unable to scream as Mina reached a hand forward, her last words on her tongue.

"I'm…sorry."

He wanted to respond. She had nothing to be sorry for. He was the one who was sorry. He was the one who hadn't saved her, who had done nothing. It was his fault she was dead.

With a pop, Mina disappeared. His heart plummeted when he

recognized the next face.

Cassian stood before him, a knife in his back. He faced away, his front toward the blood-soaked walls, the knife that had obviously dealt the killing blow teasing Kellan where he stood.

He turned, the green of his eyes brighter than he'd ever seen it. "Why?"

Kellan awoke with a start, gasping as he sat up in bed, drenched in cold sweat. He'd spent the last four days tossing and turning, having that same dream over and over. Vaida had visited him, knocking gently on his door several times. He hadn't answered.

She'd brought him a plate of food three times a day anyway.

That morning, he heard a sharp rap at the door. He slowly got up, shuffling his way to the door, expecting to see Vaida on the other side. But that was not the case—the commissioner himself stood on the other side, his half-moon glasses on a chain around his neck, the orange piping of his uniform almost too bright for his eyes.

Kellan stared at him for a moment, taken aback.

"May I come inside?" He spoke softly, as if he knew harsh words were not what Kellan needed to hear.

Kellan nodded, stepping aside to allow him inside the common area. The commissioner walked with purpose, striding into the room with no hesitation, no trepidation.

The commissioner continued, "It is perfectly normal, you know, to feel affected by the death of an innocent. In your line of work, however, these types of situations cannot always be avoided. Take this chance to reflect." The commissioner moved to sit on a couch in the common area, not even gesturing for Kellan to follow. He did anyway.

"Sir?" Kellan asked cautiously.

"I am here to tell you that you are not alone, Private. This has happened to many of us. The ghosts of those we couldn't save haunt us. They stay with you." He tapped his heart as he leaned forward, gazing intently at Kellan. "But don't let them control you. Let them guide you."

He was silent. He didn't know what to say. Was this normal behavior from the leader of their organization? He wasn't sure.

The commissioner didn't wait for his response. "You must understand. Death is permanent, yes. But you honor the dead by continuing to live and keeping them in your heart. You honor their memory by doing what you can in this world. Whether it be small or large, your impact keeps their memory from fading."

An emotion Kellan couldn't name welled in his heart, dropping through his veins into his stomach. Green filled his vision, the green of relief, the green of bittersweet emotion. The commissioner was right; it would not do to dwell on the past when the future was before him, ready to be experienced.

Because what was living if not experiencing everything? Happiness, sorrow, pain, joy…each emotion was a part of his experience because he was alive. Ignoring those emotions, pretending they didn't exist, would be an insult to the gift of life he'd been given, the one he'd been allowed to continue experiencing.

It didn't mean he would forget Mina, Tarin, Liza, or even Cygnus. It meant that he'd do everything he could to honor their memory, their lives. He couldn't stop now, not when he needed to find Leo and punish him for what he'd done to Mina.

The memory of her sparkled, her smile warming his heart just a touch. The commissioner was right, the ghosts stayed with him. But not to haunt him.

"I…" he began, stumbling over his words, "thank you, sir."

The commissioner leaned back once again in his chair, crossing his legs. His red hair was coiffed into a smooth pompadour, his salt-and-pepper beard trimmed neatly. The commissioner was older, but very much still in his prime. Kellan wasn't sure if he actually needed the half-moon glasses around his neck, but he almost never saw him without them. Maybe he thought they made him look distinguished? If that was the case, it certainly worked.

"Life comes with suffering, Private, but even so, we experience these things because we are alive. Isn't that wonderful?"

Kellan nodded, looking down at his hands in his lap.

The commissioner continued, "I have another job for you. A short one that will not interfere with your current case. Can you handle it?" He posed it as a question, but Kellan knew it was a command.

"Yes, sir. What do you need me to do?"

"I need you to assist Lieutenant Razorborn with security detail. It's a one-time event, but his usual partner is out on contract. He requested you."

Kellan's eyebrows raised slightly. "Me, sir?" The commissioner stayed silent, so Kellan continued, "I'd be happy to assist Sharr, sir."

The commissioner nodded once. "Good. You'll get the rest of the details from him. The event is in two days."

Kellan nodded as the commissioner stood. He didn't look back as he walked toward the door, his stride once again confident and strong.

But he stopped at the threshold, clutching the doorframe and turning his head to look at Kellan once more.

"You are strong, Manchester. I know you can accomplish this. I would not give you a task you can't handle. Do you understand?"

Kellan fought the urge to scoff. "Yes, sir."

The commissioner nodded once more, then shut the door behind him.

Kellan couldn't help but stare after him, his brow furrowed.

30TH OF WIND MOON

The job turned out to be simple. Sharr was thrilled that Kellan had accepted being his partner for the evening. They were on guard duty for Bethor Ironswing, the Councilor of Upper Cloud. He usually hired a few guards whenever he went out in public, and tonight's charity dinner was no different. In fact, most of the city's councilors hired guards, often from the ranks of the fourteenth and fifteenth.

It was a regular practice, and something Sharr had done hundreds of times before. It was Kellan's first time meeting the councilors, however.

Bethor was a jovial seraph man in his late fifties, with graying brown hair and piercing amber eyes. His nose was rounded and looked squishy and was red at the tip. He had a bit of a belly but wasn't out of shape. Kellan guessed he could take a man down and hold him easily if he really wanted to.

Bethor had been elected councilor of Upper Cloud nearly six years ago and was beloved by his people. The other councilors seemed to like him too, judging by the way everyone at the event was gathering around him.

Their job tonight was simply to stay out of the way but close enough to prevent anything bad happening to Bethor.

The event hall was in his district of Upper Cloud. It was ornate, to say the least. It was painted white, with mosaics of vines crawling up the walls in black tile. Gold filigree dotted the designs, giving them a shimmer wherever you looked. The chandeliers were massive, large enough to squash two people underneath if they were ever to fall. Kellan eyed them suspiciously.

Every outer district councilor was here—Bethor of Upper Cloud, Hazel of Lunadere, Roland of Northwind, Arice of Tethgir, Gen and her daughter, Erwen, from Rookford Down, and the newest councilor, Exto of Bloomside. The commissioner was absent, although that didn't surprise Kellan. He was not the type to attend events like these.

None of the councilors paid them much attention, although Arice had given Sharr a gentle nod earlier in the evening. She was dragonborn, too.

Bethor and the commissioner had asked them to don their dress uniforms tonight, which weren't much different from their regular uniforms. Sharr's dress uniform added a bright blue sash across his chest and an extra armband around his right arm, adorned with gold filigree and the symbol of the Legion. Kellan had a sash as well, his blood red and attached to his shoulder with a golden clip. Although he hardly ever had chances to wear his dress uniform, he liked the way the sash looked in the mirror.

But even with the added excitement of his dress uniform, Kellan couldn't muster the relaxed attitude Sharr was wearing with ease. His old mentor noticed.

"Something on your mind, Kellan?" Sharr asked, concern in his silvery eyes. They leaned against the far wall of the dining hall, watching as Bethor took a seat several tables away.

Kellan sighed, crossing his arms over his chest. "I don't really know, Sharr. I've got a lot on my mind."

"Anything I can do to ease it? I've got a lot of years under my belt." He glanced over to Kellan. When he stayed silent, Sharr continued, "Is it about that case you're working on? Heard it's been pretty intense."

"That's part of it, but…" He trailed off, unsure how to explain everything. Mina's death weighed on his heart still, as did the others. The commissioner's words two days ago had helped, but the weight of guilt was still a heavy burden.

And then there was Cassian. His feelings had grown too complicated for comfort. He remembered the way he'd looked in the sunlight the other morning, the way he'd reached for his hair without a second thought.

Everything was complicated and none of it was comfortable.

Sharr chuckled. "You seem to have a lot of things you're juggling, hatchling. Why not start with one? We have plenty of time."

Kellan chewed his lip. "Someone died because of me. I was careless. She was innocent."

Sharr sucked in a breath through his teeth, exposing their sharp points. He leaned against the wall too, arms crossed. "That's rough. You can't always protect everyone, though, as much as you may want to. Was it someone you knew?"

Kellan shook his head. "Not well, but it's my fault she was involved at all. She would be alive if it wasn't for me."

Sharr turned his head to Kellan, his eyes intense. "Did you kill her yourself?"

"No. What kind of question is that?"

"You didn't kill her. It's not your fault."

"But—"

Sharr cut him off with a wave of a black-scaled hand, the sharp claws glittering under the lights. "You weren't the one who made the choice to end her life. And if I know you at all, you tried saving her, didn't you?"

"Of course I did."

"Then it's not your fault." Sharr laid a hand on Kellan's shoulder, his long talons curving over his sash. "The person who killed her is the one at fault. You can't blame yourself for it forever. She made a choice to be around you, whoever killed her made the choice to do so, and you made the choice to do everything you could to save her. Do you see what I'm getting at?"

Kellan's heart squeezed. Sharr was right—he couldn't keep blaming himself for the choices others had made. All he could do now was make Leo pay for what he'd done. He was quiet for several moments before he could respond.

"I do. I have to avenge her."

Sharr smiled, revealing those deadly sharp teeth once more. "That's it, Kellan. You can choose to wallow in self-pity, or you can choose to do something about it. The decision is yours."

They stayed silent for a time, leaning against the filigreed walls and observing the party. The dinner moved forward swiftly, the drinks and salads being shuffled away for plates of food piled high. The candles in the centerpieces danced, and Kellan found himself distracted by his thoughts rushing by in a parade of revenge and death.

"You know…" Sharr's voice was soft, like he wasn't sure he should say anything. "Many of us in the Legion have experienced the same situation you have. Losing someone we should have been able to save."

"You sound like you're speaking from experience," Kellan said.

Sharr nodded, still staring at Bethor's table. "It was about a year and a half into my service. I was part of a small group assigned to protect the previous Councilor of Tethgir, Renhorn. He was a good man." Sharr stopped, breathing deeply through his nose. "He had a daughter—she was with him that night."

Kellan's stomach dropped. "Don't tell me…"

"She watched as someone shot her father through the head and didn't even get the chance to scream before she was dead too." Sharr closed his eyes as if he could erase the memory simply by not seeing. "We caught the guy, but there was nothing we could do for Jozita or Renhorn. I felt like a failure for years afterwards."

"Do you still?"

Sharr looked pensive. "I sometimes remember that night and how I could have changed things if only I'd been a little faster, a little smarter, a little more…something. But when I think about it, I tell myself that I did my best. That I made the choice to avenge them by catching their killer and ensuring that no one else would die by his hands."

Kellan chewed his lip, unsure how to respond. Sharr continued gazing out into the crowd with no more words of wisdom for Kellan.

Or so he thought.

"In the end, hatchling, the best thing you can do is what you have the power to do. I know you'll do your best to see this thing through until the end." Sharr's eyes twinkled.

He breathed deeply, then turned to face the crowd of people once more, Sharr's words filling the empty spaces in his heart. Mina's death wouldn't be left unresolved.

And when the evening was over and he fell into his bed back at the Guard, he vowed to make Leo pay however he could.

37

CASSIAN

1st of Jupiter's Moon

Cassian dreaded the next call with Ragnor. He'd updated him several times since that first phone call a month ago, but their conversations had always ended in disappointment. But he had questions this time.

Was Leo still in Ragnor's employ? What was his mission here if he was? Why was he so damn obsessed with Cassian? He wasn't even sure if Ragnor could answer that last question, but it couldn't hurt to try.

His techpad rang while the setting sun stained the sky a dark pink. He sat on the couch and answered, holding the device flat in his palm.

"Ragnor."

"Evermore." Ragnor's voice sounded annoyed. "My patience is wearing thin. I expected something out of you by now."

"Yes, sir," he began, unsure how to proceed. A blunt and direct approach would likely result in a dismissal from Ragnor and possibly force him to return to Ebenfell.

He wasn't sure why, but the idea of leaving Spiral City now was unpleasant. Kellan's face came to mind, and he blinked several times, hoping to rid himself of the image of him sleeping in his bed upstairs.

"They have invited me to a gala under the pretense of protecting the Morgensterns," he started again. "There have been some… unpleasant developments in the siblings' personal lives, and I am doing my best to take advantage."

Ragnor huffed, and Cassian could practically see the expression the man would inevitably make as he listened. "Elaborate."

"Well, Selwyn was kidnapped."

"By whom?"

He cleared his throat awkwardly. "Leonardo Whitburn."

Ragnor was silent on the other end of the line. Cassian didn't fill the silence, hoping to force Ragnor to speak first, to confirm something about the man who'd once been one of his top men.

"I hope you aren't implying he still works for me, Cassian," Ragnor finally drawled. "He left my employment nearly twenty-five years ago. I have not seen him since."

"I wasn't implying anything, sir, simply delivering the facts."

Ragnor huffed again. "And? Has he killed her?"

"No, sir. I rescued her. Her best friend, however, was killed in the resulting fight." He knew his words would inevitably send Ragnor into a rage. After all, the kidnapping would have been the perfect excuse to separate the siblings. But Cassian had acted upon instinct, and he didn't regret it.

When he spoke again, Ragnor's voice was like ice. "And why would you have done that?"

Cassian smiled, hoping to steady his voice with feigned confidence. "Isn't it obvious, sir? I saved her life. She's indebted to me."

"I don't appreciate your tone."

"I didn't mean to imply disrespect, Ragnor."

Ragnor sighed, and Cassian could hear the tapping of his rings against a hard surface—the arm of a chair or maybe his desk. He knew it was risky, being so bold with the man who owned his life, but Ragnor admired tenacity occasionally. He hoped this was one of those times.

"Very well. But I'm giving you a deadline. You have until the end of the month to get this resolved. Do you understand me?"

Cassian's blood ran cold. It wasn't enough. There wasn't enough time for him to do what needed to be done. He'd been slacking, he supposed, hoping the deadline Ragnor had just given him would never be imposed. Hoping that maybe, even though it had never happened before, the assignment would be abandoned.

He realized he liked life here. He liked Kellan, Pontius, and Selwyn. The idea of leaving it all behind terrified him. The idea of not being able to return, of not being able to see Kellan again…

Cassian drew his thoughts up short. Something undoubtedly attracted him to Kellan, but thinking about it too much would be dangerous. He couldn't afford to care about another person, not when Ragnor could use that to his advantage.

"Yes, sir," he finally replied. There was no space to argue, no chance for him to refute the order.

"Good. I expect another update as usual." Without waiting for Cassian's response, he ended the call.

Cassian leaned back against the couch, the techpad falling from his hands and down onto the cushions. He closed his eyes, cutting off the view of the plain white ceiling above him.

Behind his eyelids, Kellan came alive. The way he'd looked that night, after Mina's death. How he'd called to Cassian to stay, to not let him be alone. How he'd looked after he had finally fallen asleep, the thin skin of his eyelids twitching as he dreamed.

He remembered the way Kellan's hair had looked like spun gold in the morning's sunlight.

His cheeks flushed as he remembered sensing movement, how Kellan had reached for him just as he'd awoken. He'd pretended not to notice, but something in him had wanted to stay asleep. Just to see what Kellan might do.

Cassian realized he'd wished for his touch. It was a dangerous wish, a troubling hope. After what had happened to Aidyn, he couldn't risk loving anyone like that again.

And it wasn't like he was falling in love with Kellan, he told himself. Right?

His own thoughts sounded like excuses, ringing around in his head pathetically. He couldn't even convince himself that he wasn't attracted to the man. How in the world was he supposed to hide it from Kellan?

Cassian chewed his lip but enjoyed the warm flush of his cheeks.

He opened his eyes, sighing as he stared at the alabaster ceiling. He had a month. A month to find Pontius' weakness, expose him, and kill him. A month to finish what he'd started.

It was not enough time. But he had no choice.

38

SHADOW

10th of Jupiter's Moon

The man was finally making progress. He'd ensnared several more humans to test upon, and the serum, it seemed, worked much better on them. It wasn't ideal, but it was a start.

The girl before him was unconscious, bright red blood leaking from her temple where he'd struck her to stop her screaming. It had been a nuisance, and he hadn't been able to concentrate long enough to tweak the dosage for her small body. So he'd turned around and smacked her with the butt of his blade as hard as he could. She'd immediately fallen silent.

Alvemach had made him promise to stick to the plan he'd laid out. He'd said that Cassian would most likely attend the upcoming gala as a guard for Selwyn or Pontius. How Alvemach had known that, the man didn't know, nor did he particularly care. Demons had their ways of spying, knowing things said behind closed doors, sneaking into places sealed away from everyone else. He figured Alvemach had probably just spied upon his old acquaintance at the Morgenstern residence.

But if Cassian would be there… His fingers practically itched at the chance to go at the man once more. If he took the man Cassian seemed to like so much, maybe he'd finally get somewhere. He'd be a fantastic test subject, if his hypotheses were correct. He hadn't been able to obtain any new subjects, and Alvemach had ordered him to perfect the human's serum before he tested on other races. They couldn't risk any more legionnaires poking their noses into the discarded bodies they'd dumped around the city.

The elven man had been a mistake. The ghouls hadn't done a good job of weighing the body down, and he'd been discovered far too soon. The man had, of course, killed the ghouls responsible. Alvemach had summoned new ones as the old had disintegrated into chalky black dust. It wasn't like they'd *stay* dead, anyway. They simply returned to the hells, awaiting summons from another infernal prince or greater devil.

The man would not make that mistake twice; he'd hide the bodies on his own, dump them where he *knew* the meddlesome legionnaire boy Cassian liked so much would not discover them. The man scoffed. Love made fools of everyone, it seemed.

The girl made a soft noise, and the man returned to her side, two syringes lined up neatly. He bound her arm to make the veins pop out against her skin, then inserted the tip of the first needle in. She winced, but the man held her firm.

After the first injection, she convulsed. After the second, she stopped.

Her legs changed first, like the transformation ran from the bottom up. Her skin hardened, taking on an almost scale-like texture. Her toes sharpened into talons, although they stayed rather small and narrow. Her hands did much of the same, fingertips lengthening into sharp points that ended in gleaming claws.

And finally, her head changed. It resembled a jackal's head, her human ears shrinking and falling away to be replaced by sharply pointed ones at the top of her head. Her nose elongated, and her eyes flew open to reveal dark yellow irises where blue had once been. Her teeth sharpened into points, the canines growing slightly longer than the rest.

It was perfect. The man grinned.

"Welcome to the material plane."

The beast on the table just grinned back. She was ready for tomorrow, and so was he.

39

KELLAN

11th of Jupiter's Moon

Kellan watched Cassian twiddle his thumbs as they waited before the door to the Morgenstern mansion.

Cassian looked uncomfortable, but his outfit was sleek. He wore a navy blue suit in the trending menswear style of the city, complete with shiny gold buttons running up the left side of the jacket. The collar was structured, coming up high on his neck and cutting a V at the dip in his throat. The gold piping at the edges of the fabric seemed to sparkle under the setting sun. Kellan had a tough time looking away.

His own forest-green suit was similar in style, although his only buttoned three-quarters of the way up, revealing his black dress shirt underneath.

It had taken nearly four hours to find the right shade of green. Cassian had insisted they all looked the same, but Kellan could tell he'd been enjoying watching him test the different fabrics and styles. Something about clothing was fascinating to him—the idea that one could change their entire personality simply with cloth was a beautiful concept to him.

Cassian's suit had been the first one he'd tried on. Kellan made him try three others, but none had flattered his complexion in quite the same way as the navy and gold had. Kellan had clapped and whistled when he'd come out of the dressing room, drawing a blush up into Cassian's cheeks. He'd pretended not to notice it.

Both of them wore thinner versions of their stealth suits beneath their outfits. They were, foremost, attending this gala to protect Selwyn and Pontius and to gather information. Not to socialize.

Cassian ran a finger beneath the high collar and adjusted it for a fourth time since getting out of the taxi, and Kellan gently slapped his hand away.

"Just leave it, you look amazing," he chided gently, a smirk playing across his lips.

"It's itchy." But Cassian conceded his hand, letting it drop to his side.

"Better."

Cassian returned Kellan's smirk.

The door opened to Dean standing in the foyer, bowing deeply as he waved them inside. "Miss Morgenstern is in the powder room upstairs, please wait here for a moment while I fetch her."

Cassian nodded, and Dean headed up the ornate staircase and off to the left. Kellan looked around the space, hands comfortably resting in the pockets of his pants. Cassian stood stiffly, as if he was afraid to wrinkle the suit. Something about it was charming, he thought.

Selwyn and Pontius appeared at the head of the stairs, and suddenly, Kellan was glad they'd spent so long searching for their own outfits.

Selwyn wore an ankle-length deep green dress with embellished spaghetti straps, the cut of the satin accentuating her slim figure. Her silver shoes sparkled under the dim lighting of the foyer, a perfect compliment to the gems on her straps. The shade was like his own suit, but it looked exquisite on Selwyn, complimenting her expertly curled and styled flame-red hair.

Pontius wore a suit similar to Kellan and Cassian's, only his was white with black satin trim. It was obviously of higher quality, and it fit him like a glove. Someone had styled his hair, a slicked-back look that gathered the bulk of his hair at the back of his head, leaving his handsome face free of flyaways.

They looked positively elegant, enough to set Kellan's teeth on edge.

Selwyn glanced at the two of them with an assessing glance after descending the stairs, apparently finding their outfits satisfactory. She nodded once, then swept out the door with hardly a backward glance, leaving the men to follow in her wake.

A long black sedan waited for them in the driveway, its windows tinted so dark one couldn't see the interior of the car or who might be inside. Kellan had seen a few of these cars drive around town, and it only made sense that the Morgensterns had something like it to usher them around.

There were four seats in the back, two benches facing each other. Kellan climbed in the car first and took a seat in the back. Selwyn followed, Cassian holding her hand gently as she slid gracefully into the bench across from Kellan.

Cassian followed Selwyn into the car, sliding into the seat next to Kellan. Their legs brushed together, and he tried his best to ignore the flush creeping up his ears. He hoped desperately that Cassian would ignore it too. This was neither the time nor the place for such thoughts.

Pontius entered the car last, finally sliding in next to his sister and shutting the car door behind him with a loud thump. The partition slid down, revealing Dean as their driver.

"Ready, everyone?" he asked in a monotone voice.

"Let's go, Dean," Selwyn said, leaning back and brushing her curled hair over her shoulder to look out the window.

It was a half an hour drive to the gala's grand ballroom. The tree-lined roads whipping by eventually gave way to the streetlamps and cold steel of Northwind. They had built the district with winged creatures in mind, so nearly every building was a skyscraper, tall, looming fingers sticking up into the sky. In Northwind, you could only see the sky if you flew.

He missed flying. He still didn't have a flier's permit; they were stingy about them in Spiral City, whether or not you were part of the Legion. Kellan knew most of it was his status. It would have been a simpler matter had he not been Fallen.

He shook his head, ridding himself of the bitter thoughts of his birth and circumstances, and looked across the car to the Morgenstern siblings. Pontius looked more colorful than he'd seen him last, as if he'd gotten some of his life back.

"You look better," Kellan said to Pontius, hoping to stir some conversation in the silent vehicle.

Pontius offered a small smile. "All I can hope is that this evening is successful, then I will truly have something to smile about."

"Vengeance?" Cassian offered.

"Vengeance." Pontius nodded soberly.

"You're all ridiculous," Selwyn cut in, her voice stern. "Remember our deal. You will do *nothing* to jeopardize my agreement with Director Byre and Northwind Medical, do you understand?"

All three men mumbled something that sounded like an agreement, which was apparently not enough for Selwyn. She stamped her silver-heeled foot on the floor of the car, hard.

"Yes, ma'am," all three said in union. Selwyn looked satisfied.

Their car finally rolled to a stop before a grand hotel. It looked as if it had been carved out of a solid block of gold. He knew it was most likely an illusion spell, but it was overwhelming all the same.

The front doors opened on their own as their small party approached, ushered in by the bite of the fall wind on their heels. Selwyn didn't glance at the screen in the lobby that offered directions to the various ballrooms of the hotel, instead heading up the grand staircase before them, her heels clicking viciously on the gilded floors.

A golden elevator awaited them on the second floor just off to the right, manned by a small woman in a tuxedo. She pushed the button immediately when she saw Selwyn approach, offering her a small bow.

The elevator was open, made entirely of glass that allowed riders to look outside the hotel as they ascended. The elevator ride was not swift, instead designed to be a show in and of itself. As they ascended, the city leveled out below them, spreading out into a grid of neon and sparkle, glittering in the night like a thousand jewels dropped on a stage. It was, Kellan had to admit, quite beautiful.

"View's not so bad from up here, huh?" Kellan whispered to Cassian, who jerked in response to his voice. "This is what I'd see if I could fly around here."

"It's incredible," he breathed. Kellan could see the pulse beating in his throat.

Selwyn and Pontius both looked over the city with less wonder than Cassian, but Kellan didn't mistake the twinkle in Pontius' eye. No matter how many times you'd seen this view, it was always breathtaking.

Their slow ascent eventually came to a stop, the elevator level with the tallest buildings in Spiral City. Kellan watched as Cassian took one last, longing look before stepping out of the elevator and into the largest ballroom he'd ever set foot in.

40

KELLAN

11th of Jupiter's Moon

They all followed Selwyn into the ballroom, flanking her in a semicircle. Kellan knew they probably looked ridiculous, but Selwyn didn't seem to care as she briskly crossed the space, her heels clicking on the floor. Her brow was slightly furrowed, the only sign she was thinking of something other than the event at hand.

The director was not here yet, it seemed. They'd arrived early, but not early enough to beat a few of the donors. One such early arrival was none other than the Northwind councilor, Roland. He spotted Selwyn as she made her way across the floor, his path following her trajectory.

She slowed down to meet him, her entourage doing the same. Pontius seemed interested in speaking with the councilor as well, but both Cassian and Kellan held back.

He approached, his hand extended for a shake. Selwyn smiled at him, the small wrinkle between her brows gone as her burgundy lips spread into a professional smile.

"Miss Morgenstern, what a delight it is to see you!" Roland was tall, with salt and pepper hair and a matching beard that was closely trimmed to follow his sharp jawline. His nose was long and thin, giving a nasally tone to his otherwise deep voice. He wore a blacker-than-onyx suit, a vest in brilliant purple beneath.

"Roland, it's a pleasure to see you," she replied, grasping his hand and giving it a firm shake.

"I'm looking forward to seeing what you and the director have been cooking up over the last few months," he replied, his mouth stretched into a wide grin.

Kellan tuned out the rest of their conversation, instead taking stock of the surrounding space. The ballroom was spacious, with floor-to-ceiling windows on the massive curved wall that encompassed the entire space. The view was stunning, a perfect, unblemished look at Spiral City sparkling beneath them.

The floor was sealed concrete, complete with a small raised section just before the windows. Plush couches dotted the exterior of the room, each joined by a small cocktail table. Small candles did their best to light the space.

The room required little decoration; it was quite striking on its own. Thanks to the addition of fashionably dressed donors, the space looked positively lavish.

In the center of the room, a small dais held a microphone, ready for the speeches that would take place later in the night. Pontius was set to introduce his sister, but they had a while before that would begin.

While Kellan watched and Selwyn talked with Roland, the space filled with more and more attendees. Some socialite subsequently pulled Pontius away, Cassian following in his tracks.

Finally, the man he'd been waiting for arrived, exiting the elevator with a smooth grace Kellan was sure no one could replicate.

The director had outdone himself tonight; he was wearing a white suit that appeared to be woven with golden threads. He shimmered in the indirect light from the crystal chandeliers hanging overhead. The craftsmanship of the suit was impressive, but Kellan forced himself to concentrate on his face as he approached.

"Miss Morgenstern, it is a pleasure to see you," Director Byre said with a broad smile as he extended his hand to Selwyn. He was flanked by two burly individuals wearing form-fitting stealth suits that covered every inch of their bodies and full face masks with mirrored fronts. There was no sign of who may be beneath the masks. It made the hairs on Kellan's neck prickle.

"I'm delighted this day is finally here," Selwyn said smoothly as she took the director's hand.

"It appears everything has come together in the intended fashion," he said. "You have done a superb job in setting this up. I must commend you."

She inclined her head to him, taking his praise gracefully. "Thank you, Director. It was my pleasure to put this together."

"I believe you mentioned the speeches would take place around eight?"

"Yes, sir."

"Fantastic. I shall entertain myself with a drink from the bar in the meantime, then. Would you care to join me?"

She nodded, not daring to glance at Kellan still hovering behind her. The director didn't even acknowledge him.

They strode across the room, still slowly filling with Spiral City elite. Kellan followed her closely but didn't say a word. He knew asking anything now wouldn't make a difference. He needed to wait. Selwyn would lead him into the conversation.

"Kellan," she whispered out of the side of her mouth. "You're making me nervous, please relax."

He shook his head. "I'm here to protect you, and that's what I'm doing. If I relax, something bad may happen to you."

She huffed, but let the subject drop as she continued to follow the director to the bar.

The bar was already swarming, but the crowd parted when they spotted Director Byre and his posse, allowing even more room when Selwyn followed closely on his heels. Kellan stayed just behind, his nerves tickling. Ever since they'd arrived, a sense of foreboding had descended upon him, something he couldn't shake.

He chalked it up to nerves.

The director took a seat at the bar, the plush white cushions of the bar stool flattening under his weight. Selwyn followed his lead, taking the stool next to him. The bartender set a glass of red wine before her before she could even ask.

"Tell me, Miss Morgenstern, how well-versed are you in our research at Northwind Medical?" the director asked, leaning forward to rest his chin on folded fingers.

"As well-versed as someone signing a contract with you must be, Director," she replied, crossing her legs at the ankles before sipping from her glass.

The director chuckled at her response, lifting his own glass to his lips. He continued after taking a long drink, "I imagine you must be curious about the research that continues to pull me out of our meetings, no?"

Kellan's ears prickled, but he stayed neutral, appearing uninterested. It was strange, this conversation—this place, the timing of it all. But he couldn't place why.

"I'd be lying if I said I wasn't, sir," Selwyn replied, a calculated smile spreading across her lips.

The director returned the smile, a mixture of malice with professionalism. "Well then, perhaps you would like to see it sometime?"

"And what would I be looking at?"

Director Byre chuckled again. "Oh, Selwyn, that is very confidential information. Suffice it to say, it's nothing like what you've seen before. A completely new innovation that will change the world as we know it."

Something in Kellan twisted. It was the same feeling he'd gotten when faced with a challenging enemy, or what he imagined it would be like to step into a dragon's den. The swooping of his stomach felt tilted, jarring. He knew his suspicions about Northwind must be causing some of the nerves. He knew that, yet he could feel the blood racing through his veins, rushing in his ears, and drowning out the din of conversation flying around them.

And for some inexplicable reason, he was *terrified*.

CASSIAN

11th of Jupiter's Moon

Cassian followed Pontius as he made his rounds through the massive space, his eyes darting constantly to the giant windows. They may be high up, but an assassination through the windows would still be too easy. It made Cassian tense.

Although Pontius seemed to have gotten a little better over the last few weeks, Cassian could tell he was off. His normal magnetism was missing, his usual spark dull and dimmed. No one else seemed to notice, however; they slapped him on the shoulders and shook his hands vigorously. Pontius dealt fine with the attention, although Cassian could already see the weariness growing in his eyes after only a few minutes.

Selwyn and Kellan had retreated to the bar with the director, and Cassian found his eyes drifting there and resting on Kellan. Even from across the ballroom, he could always spot where Kellan was.

His eyes snagged on the two guards that had accompanied Director Byre. Something about them seemed *off*, like they didn't belong here. He couldn't decide if it was the full-face masks, the black combat suits they didn't even try to pass off as formal attire, or the fact that they stood with an unnatural stillness. Everything about them sent goosebumps up Cassian's spine.

He took a deep, steadying breath, focusing back on Pontius,

who was retreating to a quiet corner away from the bustle of gala attendees. Cassian followed, not leaving the other man's side for even a moment.

Once Pontius had claimed a brown leather couch in the corner, Cassian turned to face him after doing a visual sweep of the room.

"You all right?" he asked gently, watching Pontius close his eyes and lean back into the couch.

Pontius didn't answer for a few heartbeats, and Cassian thought he might have fallen asleep. But he took a deep breath in, his chest expanding and then collapsing with the subsequent release.

"I will be. Tarin and Mina loved parties like this. I used to as well, once." Pontius' voice was soft, and Cassian had to strain to hear him.

He wasn't sure how to respond, so he didn't, sensing that Pontius had more to say.

"Tarin was a good person, you know," he said after a long silence. "He wanted to help people as much as I did. He made some bad choices in life, sure, but he had a good heart. He even wanted to come with me to Rivenstorm."

"To find the resistance?" Cassian asked.

Pontius nodded. "And I told him no, that they'd be even less willing to talk to two elves."

"Do you regret it?"

"No, I don't. What I do regret is not doing something sooner." The determined set of his jaw told Cassian all he needed to know.

Pontius stayed silent as he leaned back into the couch once more, his eyes closing. Cassian stayed alert, eyes sweeping the room and snagging on Kellan each time they passed over the bar. Selwyn and the director seemed engaged in conversation, although the former looked incredibly confused. Cassian wished he had a way of listening in, but his small drop of magic wasn't enough to give him ears across a crowded and noisy room. At best, he could enhance his eyesight to read their lips, but he hadn't read lips in years. He didn't even know if he would remember how anymore.

On his fourth sweep of the room, his eyes stayed on Director

Byre's strange, black-clad guards. One appeared to be shifting on its feet in an off-putting, almost jerky motion. It was in stark contrast to their unnatural stillness before, and Cassian found himself unable to tear his eyes away as the director turned and dismissed the shifting guard.

A feeling descended upon him like a hand on his shoulder guiding him toward the retreating guard. The sensation was so strong that he thought Pontius had placed a hand on his shoulder, but when he turned to look, the man was still on the couch, eyes closed.

The feeling was like his instinctual pull he'd followed so many times before, but it was stronger now than it ever had been before.

Cassian shook Pontius awake gently but firmly. "I need you to join your sister. Now."

Pontius looked up at Cassian with bleary eyes but obeyed, standing quickly and sweeping across the room to join Selwyn at the bar. Kellan made eye contact with Cassian, nodding once to show he understood.

Cassian glanced around the room once more, then felt a pull in his gut toward a hallway nearby. He took a deep breath through his nostrils, then hurried to follow the tug.

Cassian followed the guard on silent feet down the hallway, ducking behind corners and staying far enough from his target that he could conceivably be here by coincidence. He almost needn't be so careful; the guard never glanced back once, only continued its jerky walking down the hallway, occasionally bumping into corners or tables. The tugging in his gut had stopped the instant he'd spotted the guard on his own a minute ago.

Was the guard possessed? He'd heard of spiritual and demonic possession before, but he'd never seen it with his own eyes. He wondered if this is what it looked like. Whoever was inside that suit seemed to have absolutely no control over themselves.

Suddenly, the guard stopped. Cassian followed suit, ducking into the alcove of a bathroom door to peer around the corner. And he gasped.

The guard had removed their helmet. Where their head should have been was the head of some sort of scaled dog with a pronounced snout and pointed ears. It shook its head, breath coming in short pants. It seemed the helmet had been suffocating it and it had come here to take a breather.

Whatever it was.

Even with Cassian's limited knowledge of the various races of the other continents, he'd seen nothing of this sort. This kind of creature shouldn't exist, yet here it was. What the hell was Byre doing with these things as his guards?

He ducked into the bathroom, willing his heart to calm down and keeping an ear out for footsteps. He waited several minutes before he heard the guard retreat down the hallway. He waited a little longer, ensuring the guard was truly gone before he slipped back out of the bathroom and headed back down the hall.

The air had changed—maybe it was just Cassian, and maybe it had something to do with the horrible sight he'd seen under the guard's helmet, but everything here now felt *wrong*. He could practically taste it on his tongue, its slimy air coating his lungs with every breath he took.

He walked slowly to avoid looking suspicious, especially if the guard saw him return from the same area so soon after they did. But he was wound tightly, a coil ready to spring at any moment.

When he finally arrived back at the ballroom, Pontius was already up on the stage, preparing to introduce his sister to the enamored crowd. Kellan stood at the edge of the dais with Selwyn, his shoulders tight. That air of wrongness had not dissipated. Cassian glanced around the space again, searching for the guards or any other source of this feeling.

"Welcome, esteemed people of Spiral City! On behalf of both

Morgenstern Technology Group and Northwind Medical, we are thrilled to have you join us tonight for a special gala honoring our brand-new partnership!" Pontius' voice boomed across the space, the crowd quieting to listen to him.

"As some of you may know, my name is Pontius Morgenstern. And no, I'm not the one who made this fantastic gala a reality; that honor belongs to my wonderful sister, Selwyn." A polite clap echoed through the hall. "Thanks to her hard work and dedication to creating a future where everyone can live life to the fullest, one of the most innovative partnerships to bloom in this city has officially begun."

You could never tell that Pontius had been terribly depressed over the last month with the way he spoke—his face was lit with the same fiery passion that drove so many people to back his causes and ideas. He'd captivated the audience with his enthusiasm and his words.

The tugging in his gut began again as he listened, this time pulling him toward Pontius. It was as familiar to him as his own hands, but he didn't understand what it was trying to tell him now.

Then he noticed it—no one else would have, not if they weren't looking for it. A small blue dot had positioned itself on Pontius' chest. It was miniscule enough that even Cassian could have easily missed it. As fast as his legs could carry him, Cassian dashed across the room, shoving guests aside when warranted, earning quite a few disgruntled noises along the way. The crowd was so enamored with Pontius that most hardly took notice of the man scrambling through them to get to the stage.

A shot sounded and glass shattered from somewhere behind him as he climbed on the stage and tackled Pontius, hardly caring if he broke bones on the way down. It would be better than the killing blow that was about to take Pontius' life.

A single scream echoed as they landed. Pain lanced through Cassian, then he felt nothing at all.

SHADOW

11th of Jupiter's Moon

The janitor's uniform was itchy. The man shuddered as he pulled it up over his legs and zipped the top over his chest. The man he'd taken it from lay unconscious, breathing slowly.

The man stared down at him in disgust. To have to take clothing from such a creature was revolting, but this was all Alvemach's plan. Leave no bodies this time, draw less suspicion.

He placed the long, slim case in the basket of the garbage can, pulling the bag closed over top of it. He rolled the cart slowly out into the hallway, plastering a bored look onto his face as the night receptionist glanced up at him.

"Oh, Wilson, you're a bit later than usual; I was worried something had happened to you."

The man didn't know their name. It didn't matter. "A bit of bowel trouble, nothing to worry about."

He stopped listening after she'd accepted his excuse, her rambling falling upon his deaf ears as he stepped up to the elevators and scanned his keycard. As the elevator slid closed, he lifted a hand to the receptionist, who beamed back at him.

Sickening.

The elevator slid open on the seventh floor, as high as he could go with the janitor's clearance. One of the supervisors on this floor had high-level clearance and worked late into the evening by themselves. It would be a simple task to take their card.

The man pushed the cart around the floor, not even pretending to clean. No one was here. He didn't need to keep up appearances.

Finally, he saw a sandy blonde head over the cubicles, the sound of an old analog keyboard filling the air.

The man tugged at the magic at his core, sending a small strand of it toward that head, willing them to sleep. Moments later, a heavy thump sounded, and the blonde head disappeared below the cubicles.

He took the access card hanging around their neck with a deft twist of his wrist, not even bothering to glance at their face.

The man shed the janitor's suit, tossing it into the garbage can on the cart and leaving it by the elevator. He slowly removed the case he'd stowed earlier, resting it on his feet as he rode the rest of the way up.

He made quick work of the lock to the roof, shattering it apart with a flick of his finger. Pathetic, really. The lock was mechanical, a type he hadn't seen for ages.

He hauled the case up to the lip of the roof, opening it and gleefully observing the contents inside.

The rifle was his own custom design, and it had taken months to track down the right parts when he'd put it together twenty years ago. It was just as difficult to find the right parts now with the damn council's laws against firearms. He'd needed to go all the way to Ellsemere to find the right sights.

But as he settled into place and fitted the stock against his shoulder, he knew this was the way Sol had intended for him to take lives. Not with magic, but with steel and force, gunpowder and fire. It felt *good*.

He waited patiently, cheek pressed to the stock as he watched the scene unfold through his scope. The throng of people going about their evening as if they weren't the most disgusting plague this world had ever faced. He monitored the dais in the middle. His target would be there soon enough.

He observed the rest of the room through his scope, noting the others in the room.

The heiress, who would have her day coming soon enough.

The legionnaire boy Cassian liked so much, hovering behind her.

And Alvemach, standing next to her, flanked by his two newest creations and dressed in an ostentatious white suit that made the man gag.

They'd finally agreed that she was much too distracted with her brother to be of use to them. Eliminating him now would make their objective easier.

He found their relationship disgusting.

Finally, after what felt like an eternity, the heiress' brother stepped up on the stage. The man smirked, noting the certain swagger with which he walked.

The man aligned the sights, adjusting the small pinprick of light to just below his heart, knowing the recoil would tilt the end of the barrel up slightly. No one noticed the guide.

His finger squeezed the trigger slowly—so slowly. He loved this moment, the moment right before the kill. The euphoric high he got just from aiming was better than any drug.

He pulled the trigger the rest of the way with certainty. And as the bullet left the barrel, he saw Cassian run from the crowd and leap in front of Pontius, taking the shot instead.

The man swore colorfully.

43

KELLAN

11th of Jupiter's Moon

The scream had been Selwyn, but Kellan found it hard not to scream himself.

The room was chaos, as expected after an assassination attempt. People fled toward the elevators, crowding around them as the chatter turned from expectant to terrified.

Kellan's training took over. Numbness spread down through his fingertips as he grabbed Selwyn's shoulders before she could even finish screaming. The director stood to her left, frozen in place as he stared at the stage, face unreadable. His guards moved swiftly, gathering him in their fold and escorting him away. The frenzied crowd at the elevators parted like water for him, and he disappeared quickly from the scene.

Selwyn's shoulders shook as he held on to her, shielding her from the shattered window. If the assassin tried to take a shot at her, they'd have to go through him first.

His heart was in his throat, but he was here to protect Selwyn. He needed to get her to safety before he could even hope to focus on Cassian bleeding on the dais.

"Kellan," Selwyn breathed, her voice raw. "Go, please…Pontius."

He pulled his techpad from inside his suit coat, dialing the number for the trauma team. He held Selwyn as he explained the situation, his voice steadier than he expected. When he hung up, her shaking had gotten worse.

"Let me go!" she cried, jerking in his arms as he put the techpad back in his pocket. Her struggle was weak.

He spun Selwyn around, grasping her firmly around the shoulders while keeping her away from the shattered window. "Selwyn." His voice was somehow still and steady. "I want nothing more than to run up there and help. But if I do, that would leave you open to be killed as well. I'm here to protect you."

Her mouth twisted, but he knew she would listen to logic. She stilled some, but her shoulders still jerked underneath his grip. "What if he's dead?"

"Cassian protected him. They're going to be okay." If only he believed it himself. He ignored the warning bells pealing in his head, pretending to not notice that his own hands were shaking. Not yet, he told himself. Not yet.

They stood like that until the trauma team arrived, the bright red piping of their uniforms sending a pulse of nausea through him. Two of their ranks took Selwyn away, leading her gently to the now-cleared elevators. Several others rushed past him, heading immediately toward the stage.

Kellan moved to follow but was stopped by a hand on his chest.

He recognized the girl who stopped him. She'd been there when they'd fished Tarin's body from the river. The one who'd given him some relief from the sickness he'd felt that day. Her eyes were wide, but they held his gaze steadily as he stared.

"I—" he began, but she shook her head.

"We are administering life-saving procedures right now. Stabilization magic is, ironically enough, very delicate. I can't have you interfering with the paramedic's operations."

"But..." he started again, and the numbness began fading away. Selwyn was safe, Pontius was being tended to. He had no one left to protect, and now the calm was fading from his veins. "He's my..."

He trailed off. What was he trying to say?

The paramedic smiled, although it was a sad one. "Kellan, I understand how you must be feeling." She looked behind her toward the flurry of activity and purple light that shone from the stage. "But I promise, this is for the best."

He breathed once, the panic, hot and yellow, rising in his throat like a noose threatening to strangle him. He tried to speak, tried to explain that he couldn't just wait here while Cassian was there. How could he just stand around while there was so much blood?

"You should head back to the Guard," she continued, her hand becoming firmer on his chest as she pushed. "He's in good hands."

But those hands weren't his.

"Kellan," she said again. "I know he must be special to you. But there is nothing you can do right now."

He resisted her push but didn't fight against her. So they stood in limbo, her hand on his chest, his eyes fixed on the dais. The purple glow grew stronger, then faded, then grew again. Whatever they were doing, it was a long process.

A new set of hands appeared on his shoulders. They were small but strong as they gripped his upper arms, pulling him away from the scene. He wanted to rip himself away, to fling himself across the small gap between him and the dais. They couldn't take him. He couldn't leave Cassian. He couldn't.

"Kellan," a new voice said in his ear. One he recognized. "Come on. Meridia needs to do her job, and you're being a nuisance."

He tried to speak once again, but all that came out was a choked sob.

"Thank you, Vaida," the paramedic said, finally removing her hand from his chest. "He is medically fine, but needs to leave so we can finish."

He lost whatever Vaida said to him after that—he couldn't hear anything over the rush in his ears. He focused on her hands, still on his arms, guiding him away from where he could just barely see Cassian's silvery hair. It was stained red.

She guided him gently into the elevator, turning him toward

the descending view of the city. The sparkle and splendor of it all mocked him.

There was so much blood. It had sprayed onto the microphone, the small steps leading up to the dais, and the pristine concrete floors.

His heart was too big for his chest as it thumped an uneven rhythm. The lights of the lobby were too bright as Vaida led him toward the entrance. The air outside was too thick with city smells of fried food, smoke, and excrement. He couldn't breathe.

Every sensation was too much. Every sound too loud, every light too bright.

He'd enjoyed the bustle of Spiral City ever since being assigned here—a city that really, truly, never slept. The neon signs shone at all hours of the night, always bathing the streets in a muted glow.

But tonight it was overwhelming. Tonight, it was mocking him.

If Vaida spoke to him as she loaded him into her car, he didn't hear it. If music played on the never-ending drive back to the Guard, he didn't hear it.

Or maybe he did, but it all sounded vague. What would be individual words became slurred speech, each word indecipherable from the next. What once was single notes in a song became every note being played at once.

It was like time had melted. It was all happening too fast but not fast enough. The buildings beyond the car window blurred together, streaks of blue and black and purple and green and oh god he was going to be sick.

The car stopped just as he felt the bile rise. He flung the car door open, emptying his stomach onto the pavement.

Vaida's hands were back on his shoulders as he dry-heaved out the car door, the waves passing through his body in a violent cycle of breaths in and heaving out. He could barely make out her murmuring, her fingers playing a simple melody on his upper back.

She helped him out of her car, carefully sidestepping the sickness. She flung one of his arms around her neck, then supported him around his waist.

He could walk, but he couldn't be sure where the ground met his feet. He also couldn't be sure that the absence of noise now was real or if he'd finally shut down enough to stop absorbing anything other than the feel of Vaida's arms supporting him.

They reached his rooms, the travel up to his floor immediately forgotten as soon as they reached their destination.

She helped him out of his burgundy suit, then out of the stealth suit. He forgot to be embarrassed as she methodically wrapped a towel around his waist and led him to the bathroom.

He heard only one command from her clearly. "Shower. I'll wait here."

He obeyed. He couldn't tell if the water was hot or cold; it felt like needles in his skin as he let it wash over him, dribbling into his eyes and mouth.

He didn't know how long he stood under the stream, staring at the beige tiles of the shower floor. But then the curtain was ripping back and Vaida was shutting off the water.

He heard another command, this time in a softer voice. "Dry off. Here's a towel."

He accepted the offered fabric, the scent different from the towels he usually used. It smelled like bergamot and pomegranate, a touch of lavender. If his senses were returning, it meant the panic was subsiding.

But the moment he let himself relax, the moment he thought about something other than nothing, Cassian's bloodstained hair returned in his vision.

"Come on, Kellan. You're going to freeze if you stand here like that." Vaida threw another towel over his head, drying it with a few quick rubs. The floral scent washed over him again, and he breathed deeply.

He found his voice again as they returned to his room. "How did you know?"

Vaida snorted as she opened the door. "I have friends in the

Legion other than you, you know. Meridia, the paramedic on scene, is a friend of mine."

He realized he'd never learned her name. The girl who'd held him back. Yet she'd known his, had remembered it from their brief encounter weeks before.

"I-I'm sorry."

Vaida opened his bedroom door, commanding him to sit on the bed, the towel still wrapped around his head. "You have nothing to be sorry for."

How could he explain? That he hadn't listened, that he'd been selfish, that he'd been useless once Selwyn had left?

"I just—"

Vaida stopped him with a hand, then gestured to the towel. "Stop. Not now. You've been through a hell of a day, and I don't want to hear it. You need to rest, and I already told you, apologies are unnecessary."

He obeyed, stripping the damp towel for a pair of undergarments and an oversized t-shirt. Vaida said nothing more as she pulled his comforter back, pointing to the bed like a stern mother.

When he'd settled, she pulled the covers up to his chest, then looked down her nose at him. "Sleep. And if you can't sleep, count the ceiling tiles until you can."

"Are you leaving?" A memory sparked—a similar situation, and Cassian agreeing to stay. His heart throbbed in pain.

But Vaida wasn't Cassian. "I'll be right outside. I'll sleep on the couch tonight."

He nodded as she stood, brushing off her dark, flowy pants and rolling her shoulders. Then she left, shutting the door behind her with a definitive click, and the room plunged into darkness.

His nightmare resurfaced, the knife in Cassian's back replaced by a bullet hole. Blood leaked down his navy suit, pooling in the wave that was now up to his throat.

As Cassian's blood dripped, the pool rose, covering his mouth, then his nose, then his eyes. All that was left was the silver of his hair as it continued to rise.

He choked, the metallic taste of blood filling his mouth, suffocating, blinding, and deafening him. Kellan tried to scream, to no avail.

Morning arrived quickly and brutally, the sunlight shining in his eyes. It seemed as if Sol himself was mocking Kellan, reminding him that the morning still came no matter how many people he failed. No matter how many people died because of him.

Someone knocked on his door softly.

"You awake in there?" Vaida asked through the door, her voice muffled.

Kellan tried to say something but found the words wouldn't come. Instead, a croak slipped through his lips.

The door opened, and Vaida entered, dressed and ready to go somewhere. She jostled Kellan's bedsheets. "Come on. I called the hospital, they said we can go visit now."

"He's—" Kellan could hardly form sounds through the pain and grit in his throat. "He's alive?"

She'd been there all night. She'd pushed him enough to function. She'd reminded him to calm down, to take care of himself. People considered Vaida cold, but Kellan knew better. She simply wouldn't allow you to wallow. She knew his limits and had pushed him right to the edge of them. Enough that now, in the cruel light of morning, he remembered all that had transpired and didn't feel ashamed.

What he'd done to deserve a friendship like hers, he didn't know. But the orange swell of gratitude filled his chest, nearly choking him with its intensity.

"I assume you mean Cassian, and yes, he's alive. Get up, let's go."

Relief swept through him like a cool breeze, calming his thudding heart. It hadn't stopped beating furiously since last night. "Thank Sol," he breathed.

Vaida smiled softly at him. It was the first time he'd seen such an easy expression on her face. "I know you've been worried, but they told me he's awake. Come on, put a shirt on and let's go see your boyfriend."

"He's not—"

Vaida threw a smirk over her shoulder as she yanked a shirt from his closet. "You're not fooling anyone, you know." She tossed the clothing at him casually. "Sex is good for you," she whispered.

Kellan just stared at her, open-mouthed, for several moments before she made a circle gesture with her fingers, urging him to hurry.

"Well, come on, let's go. We don't want to make him wait, do we?"

Kellan was vibrating by the time they pulled up to Northwind Medical, his nerves on fire. He was wound so tightly he was afraid a single breeze might set him loose. Vaida had driven him there, but politely declined to come up when he offered. She just told him to call her when he was ready to leave.

The medical staff on the intensive care floor were sympathetic, not commenting on Kellan's clenched jaw and clipped answers, instead responding to him with kindness. Their thoughtfulness made his chest tight. It wasn't their fault Cassian had nearly died. In fact, they'd been the ones to save him. He tried unclenching his jaw. He was only mildly successful.

The staff had hooked Cassian up to state-of-the-art machines monitoring everything from pulse to oxygen to brain activity. Everything in the room was white, from the bedsheets to the floor to the loose hospital robe they'd dressed him in. A white sheet hung from a track in the ceiling, separating Cassian's bed from another one.

Kellan nearly wept when he saw Cassian's eyes slide to meet his.

He looked as he had before, if not paler. His hair was messy, but his eyes were bright, not fogged with pain. Someone had propped him up in the bed, the frame adjusted to sit him nearly straight up. A tray sat on a small table beside him, the remnants of a breakfast waiting to be taken away. Although the air mostly smelled of antiseptic and metal, he could still pick out Cassian's musky, coffee scent through it all.

He pulled a chair from the wall and flopped into it next to the bed, his arms weak with relief. Cassian's eyes flashed, the corners of his mouth twitching as he watched Kellan's dramatic entrance.

"I thought you'd died," he breathed, feeling his eyes burn with tears. He leaned his head forward, resting it on the small space beside Cassian's legs on the bed.

He felt Cassian's hand stroke his back once before resting on his shoulder blade. "I'm fine, Kellan. I was wearing my suit, remember?"

Kellan turned his head, his cheek on the sheets. "Yeah, but they don't stop bullets. There was…a lot of blood, Cass. Not that I'm not used to it, but…" He trailed off awkwardly.

Cassian's hand began moving on his back, his thumb drawing a lazy line back and forth over his bone. He'd worn a thin t-shirt, the fabric thin enough that he could feel the heat of Cassian's hand through it. He was real. He was *alive*.

"I'm sorry, truly. I never meant to worry you."

Kellan huffed a bitter laugh, turning his face back down into the sheets. "You did what you came to do. I can't blame you for that."

Cassian's hand stopped, his fingers curling just a bit before flattening back down and continuing to stroke his back. "Thank you for worrying about me."

"Anyone would have," Kellan replied, sliding a hand under his face to look back up at Cassian again.

Cassian shook his head, a sad look passing over his face. "No, not just anyone."

Something curled in his stomach, a light and airy feeling that pushed itself up under his ribcage. "Cassian I—"

The opening of the door behind him interrupted whatever he was about to say next. A nurse entered, nodding once to Kellan as she approached the machines. She checked a few numbers, scribbling something on the large techpad she carried in her hand.

Complex charts hovered in the air before her as she worked, the projections from her techpad somehow scrambled to hide the data within. Kellan watched her work, then nodded as she left, promising to bring lunch in an hour.

Cassian's hand never left his back. He continued stroking Kellan's shoulder blade almost absentmindedly while the nurse worked, apparently not caring what she thought.

That feeling that rested beneath his rib cage swelled.

"What were you saying before?" Cassian asked quietly, his fingers distracting.

The moment was lost, though. He hadn't known what he was about to say—he'd simply let his heart do the talking.

So instead, he just shook his head. "Nothing important."

Cassian cocked an eyebrow. "If you say so."

Kellan flicked his eyes away from Cassian's intense stare, knowing if he looked too much longer, he'd say something he could never take back. "How is Pontius?"

The curtain around Cassian's bed withdrew at his question, and Kellan nearly jumped out of his skin. No one had entered the room since the nurse.

"Thank you for asking, Kellan. I'm doing well, thanks to Cassian." Pontius was apparently the other occupant of the room—and, much to his chagrin, Selwyn was here too. They'd heard everything, then.

"We're eternally in his debt," Selwyn said, nodding to Cassian. "If he hadn't intervened when he did, Pontius would surely be dead."

"Well then, it's a good thing we were there with you," Kellan replied, sitting up. Cassian's hand fell away from his back, the absence of warmth flattening the feeling in his chest.

Selwyn shifted again. "And I have you to thank as well, Kellan."

"I was just doing my job," he replied almost robotically. He'd never thought doing his job would earn him praise. He'd never expected it, had understood long ago that it would never come. After all, his job was killing, not saving.

But if that was true, what was he doing now?

Pontius turned around to sit back in his bed, his long legs folding beneath him as he met Kellan's gaze. "Even so, we were very lucky you were both there."

Kellan flicked his gaze back to Cassian and was surprised to find his jaw clenched. He met Kellan's gaze, one corner of his mouth turned slightly down. It looked like he wanted to say something, but his eyes flicked around him.

"What happened?" Kellan said, trying to be vague. He hoped Cassian would pick up on his question.

It appeared he understood. He inclined his head slightly, closing his eyes as he did. "Something you'll never believe. But the more important question is, who is after you, Pontius?" Cassian turned his gaze to the man across from him.

Kellan ignored the small voice in his head that condemned Cassian. It was Cassian's job to eliminate him. He stared at the elven man, wondering why in the world he'd chosen to save Pontius rather than let him die.

Pontius frowned, an expression that didn't suit him at all. "I'm not sure, to be honest. I'm sure I've made enemies because of my work, but I didn't think they'd be this extreme."

Cassian's brows furrowed, and Kellan resisted the urge to brush his cheek. Selwyn didn't appear surprised, though, leaning back in her chair with her arms crossed.

"Does it have something to do with what you were doing in Rivenstorm?" she asked. "Did the resistance not take kindly to you poking around in their business?"

Pontius guffawed. "They'd never take such measures."

"How do you know?" Selwyn countered.

"I just…I do, okay? They wouldn't, not against me."

"Are you sure it's even you they were targeting?" Selwyn finally uncrossed her arms to lay them in her lap.

"It was definitely him," Cassian interjected. "The target beam was directly on his chest. It was no accident. They knew he'd be there, and that's when they struck."

Kellan shifted, his leg going numb. Who would be so disgruntled with Pontius to try to kill him? He was beloved by the city. No one seemed to have a bad thing to say of him.

He had an awful thought—he remembered what Leo had said to them back at the safe house.

"Cass, what if…what if it was Leo?"

Cassian looked like Kellan had slapped him. His eyes went wide, and his lips parted. "I hadn't even considered that, but it's entirely possible. Even so, why Pontius?"

He looked at Cassian for a few moments, knowing what the answer was but not daring to speak it out loud. Cassian looked like he knew it too.

It was Selwyn that replied. "He's still after me, isn't he? I remember what he said that night…that we were important. Or at least, I was."

Cassian frowned, then swore softly. "He's probably after me, too."

Selwyn turned to look at him, her foot tapping against the floor. "I've had enough of your vague references to your own identity, Cassian. If your involvement in this is what's causing our friends to get caught up in whatever this crap is, if you're the reason Mina's dead—"

"That's rather harsh, Selwyn," Pontius began, but Selwyn held up a hand, cutting him off.

"Tell me everything. Now."

Cassian breathed, looking in that moment like a deer caught in a hunter's scope. Surprise widened his features, making him look younger. Kellan scratched the back of his neck, the tension in the room so thick he could hardly breathe. Selwyn's eyes swung to him.

"And you? Are you even Legion?"

Kellan's stomach twisted—partially in fear, partially in anger. He stood from Cassian's bedside, then turned so his back was to Selwyn, tugging his collar down so she could see the tattoo inked into his skin.

"You tell me, Selwyn. Does this look fake to you?"

She was quiet, lips pursed in a frown. Her eyes burned, and Kellan knew she was furious but had no outlet. She'd just lost her best friend, and she'd nearly lost her brother. Kellan could sympathize, but he didn't appreciate his authenticity being questioned.

He approached her to lay a hand on her shoulder. "Look, Selwyn, I know you're angry, and you have every right to be. But we're just as confused as you are. It's not like Cassian is doing this on purpose."

She stared at him, holding her breath, then let it out in one long sigh. "You're right, Kellan. I apologize. I shouldn't have blamed you."

"But she's right." Cassian's voice was rough, like he was holding himself back from screaming. "It's my fault. I'm sure Leo wouldn't be targeting you if I wasn't associating with you."

"And there's nothing to be done about that now, you know," Selwyn said. "And I heard it too—he wants me for something. It seems like this 'Leo' is doing whatever he can to isolate me. What we *need* is a plan of action."

Kellan let go of her shoulder, retreating to his chair at Cassian's bedside. "That's what we're for, Selwyn. You just focus on your brother, and we'll handle Leo."

It seemed for the moment that Cassian's identity was safe. He still didn't understand why Cassian had gone through the trouble, but he wouldn't—*couldn't*—be the one to blow Cassian's cover.

"Fine," Selwyn finally said. "I'm trusting you, conditionally. Find who did this to Pontius. After that, we will discuss this again. I am dissatisfied with your answers, but they'll have to do for now."

Cassian bowed his head. "Thank you, Selwyn. We won't let you down."

Her cool ocean eyes turned to Kellan, and he resisted the urge to squirm. Instead, he nodded. "You can count on both of us."

SECTION 5

THE HELLS AREN'T JUST FOR DEMONS

In Ileron (and, consequently, in parallel versions of Ileron's material plane), there exists another plane besides the material and the ethereal—the infernal plane. On the infernal plane, there are nine distinct sections, called the Hells.

Each layer of Hell has its own unique geography and nature, and some planes are larger than others.

Travel through the planes is not simple. One must travel through each plane to get to subsequent layers. For example, one cannot travel directly to the fourth plane of the Hells without first traveling through layers one through three.

The layers of Hell are as follows:

Avernus, made of basalt and bone
Dis, made of metal and concrete
Minarus, made of swamp and clay
Phelgetos, made of obsidian and brimstone
Stygia, made of ice and freezing water
Malbolge, made of flesh and slate
Maladomini, made of marble and decaying rock
Cania, made of snow and glaciers
Nessus, made of limestone and lava rock

Nessus is the domain of the King of Demons, Asmodeus. Very little is known about the mysterious overlord, and thus, he is deeply feared by those on the material plane.

Demons aren't the only ones that can travel to the infernal plane, but it is, once again, not easy. One must have a demonic escort in order to access the Hells. However, one can access the Hells after death. If rejected by Jupiter, a soul is sent to the Hells, where it is reborn as a low-level demon.

44

SHADOW

14th of Jupiter's Moon

They were close. So close.

A scrawny half-elf sat strapped to the chair before him, unconscious, with a trickle of blood leaking from her temple. They'd found her shooting up something in a back alley in Rookford Down.

No one would miss her, which the man had discovered was an easier way to gather specimens. Although not ideal, as they weren't as strong as healthy individuals once turned, they were still preferable to nothing. And they were always eager to follow the promise of a new high.

Alvemach was here, hands clasped behind his back as he waited for the man to finish preparations. He'd asked to sit in. Since the disastrous attempt at assassinating the elven socialite, he'd become almost overbearing.

The man scoffed silently as he remembered how Cassian had leaped in front of his target without a second thought. That sort of behavior had two sides. Some found it admirable, a trait that spoke to a person's goodness.

The thought made him sick. It wasn't about goodness. An act like that was nothing more than selfishness, in his opinion.

Everyone would die someday. Why should you bother to save

someone when your efforts would go to waste? The act of saving someone when it was their time to die? Selfishness, and nothing more.

But he was sure Cassian would see it his way someday. Someday soon.

The half-elf in the chair stirred, groaning as she shifted beneath the bonds. The man didn't look up from the table, dipping the glass stirring stick into the mixture and swirling it a few times before grabbing a syringe.

"I'm expecting results, Shadow," Alvemach's voice said from behind him. "You've pushed my patience far enough."

The man tamped down the flicker of annoyance that pulsated through him at the comment. "I'm aware, Alvemach. This will work, I'm sure of it."

The demon prince said nothing further, and the man didn't push. Faced with the multitudes of failures they'd been through already, he wasn't in the mood to speak. He was positive this would work.

The syringe filled slowly, the deep red liquid almost making the measurements on the glass disappear.

He wasn't nervous. He wasn't sure what that emotion even felt like anymore. He was simply ready for what was to come next, confident in his abilities to create exactly what they'd been hoping for this whole time.

Their test subject squirmed weakly beneath the bonds. She was finally coming to, it seemed. The man smiled as he approached, syringe in hand.

"What—" the woman in the chair began, but was abruptly cut off by the jab of the syringe in her arm.

The man smiled down at his victim. "Soon. Soon you'll be so much more."

She did not reply.

The transformation was slow but steady—a good sign. Hard scales replaced soft skin, the gray of her eyes liquefied into gold, and the tips of her fingers elongated into sharp points. Yes, all good signs.

She choked, the bonds groaning against her thrashing as the transformation overtook her body. A bit of blood spilled from the corner of her mouth, trickling down her chin and onto her neck.

Then, when the scales finally reached her face, the man stepped forward and released the bonds.

The creature before him did not move, prone on the chair and looking for all the world as if it was asleep. But he knew better.

He tugged at the cord that had formed behind his navel, tied to his magic. "Wakey wakey."

The demon's eyes snapped open, yellow meeting his with a ferocity he couldn't fabricate. Excellent.

It snarled when they made eye contact, jerking up from the chair, panting with bloodlust. The man tugged the cord, willing it to heel.

It obeyed. The man smiled. The final piece of the puzzle was in place. It was time to begin.

45

KELLAN

16th of Jupiter's Moon

They'd released Pontius from the hospital quickly, but Cassian had needed longer to recover. Kellan had gone to visit him nearly every day. They had finally released him that morning, much to their relief.

He'd made no further progress with his investigation. He still didn't know how Alvemach, Leo, and Northwind Medical were all connected.

He'd relegated himself to patrols instead. They were monotonous, but he hoped it would turn up something. He'd taken to visiting Cassian during the day and patrolling at night since it seemed the killer enjoyed dumping bodies under the cover of darkness.

This evening was no different. Cassian had sat up on his own without the support of the pillows, and the nurse had said they were nearly ready to take his sutures out. The thought warmed his stomach as a cold breeze blew down an alleyway he passed three blocks from Northwind Medical.

Kellan puffed warm air into his hands in a vain attempt to warm them up, but he could tell the winter chill was truly setting in now.

Movement caught his eye from down the alleyway, and he turned to see a young seraph man injecting himself with something. *Great,* he thought. It was his duty to take them into custody, especially since he'd just witnessed him taking the drug.

Kellan stopped at that thought—the drug. What if it was the same stuff that killed Liza and Tarin? His hands shook, and not from the cold.

He approached the man, who was now doubled over against the wall, his breath coming in short gasps.

"Hey, you! You all right?" he said, not wanting to startle the man.

He looked at Kellan as he called out, and his stomach dropped. His face—there was something wrong with his face.

Before his eyes, he watched the man's nose grow and elongate, turning from a normal, humanoid face into a horrid cross between man and dog. He took another step, and the man collapsed to the ground, gripping his hair between his fingers and pulling it out. Beneath, scales were growing.

Kellan retched slightly at the sight, but continued forward. "Can you hear me? I need you to tell me where you got that drug from!"

The man ignored him, hunched over the ground and gasping for breath as scales began covering his once-pale skin. It looked like insects were sprouting from beneath his flesh. Kellan retched again.

He finally reached the man, now almost entirely covered in scales, and noticed he'd sprouted scaled ears atop his head. When he reached a hand out to help the man up, he finally stopped writhing. Something in Kellan recoiled, telling him to run. *Now.*

The man-turned-demon lifted his head to look at him, eyes now slitted and yellow and bloodshot to hell. He'd seen eyes like that before—on Tarin and on Liza.

The demon snarled, its back curving like an angry cat's, and Kellan saw its elongated canines. Its hands had lengthened into sharp points, each tipped in a black claw that looked sharp enough to slice a man in two.

Kellan stepped back slowly, his eyes never leaving the monstrosity before him as he drew his sword from the sheath on his back.

It lunged faster than any person should be able to move,

launching itself toward Kellan's throat. He crumpled, sliding himself between the demon's legs as it careened toward him and springing up behind with his sword drawn. He had the advantage at this distance, but he absolutely could not let the demon get close, not with those claws.

It turned, its tongue wagging out the side of its open mouth, saliva dripping to the ground. It snarled and leapt again.

Kellan slashed forward, bringing his sword down in a graceful arc intended to cut someone from shoulder to hip diagonally, but was met with resistance. The demon's scales were as hard as any metal, and he didn't see any gaps. Kellan swore silently to himself. Was this how it would end?

No. He couldn't afford to panic, not now. Not when he thought he finally understood what the hell was going on here.

Northwind Medical was manufacturing demons.

The demon slashed forward again, cutting a similar arc to Kellan's previous move. He parried, the demon's claws clanging against the steel of his blade.

They continued their dance, neither one gaining the upper hand, both lunging and slashing at every chance they got. Kellan needed to think of something, and *fast,* or he was as good as dead. But no opportunity presented itself. The dance continued.

As fast as an asp, the demon lunged, hooking a claw under his blade at just the right angle to wrench it from his grasp. It went skidding across the pavement, and both Kellan and the demon paused to watch it. It came to rest several feet away from where they stood. Kellan swore out loud.

The demon just grinned, a mockery of the gesture. It looked more like a snarl, but Kellan knew it was teasing him.

He dove, rolling under the demon's extended claws in a desperate dash to recover his sword. He had a small dagger, but it wouldn't be enough to face off against the monster.

The demon must have sensed his intentions. It aimed for his throat once again. Still on the ground, Kellan got both feet in front of him and kicked with as much force as he could muster. His feet landed squarely in the middle of the demon's chest, throwing it across the alleyway. It landed with a crash on a metal staircase.

Kellan wrapped a hand around the hilt of his sword once more, victorious.

He heard a door open into the alley. Someone must be coming to investigate the ruckus. A head poked out, immediately finding a battered Kellan standing in the alley, sword drawn.

"Get back inside, *now*," he said.

The bystander's eyes grew wide, but they listened. He heard a lock click after the door swung closed.

The demon had recovered now and was shaking its head as it stalked toward him once more. Kellan's stomach grew leaden as he lowered his sword, adjusting his grip and facing his opponent.

A disturbance crackled through the air like lightning preparing to strike. Behind the demon, a purple swirl appeared. Kellan remembered the magic from what Cassian had told him and what he'd seen Leo do. But what was this portal for?

A hand reached out, then a head emerged. Kellan's jaw dropped.

"Nice to see you, Legionnaire," Leo said, his voice dripping with malice. "Give my regards to Cassian. I'm sorry I couldn't stay and chat, but our friend here needs to come with me."

Before Kellan had time to think, Leo snapped his fingers, and the demon turned toward the portal, following him through it as if in a trance. Leo's laughter echoed through the alleyway as the portal snapped closed.

Kellan swore again, sheathing his sword as he calculated the trajectory of the portal. It was facing Northwind Medical, and that made things even more complicated.

Kellan stared up at the monolithic hospital built of iron and glass. He knew what needed to come next. And he didn't like it. Not one bit.

46

SHADOW

16th of Jupiter's Moon

The magic needed to disguise oneself wasn't excessive, especially not to fool someone as trusting as the man standing just a few feet away.

He looked well, considering what he'd just been through, and that irked the man. He'd infuriatingly survived an assassination attempt and had come out the other side looking no worse for the wear.

The dark circles around his eyes were a different story.

He watched his target from the safety of an alleyway, the light fading from late afternoon into dusk. The shadows grew longer by the minute. Many found this time to be magical—he simply found it convenient.

The man breathed slowly, imagining the magic spreading out from where it lay in his navel, spreading outward like water on a cloth. It ran through his veins, his muscles, his bones, elongating his ears and shortening his hair. Better to approach as a species his target would trust.

When their last plan had failed, they'd moved on quickly to the next. It would be quite unlike Alvemach to approach any situation without several backups. This one would surely not fail, not if the man had anything to say about it.

"Excuse me," he said, willing his voice a few steps higher than it usually was. He imagined the look on the faces of his test subjects, then adopted it himself. Pity me, he thought, as the other man turned to look at him.

His brilliant blue eyes still held a bit of sparkle. The man would take pleasure in wringing that from him. "Oh, hello! Can I help you with something?"

So trusting, so naïve. "I'm afraid I'm lost, you see. I'm hoping you can assist me?"

A flash of a brilliant white smile, and he knew he'd won. "Of course, I'd be happy to."

He led the man away from the street, from prying eyes that may recognize him, that might report him. The man didn't need *more* legionnaires sniffing around. He'd dealt with them enough in recent weeks.

How Cassian could become attached to such a pathetic slave of the state was a mystery to the man. They were nothing but puppets. As he'd been, once.

But he'd broken free of those shackles. He'd gained power.

The shadows grew even longer as they wandered down a side alley, finally deep enough that he could do what needed to be done.

He chained his target the same way he'd once chained his sister, the magic flowing from his fingertips as easily as breathing. He struggled, but the man knew he'd never break free.

His portal glimmered, chasing away the shadows they'd so carefully found. But it didn't matter.

He'd won.

The final steps of their plans were crawling forward. The rest was up to Alvemach.

47

KELLAN

16th of Jupiter's Moon

He still remembered how to get to Cassian's safe house, although he thought perhaps it wasn't the best thing he knew where it was by heart.

Kellan knocked on the door loudly, hoping Cassian would hear him. The street was eerily quiet, as if it knew something heinous was about to happen.

He shifted on his feet as he waited, too aware of his sword strapped to his back. Too aware of how his heart thudded against his ribcage like it was desperate to be anywhere but in his chest.

Cassian answered, wincing as he opened the door. His wound wasn't fully healed yet. Kellan could sympathize; his own shoulder was twinging.

Although Kellan had seen Cassian in sweatpants and t-shirts before, seeing that same outfit tonight set something off in him he didn't have time for. His attraction to Cassian was the least important thing right now.

"Kellan," Cassian said, his eyebrows raised. "What—"

"I need to talk to you," Kellan cut him off, stepping up close to Cassian as an ask to come inside.

Cassian obliged, stepping aside to allow Kellan in.

He made his way to the sofa, plopping himself down

unceremoniously. How should he even explain what he'd seen tonight? More importantly, how in the world were they going to infiltrate Northwind Medical?

His head was pounding as Cassian set a cup of coffee down in front of him, cream still swirling inside.

"Thanks," Kellan said, grabbing the mug with both hands. "I don't even know where to begin."

"Try the beginning," Cassian replied. Kellan threw him an exasperated look, to which he responded with a small grin. His stomach did an annoying flip-flop.

He sighed, sipped the coffee, and set it back down on the table. "I was attacked tonight out on patrol. By a demon that was once a seraph. But before I could do anything, Leo came and took the demon."

"What?" Cassian said, practically jumping up out of his seat.

"I think I was right, but I still don't understand Leo's involvement." He leaned in close, not knowing if the walls had ears. "Northwind Medical is manufacturing demons with that drug that killed Liza and Tarin."

He leaned in, one arm snaking on the couch behind Cassian and the other dangerously close to Cassian's thighs. From this angle, he could see Cassian's pulse pounding in his throat. Cassian didn't move either, his hands gripping the coffee mug tightly. His breaths tickled Kellan's ear.

Kellan leaned forward, placing his head on Cassian's shoulder and letting the tension and adrenaline that had been keeping him awake at night for the last two months melt out of him. Just long enough to soak in Cassian's nutty scent, feel his warmth, and feel like something, *anything,* might finally go right as long as he could say by Cassian's side.

Cassian didn't move for a few moments, silent and still. He shifted, but before Kellan could lift his head, he felt a hand on his back, stroking gently down the curve of his spine and back up, leaving goosebumps in its wake.

"Cassian," Kellan whispered against his shoulder.

"Just wait," he replied. "Just wait a moment. Stay here, like this."

"Okay."

And they did, Kellan resting his forehead upon Cassian's shoulder and Cassian's soft strokes upon his back calming the maelstrom of emotions that had festered in the pit of his stomach. Something soft shone through at the touch, something light, something healing. Kellan saw it when he closed his eyes.

Cassian's hand left his back after a few moments, but it quickly reappeared under his chin, pulling his head up. Kellan's bronze eyes met Cassian's sea-green ones.

Kellan's lips parted in anticipation, but Cassian didn't pull him in. Instead, he stared. The gray of his eyes swirled away and the green around the irises dominated. His hand snaked behind Kellan's head, pulling their heads together, touching their foreheads to one another.

"I'll follow you, Kellan," he whispered. "Sol knows why, but I will follow you until death claims me or this shitstorm has ended. I promise you that."

Kellan felt the tears well up, his vision going hot and blurry at the words. This was a declaration—not only of the intent to see this through to the end, but of companionship, and dare he think it, affection.

"Until death claims us or this shitstorm is over, Cass. I promise you that too."

They stayed still, foreheads pressed together, for several more moments, Kellan letting Cassian's warmth seep into him. It drove away the last of the chill from the late fall weather and the fight he'd barely survived.

"Kellan," Cassian began, finally removing his hand from the back of Kellan's head. He didn't like the tone of worry in Cassian's voice.

"What is it?"

"I never got to tell you what I saw that night at the gala," he replied. His face was pinched with worry.

Kellan stayed silent, eyes wide with anticipation. What had he seen? Something that would help them?

"The director, he was"—Cassian paused, biting his lip—"well his guards were…ah, how do I put this? I think his guards were demons."

"So my theory is even more plausible," Kellan replied. His heart was doing a fluttering waltz behind his ribcage, the knowledge that everything was connected sending his body into overdrive. "Then that must mean—"

"That the director really is connected to all this," Cassian finished for him.

Kellan drew his hands up into his hair, gripping the short strands as he pondered the situation. There was a sense of impending doom hanging over him, and the revelation that the most powerful man in Northwind Medical was part of the plot only added weight to the heavy feeling of catastrophe that choked the air.

"So what are we supposed to do, then?" Kellan hated the way his voice sounded. Small, pathetic, like a lost child.

Cassian's hand came to rest on his knee. "I don't know, but we'll figure this out. Together."

Kellan nodded just as his techpad dinged. At the same moment, Cassian's did as well.

It was Selwyn.

Emergency—Pontius is missing.

Kellan looked up at Cassian, whose hand was still resting on his knee, the other holding his techpad and gazing at it with concern.

"We have to do something," Kellan said, then bit his lip. What if Cassian didn't want to help? He theoretically shouldn't, considering the terms of their agreement should have been violated back when Selwyn and Mina were kidnapped.

It didn't look, however, like Cassian was ready to give up or turn him down. "I'll ask Selwyn to meet us."

He dialed her number, holding the techpad to his ear as he

waited. When she answered, he set her on speaker so both of them could hear.

"Selwyn?" Kellan said. "What do you mean 'Pontius is missing?'"

"Exactly what I said," she began. Her voice sounded strained. "He was supposed to be home three hours ago, but he's nowhere to be found."

Kellan swallowed, but Cassian stayed calm. "Are you sure he's not visiting a friend or staying out later than he told you?"

Selwyn huffed. "I would check these things before calling you in a panic. I'm not stupid."

"I wasn't implying you were."

"He's not in any of his regular places. I can't contact him on his techpad either, and he's usually so good about getting back to me." She paused, the silence thoughtful. "Especially lately, we've been really careful about communicating frequently with each other."

Kellan's heart twisted. He could see Cassian's mouth twist down into a frown at Selwyn's words. He wondered if he felt the same way, that he had irrevocably broken something simply by existing in their lives.

Cassian recovered more quickly than Kellan. "Where was he last seen?"

"He was getting a checkup at Northwind Medical. In fact, I'm there now."

Kellan felt the air turn cold. Cassian's hand squeezed his knee tightly. "Selwyn, leave. Now."

"I can't, I've got an important meeting with the director. I'm about to be late. Just…please. Find my brother. He needs you."

"But—"

She cut him off. "I really must go. I'll message you when my meeting is over."

Kellan looked at Cassian, meeting his eyes as he clenched his jaw. This didn't bode well for anyone, but especially the Morgensterns. They had precious little time to find Pontius before…

Well, Kellan thought, before the worst.

Kellan clenched his jaw again. Cassian's hand squeezed his knee again before finally letting go. He missed the warmth.

"You heard her," Cassian began. "And that means we're running against the clock."

CASSIAN

16th of Jupiter's Moon

"Do you have any idea where they might take him?" Kellan asked, worry in his eyes. "I assume it's somewhere in the hospital since Leo took the demon I found in the alleyway this direction."

Cassian already missed the feeling of Kellan's leg beneath his hand, but he'd pushed his luck already by keeping it there as long as he had. They had other things to focus on. Rescuing Pontius was the most imperative.

Some part of him asked why. After all, he was here to kill Pontius, and allowing him to be kidnapped was a perfect excuse. But he still hadn't fulfilled the rest of the terms of the contract, and he knew the council would be furious if he didn't follow their instructions to the letter.

He shook his head. "I haven't had the chance to review any floor plans of the hospital. It wasn't relevant, and there are too many variables for me to simply guess at it."

"So you're saying that we need a better plan?"

"At the very least, we need floor plans. And more weapons."

Kellan's lips curled into a feral smile. It was a rather eerie one, especially on a face like Kellan's. He stared a moment too long at that smile, those lips upon which it rested.

Kellan shifted on his feet but said nothing else. Cassian could almost sense his anxiety, the desire for action *right now* rather than taking a step back and preparing properly. He couldn't let Kellan be reckless. Not now.

"Kellan," Cassian started, standing from the couch. "Promise me you won't be reckless. Let me handle Leo. You get Pontius and Selwyn out."

"But Cass—"

Cassian cut him off with a hand. "I'm serious. I can't lose you, too." He hadn't meant to let the 'too' slip. Refusing to acknowledge it, he continued, "Leo is dangerous. And he wants me. He'll take the bait while you get them out."

"When I do, I'm coming back for you," Kellan said. He'd sunk back into the couch after Cassian stood, his arms crossed over his chest. He stared at Cassian, his chin jutting forward slightly, daring him to challenge.

He did no such thing. Instead, he ignored the lurching of his stomach at the expression. "Fine, but there will be nothing left of Leo after I'm done with him."

The feral smile returned. "Be careful, Cassian, you might just make me fall for you when you talk like that."

Cassian ignored the blush creeping up his cheeks as he turned away, heading for the staircase. "I'm going to gather some weapons. Stay here. We'll figure out a plan once I'm done."

His trove of weapons was upstairs, still in the case he'd brought from Ebenfell nearly two months ago. He'd lost a few—namely, the ones he'd brought to the gala. Luckily, they had mostly been smaller daggers. Unfortunately, it meant he had no short-range weapons left. He wondered if he could borrow one from Kellan.

As he sheathed his sword upon his back, his techpad dinged. Now wasn't the time, he thought as he reached for it.

But his stomach dropped when he read the name.

Ragnor was calling.

Was he out of time? Had Ragnor finally decided to take him off the job? This wasn't their usual check-in time, and that made him panic.

"Good evening, sir," he answered as casually as he could.

"Evermore, I have a bit of news." Ragnor sounded calm. His voice set Cassian's nerves on edge. When Ragnor was calm, one could expect one of two things: imminent death, or praise. You were never sure which it was, however.

He didn't wait for Cassian to reply. "Your mission is complete. You should return to Ebenfell this evening."

Cassian nearly dropped his techpad. Complete? What the hell did that mean? He had done nothing yet. He hadn't fulfilled the terms of the contract. He knew nothing that could damn Pontius. He hadn't even laid a finger upon him.

"Sir?" He couldn't figure out how to ask what Ragnor meant. He didn't want to be blunt for fear of incurring his wrath, but he also couldn't hang up without asking.

"Did you not hear me?" Ragnor's calm voice was touched with annoyance now. "Your mission. It's complete. The conditions have been fulfilled. Return at once."

"I—"

"Cassian?" Kellan's voice called up the stairs. "Everything all right?"

"Ah." Ragnor sounded amused. Cassian wondered if he would get the wrong idea about Kellan's purpose at the safehouse. Although he approved of his contractors enjoying themselves, Cassian knew he'd be enraged if he knew who Kellan actually was.

"I will grant you until the morning, I suppose. Have your fun this evening, and return tomorrow morning." Ragnor continued.

He didn't wait for Cassian's response this time. The techpad's disconnecting click rang in Cassian's ears. It was probably for the best, anyway, that Cassian didn't address Kellan's presence.

Kellan appeared in the doorway, his brows knit together in concern. Cassian didn't know how to respond as Kellan leaned against the doorframe, waiting for his answer.

"You all right?" he said, his tone softer than it had been earlier. It was as if he could sense something had gone wrong. "Who were you talking to?"

"My mission, it's…" He trailed off, unsure how to even explain.

Did Ragnor somehow know Pontius had gone missing? But that didn't explain how he'd needed to find something about Pontius to expose him. Even if Pontius had been kidnapped by Northwind, it was all wrong. He could die before Cassian could expose him like the council had commanded him to do.

Kellan strode inside to where Cassian still knelt by his weapons stash. He glanced at the weapons, then Cassian's holsters, then closed the lid for him.

"No matter what happened, you need to stand up. We have to save Pontius."

"I—I don't think I'm supposed to."

Kellan looked taken aback. "What do you mean?"

"Ragnor, the man who owns my contract. He called. Said my mission was complete." Cassian was cold. Maybe Ragnor had simply said it was over to dismiss him from the case. But Ragnor wouldn't have sounded so calm if that was so. Ragnor might have been many things, but he was honest with his employees. Usually, that didn't bode well for them; but in rare cases like this, it meant Cassian could trust what he'd said.

Which meant he hadn't been lying when he told Cassian his mission was complete. If he was simply dismissing him, that would have been the message.

Kellan crossed his arms. "Why's that a problem? It means you're free."

"But if I end up saving him and Ragnor finds out…"

"Then Ragnor won't find out."

Cassian stood and faced Kellan. "What's that supposed to mean?"

"When all this is over, Cassian, I want to help you. I don't want this to be the end." His eyes were sparkling now, a fierce determination in them that made Cassian's heart leap. "I can't help it. I feel like I have to stay close to you."

"You do? Why?"

Kellan flushed, his cheeks turning a wonderful shade of red as he glanced down. "I-I don't really understand it myself, but—"

Cassian stepped up close to him, close enough that their breaths intermingled. His own heart pounded in his ears, keeping time with the pulse he could see in Kellan's throat.

"You feel something for me, don't you?" His own boldness surprised him, but something like relief flooded his veins. He'd felt it too, that shift.

Kellan didn't acknowledge his question. Instead, he stared, his lips parting as he breathed in large sighs.

A mischievous part of him rose to the surface. He lifted his hand as if to touch Kellan's cheek, but dropped it to the dagger strapped to Kellan's thigh instead, removing it from its sheath.

"I'm coming with you, regardless of what happens with Ragnor after this," he said, sliding the blade out carefully. "But I'm unfortunately out of daggers." Cassian, perturbed by his own boldness, leaned away, sheathing the dagger at his own thigh as he did.

Before he could get far, Kellan grabbed him by the front of his suit, fingers knotting in the stretchy, thick fabric as he yanked. Cassian allowed himself to be pulled, savoring the moment before the fall.

Their lips met, a moment suspended in time. The spark that had ignited in Cassian roared to a full flame. Every nerve sparkled, each place they touched flooding with a thousand volts of electricity. Their mouths moved fervently, like if they stopped dancing along each other's lips they might die a spectacular, fiery death.

The need filled his head, every thought of Pontius, of Ragnor, of Leo, draining out in a stream to be replaced and filled with Kellan and only Kellan.

He tasted like alcohol and something sweet, the mix of flavors dancing across his tongue. It was intoxicating, enough to make

Cassian sway on his feet. At this, Kellan pulled away, concern creasing his features.

"That was okay, right?" His lips were slightly swollen. Cassian couldn't stop staring at them as he nodded.

Kellan just smirked, his eyes half-lidded as he leaned back in to plant another kiss atop Cassian's lips.

This kiss didn't last nearly as long. Kellan pulled away rather quickly, to Cassian's disappointment, and turned toward the door, glancing over his shoulder. He threw another cocky smirk as he did.

"I had Vaida send me the schematics," he said, as if the kiss had never happened at all. He paused, letting his smirk deepen. "And, as much as I'd love to stay here and kiss you all night, we have people to save."

Cassian could feel that fire still singing along his bones, vibrating his blood, and spreading goosebumps down the back of his neck. He was simultaneously hot and cold, flying and falling.

And there, in the smallest part of his heart, he felt something growing, something that before the kiss had been small and easily ignored. But now it grew enough to blanket his heart with warmth and softness, to give him pause when Kellan's hand extended toward him. His hands tingled with the anticipation of simply *touching his skin*.

He knew this was a dangerous path to walk; beginning something with Kellan was inviting trouble. But he also didn't care. Each step he'd taken on the path to this moment had been calculated until he'd met Kellan. Every moment carefully counted and measured, each path woven with intricacies no one else could see but him. But the moment he'd seen Kellan in that garden in Lunadere, he'd felt a shift. Something had changed that day. Now he knew what it was.

He hadn't even felt this with Aidyn. It had been like a ray of sun with Aidyn, warm, comforting, small, cherished. This was a raging inferno, not quenched with a small cloud or a bit of rain. Something that roared and burned with such intensity it scared him.

But he looked at Kellan's outstretched hand, feeling like he was full of something living and entirely too big for his body, and he reached. He clasped Kellan's calloused, rough hand with his own. He felt the bones of his hand and knuckles rise and fall like the tides beneath his own fingers.

He knew at that moment that everything he'd done until now was to get him here. To be filled with this feeling that he couldn't explain. And he decided it was worth it. Worth it all to be here with him.

49

SHADOW

16th of Jupiter's Moon

He'd been busy today—first the socialite, then the demon. He had an inexorable link to those who'd turn because of their serum. He always knew where they were. And this one had turned soon after he'd dropped the woman's brother in the room next door.

That legionnaire was there, something he hadn't expected. But no matter—it was too late to stop them.

Alvemach would arrive soon. Until then, he could wait. He heard the muffled sounds of thumping in the next room and smiled to himself.

The idea had been Alvemach's: capture the girl's brother and force her into a pact as well, using him as leverage. If she refused, they'd use him for tests. Either way, it was a low-risk plan.

The original plan to kill him to chip away at her support system hadn't worked. This was Plan B.

The man they'd captured was in his own room, unbound but locked in from the outside. He'd been quite easy to take, the man thought with a little thrill of self-satisfaction.

Good people were easy to manipulate.

He heard footsteps approaching and a snippet of conversation.

"Now Selwyn, don't be difficult. I'd like for you to work with us willingly."

A laugh, bitter and cold. *"Willingly?* And why would I do that?"

"For Pontius, of course. And your sweet little assassin friends as well."

Alvemach had already gotten her down here, it seemed. She was so trusting of the man she'd thought was Ronson Byre.

Little did the heiress know, Byre hadn't existed on this plane for many, many years.

The footsteps continued, and the man turned to face the hallway from which they approached. Obviously, from their conversation, he could guess that the woman had seen her brother, locked in a lab and ready to fulfill his purpose.

The door to the main laboratory opened, a sliver of light slicing through the concrete floor and stopping where the man stood.

Alvemach flicked on the lights, and the man's smile stretched his lips thin.

"You," the woman snarled. "How dare you?"

The man shrugged. "I don't know what you mean, little heiress. You should be more specific."

She was red, her face nearly matching her hair. "You know exactly what I mean. You've kidnapped my brother! You killed my best friend!"

The man waved a hand dismissively. Such paltry things to be caught up in. She would benefit from regarding death as a step in the right direction rather than a thing that must be avoided. It was a plague, this way of thinking.

He was so very close to changing that.

Alvemach stepped into the room after her, then shut the door behind them. She didn't seem to notice; instead, she continued staring daggers at him.

The man chuckled. She'd see reason soon.

"I thought you were a woman of innovation?" he said, watching Alvemach's smile curl his lips.

She narrowed her eyes. "Not like this. Never like this. This is *wrong.*"

"Only by mortal standards," Alvemach said dismissively. "You'll realize this soon as well."

She whirled, her gaze finally leaving the man and turning to Alvemach. "What's that supposed to mean?"

The man whistled softly, and the demon he'd fetched earlier emerged from the shadows, its claws dragging on the floor. The noise sent chills up the man's neck. Delightful.

The heiress, to her credit, didn't scream. Her mouth dropped open, suspended in a gasp, her face frozen in fear. It was, he thought, one of his favorite expressions mortals could make.

"Wh—" she breathed, then recovered. "What in Sol's name is that?"

Alvemach smiled. "The future."

She looked horrified as the demon continued toward her. He didn't bother speaking again. Alvemach would handle her.

Her next words were spoken softly, as if she couldn't quite bring herself to speak at full volume. "What kind of future could you possibly want with this?"

Alvemach laughed, all honey and beauty and disgust. "Isn't it obvious, Miss Morgenstern? We will remake the world. Reborn. And we want your help to create it."

The heiress backed away, swallowing heavily as her chest rose and fell. "I want no part of this. Let me go."

This was what the man had been waiting for, the moment they'd reveal their great plan.

Alvemach smiled. "I'm afraid we can't do that, Selwyn. See, we need you to finish what we've begun. You are pivotal to the success of this. But if we cannot convince you of your own will…"

He trailed off, then nodded at the man.

"Well then, I suppose we will just need to force you."

50

KELLAN

16th of Jupiter's Moon

His head was fuzzy as they walked back downstairs, his blood vibrating inside his body.

He'd *done* it. He'd actually kissed Cassian. And he'd wanted to stay, to continue the question that the kiss had posed. But it wasn't the time. The answer that now hovered between them would simply have to wait.

"You said Vaida got you the schematics? Can you send them to me? I can pull them up on my techpad," Cassian said as he dug through a backpack on the floor by the couch.

He revealed a large tabletop techpad, one that would make finding the small details in the schematics easier. It was certainly better than trying to look at it on their handhelds.

They sat on the couch, Cassian propping the screen before them. Kellan got to work sending over the file Vaida had given him, trying not to pay too close attention to the fact that their knees were touching.

He stole a glance at Cassian's profile, his strong nose outlined by the light above them, his silvery hair curling down into his eyes. The lips he'd just tasted. It was tempting, the desire to taste them again, but he resisted.

Cassian's device dinged, and he opened the hologram,

manipulating it with two fingers.

It looked like any schematic he'd seen before, he supposed. He could make out the upper floors of the diagram and a room that looked ornate enough to be the director's office.

But there were almost *too* many floors. It was hard to tell with a massive structure like Northwind Medical, but even then, it was too much.

"Kellan, look," Cassian said, pointing at a small doorway in the diagram. "This is the main entrance."

He looked to where Cassian's finger rested, finally realizing what had seemed off about the diagram.

There were subterranean floors.

He supposed it wasn't all that surprising, really, considering the Guard and the parliament building both had them as well. But his heart still pounded in his chest.

"I didn't see any buttons for lower floors in the elevators, though," Kellan commented, closing his eyes to visualize the elevator's buttons. Although he'd only seen them once, he was confident enough in his memory.

Cassian scratched his chin. "Then there must be some other way to get there." He trailed off, searching the diagram for any sign of how that might be possible.

Kellan's eyes strained. The elevators didn't go down that far; they stopped at the main floor. It seemed the public staircases were more of the same. Every route they thought of seemed to result in a dead end.

"Wait, Kellan, look," Cassian said, pointing to the very top of the diagram.

There—it was exactly what they needed. A private elevator ran from the director's office all the way to those inaccessible basement floors.

And it seemed they were a new construction. They'd been added right as the director had taken the position a few years prior. If that wasn't suspicious, Kellan didn't know what was.

"We'll have a tough time getting into the office, though," Kellan mused. "I'd offer to fly us up there, but I'm not sure what kind of security he's got on his windows. I don't want to risk finding out while carrying you."

Cassian nodded. "Caution is best here. Unfortunately, my magic won't be enough to get us anywhere, truthfully. I can unlock simple spells, but I don't have the power to get through the security that's sure to be there."

Kellan scratched the back of his neck. Beck would have known what to do; strategy had been a strong suit of his. A challenge like this would have been fun for him. But Kellan had never been as good as his best friend. He wished, not for the first time, that Beck could be here now.

But he wasn't, and there was another person they could rely on.

"Cassian, I have an idea," he began slowly. "I think Vaida could help us. But I won't involve her if you think it's a bad decision."

Cassian cocked an eyebrow. "What does she do?"

"She was the one who analyzed Tarin's syringe for us. She's my lab technician. Much smarter than I am. She'll know what to do."

He looked unsure, so Kellan continued.

"She's indentured, like me." He didn't know if it would help, but he risked it anyway.

Cassian stayed silent, chewing his lip. If he said no, it wasn't the end, but it would certainly make things harder. Vaida could be an asset to them, especially with technology.

"Why not your other friends, the ones who helped us with Mina?"

Kellan shook his head. "Kindra's gone on an assignment again. Avalan is too hard-headed for strategic work like this. Vaida will be the best asset."

Cassian finally stopped chewing his lip, then sighed. "Okay, call her."

Kellan smiled, then dialed Vaida again on his techpad.

"V?" he said as soon as she picked up.

She sighed on the other end of the line. "You again? Didn't I just do something for you?"

His smile grew at her brusque tone. "You did, but I need another favor. Something only you can do. Please?"

"Fine, what do you want?"

"I'm going to send you an address. Can you come meet me? Bring your field gear." He hoped she'd understand his implication, but it was too risky to explain much over a call.

He could practically hear her making a face on the other end. "You're going to owe me dinner for a month. But fine. Be there soon."

"You are a wonderful creature of immense and immeasurable beauty, and I am eternally in your debt," Kellan cooed. Vaida huffed, but he knew she'd be smiling.

"Bye, dumbass," she said, hanging up with a decisive click.

Cassian was smiling vaguely after he hung up. Kellan liked the curl of his smile, the way it pinched the skin at the corners of his lips, the way his eyes crinkled in delight.

He wanted to touch him again. He wanted so badly to reach out and take his lips again, to feel his breath against his neck, to feel his hands running down his back—

"Kellan?" Cassian's voice cut through his daydream. "I'm going to make a new pot of coffee. I know you already had some, but would you like a new cup?"

Coffee might help. He was distracted. He couldn't focus, not with the temptation of Cassian always teasing him. Although he didn't love the taste, he nodded his head.

Cassian stood, and Kellan mourned the loss of his warmth beside him.

He made his coffee as usual, grinding the beans with practiced care, pouring the water in a slow circle, observing the drip as it fell through into the glass carafe. Kellan watched it too, the tension in his chest building.

The coffee brewed, Cassian poured a cup for himself, then a second for Kellan.

"Sugar? Cream?" he asked, holding Kellan's intended cup.

"Please."

Cassian nodded, adding the ingredients to the cup.

Something about the domestic nature of that moment gave Kellan a sickly pink feeling of nostalgia. A longing for a life he'd never even had. Was it possible to miss something he'd never experienced before?

He could see it. A future in which he and Cassian weren't assassins, where their lives weren't owned by others, where they could be free to simply sit and have a cup of coffee in the comfort of their perfectly ordinary home.

"Here."

A cup appeared before him, its contents swirling. He accepted the mug with murmured thanks, his fingers accidentally brushing Cassian's.

He looked up, meeting green eyes filled with an emotion that made them darker than usual. He was blushing as he turned away, his eyes falling back to the spot he'd left on the couch.

Cassian returned to it, his thigh pressing against Kellan's again.

They sat in a heavy, pregnant silence for several minutes, Cassian looking over the schematics again. Kellan simply sat, both hands wrapped around his steaming mug of coffee he was almost afraid to drink.

"Do you regret it?" Cassian's voice was soft.

Kellan flinched. "Regret what?"

A blush spread over Cassian's face, light pink and beautiful. "Earlier. In the bedroom."

He understood. He'd been so awkward in his attempt to give Cassian space, fearing he might have come on too strong. Instead, he'd sent an entirely different message.

"If you're asking if I regret kissing you, no. I don't. Not for a second."

Cassian turned back to the techpad before them, a small smile spreading across his face. "Good. I don't regret it either."

Kellan squeezed the mug in his hands. "You know, if you keep saying things like that, it's going to be awfully hard to focus when Vaida gets here."

"I know."

He sipped his coffee quietly, unable to keep the smile from his lips.

CASSIAN

16th of Jupiter's Moon

Cassian had never stopped to wonder what Kellan's elusive friend looked like. When Vaida finally crossed the threshold into his safe house, he was taken aback.

To say she was beautiful was an understatement. She was positively ethereal.

And something in him *pulled* toward her when she entered. It was a deep sense of nostalgia, as if she was something he'd once lost. He couldn't understand it, though. He'd never met Vaida before in his life.

"All right, Kellan. Explain." Her voice was firm, but he could tell she had a soft spot for Kellan by the way her eyes lowered just a touch at the sight of him.

Kellan explained the situation to her, about how the details she'd helped uncover had led him here. How his suspicions about Northwind had grown stronger and stronger by the day. How they had undeniable proof that something fishy was going on. She grew more pensive as she listened, obviously turning the details over in her head.

Finally, she spoke. "This is insane, you know."

He huffed a laugh, plopping himself casually onto the couch. "I know, but it's the only thing that makes sense."

She frowned at him, chewing her lip. Obviously unsure what to say, she turned to Cassian, cocking an eyebrow at him.

"You must be Cassian. I've heard disgustingly little about you, but I can see why he's infatuated with you." She held out a hand to him, ignoring the very obvious heat rising to his face.

"It's a pleasure," he said quietly, taking her offered hand.

Somewhere in their handshake she found approval, dropping his hand and turning to face Kellan on the couch. She lugged her bag over, taking almost no time at all to hook up her equipment.

Once she was settled, Vaida pulled the floor plans she'd sent of the Northwind Medical building up on her screen. Her fingers flew across the holographic keys as she pulled up the various construction contracts, technology agreements, and even company emails that Cassian was pretty sure she shouldn't have had access to.

"So. You need to get to the basement levels. And you want to get there via the elevator in the director's office?" She pointed a finger at the elevator shaft they'd found before.

Kellan nodded.

She sighed. "Well, unfortunately for you, there are biometric scanners both to open the doors and to call the elevator. The one to open the doors is a little less complex, so I can probably hack it, but even I can't hope to do it on the one inside."

Cassian leaned in, observing the schematic again on her screen. "What about getting us up there? Kellan can fly, but we don't know what kind of security they've got around the windows or the building."

"You're absolutely right; you can't fly directly up to that floor. However, there's a balcony three floors below. See?" She pointed to a spot on the map just below the director's office. "It wouldn't be a challenge to get you in through the door there. You'll just have to get yourselves up three flights of stairs."

Kellan sighed. "So how are we getting down after we get into the elevator? You can't send it down for us, right, V?"

She shook her head. "No, but it's a small elevator shaft. You can crawl down."

"Absofuckingloutely not, Vaida. We'll fly, I have wings."

"You won't fit."

"Won't know until we try, huh?"

"Don't say I didn't tell you so."

"I'll never give you the satisfaction of being right."

Cassian watched their verbal spar back and forth, his hands clenched in his lap. He'd done some crazy stunts in his life already; crawling down an elevator shaft was new, but not any more or less dangerous than things he'd done before.

Kellan practically vibrated as he looked at the schematics, his smile wild. It wasn't the flirty, feral smile he'd worn earlier that night, but a sort of uncontrollable thrill of emotion Cassian could tell he was having a hard time containing. Cassian, however, could feel the nerves roiling in his gut. This was the breaking point, the rock upon which his wave would break. He was afraid. So, so afraid.

"I'll be in your ear the whole time," Vaida said, handing them small earpieces from her bag. "If you get stuck, I'll do my best to get you out."

He twisted the earpiece into place, pretending the nerves weren't affecting him. He could handle this. He had to.

"All right then, let's get moving." Kellan stood, brushing his hands on his pants as he stood. He glanced once more at Vaida, and she nodded.

"I'll stay here and wait for you to get back," she said. "If you need more Legion, let me know. I can call dispatch."

Cassian shivered. "We'll handle it. The less Legion, the better. We don't want to spook Leo."

Vaida cocked her eyebrow at him, and he felt distinctly like she was scolding him silently. "Fine. But don't let your ego get in the way of your life. If I don't hear from you in an hour, I'm calling dispatch."

Cassian nodded, then checked his holsters one more time before following Kellan out the front door and into the night.

It was cold tonight, Cassian thought as they climbed a building across the street from Northwind Medical. The wind was stronger up there, and even though his suit was well insulated, each gust still sent a chill through his body.

They'd decided it would be easier for Kellan to start higher up. Rather than trying to fly up nearly a hundred floors, starting on one of the adjacent buildings would mean less time carrying Cassian and less time to be seen.

Of course, the plan still came with its risks. If someone caught them climbing up the other building, their mission would end before it began. They were blatantly trespassing, but so long as they were stealthy, no one would know.

Kellan reached the top before he did, shouldering open the old roof access door with a small grunt. No one was in the building, they'd found, and so their journey up had been easier than expected.

But this was only the first step.

The door closed behind them, and they turned their faces to the glass and iron structure that was Northwind Medical.

"You ready?" Kellan said, stretching his hands out before him. "It's going to feel good to fly again." His tone was wistful, his eyes unfocused as they stared into space.

Cassian stepped up to meet Kellan at the edge of the roof, feeling a sense of finality. No matter what happened tonight, he'd be gone tomorrow. He didn't know if he'd ever see Kellan again.

The thought scared him. Enough to prompt him to reach out for Kellan's gloved hand and grasp it in his own.

Kellan turned to him, silhouetted by the lights of the city, eyes questioning.

"Cassian?"

He squeezed Kellan's hand once, then let go. "I'm ready."

Kellan nodded, then closed his eyes. His wings sprang free, holes in the back of his suit opening to accommodate them.

They were beautiful. The scapular feathers nearest his back were nearly black, while his primaries were an iron gray. The gradient was beautiful in the night, illuminated just enough to look like they were made of pure silver.

Kellan rolled his head and shoulders, stretching his wings as if he hadn't used them for a while.

"Come here," he said, his voice lower than usual. "I need you to hold me around my neck and wrap your legs around my hips, okay?"

Cassian didn't know why it hadn't occurred to him that they'd need to hang on like this when he flew. Heat rushed to his cheeks, and a fizzy feeling bubbled low in his abdomen.

He nodded and wrapped himself around Kellan as instructed. He was warm, even in the cold night air. Cassian rested his chin on Kellan's shoulder, watching the pulse as it fluttered in his neck. Kellan wrapped his own arms around Cassian's back, his hands splaying wide enough to cover his entire upper back. Heat bloomed again in his chest, sending tingles to his toes.

He realized then he'd do whatever it took to keep Kellan in his life. Because letting go of all this was too much to bear.

"All right, I'm going to jump. Don't let go of me."

And then they were falling. The swooping of his stomach almost made him sick, but Kellan's hands on his back steadied him.

Wind rushed by his ears, drowning out the din of the city at night. His back was cold except for where Kellan's hands grasped him tightly. His front was very warm, however, pressed against the shifting muscle that was Kellan in flight.

He wished he could open his eyes to see how beautiful this flight must look. But the wind was too strong, and he couldn't bring himself to lift his head from Kellan's shoulder.

It was over nearly as quickly as it began.

"Here," Kellan said, breathless. "You can let go now."

Cassian lifted his head from Kellan's shoulder, then gradually unwound his legs from Kellan's waist. His feet hit concrete, and he made to untangle his arms from Kellan's neck, but found himself pressed against him instead.

"Uh, Kellan?"

"Just…wait a moment," he said, his breath still ragged. His hands were still on Cassian's back.

He didn't argue. He pressed himself into Kellan, nuzzling his nose into his neck. He was tempted to press a kiss there, but couldn't bring himself to do it.

Then Kellan's hands moved, leaving his back feeling cold, empty. But they reappeared a second later to cup his cheeks.

"I know you have to leave after this," Kellan whispered. "I know you have to return. But I don't want you to."

Cassian moved his own hands to cover Kellan's. "I don't want to leave either. But I must return."

His vision was nothing but Kellan. Then, the barest touch of their lips. Compared to the kiss earlier that night it was soft, chaste. It lacked the fire and passion and longing that their first kiss had.

But this one felt melancholy. Like a kiss goodbye. Cassian's heart ached.

"Then promise me you'll return to me someday," Kellan said, moving his lips away from Cassian's just enough to speak. "Promise me you'll return."

Cassian's heart squeezed painfully. His limbs felt heavy, weighed down by the chains of responsibility and the simple unfairness of life. He wanted to promise everything, wanted to give Kellan whatever he asked for. The need to be exactly what he wished for was overpowering.

But he couldn't.

"I will do everything I can, Kellan," he said. Kellan's name on his tongue burned.

They broke apart, the silence of the moment roaring like a scream.

"That's all I can ask for," he replied after a moment's pause.

A huff came through his earpiece. "Oh, for god's sake, you two, get a room. Preferably where I *can't* hear your sappy confessions."

He'd forgotten Vaida was listening in. The embarrassment was palpable, both of them blushing at the woman who couldn't see them.

"Get a move on, you two. I've unlocked the balcony door, but it will reset itself in a few minutes. If you dick around any longer, it'll lock you and me out."

Kellan sighed, cheeks puffing as he forced the air from his lungs. Then he opened his eyes and turned to Cassian, his spine straighter than it had been just a moment ago.

He held out a hand, a gesture of partnership.

"You ready?"

Cassian nodded, taking the offered hand in his own.

52

KELLAN

16th of Jupiter's Moon

They got inside the building without issue. Cassian's scent lingered in his nose; his head buzzed with it.

He'd asked Cassian to stay; he wanted him to promise he would. But it wasn't that easy, and Kellan knew he was being selfish.

He shook his head to clear the intrusive thoughts—now was not the time. Not when they had people to save.

The stairwell they needed was in the building's interior, so they would have to navigate half of the floor to access it. Luckily for them, this floor was dark. Unlucky for them, they didn't have their visors.

They moved slowly through the space, being careful not to bump into anything. Although no one was up here, it would be best for them to stay unnoticed as long as possible. Even bumping into a desk or chair wrong may send alarm signals to the building's security. They couldn't risk being sloppy.

Kellan led them through, tiptoeing around and stopping whenever he heard anything shifting. Cassian followed his lead, and they made slow progress toward the inner stairwell.

"You're close, take a left in about twelve paces," Vaida's voice whispered in his ear. Although the earpieces were already quiet, the floor was silent. She didn't want to be accidentally heard.

Kellan motioned to his left, then held up one finger, followed by another. He could barely see Cassian nod, but he knew he understood.

They reached the inner stairwell just as Vaida had instructed and opened the door. When they stepped inside, lights flickered on, making Kellan wince.

"V, you couldn't turn the motion sensors off the lights, could you?" he whispered. His voice echoed in the concrete stairwell.

"Unfortunately, no; they're not connected to the main security terminal that I'm connected to. You just need to pray no one's looking in the stairwell."

Kellan swore to himself, but they didn't have time to waste. He headed up the stairs, Cassian at his heels.

They climbed the three floors to get to the top level where the director's office was. The stairwell would spit them out outside of the office, but that was fine. A scanner on the inside of the stairwell offered access to the floor with an ID card. Vaida made quick work of the door's lock, and it turned green as they approached.

"Have I thanked you yet, V?" Kellan whispered as he opened the door.

Vaida sighed. He could practically hear her eye roll. "Now's not the time. You can sing my praises later."

Another scanner awaited them before the massive oak door into the director's office. Once again, it flashed green as they approached.

Kellan pushed open the door, and gasped.

The director's office was fully open to the city; the floor-to-ceiling windows overlooking the skyline of Spiral City were the main feature of the space. In the center rested a wood and glass desk, complete with a comfy black leather chair and two plush armchairs before it.

But the floor took his breath away. Someone had enchanted it to look like a snowy field. As they walked across the space, they left behind footprints that disappeared moments later.

It was beautiful, Kellan thought.

"Kellan, we have to get moving." Cassian's voice was soft in his ear. "But it is pretty incredible."

Kellan threw him a small smirk, but tore his eyes away from the floor to search for the elevator.

It was on the opposite wall, a single break in the massive windows. It was also enchanted like the floor, the only one of the wall panels that seemed to match.

"V, we have eyes on the elevator," Cassian said.

"Understood. I'll unlock the doors. You handle the rest."

The elevator doors slid open smoothly, and the hairs on the back of Kellan's neck raised as he saw what awaited them.

Vaida couldn't call the elevator, so they would need to climb down the shaft. Seeing it himself, he realized Vaida had been right when she'd insisted he wouldn't be able to fly down. It was small, smaller than a normal elevator, as if it was meant to only fit one person at a time. The space was rounded too, not square like normal elevator shafts.

He sighed, then stepped up to the dark space dropping below them. It went deep, deep down. A hundred floors down. If they fell, they'd die.

Panic churned in his gut as they stared down.

"You sure you can't call the elevator, V?"

"It's too complicated of a code for me to hack now. It would take me days, and I don't have a program ready. I already told you, you're going to have to climb down." Her voice wasn't harsh, but it was firm. There was nothing she could do.

Kellan swore under his breath and assessed the shaft one more time. A cable that obviously lifted the elevator itself ran down the center. They'd have to use it to get down.

"Here goes nothing, I guess," he said quietly.

Cassian patted his shoulder as he reached for the cable. "I'll be right behind you, okay? I won't let you fall."

"Right." Kellan nodded as his hand closed around the cable.

It was sturdy and thick. It would definitely bear their weight so long as they didn't jostle it too hard or do something stupid. He breathed one more time, deeply in through his nose and out through his mouth. Then he jumped.

His feet hit the other side of the shaft, rubber against metal. The impact wasn't loud, but it jarred him enough to make his teeth rattle in his head. He held on through it all, gloved hands gripping the cable as hard as he could.

They'd descend this way, feet against the shaft, gripping the cable with all their strength. It would be slow going, but it was the best they could do.

Kellan worked his way down to make room for Cassian. It jostled him around a bit, but when Cassian stopped moving, the line held. He relaxed just a touch, knowing that the first part of their elevator climb was the most dangerous. It would be easier now that they had a hold of the line.

They made their way down slowly, carefully putting hand under hand, foot under foot. Even though they wanted to move quickly, one mistake would mean plummeting to their deaths.

Kellan lost track of time as they climbed. It felt like hours. His legs burned, his shoulders burned, his abdominal muscles burned. Every muscle was on fire from the strain. He'd long ago stopped hearing Cassian's labored breathing. He didn't know if Vaida was talking to them anymore.

He moved his hand down and grabbed air.

He'd missed the cable.

His foot slid down the smooth metal of the shaft, the hand still on the cable slipping as his feet slid. Kellan's heart flew into his mouth as he fell.

But before he got too far, he felt a hand grab the front of his suit—Cassian. He'd slid down and was precariously grabbing the cable with one strong hand.

"You all right?" His breathing was slow and steady, but Kellan could tell he was exhausted. The arm that held him trembled slightly.

Kellan replaced his feet on the shaft's wall, repositioning his hands on the elevator cable. Then he nodded to Cassian. "Thank you for that."

Cassian let go of his suit, smiling. "We're almost there, I can feel it. Just hold on for a little longer."

Kellan nodded.

"You're currently on floor five, you're close." Vaida's voice was breathy, like she'd been afraid for him, too.

The last leg of the climb only made his arms burn more, but he didn't let his mind go blank. Even a fall from here would cause serious injury, and they didn't know what they'd face in the basement.

Finally, his back hit something smooth. It was the top of the elevator, parked on the lowest basement floor. They'd have to get out the floor above, but it at least gave them an idea of where Leo and the director might be.

"V, we hit the bottom. Open the doors on the fourth floor of the basement," Kellan whispered.

They both dropped, landing on the top of the elevator and standing as they waited for Vaida to open the shaft doors just above them. When they slid open, all they saw was black. Cassian gave Kellan a boost, and Kellan reached a hand down to help him up.

As they stepped into the darkness, fluorescent lights above them flickered to life, their twitching light casting a yellow glow on everything.

The floors were white and polished to perfection, and the walls were made of cold, white-washed cinder blocks. Several labs with massive windows lined the hallway. But for all the polishing and cleanliness, the place seemed abandoned. Nothing breathed or moved, save for Kellan and Cassian, their huffs seeming to almost defile the sterile whiteness of the labs.

"Cass, look," Kellan said, pointing into a lab. He'd noticed a stainless-steel table, polished as much as the floors, its surface reflecting the shelves of medical supplies. But then he'd seen something that made his skin crawl—restraints.

"Enya's fire, are those…restraints?" Cassian breathed. The back of Kellan's neck prickled.

Whatever was happening down here, it made Kellan's stomach turn. The flickering of the overhead lights made his vision swim.

"Vaida," he breathed, afraid to speak too loudly. "I've gotta send you a picture of this."

His earpiece was quiet.

"V?"

Cassian approached him, concern pinching his eyebrows together. "She said she'd be listening. Does she do this often?"

Kellan shook his head. "She's never gone dark on me before. Not like this. Something's wrong."

Cassian shifted on his feet as he rolled a shoulder back. "Do we keep going, then? If she's not able to communicate with us…"

They'd be in a world of trouble if she wasn't able to open doors or call backup. She wouldn't know where they were; she wouldn't be able to help them if they needed it.

But Pontius needed them. So did Selwyn. Any delay might spell their demise.

Kellan shook his head. "We have to keep going. We can't leave them. We'll just hope we can get out before Vaida calls in backup."

Cassian nodded, then turned toward the end of the hallway that ended in a T juncture. They had to keep moving, for Selwyn and Pontius.

The stairwell down was close by, only a turn away from where they'd exited the elevator. There was no security on the stairwell doors, which only made his heart pound faster. Kellan's hand tingled as he opened the door to the final floor.

It was more of the same—polished white floors, white cinderblock, and rows upon rows of labs with one-way mirrored windows to the hallway.

"What the hell kind of sadistic bastard would build something like this?" Kellan wondered out loud.

Cassian shook his head. "This is exactly the sort of behavior I'd expect from Leo, truthfully."

He shuddered. From the little he'd seen of the man, he knew Leo was crazy. But for him to go this far was absolutely horrifying. Fear rose in his throat, choking him with its blackness. But he shoved it down, refusing to give in.

He needed to save Selwyn, save Pontius.

Their footsteps were silent as they crouched low, taking their time inspecting each room as they passed by, hoping that Pontius would magically appear before them. He never did.

Instead, they found humans strapped to the tables they'd seen on the other floor. Most of them looked like they were asleep, although it was more likely a magically induced coma, judging by the slow rate of their heartbeat monitors. Kellan thought he might be sick looking at them.

"Cass, we have to do something," he said after they'd passed the third unconscious human.

But Cassian just shook his head, his eyes haunted. "We don't have time to save them all, Kellan, especially not when we don't know where the Morgensterns and Leo are. If we stop Leo, we can save them. But we have to prioritize."

Kellan closed his eyes, squeezing them shut hard enough to see stars. He knew Cassian was right, but it didn't make the guilt lessen as they passed room after room of unconscious people.

Kellan's stomach roiled when they reached the final room at the end of the hallway, afraid of what he might see. This time, however, the room was empty.

As they reached the end of the hallway, he heard voices. Kellan couldn't distinguish the words, but he knew Cassian must have been able to. He'd gone as pale as death.

"What's happening?" Kellan whispered, reaching a hand out to touch his arm.

Cassian flinched. He just shook his head, pressing a finger to his lips. "They're in here," he said, pointing to a black door before them. "I can hear Leo."

Kellan reached for the handle, but Cassian stopped him.

"*Think,* Kellan. We don't know who else is in there or what they're doing. We have to think about this care—"

A high-pitched scream from the other room cut Cassian off. Chills worked their way up from his legs, spreading across his back and down his arms, causing the hair to stand on end. He'd heard that scream before. It was Selwyn.

53

SHADOW

16th of Jupiter's Moon

The man retreated, gesturing for the demon in the corner to accompany him as he collected the woman's brother from the other room.

They led him back into the main laboratory, arms constricted by the long talons of the demon. The man did not struggle. Instead, he stared at the woman with wide eyes. The man could smell his fear. It had a delicious scent.

The demon forced the man onto the operating chair in the center of the room, then the man took over, strapping his arms and legs to the device.

The chair itself did little, but the restraints helped during the transformation.

"Good, now the gang's all here," the man muttered as he found the syringe.

"N-no," the woman stuttered. "Please, no, not Pontius. Leave him alone."

The sound of her begging was music to his ears.

"Miss Morgenstern…" Alvemach began. His voice in this body was pleasant and smooth, like honey. He wondered how much she would tremble if she heard his true voice, the one that sounded like lava cooling over a mountainside. Crackled. Deep.

"I thought I made myself quite clear," Alvemach continued. "You will work with us, willingly or not. Your brother's life depends on it."

Her brother had been silent the entire time. The man wondered if he'd try to scream.

"Selwyn," he breathed. His voice was rough. Maybe he'd already been screaming. "I'm not worth it. Don't."

"I won't lose you," she replied, a sob breaking through.

Oh, the pain was quite lovely. It was nourishing, sending chills up his spine, feeding him, sustaining him. Alvemach had chosen well.

The man lifted the syringe from the table beside the chair, flicking the needle tip once. "I suggest you make your choice, little heiress. Never know when my hand might…slip."

He stuck the needle into her brother's arm, right in the soft crook of his arm, but he did not push down on the syringe.

"*No!*" she screamed, lunging forward.

The demon beside the chair stepped between them, bearing its long teeth.

Tears made lines down her face. Women were so ugly when they cried. "Fine. I'll do it. Whatever you want. Just please, please let him go."

Alvemach smiled. "Wonderful. Shadow, if you please."

The man smiled again, vicious, cruel, vengeful. "With pleasure."

Her scream was deafening as he emptied the contents of the syringe into her brother's arm.

54

CASSIAN

16th of Jupiter's Moon

Even though he'd held Kellan back, at the sound of Selwyn's scream, he didn't hesitate. He kicked open the door without a second thought and burst through the room to see an awful sight.

A demon like the one he'd seen at the gala restrained Selwyn, her arms held back in an awful lock that he knew must hurt. Leo stood over Pontius' prone form, an empty syringe in his hand.

And Director Byre stood next to them, a nasty smile spreading across his lips.

They'd strapped Pontius to a chair in the center of the room, held down by what seemed like an excessive number of restraints. Cassian lurched toward him, but he felt a hand on his arm. Kellan.

"So good of you gentlemen to join us," the director purred, his voice like icicles and venom. He stood stoically, his hands clasped behind his back, as if observing this scene was perfectly normal behavior for him. "The show is just about to begin."

"The show?" Kellan's voice was surprisingly calm next to his ear, but Cassian knew his heart must be pounding as loudly as his own.

Leo cackled. "Just watch, little legionnaire. You'll see."

Cassian glanced at Kellan, a silent plea filling his eyes. The situation was worse than they'd expected—Selwyn was here,

Pontius was in more danger than they'd anticipated, and Leo looked murderous.

And then there was the director. What his role was in this whole situation was still unclear. But he didn't look distressed, which meant he knew what was happening and approved of it.

He didn't blink as he continued to watch Leo and the director observe Pontius on the chair. He took a deep breath in, let it out, and grabbed Kellan's hand to squeeze it. While the director and Leo were still distracted with Pontius, Cassian nodded.

They sprung into action simultaneously—Kellan going for the demon holding Selwyn hostage and Cassian lunging for Pontius still strapped to the chair.

Leo seemed unsurprised by the attack, only casually stepping back to give Cassian more room as he lunged. He couldn't fathom why Leo wouldn't attack him back as he reached for the restraints on the table.

Byre chuckled and stepped back. Cassian's hands paused, his head whipping toward the director.

"Oh, by all means, please continue," he said, his blue eyes twinkling with glee.

He did not continue. Their behavior was too strange for him to ignore. He remembered the syringe that Leo had been holding as they entered. His stomach dropped.

Pontius writhed on the table, bucking up against the restraints, his mouth open wide in a silent scream. Cassian stood glued to the spot as he watched the transformation take place before his eyes.

It was agony to watch. Pontius' eyes flew open and were golden with slitted pupils, terrible and angry. A spark of recognition flared in them for a single moment when their eyes locked, but it was gone in a flash as his body writhed again.

His skin hardened, turning gray as scales dotted his skin. Pontius' back arched so far off the chair that Cassian couldn't believe he wasn't hurting himself. His hands flexed and stretched. His fingers lengthened, the snap of his broken fingers echoing in Cassian's ears.

Pontius' back curved off the chair again.

The restraints broke this time, and his transformation was nearly complete. Kellan had managed to get the demon holding Selwyn to let go, but she hadn't moved. She stared at the monster her brother had become, tears streaming down her cheeks. He could see from here how badly she was shaking.

"Selwyn, get out, *now!*" Cassian roared. He didn't want her to meet the same fate, not while he could help it.

The director's voice practically trembled as he spoke. "She will do no such thing."

Selwyn's head whipped back and forth, her eyes moving from one person to the next. She backed up slowly, heading toward the wall, her breathing uneven. Her face had gone pale, her lips pulled back in a fearful frown.

Cassian didn't know whether to engage Leo, the director, or try to do something about Pontius. They didn't have enough people to save Selwyn. And it seemed the director would not let her go so easily.

Behind him, Kellan still battled the demon, his sword sending out sparks as it met the demon's razor-sharp claws. The clanging was loud enough to echo in the large space. They were evenly matched for now, it seemed. He just hoped Kellan could keep it up.

Leo would have to be his first target, Cassian decided. He posed the biggest threat. Selwyn was relatively safe, as the director would need to get around Kellan to reach her. And the demon itself was being handled by Kellan.

All that was left was Pontius, but he hoped by getting Leo out of the way, he could more easily stop whatever was happening to Pontius.

A voice in the back of his head urged him to continue, to fight. He didn't need the encouragement, but he listened anyway.

Cassian drew his sword, slowly positioning himself to keep Pontius as far from harm as he could. Leo saw his stance and chuckled.

"Come now, Cassian, I'd much rather talk to you than fight you," he said, his voice low. He was nearly trembling with excitement.

He lowered his sword tip toward the man, a frown forming on his face. "I have nothing to say to you."

Leo spread his arms wide. "Don't you wonder why I have so much power? Don't you want that for yourself? I have always watched you, Cassian. You are destined for greatness. I can help you achieve it."

He sprung, not waiting for Leo to finish his speech. If he had been anyone but Leo, he would have cleaved them in half from shoulder to hip, but the other man was entirely too quick. He instead slashed a line through the fabric of Leo's shirt, exposing his bare chest. Beneath lay a sickening congregation of blackened veins, pulsating beneath his skin like a twisted maze of darkness.

Blood welled from the shallow cut he'd landed, but the blood was not the red of mortal blood. It was black, viscous, and unlike anything he'd seen before. Bile rose in his throat. But worse, he watched as the shallow cut knit itself back together before his eyes.

"What the—"

"Like what you see?" Leo said, arms opened wide. His torn shirt opened even further with the movement, exposing more of the horrible blackened veins. "Aren't I beautiful?"

"What did you do to yourself, Leo?" Cassian whispered, lips parting the longer he looked at Leo.

"The beauty of pact magic, Cassian, is that it transforms you. Irrevocably. It has made me into a being of immense power. More than you could ever imagine. The power that flows through my veins makes me like this, and I relish the change that happens each time I grow stronger."

Cassian shook his head. He *enjoyed* this horrific transformation? This disease that made him look as if he was rotting from the inside out? He remembered seeing Leo's blood at the safe house; it had looked darker than usual. What sort of sickness was consuming him?

He'd heard of pact magic, a cursed form of heightening existing magical power through a pact with a demon. It was taboo, looked upon as a dirty way to gain power quickly.

But he'd never known the cost. A sickness that turned your blood to sludge seemed like a horrible trade for greater power.

"Aw, have I taken all the fight out of you?" Leo said, cutting through Cassian's thoughts. He had gone back to stroking his whip. "Come now, don't you want to hear what I have to say?"

"No."

Leo laughed, then glanced at Kellan, still fighting against the demon, a devious smile spreading his lips apart. "Maybe you'd be more willing to listen if that obnoxious legionnaire was out of the picture."

Cassian's vision flared red. "You won't touch him, Leo."

"Is that a weakness I sense, Cass? Such a shame. We'll have to beat that out of you."

"You're sick."

"No," Leo replied, his voice suddenly serious, "I am powerful. There is a distinction. And I will have you by my side, willing or not."

KELLAN

16th of Jupiter's Moon

Kellan's sword struck the demon's claws, sending up sparks. That couldn't be good for the blade.

His fight was not going well, but it also was not going poorly. They were evenly matched, the game of give-and-take almost perfectly balanced. The demon seemed almost unsteady, frequently wobbling on its legs, like it hadn't totally gotten used to its body yet.

He wondered if this was the same demon that he'd spotted in the alleyway just a few hours ago. It seemed like a lifetime ago at this point.

The demon growled, the animalistic noise grinding out from low in its throat.

He swung his sword again, cutting an arc through the air. The blade whistled as it came down, clanging off the demon's hard-as-iron scales. There had to be a place it was weak, he just needed to figure out where.

Selwyn still stood at the edge of the room, her horrified expression causing her to withdraw into herself. Unfortunately, she couldn't escape; she was as far from the door as she could get now. And until he took care of this demon, she would continue to be stuck.

Their dance continued, and he watched Cassian out of the corner of his eye facing off against Leo. They didn't seem to do much, instead just talking. Kellan wondered what they were saying when Leo's eyes flicked to him, meeting his stare. Leo just smirked, turning back to Cassian.

The demon took advantage of his momentary distraction to swipe at him. He leaped out of the way, but not before its razor-sharp claws sliced open the front of his battle suit.

He swore under his breath, dancing out of the demon's reach again, forcing it to follow him clumsily. If he could just knock it over, he could find a weak spot. Maybe its neck?

He circled in close, holding his blade before him in a defensive position. He couldn't afford to get distracted again, especially since his suit was shredded. The demon wouldn't hesitate to disembowel him if given the chance.

Kellan flitted forward and backward, keeping just ahead of the demon's claws. The more he spun, the more unsteady the demon became. Finally, he saw his opening.

As the demon turned once more to face him, he lashed out, swinging himself low with his legs in front of him, aiming for where he assumed its knees were. It was already wobbling, and he knew a well-timed blow to the side would knock it over.

His plan worked—the demon wobbled, then toppled over on gangly limbs as he connected. He scrambled to sit atop it. He kneeled on its arms, relying on the strength of his legs to keep it pinned, his sword at its throat.

"If you value your life at all, you'll stop struggling," he said, unsure if it knew what he said.

"It doesn't understand you." The smooth voice in his ear made him jump.

The director stood next to him, a coy smile on his face, his hands tucked behind his back. He observed Kellan with a coolness that didn't fit the situation, and it made Kellan sweat.

"You," Kellan replied, his sword still at the demon's throat.

"What are you?"

Byre laughed, leaning backward and exposing his throat. He was very confident in his abilities to allow such vulnerability to show so obviously. "You mean you haven't figured it out? You were so close."

His eyes narrowed, searching his mind for the missing puzzle piece, the one he hadn't been able to place yet. The demon struggled weakly beneath him, but Kellan stayed firmly atop it.

"Think, dear boy. You really don't know?"

That was it. The last piece he still hadn't figured out. The demonic prince Alvemach. But that couldn't possibly...

"You're..." Kellan started, pulling back.

"Say what you know in your heart to be true, legionnaire."

"You're him. Alvemach."

Byre's composure finally melted as he lifted a hand to his face, his lips trembling with suppressed laughter. He covered his eyes, tilting his head back once more and letting out a small chuckle that built and grew and crashed upon him like a wave until he was laughing deeply and loudly. The maniacal sound raised the hairs on the back of Kellan's neck.

"You do not know how good it feels to shed this skin now that you know," Byre said. Kellan watched in horror as the well-dressed, trim man before him melted away, revealing what could only be described as a beast of hell.

The Demon Prince Alvemach lived up to his name. He made the demons they'd been dealing with look like puppies.

Rather than the head of a jackal, Alvemach had the head of a boar. Its tusks were long and sharp, and rather than bone-colored, they were black that faded into a blood-red color. His black skin crackled and pulsated, looking like a barely withheld volcanic eruption. The ensemble was horrifying enough to make Kellan lose his grip on the demon beneath him.

It surged up, knocking him off and swiping a claw across his thigh. Kellan cried out but scrambled to his feet anyway, gritting his teeth. He'd be damned if he'd go down now, even with the terrifying

Alvemach now before him.

He settled once more into a fighting stance, his sword prepared to strike in front of him. He needed to go on the offensive now and end this before they locked him into a long battle with a prince of Hell.

Alvemach smiled, or what seemed like a smile with a boar's head. It was more like he opened his mouth and pulled back his lips, but Kellan could sense his glee. His knees trembled against his will.

"I'll kill you where you stand, boy," Alvemach said, and his voice was like raging fire and boiling lava, not like the smooth, honeyed voice he'd had as Byre.

Alvemach surged forward, and it was all Kellan could do to scramble backward and lift his sword before the demon prince crashed into him with enough force to send him flying into the wall. He heard something crack as he landed, and pain blossomed across his shoulder a moment later.

He knew Alvemach was coming for him, but he couldn't find the energy to stand. The blow had knocked all the air from his lungs, and he could scarcely breathe, never mind move.

At least he'd kissed Cassian before he died.

56

CASSIAN

16th of Jupiter's Moon

"You haven't even asked why I'm here," Leo continued, pouting. The sheer ridiculousness of the conversation had Cassian lowering his sword a fraction of an inch.

He didn't respond, staring Leo down as he clenched his jaw.

Leo smiled, his pointed canines catching his lower lip. "You could be so much more, Cassian. You have such potential; I can smell it on you. I can practically hear your blood calling out to me."

"My blood isn't calling out to anyone," he retorted, adjusting his grip on his sword. "What is your fascination with me?"

"I just told you—I can feel your potential, and I want to see what it will do with a little…coaxing."

"What does that even mean?"

A crash cut through his response, and he looked to Kellan, who'd pinned the demon he'd been battling to the ground. Pride swelled in his chest.

Leo snapped his fingers, drawing Cassian's attention back to him. "Eyes on me, Cassian. No one else."

Cassian gritted his teeth.

"You've seen what I can do. What *you* could do if you only came with me."

Cassian balked. "You want me to make a pact with a demon and become one of your cronies? Never going to happen."

"Never say never."

"*Never*," Cassian repeated, eyes narrowing.

Movement caught his eye, and Cassian glanced over Leo's shoulder before he could stop himself.

Cassian watched in horror as Byre shed his skin and transformed into a demonic beast. It was a horrible sight; the monster was massive, emitting heat that warmed the room from what looked like lava beneath its skin. Is that what had been hiding under the director's face this whole time?

Leo still hadn't moved, standing in the same spot as before with a cocky grin on his face.

"Will you listen to me now?" Leo said, never glancing back once.

He moved toward Kellan to stop the beast from getting to him. But he didn't get more than two steps before Leo's hand stopped him at his chest.

"I know what you're thinking, Cassian," he said. "There's not much you can do. You can't save him. Just like you couldn't save that boy you loved so long ago."

Anger welled in the pit of his stomach, churning right behind his navel. It had been Leo. Leo had told those men where to find Aidyn. He'd always suspected, but hearing Leo confirm it made the world go red.

He slapped Leo's hand away and continued toward Kellan. He wouldn't lose him. Not when he had the power to do something about it.

An invisible wall stopped him in his tracks, and the anger in his stomach raged into a storm.

He whirled on Leo, whose hands glowed purple as they held the barrier keeping Cassian from reaching Kellan. His anger was no longer red—it had turned white hot, spilling from his gut in waves.

The instinct spoke to him again, the one that had pushed him so many times before. It told him to release, to let go, to *rage*. The man stopping him had ruined his life before. It was time to stop Leo from doing something Cassian could never recover from.

He felt his right hand grow hot, then his arm, then his body, until finally, he couldn't contain the storm any longer.

And from Cassian, holy fire exploded.

It flowed out of him in waves, pulsating from every part of his body and setting his surroundings ablaze. He was vaguely aware of Leo yelling, of a sickening *crunch,* and of glass shattering. He didn't know if he'd opened his eyes or if he'd kept them squeezed shut. He could see nothing but pulsating light, and he didn't know how to stop it.

He felt like he was floating, like he was lying on his back in a warm pool of water. Where had this fire come from? It was unlike any spell he'd ever seen, unlike any power he'd ever had before. But it didn't feel foreign. No, it felt like a missing piece of him had finally clicked into place.

The fire emanating from him felt *good.* It was a release he hadn't known he needed.

He remembered other moments he'd felt this good—observatory trips with his mother, nights spent with Aidyn at his side, Kellan's lips on his in the safe house, the warmth of wrapping his arms around Kellan's neck as they flew.

With a jolt, Kellan's face returned to his mind, the image of him smiling warmly, his brown eyes crinkled in delight. He felt fear then, fear that he'd inadvertently hurt Kellan with this new, strange power.

With that, the fire stopped. It sucked itself back into Cassian like water down a drain. He frantically blinked the spots from his eyes, desperately praying to Sol that he hadn't done something he could never recover from.

He noticed the blood first—the blackish-red blood that sluggishly seeped out onto the floor next to his left foot. Then he saw the black-as-night blood that plastered the walls and ceiling to his right, dripping rhythmically into a massive puddle on the floor. The headless body of the Byre-demon twitched on the floor.

Slowly, Byre's body dissolved, sending flecks of what looked like black sand up into the atmosphere as if it was being pushed by a light, lazy wind. Leo's body lay motionless behind the chair, black blood pouring from a wound on his face.

Pontius was still shackled to the chair, untouched.

He'd done *that?* With a jolt of fear, he searched for a sign of Kellan, frantic now that he'd seen what his power had done.

He lay in the same place as before, unscathed. His face was pure shock, staring at the body of the Byre-demon dissolving on the floor before him. Selwyn stood where she'd been the whole time, backed against the wall, a hand pressed to her chest.

After a moment, Kellan's eyes found Cassian's, and he released a breath.

"Have you always been able to do that?" he asked, his voice soft with disbelief.

Cassian shook his head slowly. "No. Never."

Kellan stood shakily, coughing as he did, still out of breath from being thrown into the wall. Cassian rushed to his side, ignoring the splash as he ran through a puddle of demon blood.

They crashed into each other, Cassian finally allowing himself to relax. He shook as he held Kellan, wrapping his arms around him and burying his nose in Kellan's neck. Kellan held him back, dropping his sword in favor of wrapping both arms around him. His heart thudded almost painfully against his ribcage, and he knew Kellan could feel it but he didn't care. He was safe, and that was all that mattered.

Kellan smelled of blood and sweat, but his neck was soft. He breathed in deeply, closing his eyes as he held Kellan close. Their heartbeats felt syncopated—when one beat, the other followed close behind. It was as if they spoke to each other, telling the other that it was all right, that they were still alive, to keep beating.

Kellan's warmth against his chest felt comforting, like a piece of him had been missing. Like the best part of him had finally come home.

From behind him, a growl cut through the air, then a scream.

Cassian released Kellan, goosebumps traveling their way up his arms as he faced what had once been Pontius, claws dragging along the floor, now freed from his bonds.

Pontius lunged toward Kellan, and before he could think, Cassian leapt in the way of his extended claws.

57

KELLAN

16th of Jupiter's Moon

Kellan felt the scream shred his throat as Cassian fell back, sagging to the ground before he could get a grip on him.

Pontius retracted his claw, a snarl crossing his lips as he stretched out his hand to strike again. But before he could, he heard a small whimper, a cry so quiet he was surprised he heard it at all.

Kellan crouched slowly, reaching for his sword. He didn't care if the demon had once been Pontius. He had to protect Selwyn, protect Cassian.

Selwyn looked as if she finally registered the situation before her. Tears streamed down her cheeks as she covered her mouth with both her trembling hands.

She whimpered once more. "Pontius, no."

The demon swiveled its head to her, pausing as if in recognition.

Kellan sprang, swiping his sword at Pontius' back as Selwyn shrieked. He didn't care—the anger burned in his stomach, the grief brilliant and all-consuming and rendering him unable to think of anything but revenge.

He couldn't lose Cassian. He needed to save him. Killing Pontius was the only way.

But his sword was useless. It glanced off the hardened scales running along Pontius' back, vibrating so hard Kellan lost his grip on it once more.

"Stop," a voice echoed behind him. Cassian's.

He whirled to see Cassian propping himself up on an arm, clutching his bleeding stomach with another. Kellan went cold at the sight.

"Stop it," he said again.

"But I have to—"

"Look." He pointed at the demon, who hadn't moved. It was as if something rooted him to the spot as he stared at his sister. The demon didn't seem interested in Kellan any longer; it turned the rest of its body to face Selwyn.

She didn't appear scared of him even now. One hand held the wall as the other clenched over her heart in a tight fist. Her brow was furrowed in sorrow.

"Selwyn…" Kellan said, but she didn't seem to hear him, her eyes locked on her brother.

The demon took a single step forward, showing no signs of aggression as he approached. His claws dragged on the ground, the one still coated in Cassian's blood leaving a trail across the floor.

"Kellan," Cassian's voice said from behind him, "he's still in there. He knows Selwyn."

Kellan clenched his jaw, then turned to crouch next to Cassian, sitting on the ground next to him. "But he hurt you."

Cassian's green eyes were blurry with pain. Kellan shuffled himself beneath Cassian's head, letting it rest upon his thighs as he tore the top of Cassian's shredded suit off, wadding it against the puncture in his stomach.

"I know, but"—he stopped, coughing as a fresh wave of blood poured from his stomach—"you can't. Not now."

Cassian knew. He knew Kellan would regret it for the rest of his life if he hurt Pontius when there was still a chance they could save him. But the feeling of hopelessness cascaded over him as he glanced down at his lap.

They'd been robbed. Robbed of so many things—a happy

life, the chance to properly love each other, the opportunity to be something more than just killers. Before, they might have had the chance to change it.

But now, faced with an end he'd never expected, they had no choice.

He glanced up once more to check the advance of Pontius toward Selwyn. He'd only gotten about halfway across the room. As he watched, it looked as if Pontius was straining against something, like he was walking through water or deep snow. But nothing appeared to be holding him back, at least not that Kellan could see.

"Kellan," Cassian's voice came again as he felt a wet hand cradle his cheek. "I wish we'd had more time."

He leaned into the touch, the wadded suit beneath his hands becoming more and more soaked. "Stop talking like you're dying."

"But I am." A wet chuckle, followed by a stroke of his thumb on Kellan's cheek.

"You're not, dammit!" He sucked in a breath, unable to keep his voice steady. "Please, just hold on a little longer. For me."

Cassian smiled, a tear rolling down his cheek. Kellan watched as it started clear, then gradually turned pink and then deep red as it made a trail down his face. Cassian squeezed his hand, his breathing slowing to a crawl as his eyes closed, the rise and fall of his chest slow but steady.

Kellan kept holding his hand, lifting it to his forehead. He let the tears flow freely then, dribbling to the ground like summer rain. Several landed on his knees, soaking into the thick fabric of his suit. The others landed on the blood-slicked floor beneath him, mixing to create pink swirls.

"Don't leave me," he whispered, unsure if Cassian could even hear him anymore. "Don't leave me here without you, Cassian, please."

Leo had caused this—all this blood, this pain, this *grief*. And Kellan would be damned if he let him get away with it. He refused to lose Cassian, and if that meant killing Leo with his own bare hands, then so be it. He'd do anything to see Cassian live, even if it meant giving himself up as tribute.

"Interesting," a voice said, ringing clearly from behind the chair where Pontius had been turned. "Such a touching scene from you two. Bravo, bravo."

A jagged cut had sliced Leo's face in half—it was covered in inky blood that dribbled down and cleaved his rugged face into something out of a nightmare. Had Cassian's fire done that?

He'd seen Leo's other wounds heal themselves, but this one wasn't closing.

"It seems my friend has been holding something back from me," he said, gesturing his chin down to where Cassian lay in Kellan's lap, ignoring the blood dribbling down his own face. "No matter, all will be revealed soon."

"Is Byre dead?" Kellan asked. His body had completely dissolved by now, the only trace of him the black blood staining the walls.

Leo ignored Kellan and flicked his hand at Pontius, still straining his way across the room to his sister. He immediately halted, the muscles in his thick, scaled neck still straining. It appeared he could not go against Leo's command.

"Not now," he said, directing his words at Pontius. "You're going to be troublesome, aren't you? Hmph." He flicked his hand again, and Pontius dissolved, too.

Selwyn had been silent while Pontius made his slow trek to her. Upon his disappearance, she sank to the floor, silent as she stared at the place he'd once been.

"The wound is fatal, legionnaire. You won't save him," Leo said, his arms crossed before him.

He hadn't even noticed Leo's attention had turned back to him. He'd focused on Selwyn, now crumpled in the corner, head in her hands.

Kellan knew what Leo said was true, that he wasn't lying about the wound being fatal. He'd known it himself and had refused to acknowledge it. Grief flooded his senses, filling his mouth with its iron-rich taste, coloring the world a shade of blue he hated. He breathed slowly, the air catching in his throat. His pulse quickened, undeterred by his struggle to stay calm.

Leo's face was slowly healing, the cut knitting itself together as Kellan watched.

He spoke again, holding a hand out to Kellan. "Give him to me; I can do what you cannot."

Kellan's eyes narrowed as he instinctively curled around Cassian, shielding him from Leo's gaze. "And why would I do that?"

Leo chuckled, gesturing to his face. "You've seen what I can do. You know the power I wield. I can heal him."

"No," Kellan said. "It's your fault he's like this to begin with, why would I trust you?"

"Because, like I said, it's fatal. He'll die without my intervention."

"I don't trust you. I will never trust you."

"You don't *have* to trust me, you just need to give him to me."

"And if I do? Will I ever see him again?"

At that, Leo laughed. It was a terrible chuckle, starting low in his throat and bubbling to the surface like a volcano threatening to erupt. The sound sent shivers down Kellan's spine.

"Oh, you'll see him again," Leo finally said. "Now hand him over."

"*Don't do it!*" screamed Selwyn.

Her scream reverberated through the room, the echo bouncing off the cold metal walls and ringing in Kellan's ears. He knew Leo was right—there was no way he would get Cassian back down the hallway and up to the hospital without worsening his condition. Only magic could stabilize him now, and Kellan didn't have a drop.

It was the type of impossible dilemma they'd discuss in logic or strategy classes. Both routes are terrible choices. Both will lead to death, to pain, to heartache, to loss. Both options won't give you the ending you want or need. The choice was impossible.

But Kellan knew that he'd pick the choice where Cassian would live even if it meant never seeing him again. He would choose that path again and again, relive this moment for the rest of his life if it meant Cassian would continue breathing.

And that was exactly what he would do.

"Fine. Take him."

"Kellan!" Selwyn screamed again.

"You've made the right choice." As soon as he heard those words, the world went dark.

He awoke to soft hands cradling his head and someone's legs beneath him. Fluorescent lights gleamed too brightly above him.

"Cassian?"

"Sorry to disappoint, it's just me." Selwyn's voice was soft but ragged, like she'd been crying for hours.

"What happened?" He tried to sit up, but she placed a hand on his chest, gently shoving him back down.

"Don't move; you got a really nasty whack to the head," Selwyn said, and her face finally appeared in his vision. Her eyes were ringed in red. "Everyone is gone. Leo, Byre, Cassian, Pontius…" Her voice snagged on the last one.

His heart cracked. Cassian was truly gone, then. He'd let Leo take him. He didn't even know if he'd survive whatever Leo wanted to put him through, but he knew one thing for sure—he would never see Cassian again.

But the corridor was loud, bustling with activity. He turned his head to see what seemed like hundreds of black-suited figures stomping down the hallways. The frenetic activity of his comrades was jarring compared to the quiet stillness that was Selwyn.

"Legion?" he whispered.

"They said someone named Vaida called dispatch about twenty minutes ago."

But they'd been too late. Cassian was gone.

It wasn't Vaida's fault—he knew that. But he couldn't focus on his own thoughts long enough to form a single coherent thought.

Cassian was gone.

Cassian was *gone*.

And it was his fault.

"Kellan?" Selwyn asked, her voice shaky. "What happened to Director Byre?"

Kellan remembered the man shedding his disguise and becoming the demon prince. The memory of his gruesome visage sent shivers down his spine.

And so he told her; at the mention of Byre's true identity, her eyes went wide. He felt bad for her. She'd lost everything.

The tears came of their own accord, sliding down his cheeks, carving hot lines into his face. Selwyn's brow furrowed to keep her own tears from falling, but it was in vain. They splashed down onto Kellan's face, mixing with his own.

They sat in mutual sorrow, allowing their tears to fall in the comfort of each other's presence.

A pair of shoes so shiny he could see the fluorescent lights reflected in them stepped up before them.

"Kellan," the commissioner said, his voice gentle.

Kellan sat up, wincing as he did. This time, Selwyn let him.

"Sir," he said weakly.

The commissioner crouched down to meet him, his steel-gray eyes hardened with concern. "What in Sol's name happened?"

He swallowed. "I can explain, but…"

The commissioner nodded, concern furrowing his brow. "We can discuss that later, then. Are you both all right?"

"No," he wanted to reply. Everything was gone. But explaining everything that had transpired with Cassian over the last few months wasn't a conversation he wanted, especially not with the commissioner.

"A few scrapes and bruises, maybe a broken rib, but I'm fine." It was the most he could muster. Selwyn's hands tightened in her lap.

The commissioner's eyes flicked to Selwyn. "And you, Miss Morgenstern?"

He worried for a moment that Selwyn might not follow his lead, that she might spill everything here and now. But she knew better.

"I'm fine, commissioner. Thank you for asking." Her voice was steady as she returned the commissioner's gaze.

He nodded, then stood. "I'll have a trauma team member over here in a moment to scan you both." His eyes found Kellan's again. "I'm glad you're all right, Kellan."

Without waiting for him to reply, he retreated into the throng of Legion swarming the hallway. Kellan stared after him, mouth agape.

Selwyn breathed once more. "Is Pontius going to live?"

His heart broke for her. In the matter of a few months, she'd lost not only her best friend, but her brother and a goal she'd worked so hard to achieve. He couldn't stop himself—he leaned forward, embracing her around her shoulders.

She froze for a heartbeat, undoubtedly surprised. But she gave in, wrapping her arms around him and burying her face in his shoulder. He couldn't find the strength to be embarrassed by the gesture. Instead, he let her sob again, stroking her hair and willing the tears filling his own eyes again to stay away. He'd been weak for as long as he could; Selwyn needed him to be strong now.

"I don't know, Selwyn," he finally said. "I don't know if he's dead or alive, but I will do everything it takes to get him back. I promise."

Her hands curled into fists on his shoulder blades, then relaxed. She pulled away, and Kellan let her so they sat face-to-face on the cold tile floor.

"I expect nothing less than that, Kellan Manchester."

58

CASSIAN

Unknown

The pain was unbearable. His stomach was hot like it might explode.

The air was freezing cold, though.

"I can't believe this is what you brought me, Leonardo. I'm disappointed." The voice was cool, like the ocean in winter. He was sure he was hallucinating the sound. Was this what death felt like? "He's on death's door. Why not just make him one of your little demons?"

"I need him alive," Leo snarled. He'd never heard Leo be so angry with anyone before. Not even he could get a rise out of Leo like that.

But why was Leo here? Had he died, too?

The other voice just laughed, cool and even. "Interesting. Why me, though?"

"Alvemach said I should. Stygia's the only one without a pact right now, anyway."

The voice laughed again. He found he liked the sound, even if it wasn't real.

"Then I'll take him." He felt his cheek being poked. "You. Do you want to live?"

He thought he was dead. Why would they ask that?

The finger poked his face again. "I need you to say it out loud."

"Yes." His voice felt like sandpaper.

"Wonderful. Then it seems we agree." A bloom of pain in his stomach followed. It seemed as if someone was poking at the hole in his abdomen.

He was sure he'd died, then. The air went still, like he was in a vacuum, and the pain worsened. He could hardly expand his ribs enough to breathe, and the motion hurt. Wasn't death supposed to be painless after a while? If this was how his victims had died, he felt it was just punishment.

Memories came back, hazy and unfocused. Blackened blood smearing the walls, golden brown eyes filled with worry, a single scream. They blossomed in him, returned to him like they were being fed through a water-logged screen. The sound was fuzzy, unfocused.

Kellan's face appeared then, clearer than any other image that fluttered around in his subconscious. His hair was longer. He sat with a dark-skinned woman on a couch, his face twisted in pain. He ached—a different sort of ache than the one that plagued his stomach. It was the ache of longing.

He wanted to hold Kellan, to ease his pain, to make his expression turn to one of joy, one of love. He wanted to erase whatever was making Kellan feel that pain.

He realized with a jolt that it was probably him—he was the reason. After all, he was…wherever he was, and Kellan was not.

The cold had seeped into his bones now. His stomach didn't feel hot anymore, either. It was just as cold as the rest of him. Maybe he really had died.

A burst of purple light had him blinking spots from his eyes. Wait, why was he blinking? Can the dead still see? He'd never known if they could or not. He wondered if Jupiter would look like her statues.

The cold gradually flowed out of his body, leaving him not warm but not cold. He sat up, inspecting his surroundings. The ice beneath him wasn't cold to the touch.

This was not what he'd expected the ethereal plane to look like.

Before him swirled an endless gray ocean, pushed and pulled by invisible currents. Beneath him, a single slab of ice stood firm in the middle of the water. And beside him sat a person.

Ze was quite attractive, with dark brown skin, ice-blond hair, and matching eyes. Zir lips were full and tinged slightly blue. Ze wore a white sweater to match their hair. As he stared, ze smiled, revealing pointed canines.

"Ah, you're awake," ze said. Zir voice was the one he'd heard Leo speaking to earlier. So it hadn't been a dream?

"I'm dead, aren't I?" he asked.

"Oh no, my dear Cassian, you're not dead." Ze smiled. "My name is Zalmelloth. Welcome to Hell."

EPILOGUE

BECK

Kettleguard
Evergreen Moon

"Your new mission will take you out of Kettleguard, and I expect you will be away for some time. The council will extend the range on your mark, but this does not mean it's broken. Am I clear?"

Commander Aluin was a hardass but had taken a liking to Beck over the last year. That much was clear, considering this new directive.

Beck had been with the Red Guard for just over a year now, and it was almost completely unheard of to send a draftee out of the city on official business aside from war. He assumed this wasn't war, considering he was the only person in the expansive, brick-walled office overlooking the Lanaheim River.

Had he been born any differently, Beck might have joined the Red Guard of his own free will. As it was, he didn't entirely hate the fact that the council had assigned him here, aside from the fact that he hadn't seen Kellan except during their infrequent video chats. His heart ached.

"Crystal, sir."

Commander Aluin nodded, turning his sharp gaze back to the paper before him. "I know you know our contractual agreements well. This is a particularly…how should I put this? A *delicate* one."

Beck stayed silent, hands clasped behind his back and feet wide in the traditional Guard stance.

"It's a two-prong mission involving a double elimination and a long-term undercover assignment. You have proven your worth while protecting Countess Galina, and she recommended you for this job. You should thank her."

"I will do so, sir."

"Good. I have sent the details to your techpad. It is encrypted, so please take care with this information. I will know if you mention details of the case to anyone other than myself or Ragnor."

Ragnor? Who was that? He knew better than to ask now, though. "I understand, sir."

"You are dismissed, Aenmar."

Beck bowed his head incrementally to his commander before turning on his heel and exiting the office. He was dying of curiosity, but he knew better than to look at his techpad now.

He returned to his room in the west wing of the sprawling Red Guard complex, nodding and bowing his head several times along the way when he encountered other generals and sergeants. They rarely returned the gesture, instead gazing at him out of the corners of their eyes with obvious disdain.

His room was sparse but cozy. A fire burned in the small steel furnace in the room's corner, and the building maids must have changed his checkered comforter while he was away. He took a seat in the chair by his desk and flipped on his techpad.

Infiltration Mission, to be assigned to Beck Aenmar.

Locations: Ebenfell, Rivenstorm.

Targets: Eliza Evermore and Rosalie Delacour.

Eliza Evermore—Cassian Evermore's birth

mother. Owes debts to Ragnor LaRoche, a contractor for the Red Council. Used as collateral for Cassian's cooperation, but he has not returned. Debt collection is her death, as agreed upon between parties. If Cassian resurfaces, his elimination is requested as well.

Rosalie Delacour—believed to be the rebel movement's head. Elimination is of the utmost importance.

Infiltration into the rebel organization is the main objective. Attain their secrets, understand the structure, and eliminate its leader. Your timeline is five years.

Five years? Beck set the techpad down on the desk and rubbed his eyes with the heels of his palms. Aluin wasn't kidding when he said a long-term assignment. And what was with killing this poor guy's mother?

He knew he must if he wanted to continue living. Even though killing her felt wrong, he had no choice.

There was more to the file after the page he'd just read, but he needed a moment to process. Beck reached up to touch the tattoo on the back of his neck. A shackle, no more, no less. He'd gotten other tattoos to hide the appearance of it, but it didn't matter. He still knew it was there, and the magic was as strong as the day they'd marked him.

He closed his eyes, leaning back in the chair and rubbing his face once more. He desperately wished he could talk to Kellan about the case, but he knew he couldn't do that, either.

The next day, Beck packed the last of his belongings into a duffel bag. He brought little, as Ragnor would outfit him once he arrived in Ebenfell.

His stomach flipped as he exited the Red Guard complex and again when he boarded the train. He was truly leaving Kettleguard for the first time in a year.

A small part of him chided himself for being excited when he was on his way to kill someone's mother, but he couldn't help himself.

It may not be freedom, but it certainly tasted like it.

Acknowledgements

I owe so many wonderful, beautiful, talented, and amazing individuals my undying gratitude for their time and pieces of their souls left behind in this work.

First and foremost, I owe the biggest debt of gratitude to my husband, Ryan. Although you don't quite understand the world of authoring, you never once laughed at my dream or told me I couldn't do it. For all the times you bragged about me to your friends, family, and co-workers... I am eternally grateful to you and every moment you spent being my rock. You have, undoubtedly, been one of the primary reasons I didn't give up on this journey. Thank you, with every piece of my soul, every beat of my heart. I love you more than life itself.

Secondly, to RaeAnne, Stefanie, Lindsay, Rachael, and Hannah. You made this journey easy, which is saying something for self-publishing. Your high quality work, extreme professionalism, and easy going natures made this whole process a heck of a lot easier than it could have been. I chose my partners in this thing well, and I appreciate every single second you dedicated to helping me realize this dream.

And of course, to the swaths of incredible, supportive, generous, kind, WONDERFUL people I met along the way.

To Judith, Rae, and Jason - you three have been my light in the dark. My shining pillars, my beacons of hope. Without your unfailing love, support, and encouragement, this book would not be what it is today. Your feedback and obsession with Kellan, Cassian, Pontius,

Selwyn, Mina, and Vaida has kept me plugging away, even when I was at my lowest during this journey. I cannot express my gratitude to the three of you enough. As John Mayer put it so beautifully: parts of me were made by you. Your parts in my journey are the reason I am where I am. Thank you, eternally, and perpetually.

To Paulina - having you in my corner has been a blessing I am thankful for each and every single day. Your ideas, encouragement, and sass-talking kept my spirits high even when it felt like I might not be able to continue. How I got so lucky to have someone like you on my side and in my life is a wonderful gift from the universe. Thank you for being there for me, always.

To Lindsay - whoever said internet friends aren't real friends was a liar. I am the luckiest person in the world to have met you. Thank you, over and over again, for your love, support, guidance, and friendship. You existing in my life was a wonderful blessing, and OBBT would not be what it is without you. You're a rock against the stormy sea that is self-doubt, and have never once been afraid to give me encouragement and love when I needed it most.

To Alex - where do I even begin with you. My soul sister, my chaos twin, my sounding board and voice of reason. You have been such a saving grace through writing this book. I have no idea how I got so lucky to have met you, but all I know is that I am forever grateful for the universe bringing us together. You are the best cheerleader and supporter anyone could ever ask for. Thank you, from the bottom of my heart, for being you and for sharing that with me.

To Jess - I can't express what you and your friendship have meant to me during the course of publishing this book. From being a sounding board when all I want to do is complain, to hyping me up when I needed a bit of a boost, your support and love has kept me afloat. I don't know where I would be without you, but that's not a place I want to see. Thank you for your dedication to loving my characters and me.

To Rachel - your brand of support is one I needed so desperately. The quiet Sunday mornings spent at a coffee shop just writing and chatting. The random weeknights spent on Discord listening to music and chuckling about our silly dogs. You made me feel supported and loved and encouraged in these quiet moments of mutual work. I appreciate you deeply, and I am honored to be your writing buddy.

To Gina - I cannot express my thanks to you deeply enough. Your feedback made my writing stronger, more organized, and more interesting to read. Even the sarcastic and sassy comments on my beta draft made my writing better. Having you read my draft made me a better writer, and I can never thank you enough for that. You are an incredible human, and a fantastic friend.

To all my author friends - you are my heart. Publishing sometimes can feel like such a lonely endeavor, but having you all in my corner was a blessing I didn't even know I needed, but I cherish with every piece of my heart. You kept the lights on, the train moving, and the inspiration flowing. Without you all, I surely would have been worse off than I am now. I hope each one of you knows how important of a role you played in making my dreams come true.

To my street team - I am in awe of all of you. I still can't believe there were so many of you that wanted to help me market my queer chaos children to the world, and the fact you stuck around through it all gives me butterflies. The fact anyone knows about this book is because of you, your excitement, and your dedication to sharing my babies with the world. I am eternally grateful for every second you spent helping me share this book with the world. Thank you over and over again.

And finally, to you. My readers. I can't fully call myself an author without you. The fact you hold this book in your hands is a testament to the fact that I wrote something you wanted to read. That I created a world you were interested enough in becoming part of that you spent your hard-earned money purchasing my weird little brainchild. I am eternally grateful to you and your role in making this dream of mine a reality.

ABOUT THE AUTHOR

Photo by Audrey Rice

T.M. Ledvina is an avid reader and writer, and lover of all things fantasy and romance. They live in Madison, Wisconsin with her husband, Ryan, and retired racing greyhound, Addy. When she isn't writing, you can find them watching anime, playing Dungeons and Dragons, or playing video games. Of Blood, Bones, and Truth is her first full-length completed novel.

tmledvina.com
On Instagram: @tiamae.books